LOVE ON THE D-LIST

J.R. BARKER

Copyright © 2023 by J.R. Barker

All rights reserved.

No part of this publication may be reproduced, distributed, or transmitted in any form or by any means, including photocopying, recording, or other electronic or mechanical methods, without the prior written permission of the publisher, except as permitted by U.S. copyright law. For permission requests, contact jrbarkerbooks@gmail.com.

Book Cover by Ashley Santoro

CONTENT NOTE

Please be aware: While this story delivers humor and a happily ever after, it also discusses topics that could trigger certain audiences, such as public shaming, secondary characters with cancer and Alzheimer's, characters who've lost a loved one to suicide, characters who've experienced homophobia in their pasts, and graphic, steamy depictions of sex.

To Mom and Dad

CHAPTER 1
WILL

Will's stomach lurched as the elevator began the ninety-five-story climb to the penthouse. This was going to be mortifying. Will had no business attending his brother's star-studded bachelor party—even if he was the best man.

"Come on, cheer up. There's going to be an open bar," Miles said. "Plus, there are going to be a million self-absorbed, self-conscious celebrities there, and if I don't get another high-profile client soon, we're going to have to move to Staten Island."

Right. This wasn't just about Will. And attending an industry party full of potential clients was the least Will could do for Miles, who was not only Will's best friend, but also his roommate and personal trainer.

"Why does he have to do it in front of an audience? Why can't he just announce it in private?" Will asked. That was probably an oxymoron, a private announcement, but tonight was supposed to be about celebrating his brother Andy's forthcoming marriage to a gorgeous supermodel, not Will's doomed comeback.

"Because your dad is a self-centered ass who can't do anything without an audience. And remember, this is a good thing. You served your time. You deserve this."

Will wouldn't go that far. He deserved prison time. Ten years ago, he'd gotten blackout drunk and almost killed his co-star. Now, his father—legendary actor, Robert Chapman—wanted him to make a glorious comeback, claiming comeback narratives were Oscar gold.

But Will wasn't sure he wanted to leave the safe bubble of his relative obscurity. It had taken him years to get out of the tabloids—years spent studying, working, and hiding in his apartment.

Sure, his students and the principal gave him hell on a regular basis, no one wanted to date or be seen with him, and the highlight of his day was watching porn before bed. But it was still a hell of a lot better than death threats and unfounded rumors about giving toothy blowjobs.

Would the ridicule start all over again if Will got a supporting role in his father's next Oscar bait movie? Probably. Of course, nothing was official yet, so there was no need to panic. All Will knew for certain was that he had to be at his brother's bachelor party for some "big announcement."

"We don't even know if it's going to happen," Will said.

"Of course it is. Your dad just wants to make a self-congratulatory spectacle out of it. Trust me, tonight's going to be awesome. Just hold your head up high and show those assholes you're back and taking names."

Miles was probably right. Will's father did like to make a self-congratulatory spectacle. And even if Will didn't deserve this opportunity, or like the way his father was going about announcing it, he was still grateful for the second chance. Acting had been Will's dream for as long as he could remember. It was all he'd ever wanted to do and the only thing he was any good at.

"Jesus Christ, fine. But do I really have to wear this shirt?" It was light pink and skintight. "I can't breathe. And you can see my nipples."

"Hey, stop whining. Pink is a soothing color. Why do you think they paint hospital rooms pink? And you've got really cute nipples. Don't you want to show them off?"

Will wanted to be at home in sweats, his nipples hidden behind a book.

"Come on, once everyone sees that tight little body of yours, they're going to be like, 'Who's your trainer?' And you'll be like, 'Have you heard of Miles Greene? That man's an artist. I mean, sure, those other guys are fine if you want a bit part on *Days of Our Lives*. But if you want a Golden Globe, if you want a body that fits you like a costume, you have to see Miles Greene.'"

"I'm not saying any of that. I want no part of your mission to perpetuate unrealistic body standards."

"Yet you have no problem perpetuating unrealistic hot teacher standards."

Will rolled his eyes. He knew what Miles was doing, and it wasn't going to work. No amount of self-confidence was going to make this night okay.

"No one is even going to talk to me. I'm just going to stand there in the corner sipping vodka sodas, praying I don't leave a watermark on the wall. Do you have any idea how sweaty my ass is right now?"

"Fine, but don't get mad at me when we end up in a railroad apartment in Staten Island, and every guy I bring home has to walk through your room to get to mine, and then back through your room again to get to the bathroom, and then back—"

"Maybe we should just go home. We can stop and get new batteries for the Bop-It."

Miles set his giant hands on Will's shoulders and started kneading the tight knots coiled under his skin. "I knew you'd be like this. That's why I saved the best news for last. Tonight, you get to drink all the beer you want. Get a fucking twenty-ouncer even. Go all out. When they see that beer in your hand and then look down at your flat stomach, they're going to be like, 'Damn, who's that boy's trainer?'"

"You're ridiculous and unethical and—"

"Adroit?"

"What?"

"I'm pretty sure the word you're looking for is adroit."

"No, I'm pretty sure it's not. Would you please stop skimming that word-a-day book. Either read it or don't read it."

Miles spit into the palm of his hand and started styling Will's unruly black hair. "No way. What if I land one of those British dames, you know, like Kate Winslet or Nicole Kidman? That'd be sick. Or should I say apropos?"

"No, you definitely shouldn't say apropos. That's not how you use that word. And Nicole isn't even British. She's Australian."

"What, they don't like words in Australia?"

The elevator started to slow, and Will grabbed Miles's wrist. "Please don't abandon me tonight."

"Relax. I'll be by your side the whole time. You've got this. And remember, no one at this party is out to get you. They just want to have a good time, same as you. All you have to do is join them. Just smile and act like you belong—because you do. Now, let me hear you say it. Stand in your superhero pose and say, 'I belong.'"

Will rolled his eyes, and the elevator doors slid open.

THE CROWDED PENTHOUSE was all big windows, hardwood floors, and white walls. The only color in the room came from bright throw pillows and giant canvases of modern art. Well, that and the massive pink cock in the center of the room, which appeared to be one of those bucking bronco rides you find in country western bars.

The moment Will stepped out of the elevator, whispers of his arrival began to spread through the party like an infection. There were two types of people in attendance—those who couldn't help but gape, like Will was a walking car crash, and those who pretended he didn't exist. Or maybe Will was just being paranoid.

"Holy shit, is that Jake Gyllenhaal?" Miles's eyes locked on a man on the far side of the room. "And who's that he's talking to? Is that Harry Styles? I have a dream that starts just like this, only we're on this cold, stormy coastline in England looking for fossils."

Will snatched a glass of champagne from a passing tray and scanned the room for his father and brother. His father probably wasn't even there yet. He was probably waiting to make a grand entrance.

Miles ripped the glass from Will's hand. "We already talked about this. Don't drink that low calorie shit. Tonight's a beer night."

Miles set the glass back on the tray and grinned at the caterer, who, now that Will looked at him, was absurdly attractive. He had bright green eyes and a warm, easy smile, like one of those hot dads you see at the park carrying a toddler on his shoulders.

He was probably in his mid-thirties, with dirty blond hair and a lean, muscular body, like a soccer player. His face had a salt of the earth boyishness to it, but the tiny flecks of gray in his rusty brown beard placed him firmly in the daddy zone: Will's weak spot.

Jesus, leave it to Will to enter a room full of gorgeous celebrities and immediately get hung up on one of the caterers.

"Any beer at this party?" Miles asked.

"Uh, yeah, of course." The caterer smiled back at Miles and then turned to Will. The moment he recognized him, his smile vanished. Will was used to being a pariah, so he wasn't surprised. But it still stung.

"No shit, like a keg?"

The caterer did his best to return the smile to his face. "Yeah, behind the bar."

Miles leveled his gaze at Will. "You think you can do ten handstand pushups on a keg? If you can't do at least ten, there's no point."

This was a mistake. Will never should've come. He never should've agreed to be Andy's best man in the first place. He should just leave. Miles would be fine on his own, and Andy would understand.

Will was about to turn and go when someone grabbed him from

behind and lifted him two feet off the ground and shook him from side to side like a dog toy. "I knew you'd come, papi. Andy was sure you were going to bail, but I knew you'd come through. You always do."

"Jesus Christ, Enrique, put me down."

Enrique Navarro was not only the owner of the swanky penthouse Will found himself in, but also Andy's best friend. Enrique co-starred with Andy in the billion-dollar buddy-cop franchise, *Hollow Point*. He should've been Andy's best man, not Will. Everyone loved Enrique.

"Damn, papi, you're looking good. You feel good, too. Solid. You want a drink? There is champagne going around and two bars, one in here and one out on the balcony." Enrique leaned in and filled Will's ear with a champagne-wet whisper. "And there are a few choice delicacies in my bathroom. I recommend the little red ones."

According to *Entertainment Weekly*, Andy and Enrique shared an onscreen chemistry that rivaled the greats—Kate and Leo, Bogart and Becall, Jay and Silent Bob. Unlike Will, whose dark hair and pale skin made him look like he belonged in the Addams Family, Andy had inherited their mother's ginger hair and their father's delicate bone structure, which made him the perfect counterbalance to Enrique, who was all chiseled and masculine and full of that dudebro charm audiences couldn't get enough of.

Enrique clapped a hand on the back of the six-foot-five brick of muscle at Will's side. "Miles, you're looking even more ripped than the last time I saw you."

"I have one question for you, Enrique. Do you do your own ass work? And if not, do you want to?"

"Huh, what? Is this guy for real? That was two questions."

"Will, show him your ass."

Miles tried to spin Will around—like he was a mannequin on a pedestal—but Will pushed him off and jumped away.

Unfortunately, at that very moment, the hot caterer walked by, and Will smacked right into him, upending his tray. Glass after glass of champagne fell and shattered on the floor, loud as gunshots. The whole room went silent, and everyone turned and stared.

"Oh my god. I'm so sorry," Will said. "I'll clean this up."

The caterer was too stunned to move. He just stood there in a daze, champagne dripping down the front of his black pants.

"Are you okay?" Will asked. "I'll buy you a new pair of pants. Enrique, where's your broom? I'll sweep this up."

The caterer looked up from the devastation—a bubbling soup of broken glass and expensive champagne—and met Will's gaze, his green eyes blazing with irritation. "It's fine, sir, don't worry about it. I'll take care of it."

Will was pushed aside as other caterers rushed over to help. Jesus, Will hadn't even been there two minutes, and he'd already made a scene.

"I'm so sorry, Enrique. I'm such a—"

"It's all good, papi. Accidents happen. And there's plenty more champagne where that came from. Now, it's time to get fucked up." Enrique started shooting pistol fingers at them as he backed away. "Best man gets to be the first cock jockey."

Enrique disappeared into the crowd and, thankfully, took most of the party's attention with him. Still, Will could feel the whispers growing like a storm. He needed to find a place to blend in until his father showed up, a place where he hadn't just made a complete jackass of himself.

"Let's go out on the balcony," he said.

THEY FOUND a couple of seats at the outside bar, which, while more modest than the inside bar, was still long enough to comfortably seat ten. Will ordered a beer and drained the first three inches in a single gulp. *Fuck, that was good.*

"Come on, man. You're a Golden Globe winning actor. Act like you're having a good time." Miles pulled the edges of Will's mouth into a smile.

It had been ten years since *The Beautiful*. Will had been nineteen when it had come out, and for one glorious year, he'd been beloved. Guys had wanted to date him. Directors had wanted to cast him. Little gay boys had wanted to grow up and be just like him. But then Will had to go and throw it all away for a few drinks and a guy who thought he was nothing more than a "pathetic fuckboy."

"Wow, look at that hottie." Miles nodded towards a squat man on the far side of the balcony who was so furry Will could see the hairs on his knuckles from a hundred paces. He was totally Miles's type.

"Yes, he's perfect for you, but please don't abandon me." The last thing Will needed was to be the guy in the skintight pink shirt drinking alone at his brother's bachelor party.

"Stop worrying. I'm not going to abandon you."

It took all Will's discipline not to chug the rest of his beer and order another, but he wasn't going to let himself get drunk tonight. There were so many things out of Will's control—his students' behavior, his principal's frustration, his parents' disappointment, his bad reputation—but there was one thing he could control: his body. At least, he could when he was sober.

Will didn't work out six days a week because he wanted to be accepted back into Hollywood or because he wanted to get laid—although he wouldn't say no to either of those things. He worked out because the endorphins he got from exercise kept him from sinking into total despair. Plus, it made Miles happy.

"Hey, Will. You made it. Andy said you might not come." Ryan Ashbury, Andy's third groomsman, sidled up to the bar. Ryan starred in *Blood Brothers,* a campy teenage vampire show.

It was total type casting because Ryan looked exactly like a vampire. He had naturally pointy incisors, supernaturally blue eyes, and voluminous blond curls that defied the laws of physics. They bounced. They gleamed. They never tangled.

"Do you have a sec?" Ryan asked. "There's something I need to discuss with you in private."

Miles gave Will's shoulder a reassuring squeeze. "Why don't I let you boys talk? But don't worry, I'll be right over there if you need me, okay?" Miles nodded towards the little bear cub on the other side of the balcony.

It wasn't okay, but Will let him go.

Once Miles was gone, Ryan glanced around nervously, no doubt self-conscious at being seen alone with Will. "Uh, let's go into one of the bedrooms."

Will nodded and picked up his beer, wondering if Ryan was going to ask him to leave. Just then, Andy came barreling through the balcony doors.

"Holy shit, holy shit, you're here." Andy threw his arms around Will. "I don't even care that I owe Enrique a lap dance. You came. Do you have any idea how happy this makes me? Bartender, three shots of Patron, please."

"I can't do shots," Will said.

"Come on, it's my bachelor party. You have to. One shot won't kill you."

"Fine, one shot."

A minute later, Will held the shot in his hand, eyeing the clear liquid like it was poison. He really shouldn't be doing this. His stomach was already a smoldering ball of nerves, and now he was about to throw gasoline on the fire.

Andy raised his glass in toast. "To Will's big comeback."

Will grimaced, really wishing Andy hadn't just said that. But Andy deserved at least one shot with his best man, so Will clinked glasses with the others, opened his throat, and tossed back the shot.

"When do you think Dad will get here?" Will asked, pulling the lime wedge from his mouth, trying to sound casual, like his whole life didn't hinge on his father's announcement.

Andy shook his head. "He's not coming. Says he's not feeling well."

A wave of relief—really more of a tsunami—washed over Will. *Thank God*. But what was his father's deal? Was his "big announcement" just a ploy to get Will to attend the bachelor party? Was Will even getting the role?

"Let's go do body shots off the strippers," Andy said, putting one freckled arm around Ryan and one around Will.

"Uh, you two go," Will said. "I have to go find Miles and ask him something."

Andy gave Will a dubious look. "Fine, but don't you dare run away. You're not leaving here tonight until you ride that big pink cock. You hear me?"

CHAPTER 2
JAMES

James Barrett was a jack-of-all-trades. He'd had many careers in his lifetime—dairy farmer, plumber's assistant, paparazzo, private investigator, stripper, and now, senior associate for an elite domestic staffing agency. In other words, James did odd jobs for celebrities, everything from dog-sitting and yard work to catering and security. That was how he'd secured the gig at Andy Chapman's star-studded bachelor party.

But James wasn't there to ogle the *Hollow Point* boys, Andy and Enrique, or even the curly-haired heartthrob, Ryan Ashbury. James was there for William Chapman, the entitled little peckerhead who thought he could use James's movie to mount a comeback.

James studied the disgraced actor sitting alone at the outside bar. He had tousled black hair, a tight pink shirt, and quite possibly the finest ass James had ever set eyes on. James hadn't been expecting William's ass to be so perky and round. But even homicidal brats had to have some redeeming qualities.

William looked pathetic drinking alone, like he was actively trying to be the biggest loser at the party. Why wasn't he doing body shots off the strippers like everyone else? Wasn't he supposed to be the best man?

Whatever. James wasn't getting involved. He wasn't. He was there to do his job and nothing more. The rest was out of his control. Or was it? *Shit.* Was William Chapman making a break for it?

The actor left his lonely perch at the bar and started weaving his way across the balcony. He stopped at the entrance to the living room, looked left and right, and then opened the doors just wide enough to let his wiry frame slip through.

He didn't head for the kitchen, where the strippers were laid out like a sushi train, but hurried in the opposite direction, towards the elevator. *Was he really leaving the party?*

James chanced a glance at the Korean-American reporter currently posing as a stripper with fishnets and neon green nipple pasties. Was Esther catching this? How was her plan supposed to work if William left the party early?

James never should've let Esther talk him into this. Yes, he needed the money. And yes, William Chapman deserved all the bad press he had coming. But if James got caught sneaking a reporter into an event, he'd lose his job. And he couldn't afford to lose his job, not now. On the other hand, didn't he owe it to his brother's memory to make sure William Chapman didn't ruin the movie?

Before James's brother died, he'd written a book, a book that was about to be made into a movie, a movie that was about to be ruined by casting William Chapman as the banished gay son—the character based on James.

James faced away from Esther, not wanting anyone to make the connection between them, and watched William Chapman skirt around the edge of the room. Was he ghosting his own brother's bachelor party? Some best man he was.

James had to do something fast or Esther's plan to get William Chapman booted from the film would crash and burn before it even got off the ground. He set his new tray of champagne down and hurried across the room.

He slid between William and the elevator doors just as they opened, preventing William from getting on.

"Hey, where are you going?" James flashed his most charming smile, the one that never failed to get him out of tricky situations. But instead of blushing, like most guys did, William flinched. Was James losing his touch?

"Uh, nowhere"—William cast his eyes to the floor—"just home. I'm so sorry I bumped into you earlier. I'll cover your dry cleaning costs, or, like I said, I can just buy you a new pair of pants. Do you have Venmo?"

"It's okay, man. They're already practically dry. And it was just champagne." James smiled and watched in amazement as William's posture relaxed, like he'd been expecting James to hit him or something. "You're William Chapman, right?"

"Yeah, sorry."

"Seriously, I don't care about the pants. Let it . . . Wait, did you just apologize for being yourself?"

"Uh . . ."

"That's fucked up, dude. I mean, I get that you have a past and all that, but you can't spend your whole life being sorry."

"Sorry."

"Wow. That bad, huh?"

William shrugged. He had the darkest eyes and whitest skin James had ever seen. He looked like a domino. Although, he'd really grown into his looks—dark brows, high cheekbones, a little ski jump nose, a strong, angular jawline. James had never seen William's movie, *The Beautiful*, but he'd seen the guy in enough tabloids to know what he looked like—or what he used to look like anyway.

"Sorry," William said for the fourth time in almost as many seconds.

James narrowed his eyes. "Are you joshing me right now?"

"Joshing you?" William glanced towards the kitchen and then back at James, only instead of making eye contact, he stared at James's collarbone.

James sighed. This was a disaster. Seriously, was it too much to ask for William to say or do something deplorable so James didn't have to feel so guilty?

"Let's try this again," James said. "I'm gonna ask if you're William Chapman, and you're gonna look me in the eye and say, 'Yes, I am.' And smile when you do it. You do know how to smile, don't you?"

William frowned. "Yeah, I know how to smile."

"Prove it." James crossed his arms over his chest and leaned against the wall. He'd spent the better part of the past month hating this guy, only to find out he was actually kind of endearing—well, in a wounded-puppy-slash-lost-orphan sort of way.

Of course, that didn't change anything. James needed the movie to succeed. If the movie was a success, the book would become an instant best seller, and James needed the book to sell, needed the money it would generate so he could continue supporting his brother's kid. And that wasn't going to happen if William Chapman was in the movie, even if he was kind of sweet and cute and oddly sexy. Let William mount his comeback with some other movie.

"Go on," James said. "Give me that movie star smile."

"What? Why?" William lifted his gaze from the floor, and their eyes locked.

William's irises were so dark they were almost black. But instead of hiding William's secrets, they laid them bare. It was like James had accidently stumbled upon William's sex drawer, fondled all of his dildos, and then read his diary.

Guilt landed in James's stomach like a brick, and he had to look away. *Shit, this was a mistake, wasn't it?* Should he call it off, tell Esther to go home?

Whatever. Esther wasn't going to get anything on William anyway. The guy was as strait-laced as they come. Plus, she was cutting James in for fifty percent of whatever dirt she published on the others, and James needed the money.

"I just wanna see it, that's all," James said, swallowing past the lump in his throat. "I bet you've got a great smile."

A whoop of laughter erupted from the kitchen, and William flinched again. "I'm sorry. I really have to go."

"You're not leaving, are you?"

Beads of sweat gathered on William's forehead, and even sweaty he was kind of adorable. "I have to go home and pee."

"Who goes home to pee? There's a bathroom right down the hall. Are you pee shy or something?"

"Pee shy?"

"My brother was pee shy. He couldn't go if anyone was even within earshot."

William crossed his hands over his crotch, which James was definitely not staring at. "No, I'm not pee shy."

"Hey, there you are." Ryan Ashbury set a hand on William's shoulder, and William jumped about a foot in the air. "Sorry, I didn't mean to scare you. Is now a good time to talk?"

William's gaze flicked to the elevator doors and then back to Ryan. "Uh, yeah, sure."

Ryan finished his drink and handed his empty glass to James, reminding James that he was at work right now. "Let's go into the studio," Ryan said. "I don't think anyone's in there."

William gave James a bashful nod. Then he and his perky little ass disappeared down the hall.

James fell back against the wall and exhaled in relief. It was out of his hands now. The rest was up to chance. Well, chance and a plucky Korean-American lesbian with cameras hidden in her nipple pasties.

CHAPTER 3
WILL

Will walked several paces behind Ryan and tried to ignore the pang of jealousy in his chest. He, too, used to strut through crowded parties like he was a prince. Now, people glared at him like he was an unattended package left on the subway. His very existence seemed to inspire a *see something, say something* mentality in people.

You'd think, with all the concerned looks he was getting, he was luring Ryan Ashbury into a windowless van, not trailing after him at a respectful distance.

What did Ryan want anyway? Maybe he and Enrique had decided one of them should give the wedding toast.

Ryan closed the door behind them, and the party noise dimmed to a low roar. The hardwood floors in the studio gleamed in the bright lights, and Will's own reflection glared back at him from the wall of mirrors, asking, *Why are you wearing that ridiculous shirt? And why does Enrique have a dance studio in his apartment?*

Ryan leaned an elbow against the wooden barre and lifted his gaze to meet Will's. "There's something I need to tell you, and I want you to hear it from me first. I got a call from my agent this morning, and—"

Before Ryan could finish speaking, Andy and Enrique burst into the studio as if pursued by wasps.

Enrique slammed the door behind him and leaned against it. "Will, you're not going to believe who is on his way up here right now to see you."

"It's Derek," Andy said. "He says Dad sent him."

Andy and Enrique continued talking—something about Derek's manager, Tony, wanting to speak to Will first—but Will wasn't listening.

Derek was at the party! A cold sweat covered Will's body.

Derek Hall and William Chapman were two sides of the same coin, like Batman and The Joker or Nancy Kerrigan and Tanya Harding. They hadn't seen each other in a decade, but you couldn't mention one name without the other. They were inextricably linked, first by their hit movie and then by their catastrophic falling-out.

Will had been seventeen when he'd been cast opposite Derek Hall in the small indie film, *The Beautiful*. Derek had been the twenty-eight-year-old shirtless hunk on the cover of GQ, and Will had been the scrawny, awkward child of two famous movie stars.

"But if you really want to go through with it," Enrique was saying when Will tuned back into the present conversation, "you're more than welcome to talk to Tony in here. It will at least give you some privacy."

Ugh, Tony Wallingford. On paper, Tony was Derek's manager, but in reality, he was so much more—his agent, his publicist, his gay father figure.

Will would never forget the first time he'd been alone with Tony. It had been two days after Will's eighteenth birthday, and he'd just finished showering. He'd stepped out of his tiny trailer bathroom in a billow of steam and almost dropped his towel. Tony was sitting on his couch, fiddling with his earring. "Jesus, you scared the shit out of me."

"Sorry, William. I just thought it was time we had a little chat." Tony's eyes roamed up and down Will's rail-thin body. "I thought your mother was getting you a personal trainer."

Will tightened his towel and cast his eyes to the floor. She had gotten him a trainer. But Miles could only do so much in such a short amount of time.

"Listen, William." Tony stood and smoothed his finely tailored suit. "You're eighteen now, so I'm going to speak to you like an adult. It's no secret you've developed certain feelings for Derek, which is understandable. You're gay, and Derek is Derek. It was actually for this very reason that I wanted them to cast another straight actor in the role of Chase. But here we are. Now, Derek would never say anything to you directly, but I know him better than anyone, and I can tell how uncomfortable you're making him. Your crush is creating a hostile work environment."

Will's face burned with mortification. Was it that obvious? "I don't know what you're talking about."

"I think you do. So, just rein it in, okay? Otherwise, we might have to get HR involved," Tony had said.

"So, what should we do?" Andy asked, placing his hands on Will's shoulders and shaking him back to the present.

"I . . . I . . ." Will wanted to speak, but he couldn't find the words. Derek was on his way up to see him! Was this really happening?

Time tripped again, and Will was back on the set, about to kiss Derek for the first time.

"I'm not going to fuck you again," Derek said, "not until you kiss me."

"I told you, I don't do that."

"Good, Will," their director said. "Now, take two steps back and feel for the doorknob behind you. Yes, like that. Now, Derek, close the distance in one big stride and cup Will's face in your palms."

Derek's touch was gentle, warm, and confident.

"Resist, Will. Look at the ground. Make Derek force your face up."

Even though Will's body was liquid with desire, he set his jaw and kept his gaze fixed on the floor.

"Now, sink to your knees, Derek. But don't look at his crotch. This isn't sexual. You just want your eyes to be in line with his. Good, just like that. Now, slowly rise again, forcing Will to lift his head to maintain eye contact. You're moving him, not with force, but with the intensity of your stare. Excellent. Now, Will, absentmindedly lick your lips. Yes, just like that. Okay, now, Derek, let two beats pass. One. Two. Then, before Will can change his mind, kiss him."

Derek's lips smashed into Will's, hot and wet, and it was better than anything Will could've imagined, the prick of Derek's stubble, the sour taste of his breath, the hulking mass of his body towering over Will.

"No, Will, don't melt like that. Make him work for it. Just stand there. Make him think he's kissing a statue."

Will scrunched his eyes closed and tried to banish the memory. When he opened them again, he was back in the brightly lit studio.

"Maybe I should call Dad and ask him what this is all about?" Andy said. "Maybe he thinks this will help, show that bygones are bygones and all that. I mean, hasn't Dad been hinting at some big surprise for months now? Maybe this is it."

Will nodded like he understood, but his brain was incapable of making sense out of anything right now.

"I think we broke Will," Enrique said. "Should I get him some whiskey?"

"What? Why? He's not a frozen corpse on Mt. Everest."

"I'll get him some whiskey." Enrique opened the door to flag down a caterer.

Yes, whiskey. That was what Will needed. But, no, it wasn't safe. He'd been drinking whiskey the last time he'd seen Derek, and look how that had turned out.

Everything had been going great before the Golden Globes. Their low budget indie had proved to be a major awards contender, and he and Derek had been on track to get their first Oscar nominations—

Derek in lead and Will in supporting. But then the Golden Globes went and messed everything up by bumping Will up into the lead category, forcing him to compete against Derek.

It would've been fine if Derek had won. Only, he hadn't won. Will had.

Will had been sneaking sips of Derek's drinks all throughout the ceremony, but as soon as he'd found Derek at the after party, he'd commandeered Derek's entire glass of whiskey.

"Give me that." If Will was old enough to win Best Actor, he was old enough to have his own drink.

"You might want to slow down," Derek said. "You don't weigh very much, and bourbon is strong stuff."

"Are you sure you don't hate me? I really didn't want to win. I wanted you to win."

Derek laughed. "Of course I don't hate you. How could anyone hate you? Come on, why don't we get out of here? I've got some wine decanting in my room upstairs, and there's something I want to ask you."

Will almost choked on the whiskey. Was he dreaming? Did Derek really just invite him up to his hotel room? "Yeah, okay, let's go," Will said, doing his best not to squeal like a child on Christmas morning.

They were just reaching the elevator doors when Tony, Derek's manager, intercepted them.

"Congratulations, William. That might be the biggest upset in Golden Globes history. Not a lot of nineteen-year-olds can pull off a win in the lead actor category. My offer still stands, by the way, if you're looking for representation. After tonight, you're going to need it. Why don't you think about it while I steal Derek for a minute? He and I need to finish our conversation."

Will didn't need to think about it. His mother had already made it perfectly clear that he was to have nothing to do with Tony Wallingford.

"Not now, Tony," Derek said. "We'll talk tomorrow."

Will could remember little bits and pieces of the trip up to

Derek's room—the feel of Derek's hand on the small of his back, the ding of the elevator reaching Derek's floor, but that was it. The moment Will stepped into Derek's hotel room, his brain stopped recording memories.

Had the alcohol erased his brain, or had his crime been so heinous he'd blocked it out? Either way, Will's next conscious memory was waking up in his hotel room surrounded by police officers.

"Dad's not answering." Andy, who'd broken his own no cell-phone rule, put his phone back in his pocket. Will tried to pull himself out of his head and meet his brother's gaze, but all the freckles made him dizzy. "But it makes sense, doesn't it? This way you can put the Derek stuff behind you and focus on the movie."

"Andy, can I talk to you for a sec?" Ryan dragged Andy out of the room and left Will alone with Enrique and a head full of painful memories.

The police had handcuffed Will thirty seconds after he'd opened his eyes, saying Derek had been attacked and that Will had been the one to attack him. They had dragged Will to the police station through a swarm of press, and he had spent one night in jail before being released.

There hadn't been enough evidence to charge Will with the attack. The security footage from the hotel had gone mysteriously missing—no doubt Will's mother's doing—and Derek had suffered a traumatic brain injury and couldn't remember who'd attacked him, just that it couldn't have been Will because he'd already left Derek's room at that point. Naturally, the media had a field day with their tale of dual amnesia, comparing it to a spoof of a bad soap opera.

There had been one reliable data point from that night, however. An elderly couple across the hall had overheard Derek screaming at Will, saying words Will couldn't fathom Derek ever saying.

"You're just a pathetic fuckboy. You're so fucking entitled you think you deserve everything, even me. But I'm not yours, Will. I don't belong to anyone but myself. Now get the fuck out of my bed."

The first two months following the attack had been the loneliest months of Will's life. His parents, not wanting to be seen with him, had sent him to rehab. From there, on his small TV in his small, barren room, he'd watched the world tear him apart like a carcass on the savannah. It hadn't just been late-night jokes and far-fetched conspiracy theories. His best friend, Ariel, had gone on CNN to talk about Will's obsession with Derek. She'd even read his emails and texts aloud.

Will had done his best to suffer in solitude. But on the night of the Academy Awards, after he'd watched Derek accept the Oscar for Best Actor and the camera had panned from the white scar slicing Derek's eyebrow in half to Will's father standing and applauding in the audience, he'd broken down and called Miles. "Can you come get me? I don't want to be here anymore."

Hands landed on Will's shoulders, and dark brown eyes bore into him, pulling him back to reality. "Should I maybe go get Miles?" Enrique asked.

Will couldn't find the words to speak. What would he say to Derek? What would Derek say to him?

"I'll go get Miles."

Enrique left, but Will wasn't alone for long. The hot caterer from earlier came into the studio with a bottle of bourbon and a tray of crystal tumblers.

Wait, Will couldn't see Derek. Derek had a restraining order against him. Will wasn't allowed within three hundred feet of Derek.

"Are you okay?" the caterer asked, pouring three fingers of bourbon into a glass. "Your eyes are kinda doing this twitchy thing."

Will took the glass from the man without thinking and downed the amber liquid in one gulp.

Andy and his father were right. Will had no prayer of launching a comeback without Derek's approval. But why hadn't his father warned him?

"I found Miles," Enrique said a few minutes later, and before Will could even blink, his face was pressed into his best friend's chest.

"Derek's here," Will mouthed into the hollow between Miles's pecs.

"I heard. It's going to be okay, though, I promise. He's probably just here to congratulate you."

Will pulled himself free of Miles's embrace and caught the handsome caterer's green eyes staring at him. They weren't just green. They were kind, too. The man smiled, and something in Will, probably mirror neurons, made him smile back.

"Can I have another?" Will asked, holding out his empty glass.

The caterer refilled Will's drink without judgment just as the door opened and Tony Wallingford strode into the room.

CHAPTER 4

JAMES

James sank back against the wall as a handsome middle-aged man entered the room. He wore a charcoal gray suit over a black shirt and walked with authority, like the CEO of some multinational corporation. He had artificially silver hair and a small gold hoop in his right ear.

He strode right past William and offered his hand to Enrique. "Your home is beautiful. Thank you for letting us crash the party. I promise this won't take long."

Enrique shook the man's hand. "Do you want a drink or something?"

"No, thank you, just a quick word alone with William, please."

James started to follow Enrique out of the room, but he stopped when William's eyes landed on him.

"Stay," William said.

James doubted William was talking to him, but he stayed anyway, unable to ignore the tremor of fear in William's voice.

The silver-haired man let out a rumbly, throaty laugh. "Really? You'd think if anyone would want a witness present, it'd be me. I'm only doing this as a favor to your father, you know. He thought it would be a good idea if you and Derek were seen together before tomorrow's announcement. So, here we are."

"What announcement?"

"This is obviously going to stir up old wounds. How could it not? Your father just wants to get ahead of the story. I doubt it will work, but you never know."

"Ahead of what story?"

The door flew open before the man could answer, and Andy Chapman and Ryan Ashbury came sprinting into the room.

"I know why Derek's here, Ryan just—" Andy stopped in his tracks when he saw the silver-haired man, who was smiling like a Cheshire cat.

"No one's told you yet, have they?" The man took in the room full of blank stares. "Well, let me do the honors, then. Derek has agreed to take the role of Travis in your father's movie. While he doesn't normally take supporting roles, he's decided to make an exception this one time."

Now, it was James's turn to freak out because—holy shit!—he was talking about James's movie, the one based on Travis's memoir.

The glass slipped from William's fingers and bounced several times, drenching the wooden floor in amber liquid. "Derek and I are going to play brothers?"

William was right to be stunned. This was huge. Getting Derek Hall and William Chapman to star in another movie together was like getting Kanye West and Taylor Swift to co-host the Grammys.

"You know, if you hadn't tried to kill my number one client, I might actually feel sorry for you right now. Did your father really not tell you that they offered the gay brother role to Ryan?"

"I'm sorry, Will," Ryan said, stepping forward. "I was trying to tell you earlier. I didn't want to take it, but this is my chance to make the switch to movies, and—"

"It's okay, Ryan. Don't worry about it."

Wait, William Chapman wasn't going to be in the movie? Ryan Ashbury was? *Holy shit!* James's nephew, Theo, was going to flip his shit when he found out. The kid was only Ryan Ashbury's number one fan.

"Don't you think Ryan and Derek will look great on screen together?" the silver-haired man said. "They'll be the hottest duo since, well, since Andy Chapman and Enrique Navarro."

A sob erupted over by the door, and James turned to see Andy Chapman balling his eyes out. Like, full on gushing tears. His face was all red and blotchy, and snot dripped from his nose. Was he really that upset about his brother missing out on a part in a movie?

James looked away, embarrassed for Andy. But when his eyes landed on William, he felt the brick of guilt settle in his stomach again. William wasn't crying, but his face was so still it hurt to look at.

"This isn't about you, William. Don't be selfish," the silver-haired man said. "You'd have destroyed this movie, and you know it. But look on the bright side. This is still a big first step for you. And all you have to do is go out there and shake Derek's hand."

Will swallowed, and the bones of his sharp jawline protruded, like he was grinding his teeth.

"This brings me no pleasure, William. You must know that. I can only imagine how you're feeling right now. But actions have consequences, and it's going to take time, a lot of time. But the healing process has to start somewhere, right? So why not here? Why not now? Who knows, maybe in another ten years, things will be different."

William still didn't move, and neither did anyone else. Why weren't his friends rushing to comfort him?

"Let me clean this up," James said, desperate to do something. He set the tray of glasses down, removed the towel from his arm, and crouched to clean up the mess at William's feet.

When he was finished, he chanced a glance upward and found William's black eyes staring down at him with wonder and gratitude, like James had just pulled William's child from a burning building.

William exhaled. "What do you want me to do?" he asked, lifting his eyes to face the silver-haired man.

"Just shake Derek's hand and walk away. Derek is not interested in being your friend again. And it was never more than friendship, William. You know that now, don't you? In fact, friendship isn't even the right word for what you two had. It was more like he thought of you as an annoying little cousin."

William glanced at the closed door. "Is he out there right now?"

"He's waiting in the car, but I'll text him and have him come up."

The others left to greet Derek and set the stage for the epic reunion, but William and the huge Black guy he'd come with—Miles was his name—stayed behind with the silver-haired man.

"That's an interesting shirt you're wearing," the man said. "Bit of advice, though. Maybe don't try so hard next time. If you want to get a boyfriend, you have to play hard to get."

"Shut the fuck up, Tony," Miles said, stepping in front of William. "That shirt's rad. And for your information, Will's already got a boyfriend, and he's a million times hotter than Derek."

"I'll admit, you're very handsome. But didn't I just see you with your hand up some furry man's ass?"

"Not me. I'm Will's roommate and personal trainer."

Tony turned his bemused smile on William. "You live with your personal trainer? That's adorable."

CHAPTER 5
WILL

Tony left the room, but his cologne, a suffocating combination of patchouli and sandalwood, lingered.

The moment he was gone, Will's stomach revolted. All the beer, tequila, and whiskey churning inside of him started to come up. Will's cheeks filled, and he lunged for the trash can. He almost made it, too.

"It's okay," Miles said. "You got most of it in there. And I've got gum."

"I can't meet Derek looking like this." Will stood and looked down at his shirt, which was splattered with vomit.

"Sure you can. Here, you can wear my shirt."

"What are you talking about? We're not even remotely the same size."

Miles's face scrunched up, and thick lines appeared on his forehead, which was never a good sign. He looked over at the caterer and smiled.

"I'm not going to ask the caterer to give me the shirt off his back. I've already ruined his pants."

"Why not? He's not much bigger than you are. And he doesn't

mind. Do you?" Miles pulled his wallet from his pocket. "How about I give you two hundred dollars for your shirt?"

The man took a step back and furrowed his brow. "I'd love to help, but this is my uniform. I'm at work right now."

"Nah, it's fine. We just need to borrow it for like ten minutes. But I only have a hundred and twenty on me, so I'll have to pay you the rest later. What's your name, by the way?"

"Uh, James."

"Thanks, James. You're a lifesaver." Miles thrust the wad of cash at James and clapped him on the back, as if by stating his name he'd agreed to Miles's ridiculous plan.

"Uh, I don't think this is a—"

"Of course it is. You'll probably get a promotion for going above and beyond. Now, hurry up and strip."

The man, James, looked down at the cash in his hand and then up at Will. He sighed, pocketed the money, and started removing his vest. He draped it over the dancing barre and got to work unbuttoning his shirt. He had a white tank top underneath, and Will couldn't help but stare at his muscular shoulders and arms.

"Here you go." He held the shirt out to Will with a smirk.

"Thanks. You must think I'm a total loser. And you're not wrong."

"Nah, I don't think that at all. I actually think you're kinda brave. Have you really not seen Derek since . . . ?"

Will shook his head.

"Yikes, dude. That's intense."

Yeah, that pretty much summed it up.

Will looked around for a place to change, but there wasn't one. He was in good shape, and he knew it. But he didn't like people seeing him undress. After everything that had gone down with Derek, Will's nudity in the movie had morphed in the public eye from something sexy and brave to something ugly and shameful. How could a scrawny sack of bones like William Chapman ever think he was good enough for Derek Hall?

But as much as the body shaming had hurt Will, it had hurt Miles even more. He'd taken the attacks personally and had spent the next ten years trying to finish what he'd started.

"I'm sorry, but would you mind turning around?" Will asked, casting his eyes to the floor.

"Relax, man, you're not exactly my type." James stood with his hands on his hips and a crooked grin on his face, like Will was joking. But when Will made no moves to start changing, James pulled his smile back and turned around.

Will ignored Miles's eye roll and made fast work of switching shirts. The white button down was big on him, but Will preferred it that way, and it smelled nice, like laundry detergent and some kind of citrusy cologne.

"Thank you. I know it's kind of weird. I just—"

"It's okay, man. You don't have to explain yourself to me."

James turned back around and watched with thinly veiled amusement as Will and Miles fought over how many buttons to leave undone. They settled on two, which was a pretty significant victory for Will, given Miles started negotiations at five.

"You ready?" Miles asked.

Will was nowhere near ready. "Yeah, and then we go home."

Miles brushed the hair off Will's forehead and nodded. "And then we go home."

Will focused on the rise and fall of Miles's footsteps as he followed him out of the studio and down the hall. He felt a strange, almost feverish disembodiment. He could hear the blood rushing over his temples and feel the nauseous churn in his gut. But it was like it was happening to someone else, or some other version of himself. It was like he was watching a scene he'd already filmed. It was him, yet he was powerless to turn and run because that wasn't how the scene went.

Will stepped into view, and all conversation dropped off a cliff. He lifted his eyes from the floor and chased the silence down the stairs and into the recessed living room, where Derek stood beside a beautiful blonde woman. She held a glass of red wine in her long, delicate fingers and looked like a model or aspiring actress. Derek loved models and aspiring actresses.

Derek looked exactly the same as he had ten years ago, only now, instead of letting his hair curl over his ears, it was buzzed short on the sides and left textured on top. His square jaw and cleft chin were dusted with a five o'clock shadow, and his hand rested on the curve of the blonde's hip. He looked like he'd just stepped out of a Ralph Lauren catalog in cuffed jeans and a vertical-striped polo.

The girlfriend spotted Will first, and her eyes went wide before narrowing to slits. Derek must've noticed the change in her expression because he dropped his hand from her hip and turned to face Will.

Will had seen Derek's scar in pictures and movies, a thin white line slicing his left eyebrow in two. But it knocked the wind from him, seeing it in person.

Derek didn't smile when his eyes found Will's, not like he used to. Derek used to laugh the moment Will walked into the room, like he was watching a scene from his favorite movie and already knew something funny was about to happen.

But he didn't frown either. That was something. Instead, he stared at Will the way one might stare at a stray cat that's just climbed unbidden through the window, like he wasn't sure if this was a one-off inconvenience he could handle himself or something that might require backup and rabies shots.

Will stayed frozen in place at the top of the stairs for what felt like minutes—though it was probably only seconds. Then Derek took a step forward and broke the spell. Will took an answering step, and though he could feel every eye in the room on him, he continued walking until, by some miracle of physics, he stood within arm's reach of Derek.

It was a good thing Will was merely a disembodied spectator. Otherwise, he would have forgotten his line. But, as it was, he held out his hand—just like Tony had instructed him to do—and said, "Hi."

"Hi." Derek had one of those deep bass voices that made your balls ache. He stared at Will's outstretched hand for a moment and then lifted his own in turn. A simple twine bracelet circled his tan wrist, and his thick forearms were corded with muscle and lined with veins.

Derek's hand closed on Will's, and to Will's surprise, Derek's palm was as sweaty as his own. Derek didn't squeeze, not at first. His grip was soft and tentative. But as they looked up from their joined hands and locked eyes, Derek's grip solidified, and Will allowed himself to breathe for what felt like the first time in hours.

"That's enough," Derek's girlfriend said, walking through their joined hands like it was a ribbon at the end of a race. "Now, go away."

Will's face fell, and he took a step back.

"Excuse me?" Enrique said. "Will's not going anywhere. If you have a problem, you go away."

The woman turned to Derek. "Are you going to let him talk to me like that?"

Derek didn't say anything. He just gaped like a codfish.

"It's okay, Enrique," Will said. "I was going to go home anyway. I've got report cards to finish."

"It's not going to work, you know," the woman said. "People aren't going to forget what you did just because you teach a bunch of disadvantaged children."

"Seriously, Derek," Enrique said. "Get her out of here."

"Whatever. I don't want to be at this stupid party anyway." Derek's girlfriend flipped her hair and started walking away. But she stopped when she realized Derek wasn't following her.

She strode back to get him, and on the way, she pretended to stumble. "Woops," she said as her glass of red wine spilled down the front of Will's shirt—which wasn't even Will's shirt.

"What the fuck, Sharron?" Derek said.

"It was an accident. I didn't mean to."

The wine was cold against Will's skin, and the now pink fabric clung to his stomach and chest. Will tried to catch the runoff so it didn't destroy Enrique's carpet, but it was hopeless. There was too much wine.

"These things happen," Tony said, setting his hand on Derek's shoulder. "William, send me the dry cleaning bill. I'll take care of everything."

Nervous laughter simmered through the crowd as Tony escorted Derek and his girlfriend out. As soon as they were gone, every eye in the room turned to Will, as if they expected him to make a speech.

"Let's go home," Miles said, wrapping his arm around Will's shoulder.

"Don't leave," Andy said, his eyes brimming with tears. "You can just borrow one of Enrique's shirts."

"Yeah, help yourself to anything in my closet. And then come ride the cock." Enrique slapped the flank of the huge pink phallus in the center of the room. "We got it just for you, you know."

Will hated to disappoint his brother and Enrique, but he couldn't fathom staying at the party a second longer, so he just stood there, mute with indecision.

"Let him go, Andy," Ryan said, taking pity on Will. "My driver is right out front. I'll take him home and come right back."

Andy nodded, shaking fresh tears from his eyes. "Yeah, okay." Andy pulled Will into a hug, not caring that Will was drenched in wine. Andy had five inches on his big brother, but he buried his face in Will's shoulder anyway. "Call me tomorrow, okay? We'll hang out."

"Yeah, okay."

As they waited for the elevator, James stepped out of the studio wearing his black vest over his white tank top, which made him look like an exotic dancer halfway through his routine. He stopped when he saw Will, and his mouth fell open. But he recovered quickly, shaking his head at the huge wine stain, like Will was a mischievous child who'd gotten dirt on his church clothes and not a public menace.

"I'm sorry," Will called to him. "I owe you, like, a whole new outfit now."

"It's all good, man. Don't worry about it," James called back. "It's actually kind of a sexy look on you."

Will wouldn't have thought himself capable of blushing in that moment, but he was. His cheeks warmed, and he almost laughed.

Inside the elevator, Will slumped against Miles and sighed. "Well, that was a huge success. I should really get out more often."

Miles laughed and pulled Will close. "I know you're joking, but you're not wrong. You really do need to get out more often. Tonight was just a fluke. You'll see."

CHAPTER 6

JAMES

James could've used four more hours of sleep, but Theo was up, and the aroma of coffee was too powerful to resist. And were those sticky buns James smelled? He pulled on a pair of basketball shorts and a T-shirt and padded down the hall to the coffeemaker.

Last year, when Travis passed away, James took over sole custody of his nephew, Theo. But now that Theo was eighteen, he was his own legal guardian—a terrifying thought.

James doubted much would change. Theo never listened to him anyway, and it wasn't like he was flying the nest any time soon. He was a senior in high school with exactly one plan for his future—form a rock band with his friend Raj and become disgustingly rich and famous.

"How was Coney Island?" James asked, pouring hot coffee over a mound of white sugar.

"It was okay."

"Just okay?"

Theo shrugged, and James knew right away it was boy trouble.

"Did something happen with what's-his-face?" James had

trouble keeping track of Theo's high school romances, which tended to burn bright for a week or so and then flame out.

"No, unless you count showing up to my birthday party with Chad Hollister as something."

Theo tended to use full names like James had a clue who he was talking about. "You're kidding."

"I'm not. I mean, yeah, we talked about opening up the relationship. But we never made it official. And it was my fucking birthday."

"I'm sorry, bud. That sounds awful. And sorry I had to work."

Theo pulled a plate from the cupboard and served James a huge, gooey sticky bun. "It's okay. It's probably better you weren't there anyway. Brice showed up, and—"

"Brice was there?" James didn't mean to sound surprised, but it wasn't every day your ex attended your nephew's birthday party. Of course, that was fine. Brice didn't need to stop being friends with Theo just because they weren't together anymore.

"I don't think he wanted to break up with you," Theo said, switching to his second favorite topic after his own love life—James's love life. "I think he just wanted you to fight for him. He just wanted to see if you cared enough to stop him."

It was too early for this. If Brice didn't want to break up, then he shouldn't have asked to break up—simple as that. James was too old for games. Of course, if Travis were still alive, he'd tell James, *That's what you get for dating a twenty-two-year-old.*

"If you want him back, all you have to do is make some grand gesture. He told me he's not seeing anyone else."

James closed his eyes and washed down the gooey glob in his mouth with a gulp of scalding coffee. "That's not how adult relationships work."

"Yeah, well, adult relationships are boring. There's no passion, no excitement, no risk. And you know what that means? No rewards either."

James shrugged. What did Theo expect him to do, serenade Brice at the skatepark? James was thirty-eight and no longer had the hormones for drama. But Theo wouldn't understand that. He was eighteen and still believed falling in love was magical and fated and not just a cocktail of lust, hormones, and a need for validation.

"Oh my god, did you see TMZ?" Theo asked, changing the subject yet again. "You're not going to believe this. You know that guy who's gonna play you in the movie, William Chapman?"

James's heart thudded in his chest at the mention of William's name. "Yeah, what about him?"

"Well, apparently, he's dating Ryan Ashbury, which is just ridiculous. I mean, he's nowhere near good enough for Ryan. He's not even that hot. I think Ryan must have a secret death wish. Like, he looks all sweet and innocent, but really he's a kinky motherfucker who gets off on bad boys and homoerotic asphyxiation."

James was pretty sure Theo meant autoerotic asphyxiation, but he wasn't about to correct him. He also wasn't going to tell him that TMZ was full of shit. William Chapman—who was about as far from a bad boy as you could get—was definitely not dating Ryan Ashbury, and he wasn't going to be playing James in the movie either; Ryan was.

Theo handed James his phone, which showed a picture of Ryan Ashbury holding the car door open for William Chapman. William's back was to the camera, so James couldn't see the wine stain, but that was James's shirt alright, which meant the picture must've been taken as William was leaving the party. The headline read, *Ryan Ashbury Spotted Getting Cozy With Disgraced Actor, William Chapman.*

Man, James wished he could tell Theo the truth. The kid was going to go apeshit when he found out about Ryan being in the movie. But James's position at the agency demanded discretion, and Theo was the exact opposite of discreet. The kid had no filter. He just said whatever popped into his head. Plus, James had to be extra careful when it came to William Chapman. In a little over a month, he'd be working for William's mother, former Bond girl Donna Wells, who was producing Travis's movie.

James had had to pull some strings to get himself hired on as

Donna's domestic assistant, but he'd managed it. Now, he was going to be responsible for taking care of Donna's medically fragile dog and overseeing the general setup and maintenance of her house on location in Vermont that summer. It wouldn't be the same as being on the set itself, but it was better than nothing.

For some reason, the studio didn't want James to watch them film, claiming the "intimacy of the difficult subject matter" necessitated a completely closed set, as if the difficult subject matter wasn't James's life.

James wasn't one to take no for an answer. Sure, he was a little worried Donna would make the connection and fire him. But he went by his mother's maiden name now, and even though he'd helped Travis write the book, his name was nowhere on it. There was no reason to think Donna would make the connection between her dog-sitter, James Barrett, and the character in the movie she was producing, Jimmy Young.

The only downside was figuring out what to do with Theo for two months. James didn't trust him on his own, and they needed to sublet the apartment for money. James wanted to ship him off to Florida with his grandmother, but Theo refused to go, saying he wasn't going to spend his summer playing bingo.

"I brought you home a present," James said. "It's on top of my dresser."

Theo scowled, probably because James had already given him his present—drivers ed lessons. The kid was eighteen, and it was high time he learned how to drive a car.

Theo disappeared down the hall and came back with the crystal tumbler in hand. "You bought me a glass? What the fuck? It's not even clean."

"That right there is the very glass a certain curly-haired vampire, who shall remain nameless, drank from."

Theo's eyes bulged, and his mouth fell open. "No way. You worked at Andy Chapman's bachelor party last night? Did you see

Ryan? Did you touch his hair? Is he really dating William Chapman? You have to tell me everything."

James shook his head. "You know I can't discuss work stuff with you."

Theo held the glass up to his nose, closed his eyes, and inhaled. "I think I can smell his lip balm. Do you think it's coconut flavored? I bet it's coconut flavored."

He threw his arms around James and squeezed him as hard as he could, like he used to when he was four. "This is the best birthday present ever. We need to make a shelf to put it on. You know how to make a shelf, don't you? Ooh, or maybe a pedestal, like one of those ones that normally has a marble bust on it. And we'll need proper lighting, too, like something warm that makes the crystal glow. Or maybe a blacklight. Do chapstick smears show up under blacklight?"

"I don't know, bud."

James's phone chimed in his pocket—cha-ching—and he almost shat his pants when he saw how much money Esther had wired him. And that was only half of it. Damn, maybe he should've stuck with the paparazzi business, after all.

"Is everything okay?"

James ignored the brick of guilt in his stomach. "Yeah, everything's fine."

Before heading home from the bachelor party, James had called Esther and begged her not to publish anything about William, but Esther had refused.

"Are you kidding me?" she'd said. "Do you have any idea how much I'm gonna be able to sell this story for? Some of us gotta eat, you know."

"My mom called me last night." Theo carried his empty plate over to the dishwasher as if he hadn't just pulled the pin from a grenade and set it in James's open palm.

"What? How did she get your number?"

"I gave it to her. She DM'd me on Instagram."

James would have responded, but Theo had rendered him speechless. What the hell was Emily up to?

"She said I can come stay with her this summer, so now you can shut up about Florida."

"I don't think that's a good idea."

"Did you know I'm gonna get two and a half percent of the movie's budget? Oh, and apparently, I have a little brother. He's almost three. His name is Wyatt, which makes him sound like a cowboy. But he's not. Though, he is really into Spider-Man."

How the hell had she even found out about the movie?

"You're gonna need that money to pay for school and buy a house and—"

"I already told you. I'm not gonna go to college."

James deflated. They'd already had this argument a hundred times. Theo didn't want to plan for the future. He wanted to live in the now, which James understood. He really did. Theo was afraid he was going to follow in his father's footsteps, and he wanted to make the most of whatever time he had left.

James couldn't fault him for that. He just thought Theo was taking it too far. There was a fifty percent chance Theo would be just fine, in which case he was going to need to be able to support himself. The money from the movie and Travis's life insurance wouldn't last forever.

While Theo had been a minor, the doctors wouldn't test him for the mutated gene. But now that he was eighteen, it was up to him, and James prayed to God he wouldn't go through with it.

When they'd found out their father's early-onset Alzheimer's was genetic, James and Travis had both gotten tested right away, not even considering the consequences.

It had worked out for James; he hadn't inherited the gene. But Travis had, and he'd never been the same after finding out.

"She just wants your money, Theo. And it may seem like a lot to you now, but it's not."

"No she doesn't."

"And you can't be lending it to people."

"I'm not. She hasn't even asked me." Theo turned on the Switch and passed a controller to James. "She just wants to hang out. And she's got her own house now. It's in St. Albans, which is just—"

"I know where St. Albans is." James selected Ryu. What was he supposed to do now, forbid Theo from going? Would Theo even listen?

Theo chose Link. "Apparently, it's close to the lake and you can go boating and everything there."

"We'll discuss it later." Just what they needed, Emily trying to get her drug-addled hands on Theo's meager inheritance.

"Oh, and Brady might come stay with us next weekend." Theo was just full of surprises that morning.

"Are you two getting back together?" Brady was Theo's first love, but he lived out of state.

"No, of course not. We're just gonna hang out."

"Will he be sleeping in your room?"

Theo rolled his eyes. "Just because your heart has the attention span of a goldfish doesn't mean the rest of us are the same way. It doesn't always have to be all or nothing. It is possible to still love someone even after you realize they're not your forever person."

"Alright, whatever you say."

CHAPTER 7
WILL

"I can't believe I finally get to meet your mother." Tiffany snaked her arm through Will's. "Though I feel bad. All I really know about her, thanks to you, is that she used to be hot, which is not exactly the best conversation starter. Do you think she'll be offended that I haven't seen any of her movies, but I've seen, like, all of your dad's?"

"She was a Bond girl, not Meryl Streep. She gets fucked and then murdered. There, saved you the trouble."

Will had been shocked when Tiffany had shown up at his doorstep that morning, waving the TMZ article in his face and demanding to know why he'd never told her about Ryan Ashbury.

Will had almost puked when he'd seen his picture and name in print again. But, as far as tabloid stories went, he couldn't have asked for a better one, especially given the night he'd had. And, as a consolation prize, Tiffany was now going to brunch with him instead of Miles, which meant his mother was going to have to pretend to be nice.

"That's just one movie, though."

"Okay, fine, you want a detailed account of her filmography? In

Delta Delta Delta, she played a sorority girl who gets tricked into fucking the wrong guy in a hot tub, and then she exacts revenge by getting her sorority to win a fundraising game of strip football. Then, in *Alley Girl*, she played a sex worker, named Alley, who gets mistaken as the new governess for this wealthy family. Think *The Nanny* meets *Pretty Woman*.

"My dad must've really liked that one because here I am. Then she tried her hand at the small screen, filming three separate pilots in five years. In the first, she played a detective who was also a mom. In the second, she played a lawyer who was also a mom. In the third, she played a mom who was also a Russian spy. Of course, none of them were picked up, so probably best if you don't mention them.

"Then, after almost ten years of marriage, essentially the longest relationship in Hollywood history, she divorced my dad. That's right, she divorced him. My dad, who used the divorce to garner as much sympathy as possible, continued racking up Oscar nominations—no wins, of course—while my mom, who was pushing forty at that point, and thus at the end of her fuckable years according to Hollywood, was reduced to starring in Hallmark movies. You know the deal. She gets stranded in a small town with a large budget for Christmas decorations and gives up her high-powered career to help raise the kid of a widowed mechanic.

"Now, she's in that awkward stage where she's too old to be the heroine and too hot to be the grandma, so instead, she produces movies and fucks aging European models, and by aging I mean, like, thirty-five. She likes to get them right when their careers are over and their self-esteem has sunk to the level of their employment potential."

Tiffany steered them down 58th. "So your mom's a cougar. That's so cool."

"She's a ruthless bitch."

"God, Will, don't talk about your mother like that. She sounds awesome to me."

"Well, anyway, now you know her whole career."

There was no use defending his honest assessment of his mother's character, no use describing what his childhood was like while his mom was off learning the value of family and his dad was trying every trick in the book to win an Oscar, including dying in the Holocaust, wearing a false nose, overcoming paralysis, and playing an autistic savant. Tiffany would find out soon enough.

"Do you think they'll let me in like this?" Tiffany wore shorts and flip-flops, showing off her dark, toned legs and bright red toenail polish. "I wasn't planning to go to a fancy restaurant today."

"Shit, did that guy just recognize me?" Will ducked his head and pretended to look at something on the ground.

"No, he probably just thinks you're hot. Or maybe he's wondering why you're so sweaty. It's not like anyone watches TMZ."

Will glared at her.

"I only know because I got Jennifer those Ryan Ashbury pillowcases for her birthday last year and now Google thinks I need to be kept abreast of everything Ryan Ashbury. Did you know he's a vegetarian and owns his own pit bull rehabilitation center?"

THEY ARRIVED at the Four Seasons five minutes early and were shown to their table in The Garden. Will's mother, who liked to make an entrance, showed up ten minutes late. She wore a long white dress that showed off far too much freckled boob and large two-toned sunglasses, which she pushed up into her glossy red hair the moment she stepped into the restaurant.

Her high heels tapped across the wooden floor like snare drum flams. "I thought you were bringing Miles."

"Nope, this is Tiffany."

"It's an honor to meet you, Ms. Wells." Tiffany stood and did some cross between a bow and a curtsey.

"Call me Donna." His mom shook Tiffany's hand. "You have really nice skin."

Tiffany acted like his mother hadn't just said something racist and held her hand out like she was showing off an engagement ring. "Thanks. I recently discovered this hand sanitizer that's also a lotion. I use it, like, a hundred times a day."

"I take it you work with my son, then?"

"Yeah, I also teach kindergarten."

It was generous of Tiffany to use the word *also*. But it wasn't accurate. Tiffany actually taught kindergarten. Her students sat at circle, read from their book-baskets, and did their writers' workshop. Meanwhile, Will's students ran around the room dipping their shaving cream coated hands into the sand table and soiling the Jurassic Sand, which was very expensive, a fact Will's principal never failed to mention whenever she popped in to see what all the screaming was about.

"That's good," his mother said. "It's important for those kids to see someone who looks like them in a position of power and respect. Are you looking forward to summer vacation?"

"Definitely," Tiffany said. "Though I've got two teenage daughters at home, so it's not really going to be much of a vacation."

Will's mother stared at Tiffany in awe, trying to decide if she looked good for her age or if she'd gotten knocked up young. Then she turned her critical gaze on Will.

"I see you made it to the bachelor party. Andy was sure you were going to come up with some excuse not to go." She frowned and studied Will like he had spinach in his teeth. "You should drink more water. It will help reduce the bags under your eyes."

Will, who was about to take a drink of his water, set his glass back down.

"How are you holding up?" his mother asked, as if she cared.

"Fine."

"Good, your father still needs you. So don't go making any plans for the summer." She pulled her phone from her bag and checked the time.

"What?"

"Well, you know he can't play a man dying in front of his sons without at least one of his sons present. And Andy's busy with the wedding. Plus, you know how much he likes running lines with you. It will be just like when you were a kid."

"Since when do you give a shit what Dad needs?" Will couldn't go to Vermont. Derek was going to be there.

"Since I'm producing."

"You're producing? Why?"

"I can't say." She smiled at Tiffany. "No offense, honey, but this is all very hush hush." She patted Tiffany's hand.

"None taken." Tiffany looked between Will and his mother as they stared each other down.

"I'm just going to tell her anyway."

"I wish I could, hun. I really do. But I'm not even supposed to tell you."

"I can just go to the bathroom or something," Tiffany suggested.

"Don't you dare." Will pinned Tiffany's hand to the table. "What is it, Mom?"

"I'll tell you this much. I bought a house up there, and it's only a mile from the set."

Of course she'd bought a house. "There is no way I'm spending my summer in the middle of the woods just so I can read lines with Dad." And there was no way in hell he was going to share a house with his mother.

"Don't worry, I'll hardly be there," his mother said, reading his mind. "I'm headed to France and then Italy. But I'll be in and out. Oh, and I need you to watch Atticus for a couple of days." She glanced at the floor where she'd set her purse. Inside, Atticus, who was more like a ten-thousand-dollar house plant than a living creature with agency, sat wide awake and completely motionless. "He had an appointment this morning, and the vet says he's got inner-ear problems and shouldn't fly anymore."

"I'm not babysitting your dog."

"Oh, stop. It's just for a couple of days. I already called the agency, and they're going to send someone to collect him. Besides, I already sent his stuff over to your apartment."

Before Will could protest further, the waitress came to get their orders. He and Tiffany had already decided to split the "legendary" ricotta pancakes. But his mother found this objectionable.

"Oh, stop. It's on me. Get whatever you want."

Tiffany, who for some reason cared what his mother thought, felt guilty and ordered the cauliflower steak. Now Will was going to have to eat all the pancakes himself.

"Just an iced tea for me," his mother said. "I can't stay. I have a four o'clock flight."

As soon as the waitress was out of earshot, Will turned on his mother. "Why did you drag me here, then, if you can't even stay?" They were supposed to be discussing agents and publicists, not being his father's unpaid intern.

His mother took a sip of her water, and her rings clanged against the glass. "I invited you to breakfast, not lunch. It's not my fault you were too busy drumming up a scandal to get up on time. This is the last thing your father needs, and now you've dragged Ryan into it, too. This whole movie is going to be a disaster." She turned her ice-cold stare on Tiffany. "Don't tell anyone I said that. Actually"—she reached into her purse and pulled out a manilla envelope—"I brought this for Miles to sign, but you should probably sign one, too."

"What is it?" Tiffany asked.

"It's an NDA, a non-disclosure agreement."

Will threw his hands in the air. "You're un-fucking-believable."

"No, this is awesome." A large smile spread across Tiffany's face. "I've never signed one of these before. Do you have a pen?"

"Yes, right here." His mother pulled a pen from her purse. "You should come up to Vermont, too. Bring your daughters. There's plenty of room. And it's a perfect place for kids. There's a boat, and the stables are less than a mile away."

"Can we, Will?" Tiffany batted her long eyelashes at him. "Please."

"Absolutely not."

"Besides, we could really use your help with the wedding. Bring Miles, too. We had to promise Nandi there would be swans in the marsh to get her to change the venue at the last minute. Do you have any idea how mean swans are? I'm going to need my son-in-law there for protection."

"Son-in-law?" Tiffany's eyebrows shot up in surprise.

"He's not my husband." Will's hangover headache came roaring back.

"Just because you have an open marriage doesn't mean it isn't real."

Tiffany clicked the pen like a metronome. "What is she talking about? You're married?"

"No, Miles just needed this operation a while ago, and he's got really shitty insurance because he's self-employed, and—"

"Oh my god! How did I not know this? This explains so much."

Will threw his hands in the air. "Just sign the NDA already."

Before the food arrived, Tiffany pulled Will's hand from her thigh and announced she was going to the bathroom. He gave her a *don't you dare* stare, which she responded to in kind, flashing him a *don't be a little brat* glance that hit like a viper strike. No wonder her class was so well behaved.

Wasting no time, his mother got right to work, weaving her manipulations and guilt trips.

"It's not my place to tell you this. And I promised your father I wouldn't. But like you said, when have I ever given a shit what he wants? I'm the one who's going to be left cleaning up the mess."

"You know what, Mom, save your breath. I don't care."

She set her hands flat on the table. "The cancer is back. And this time he's decided not to fight it."

"What?" There was only enough air in Will's lungs for one word.

His mother reached out to take his hand, but he pulled it away. "That's why everything is so rushed. Originally, the doctors said six months, maybe a year. But now they're saying it might be less."

Will sat there in stunned silence.

"Andy doesn't know yet. Your father wants to wait until after the wedding, you know, so he doesn't draw focus."

Will's nervous sweat turned cold. Too many thoughts raced through his mind to settle on any one. His dad was dying—like, for real this time. Was that why Will wasn't being cast? Was this all just another ploy for an Oscar? Was his father refusing chemo just so he could actually die while he portrayed a dying man?

"He really wanted you to have the part, you know. He just couldn't put you through it." She lifted her phone and checked the time again, like she couldn't wait to get out of there. "Just spend time with him. Read lines and critique his accent, like when you were a kid. He always used to say he gave his best performances rehearsing in the library with you, even when you were too little to talk."

Will's dull headache turned into a stabbing pain. "And what about Andy?"

"What about him?"

"Don't you think he might want to spend time with Dad, too?"

"You know how sensitive he is. He's not like us. This will crush him."

Will closed his eyes and bit his lip, afraid he was going to cry or scream or do something else that would wind up on the front page of some tabloid.

When he opened his eyes again, he noticed his mother had placed a leather-bound notebook before him. "I had my secretary make you a manual for Atticus. Everything you need to know is there."

"Does Derek know?"

His mother took a breath before answering. "He does. Your father is planning to tell the cast and crew, but no one else. We're not even letting the Young family come and watch filming. If this gets out, the set will be swarming with paparazzi, even up in Vermont, so don't tell anyone, even Miles."

Tiffany was making her way back to the table.

"Did you know Derek was going to be at the party?"

His mother sighed, and she almost looked sympathetic. "No, you have your father to thank for that."

Tiffany sank into her seat beside Will, and she must have sensed something was off because she set her hand on his knee and squeezed.

"Do either of you need any supplies for your classroom, an overhead projector or something? A girlfriend of mine just got her grandson this inflatable bounce house. Do you think you could fit one of those?"

"Jesus Christ, Mom."

"I'll take a bounce house," Tiffany said.

CHAPTER 8
JAMES

This was where William Chapman lived? The location was decent, but the building wasn't any nicer than James's place in Queens.

James knocked twice on the door and took a step back. He'd agreed to take Donna Wells's dog a month early because she was going to Europe and the little guy was too fragile to fly. But he wasn't sure he'd be able to keep the job in Vermont after all, not if it meant letting Emily anywhere near Theo.

The door opened, and William Chapman's big, dark eyes peered up at him. "James? What are you doing here?"

The man before James looked nothing like the man at the party. Instead of a pair of tight-fitting chinos that gripped his perfect ass, William wore baggy sweatpants. Instead of a form-fitting T-shirt, he wore an oversized monstrosity that hid every curve and muscle. Instead of glossy, tousled black waves, William's face was framed by dry wisps of product-free hair.

"I came to get—"

"Shit, you're here for your shirt, aren't you? I'm sorry. I took it to the dry cleaners this morning."

"Actually, I came—"

"You probably don't even want it back, though, do you? I don't blame you. There's no way they're getting that stain out. How about I just pay you? Is a hundred enough? I could probably swing two hundred."

James considered telling William the truth, that he was there to get the dog, but he was curious how high William would go. Would he offer James a grand for his thirty-dollar shirt? "Mind if I come in?"

William's face scrunched up in confusion, as if no one had ever asked him that question before. "Uh, okay, sure."

The apartment James stepped into was shockingly average. The fridge was covered in children's drawings, like when Theo was a little boy, and James recognized the IKEA couch and cube shelf.

A small dog—a little brown yorkie—came trundling up to James and crashed right into his shoe.

"Sorry, that's my mom's dog, Atticus. He's super old, and he can't really see, or hear, or smell. But he's nice."

James bent down to pet the dog. "Aww, poor little guy."

"Trust me, Atticus doesn't need your sympathy. That dog has a better life than most people could ever dream of. In fact, someone's coming by soon to whisk him away to my mom's new lake house in Vermont. Plus, he's older than dirt."

James couldn't have asked for a better segue into why he was really there, but he decided to have a little fun instead.

"Wait, are you saying your mom's dog has his own personal assistant? That's gotta be the most degrading job ever. What kind of loser would take a job like that?"

Will shrugged, but he didn't take the bait. "Oh, I don't know. I suppose it depends on how you look at it. People will do almost anything for a paycheck, and at least this job doesn't kill people or destroy the planet. I mean, I'd way rather be my mom's dog-sitter than some crooked politician, voting whichever way the money blows. Do you have any idea how scary it is to run active shooter drills with a bunch of five-year-olds?"

"Huh, I never thought of it that way. Still, this dog-sitter guy can't have much self-respect or ambition. He's probably hideous, too. I bet he lives in his mother's basement and uses her handicap pass to get better parking."

"Or he's a genius who's figured out that there's more to life than buying shit. And I'm sure he's not hideous. In fact, I bet he's super hot."

James couldn't help but smile, even though the compliment wasn't meant for him. "Oh yeah, why do you say that?"

"Because my mom's idea of feminism is to act like a pervy old white man. Let me put it to you this way. If you want a job working for my mom, you don't need an impressive resume. You need an impressive headshot."

James puffed out his chest and gave William his most rakish smile. "What about me? Do you think I'd get the job?"

The color that flooded William's pale cheeks was as red as a strawberry. "Oh, yeah, you'd be my new daddy for sure."

James couldn't help but laugh. So, William Chapman did find him attractive.

James scooped up the dog and carried him over to the couch, determined to drag his visit out a little longer, but there was no place to sit. The cushions were covered with black and white composition notebooks.

"What are all these?"

"Oh, those are just my students' homework books. If I don't draw a smiley face on every page, they get upset." William started stacking the books on the coffee table so there was a place for James to sit. "It takes forever, but it's my own damn fault for doing it once. Now I can't stop."

James plopped down onto the spot William had cleared for him. "Want some help? I'm pretty good at drawing smiley faces."

"That's okay. It's not very hard."

"I didn't ask if it was hard. I asked if you wanted help."

William perched on the arm of the chair opposite James and

rubbed the back of his neck. His shirt sleeve rode up and revealed the pale curve of his bicep. He wasn't jacked, not like his friend, Miles, but he was cut.

"I appreciate the offer, but it's probably better if I do it myself. It's a confidentiality thing. I'm not even allowed to tell you their names."

"Oh, that makes sense." James situated the dog on his chest and stroked his hand down its bony back. "How are you doing with everything? I heard about what happened with you and Derek's girlfriend."

William grimaced. "I'm fine. I'm used to it."

"You don't have to pretend with me. How are you really?"

James wasn't sure why he was such a glutton for punishment, but he had to know. Esther's story was set to be published in two days, and James couldn't stop obsessing over his role in throwing William Chapman under the bus.

"I'm not pretending. I'm totally fine." William must have seen the skeptical look on James's face because he started rattling off ridiculous excuses. "I know I puked and freaked out a bit, but that was just because I drank too much and skipped dinner. I'm good now. Besides, I have bigger fish to fry, like all this shit with Ryan. I mean, it's ridiculous. All the poor guy did was give me a ride home, and now his publicist is running around doing damage control. I mean, Jesus, are people really so gullible? Who in their right mind would honestly believe that Ryan is dating me?"

"Wait, so you and Ashbury aren't together, then? I assumed he was the boyfriend Miles was referring to, the one who's 'way hotter than Derek Hall.'"

William scoffed. "No you didn't. Stop lying. You know perfectly well I don't have a boyfriend. Miles is just an asshole."

Heat bloomed in James's chest. *So, William Chapman was single.*

James may have never believed the William Chapman Ryan Ashbury rumors, but that didn't mean William didn't have some other hot boyfriend. Why wouldn't he? The guy was rich and famous—or infamous, at any rate. He probably had his pick of hot guys.

"Anyway, I can give you two hundred now, and I get paid next week, so I can give you the rest then. Do you have Venmo?"

Okay, so maybe William Chapman wasn't rich. But he was definitely famous, not to mention sexy as fuck. He had that whole *I'm a broody bad boy who's secretly sweet as hell* vibe down pat.

"I'm not here for your money, dude. Your bodyguard already paid me for the shirt, remember?"

"Yeah, but not all of it. And you didn't even really agree. Miles basically forced you into it."

"He didn't force me. I wanted to help."

"Why?"

It was obvious William didn't mean to say that. As soon as the word was out of his mouth, he jumped to his feet and started folding the blanket draped over the back of the chair.

"Because you dumped champagne all over me and immediately took responsibility. You even offered to clean up the mess."

"Come on, anyone would do that."

"I don't know, man. You'd be surprised."

William set the folded blanket back on the chair and crossed his arms over his chest. "Well, if you're not here about the shirt, then why are you here? Are you looking for Miles? He's out on a date right now, and I don't know when—"

"I'm actually here to pick up this guy." James rubbed his nose against the dog's and let the little rat lick his face.

"What? Really? You're my mom's new dog-sitter?"

"That's right. You and I are going to be roomies this summer." James smiled up at William, expecting William to smile back.

But James's declaration had the exact opposite effect. All the color drained from William's face, and he scowled.

"Well, assuming I can figure out what to do with Theo for the summer," James added, trying to fill the awkward silence. Had he read William wrong?

"Who's Theo?"

James was about to tell William the truth, that Theo was his nephew, but he decided to change course at the last second, not wanting to leave any clues about his connection to the movie.

"He's my son. He's eighteen now, so, in theory, I should be able to leave him at home alone. I just don't trust him not to burn the place down. Don't get me wrong. He's a good kid. He's just kind of a free spirit."

"Why don't you bring him with you, then? My mom won't care. She'll probably put him to work, make him skim bugs from the pool and freshen up her drink."

"He actually is a pretty decent bartender, not to mention a phenomenal cook."

"See, there you go. I'm sure my mom is planning to hire a personal chef anyway. Just tell her your son will do it."

Would that work? No, James couldn't bring Theo. Theo would blow their cover on the first day. And even if he did manage to keep their secret, James didn't want him there. It wasn't good for Theo to immerse himself in their family drama.

"What about you? Would you wanna eat food prepared by an obnoxious teenager?"

"Don't worry about me. I might not even go. And if I do, I'll probably just cook for myself."

"What do you mean you might not even go? Your mom said you'd be there the whole summer. Aren't you gonna be helping your dad run lines and stuff?"

"It's complicated."

William may have only said two words—*it's complicated*—but his eyes spoke volumes.

"You mean because of Derek?"

William winced. "Yeah, among other things. Here, I'll help you carry Atticus's stuff down. Did you drive or take a cab?"

James didn't want to let William change the subject, but he

didn't want to push his luck either. "I drove. My car's just a couple blocks away."

It took them two trips to get everything down to James's car. The dog had so much shit it was unreal: pill boxes, orthopedic pillows, pee pads, four different dog beds, a six-month supply of wet food, two toothbrushes, beef flavored toothpaste, a suitcase full of toys, diapers, a crate, all sorts of snacks and treats, a mortar and pestle, and what appeared to be an IV drip. He even came with a leather-bound manual.

James leaned against the side of his car. "Now, I know I don't get a vote, but, for what it's worth, I hope you decide to come up and keep me company. It can get pretty lonely out in the sticks."

William blushed again—this time as red as a tomato. It didn't make any sense. Was William into him or not?

Whatever. It didn't matter. It wasn't like James wanted to get tangled up in William Chapman's never-ending drama anyway. James had enough drama of his own to deal with. Plus, it was never a good idea to mix business with pleasure.

"I don't know," William said, dropping his gaze to the sidewalk. "We'll see."

"Mind if I drop by in a couple days and grab the shirt? I think it'll make a cool souvenir." James didn't actually care about the shirt. He just wanted an excuse to check on William after Esther's article ran. At least, that's what he told himself.

"Uh, sure, no problem."

CHAPTER 9
WILL

Will moved fast, but not fast enough to stop Julian from bashing Yareli's head against the wall.

"Stop!"

Will's instincts told him to grab Julian and restrain him, but that wasn't what he did. He did what the textbook told him to do; he went to the victim first. The idea was to deny the aggressor negative attention.

He scooped Yareli up and held her to his chest. "Are you okay?"

Great, now they were in for it. With Yareli out of the way, Julian moved on to trashing the room. He started with the math manipulatives, and in a matter of seconds, every counting bear, tangram, unifix cube, chain-link, and pattern block was on the floor.

"Julian, go to your safe space and take some breaths." It took all Will's strength to remain calm.

"She took the blue one. I wanted the blue one."

After school, Will was removing everything blue from the room —every book, every block, every shovel, you name it. Julian was obsessed with the character Catboy, who was blue, and firmly believed everything blue belonged to him. And if he didn't get it, he lost his shit.

"Julian, walk over to your safe space and take some breaths."

"You're a fucking bitch, and I'm gonna make you sorry." Julian threw a pair of scissors at Will's head and barely missed him.

Will walked over to the phone, still holding Yareli, and called the office. "I need support in 203."

Mary, the school secretary, gave Will a knowing shake of her head and a sympathetic, "Ay, papi," as he walked past her into Principal King's office during his prep period. A few more weeks and it would be summer vacation: Jones Beach, Coney Island, and waiting all day for free Shakespeare in the Park tickets. He just had to survive. He just had to sit through another one of King's lectures.

Will sat in his usual chair and stared up at the giant inspirational poster of Theodore Roosevelt on the wall. *People don't care how much you know until they know how much you care,* it read.

Principal King sat across from him. She was a smoke-stained, leather skinned, wildly unpredictable woman. One day she'd suggest the kids needed more love and snacks, and the next she'd scream at Will for not yelling more. *Sometimes you have to raise your voice to be heard, Mr. Chapman.*

She folded her hands and smiled at Will from behind her desk. Her brittle auburn hair curled an inch above her shoulders, and Will could tell by the way she kept glancing out the window that she was jonesing for a cigarette.

She didn't say anything for probably twenty seconds. Then she opened her drawer and pulled out a copy of *US Weekly*. "Looks like you had a fun weekend."

"It was alright." *Jesus, US Weekly picked up the story, too?*

King flipped through the magazine until she came to the page she wanted, the photo of him getting into Ryan's car. "Why exactly are you still here, Mr. Chapman?"

"What?"

King stood and walked over to a low bookshelf and flicked on an electric kettle. "Well, you're not exactly doing yourself any favors. Or your students, for that matter." She pulled a wet tea bag from her mug and dropped it in the trash. "This isn't just a job, William. It's a lifestyle, a calling. It's not an experiment, or penance."

"That's not—"

She held up a hand, silencing him. "It's no secret this has been a difficult year for you. A difficult couple of years, really."

"I've had a few hard classes, but—"

"Let me give you some advice, Mr. Chapman. Don't blame the kids. Don't ever blame the kids. It's not the kids. It's never the kids."

"Well—"

"I don't think you're a bad teacher. Sometimes, I walk by your classroom and hear you playing the guitar and singing and think, give this man his own kids' show already. They would absolutely adore you in Westchester or Long Island. Hell, I'd put my own grandkids in your class. But this isn't Westchester or Long Island. This is a different population."

"What happened to it's not the kids?" Will said.

"It's not." Will thought she was going to go all Mr. Hyde on him. But she smoothed her skirt and stood there waiting for the kettle to boil. "If you'd like to apply for a job elsewhere, I'd be more than happy to write you a glowing letter of recommendation."

"That's good to know." *Just a few more weeks.*

King dropped a fresh tea bag into her mug. "Just something to think about. I think you'd be happier. You're going to burn out at the rate you're going. I've seen it happen time and time again." She looked out the window, no doubt picturing her next cigarette. "I wonder how you'd do teaching fifth grade next year?"

She wouldn't.

The door flew open, and Julian came running in, followed closely by Mrs. Cruz, one of the lunch aides.

"I'm so sorry," Mrs. Cruz said, reaching for the boy, who was now firmly wrapped around Will's waist.

"Excuse me, young man," King snapped. "We're in the middle of a private meeting. Out of my office this instant!"

Julian's eyes went wide before welling with tears. Why was King yelling at Julian? He didn't do anything to her.

"I understand your tone was meant for me," Will said, breathing through his anger. "But can you please ask nicely next time?"

Will turned his attention away from his boss and focused on Julian. He didn't need to ask the kid if he'd had another accident. He could smell it. "Julian, go with Mrs. Cruz to the nurse's office. I'll meet you there with a change of clothes and help you get cleaned up, okay?"

Julian only trusted two people to change him, his grandmother and Will. He looked up at Will with tears in his eyes, not believing Will would actually come.

"I promise, I'll be right behind you."

Julian still didn't want to let Will go, but Mrs. Cruz was able to pry him off.

Before they left, King stepped around her desk and crouched down to Julian's level. "I'm sorry for yelling. I shouldn't have done that. Mr. Chapman is right. I should've asked you nicely. If I promise to ask nicely next time, will you promise to knock before coming into my office?"

Julian looked to Will for guidance, and when Will nodded, so did Julian.

"You know, if you could advocate for yourself half as well as you advocate for your students, you might actually be a halfway decent teacher," King said when they were alone again.

Will swallowed the lump of bitterness in his throat. "I should probably go help Julian get cleaned up."

King took a sip of her tea and smiled over the rim of her mug.

"Thank you for your time, William. Think about what I said. You have more options than you think."

Will didn't know what to say to that, so he just stood, nodded, and left.

"Mr. Chapman, I feel terrible asking you this"—Mary started unrolling a large poster—"but I promised my daughter I would." Ryan Ashbury's face stared back at Will, his lustrous blond curls spilling from the curve of the poster. "Is there any way you could get this autographed for her? She's obsessed with *Blood Brothers*."

Will took a deep breath, closed his eyes, and held out his hand. "Sure, no problem."

TIFFANY ADDED another armload of blue to the pile at the end of the day. "So, have you decided if you're going to Vermont or not? Miles tells me the dog-sitter your mom hired is smoking hot."

Will grabbed the job chart off the wall and started rotating everyone down a spot. "Why would I want to waste my summer taking everyone's coffee orders?"

It was ridiculous. His dad was dying, and he wanted to run lines like everything was normal, like Will was a little kid who couldn't wait to grow up and be just like Daddy. And so what if the dog-sitter was hot? All of Will's mother's assistants were hot. Besides, James was straight. He even had a kid.

"Yeah, but it's right on the lake, and there are horses and boats and Ben and Jerry's."

"You know we have all that shit right here, don't you?" Will picked up his guitar and started tuning it because Awa had turned all the knobs again. "You can still go without me. My mom would be thrilled to have you. You could help her plan the wedding. I'm sure you'd be great at wrangling swans."

"That's true. I really would say boo to a goose." Tiffany made her way to Will's library, where the books were spilling from their baskets. "What did King want? Let me guess, you're getting a new student?"

"Even better. She threatened to move me up to fifth grade next year if I don't apply for a new job on Long Island. But don't worry, she'll write me a glowing letter of recommendation." Will set his guitar down and headed over to the easel to write the next day's morning message.

"You're not going to do it, are you?"

"I don't know." Will pulled the cap off the blue expo marker, and then, catching himself, tossed it onto the growing pile.

"Come on, we'll finish up here, and then I'll buy you a margarita and some nachos." Tiffany started shoving all the blue stuff into garbage bags for storage.

"I can't."

"Too many calories? Is Miles going to give you a spanking?"

"Probably, but that's not why. I told my brother I'd meet him for dinner."

"Oh, poor you. I can't believe you have to go have dinner with your movie star brother at some fancy restaurant."

Tiffany was right, of course. Will had no right to complain. Still, he wasn't looking forward to lying to his brother all night. Andy was going to be furious with him when he found out Will knew their father was dying and didn't tell him.

Tiffany pulled a peanut butter cup from her purse and tossed it to Will. "Are you still coming to trivia on Thursday?"

"Yeah, I'll be there."

CHAPTER 10
JAMES

"Don't tell me you're feeling guilty," Esther said. James had her on speaker phone because he was giving Atticus his fluids. The dog was prone to dehydration, and James had to stick a needle in his back and shoot water directly into his body. How the hell that worked was beyond him.

"He's just a regular guy, Es. I was at his apartment, and it's small and totally average. Plus, he's a friggin' kindergarten teacher."

"He tried to kill someone and got away with it. Trust me, being the story of the week is a hell of a lot better than going to prison. If you ask me, he's getting off easy. Plus, this was your idea. I was just doing you a favor."

Esther was a master manipulator. James may have complained about William Chapman ruining his movie, but it was her idea to try and get him fired. "Yeah, but he was never even gonna be in the movie in the first place."

"How were we supposed to know that? Just relax. This is all gonna blow over. Trust me, William Chapman is gonna go right back to biting dicks like none of this ever happened. But, if you're really that worried about it, there is something you could do."

"Oh yeah, what's that?" James pulled the needle from Atticus's back and pinched the skin to keep the liquid from leaking out of the hole.

"Well, you said he's gonna be staying at his mom's, right? And Derek will be around, too, not to mention his dad. You'll be in the perfect position to solve one of Hollywood's greatest mysteries. Do you have any idea how much money you'd get for a story like that?"

"And do you have any idea how much trouble I'd get in for breaking my NDA?"

"They don't have to know it was you. And you'd be doing Chapman a favor. According to him, he doesn't remember what happened that night. He was blackout drunk. Think about it. You could help him fill in the gaps, give him the closure he so desperately needs."

A key turned in the lock. "I gotta go, Es. Theo's home."

"Alright, I'll swing by later and drop off his birthday present. He's gonna love it."

Theo tossed a copy of *Star Magazine* onto the coffee table. "How could you not tell me? This is huge. Ryan Ashbury is gonna be playing you in the movie. Do you have any idea how amazing this is?"

James looked away from the cover, where William stood, wide-eyed and wine-soaked. The picture Esther got was brutal. It not only showed William's utter disbelief, but also Derek's righteous anger. No wonder they'd paid her so much money for it.

"Pretty amazing," James said.

"Now you have to bring me with you. You have to."

"No, I don't."

James had already run the idea by Donna, who was fine with it as long as Theo signed an NDA and was comfortable cooking paleo.

"Well, then I'll just steal Mom's car and drive down. I already looked it up. She only lives, like, an hour away."

"You will do no such thing because you'll be in Florida." Since when had Theo started calling Emily Mom?

Theo smirked and shrugged his shoulders. Teenagers were the worst.

"You'd have to sign an NDA, and we both know you'd break it in two seconds. And it's not like Ryan is gonna drop by the house. You'd never even see him."

"Yeah, but I'd be in the same town." Theo pushed his dark-rimmed glasses up the bridge of his nose and sank onto the couch with a starry-eyed gaze.

"I'll think about it."

CHAPTER 11
WILL

Will was having a fantastic day, at least by his usual standards. Three students were absent, including Julian, and Will had managed to get through all his reading groups during explore time for the first time all year. Therefore, he was somewhat surprised when Principal King stepped into his classroom.

"I need to see you in my office," she said, her expression unreadable.

"Now?" Will looked down at his kids, who, for once, were sitting on the carpet like angels.

"Yes, now." King stepped out of the way, and Mrs. Hernandez, the movement teacher, walked into the room. "Sorry to change your schedule, friends, but today is your lucky day. You're getting two specials."

The kids cheered, always happy to see Mrs. Hernandez, and Will walked from the room, wondering what he'd done now. It wasn't Julian, was it? Had something happened to him? Was he going back into foster care? What about his grandma?

King opened the door to her office, and Will was surprised to see an elderly Black woman with red-rimmed glasses sitting on the leather sofa.

"William"—King gestured to the woman—"this is Superintendent Spencer."

"Hi," Will managed to say before his mouth went dry. Was he getting fired? And what was going on outside? It sounded like some kind of protest or street festival.

King walked over to her window and parted the blinds with her fingers. "This is an elementary school, William, not *The Real World*."

Will was aware of that.

The phone rang, but King ignored it. "To be honest, I'm surprised you've gotten away with it this long." She sat down behind her desk and gestured for Will to sit in his usual chair.

Will cleared his throat. "I'm sorry, I think I'm missing something. Get away with what?" He looked from King to the superintendent, but neither of them spoke. "Is this about Ryan? I'm not dating him. I barely even know him. He's just one of my brother's groomsmen. He gave me a ride home, that's all."

"Have you checked the internet lately?" King asked.

"No, why?" Will's phone was off—as was school policy.

"There was another article, William, and it's not good. It even mentions the school."

King spun her computer monitor around, and there Will was, standing in the center of Enrique's living room under the headline, *UNFORGIVEN!* His shirt was drenched in wine, and he wore this dazed, deer-caught-in-the-headlights expression. Off to his right, Derek stared on, his eyebrows pinched in anger, looking like he wanted to throttle Will. But, no, the picture was a lie. Derek wasn't mad at Will. He was mad at his girlfriend.

"There is a sizable crowd forming outside, and between the press and concerned parents, the phone hasn't stopped ringing all afternoon."

As if on cue, the phone rang again.

This couldn't be happening. Who had even taken that picture?

No one was supposed to have their phones at the party.

King spun the monitor back around before Will could read the article.

"There are only a few weeks left in the school year. And we think it would be in everyone's best interest if you took a short leave of absence, at least until everything settles down. You have more than enough sick days to get you through the rest of the year."

"You're firing me?" Will's throat was so dry it felt like he'd swallowed sand.

"No, William. I'm not firing you. I'm just asking, as someone who cares about you—and whether you believe me or not, I do care about you—to voluntarily take the rest of the school year off. If not for your own sake, for your students'. Superintendent Spencer has already okayed it. It won't affect your pay or benefits, or anything like that. It won't even go on your record. It's just a leave, like maternity leave. Or we can call it a sabbatical if you'd like."

"But my class—"

"Your class will be fine. Mrs. Hernandez will take over for the rest of the year." King walked over to her electric kettle and flicked it on. "Is there someone you can call?"

"What? No. Why?" Will wanted to look out the window, but he couldn't bring himself to move. This couldn't be happening. Not again.

"Ms. Smith usually drives. Maybe she'd let you borrow her car or give you a ride home. Or, I can call you a cab." King sighed, and for once Will saw genuine sympathy in her eyes instead of irritation. "It's not just the press, William. There are angry protesters out there, too. I don't think it's safe for you to take the subway home." King pulled a second mug from the shelf and set it next to hers.

Will looked at the floor and probably would've started crying if he hadn't spotted the purple marker on his white tennis shoes. So that's what Brianna had been doing under the table.

"I'm making you some tea," King said. "Do you want Jasmine Green or Earl Grey?"

Will didn't respond. He closed his eyes and breathed in slowly.

"I was really moved by your performance in *The Beautiful*," Superintendent Spencer said, speaking for the first time. "You're very talented. And I know it may not feel like it now, but this isn't about punishing you. It's about protecting the kids."

Will walked back into his classroom and was greeted by a thousand bids for his attention. He addressed what he could and ignored the rest. Then he did the only thing he could think of. He grabbed his guitar and invited everyone to join him on the carpet. It was time for closing circle anyway.

"I have some sad news, friends." Will smiled to fight back the tears. "Something has come up, and I have to go away for a few weeks. I'm so sorry, but I'm going to miss the end of the year."

His tears betrayed him and started flowing down his cheeks. "But Mrs. Hernandez is going to fill in for me. She's going to keep you safe and make sure you have a lot of fun. And I'm going to miss you so much."

The tears were like rivers now, and Brianna got up off her spot and hugged him, and then they all did, all twenty-two of them. And they cried. They all cried, even Mrs. Hernandez. Will never should have gone to that fucking party.

"Let's sing our closing song one last time." It took a minute to get everyone seated again, and then they sang:

Now it's time to say goodbye
I'm going to look you in the eye
And tell you I'm going to miss you

Now it's time for us to go
I'm going to smile and let you know
Just how much I'm going to miss you

So take my hand and let me down easy
Because you're my Mario and I'm your Luigi
I'll get you a tissue if you're feeling sneezy
I'll help you breathe if you're feeling uneasy

And when we're far apart
I'm going to keep you in my heart
And I'll see you again soon
Like the sun, the stars, the moon

"Do you want me to come up?" Tiffany asked.

"No, I'm fine." Will just wanted to climb into bed and pass out. And when he couldn't sleep anymore, he'd drink. And when he couldn't drink anymore, he'd sleep.

At least the paps didn't know where he lived. Not yet, anyway.

He retrieved his guitar from Tiffany's trunk and hurried into the building. He pressed the button for the elevator, and as he waited, he closed his eyes and tried to remember how much bourbon was left in the bottle.

"William, is that you?"

Will spun around and found James walking towards him in a three-quarter sleeve baseball tee and faded red trucker hat, looking like a blue collar dream. Will didn't mean to stare, but come on! Most of Will's favorite pornos started just like this.

"It is you," James said, answering his own question. "Just the man I was looking for."

Really? Why? Oh, right. "I've got your shirt upstairs, but it's totally fucked. Sorry."

"I don't care about the shirt. How are you doing?"

"Me? I'm fine."

James tilted his head to the side and cocked an eyebrow. "Are you really?"

"Listen, I get you're my new daddy and all that, but you don't need to be so nice to me. I'm sure my mom will still buy you a sports car."

"What?"

Will looked away from James's piercing green eyes and stepped into the elevator. Now that he knew James was his mother's new houseboy, it explained a lot, like why James had approached Will at the party and why Will wanted to climb him like a tree.

Will and his mother had almost nothing in common, except their taste in men. And she'd really outdone herself this time. James was the whole package—rugged, handsome, and kind. What would that beard feel like on Will's inner thigh? What would those hands feel like gripping his waist?

"I'm not dating your mother," James said, following Will into the elevator.

Will shrugged. *Not yet, maybe. But just give it time.*

"What are you doing home so early?" Miles turned off the TV. "It's not even four."

Will set his guitar down. "Hold on a sec. I've got to give James back his shirt."

"James is outside? Why didn't you invite him in?"

Will ignored his roommate and retrieved the shirt from his closet. "Here you go," he said to James, closing the door behind him. "I bet you can get some good money for that on eBay."

James let out a nervous laugh. "Nah, I think I'll just keep it for myself."

Will shrugged. "Okay, well, have a good night." Will turned to leave, but stopped when James reached out and gently gripped his arm.

"I'm sorry about the article, man. That was bullshit. You didn't deserve that."

Will pulled his arm free, doing his best to ignore the warm tingle of James's touch. "It's fine. I'll get over it."

"No, dude, it's not fine. Stop pretending everything is fine all the time. Sometimes, things aren't fine."

Was this guy for real? Was he really giving Will a fatherly pep talk right now? "Listen, I know you mean well, but you can knock off the dad shit. You're, like, two years older than me."

James's eyes went wide, like Will had slapped him. "I'm not—"

"Shit, I'm sorry. I didn't mean to snap at you. I don't know why I just did that. Ignore me. I'm having a—"

"Stop apologizing. You have every right to be upset. That article was total BS."

"It's fine."

"No, it's not."

"Listen, I'll put a good word in for you with my mom. But right now, I just need to go inside and get drunk."

James's nostrils flared, and a vein pulsed in his forehead. "I don't need you to put a good word in for me. That's not why I'm here. I just wanted to check on you."

"Okay, well, now you have. And, as you can see, I'm fine."

"So you've said." James rocked back on his heels, and Will expected him to turn and leave, but he just kept standing there. "So, have you decided? Are you coming up to Vermont for the summer?"

"I don't know, maybe. I'll probably have to now." Will wasn't going to be able to go anywhere this summer without being photographed and harassed—maybe even assaulted. Rural Vermont was probably going to be his best option.

"What does that mean?"

"It means . . . You know what, it doesn't mean anything."

"Just come up, then. It'll be fun. I'm from Vermont, so I can show you around. Do you like cliff jumping? I know where there's this old granite quarry. There's even a rope swing."

"Did you just ask me if I like cliff jumping?" Jesus, James was going to be even worse than Sergio, the Spanish matador Will's mom used to date. Sergio had loved to go rock climbing and had always insisted fifteen-year-old Will go with him, which Will had done because Sergio had sleeve tattoos, smokey gray eyes, and thick black hair.

"Yeah, it's pretty fun. We can start small, though. You don't have to go for the high ones right off the bat. There are a few ten-footers, too."

"Ten-footers? Well, that's good to know."

"Just please come to Vermont. I promise you'll have a good time."

James could make all the promises he wanted, but it wasn't going to change the fact that, no matter what Will decided, this summer was going to suck balls—and not in the good, literal way either. There was a reason Will didn't still live with his mother and pal around with her boy toys.

"I'll think about it."

James took a step towards Will, and before Will knew what was going on, James was hugging him. He pulled Will close, and Will could feel the hard muscles under James's shirt and smell the sweat on his neck.

"Just don't give up, okay?" James gripped Will tighter. "Your day is coming. I know it."

Will decided to bypass the booze and nosedive into his pillow instead.

"Are you sick?" Miles came into the room and gingerly stepped over the books and dirty clothes that littered the floor. "Want me to make you some soup or something?"

Will pulled the pillow over his head. "I'm fine. I just want to lay here and feel sorry for myself."

"Did James say something to piss you off?"

Will shook his head. Screw James and his moss green eyes and rusty brown beard and amazing hugs.

The mattress caved under Miles's weight. "Is this about Ryan taking your part? Just say the word, and I'll make your dad give it to you. You took ten years off, just like he asked you to. It's the fucking least he could do."

"He's dying." Will wasn't supposed to tell anyone, even Andy. But there it was. His dad was dying. Will was never going to make him proud or prove him wrong. They were never going to be in a movie together like Jane and Henry Fonda. In fact, if the article in *Star* was any indication, ten years had done nothing to sponge Will's record. He'd probably never act again.

"What?"

"The cancer is back." Will tried to hold the pillow in place, but Miles was too strong. "It's all very top secret, so don't tell anyone. You'll ruin his master plan. He's got a plan, you know. He's finally going to win that fucking Oscar."

"What?"

"It's all very method. His character is dying in the movie, so it will play a lot better on screen if he's actually dying in real life. Sure, he could probably do chemo again. It worked last time. But his character is dying of Alzheimer's, and chemo doesn't treat Alzheimer's, so it just wouldn't make sense to go that route."

Miles set a hand on Will's leg. "Are you serious?"

"It's kind of stupid, though, don't you think? I mean, he's going to be dead long before the Oscars, so what does it matter? He's not going to know if he won or not."

"Fuck, dude. And that's why he wants you to go up to Vermont this summer?"

"Yup. His character dies in front of his son, so, you know, it only makes sense."

"Then why the fuck didn't he give you the part? Why did he choose Ryan and Derek over you?"

The answer was obvious. "He doesn't think I'm good enough. He doesn't want me ruining his last chance to win an Oscar. And this way, with Derek in the movie, he can pretend he's doing me a favor."

"Jesus, that's fucked up." Miles lay down beside Will and spooned him. "Are you going to go?"

"I think I might have gotten fired today."

"What do you mean?"

"Well, she can't technically fire me. I haven't done anything wrong. But she can still make my life a living hell until I quit. She's forcing me to use my sick time for the rest of the year, and then, next year, if I try to come back, she's going to stick me with fifth graders. Do you have any idea how big and scary fifth graders are?"

"They're, like, what, ten or eleven?"

"Exactly."

"But aren't there only a few weeks left? Why is she making you use your sick time now?"

"I take it you haven't read *Star* today. Someone at the party got a shot of Derek's girlfriend giving me the diva slap down. And Derek is just standing there, glaring at me like I murdered his dog."

"What? That's impossible. No one had their phones. I would've noticed if someone was taking pictures."

Will pulled the pillow back over his head.

Miles didn't move or speak for several minutes, and Will thought he'd fallen asleep, but then he asked again, "Are you going to go?"

"He's my dad." Of course Will was going to go. He'd tell his father all the things his father needed to hear, like how he was definitely going to win this time, and how he'd probably get a standing ovation.

But when Will wasn't blowing smoke up his father's ass, he was going to get to the bottom of what really happened the night of the Golden Globes. Why had Derek said all those horrible things to him? *Pathetic fuckboy?* Will had practically been a virgin back then.

It made no sense. What could Derek possibly have said or done to make Will want to hurt him? Was it really nothing more than rejection? Had he really taken it that badly?

Bottom line, if one drunken night was going to dictate the rest of Will's miserable life, he had a right to know why.

CHAPTER 12
JAMES

It was good to be back in Vermont, where the air smelled like lilacs and fresh cut grass, where, instead of the bustle of traffic and the bitching of strangers sharing their bad days with the rest of the world, there was the chirp of crickets and the tremolo of peepers in the grass. It even tasted like home, maple creemees and apple cider donuts.

Theo wasn't quite so enamored with life in the sticks, and getting him to leave the house was like pulling teeth. But James had all summer to show him there was more to life than video games, cooking shows, and guitar riffs.

The house was gorgeous, a six-bedroom, seven-bath refurbished farmhouse on the lake, which they pretty much had to themselves. Donna had only spent one night there in the past two weeks. Of course, that had been all it had taken for her to fall in love with Theo. She'd even put him in charge of outfitting the kitchen.

You'd never know the kid grew up with Goodwill frying pans by the way he shopped the Williams Sonoma catalog. The little shit spent almost five thousand dollars on a 24-piece cookware set.

"It's got a copper core," he'd said. For that much money, it should have a diamond core.

The evening William Chapman was set to arrive, James came into the kitchen to get a fresh beer and found Theo hunched over the oven. "What are you doing?"

"I'm making bread."

That much was obvious. But why? Theo had already marinated enough chicken to feed an army.

"You do realize he's not gonna murder you in your sleep if you don't serve him a five-course meal every night, right?"

"You don't know that."

They'd already had this argument a hundred times. Over the past couple of weeks, Theo had read every article ever written about William Chapman and was convinced he was Satan reborn. He was positive the only reason William was coming to Vermont was to finish Derek off, and probably Ryan, too.

"He's a kindergarten teacher, Theo, not a comic book villain."

Theo scoffed. "That remains to be seen."

CHAPTER 13
WILL

Will must have driven within range of a cellphone tower because he got six text messages at once. They were all from Miles. He wanted Will to send nudes every morning so he could adjust his workouts. He got him a local gym membership. And he wrote four separate messages forbidding Will from drinking beer.

Will tossed his phone onto the passenger seat and glanced over at the navigation screen. Almost there.

Getting to Derek was going to be tricky. He was staying at the same inn as Tony, his overprotective manager, and Tony had already made it perfectly clear Derek had no interest in being Will's friend again.

Whatever Will did, he couldn't seem too desperate. The whole world already thought he was a homicidal stalker.

But if he bided his time and played it cool, showed Derek he was only interested in friendship, maybe Derek would come to trust him again. Derek used to tell Will everything. He used to lay on the couch in Will's trailer and complain about the women he was fucking. Sometimes, he'd even fall asleep there.

The exit ramp to Chelmsford, Vermont, dumped Will out on a pale gray road stitched together with veins of black tar. Across the street was a gas station that sold guns and tackle, whatever the fuck tackle was. Will turned left and drove down the narrow street, which was so faded and weather-beaten he could hardly see the yellow lines running down the middle. Wasn't Vermont supposed to be quaint?

Will kept expecting a town to materialize, a restaurant, a hotel, a McDonald's even, but other than one Dunkin' Donuts, there was nothing. And what was with all the orange lilies? Every sagging white house had a log fence out front surrounded by a row of tall orange lilies.

"In one mile, turn right onto Wild Oaks Road," his GPS said.

Will was pretty sure he'd signed something saying he wouldn't drive his rental car on any dirt roads, but what was he supposed to do, park and walk?

Wild Oaks Road was so poorly maintained, a line of grass ran down the center. Trees with trunks as thick as elephants stood sentinel on either side. They arched overhead and created a long, continuous canopy. It was like the Norman Rockwell version of the Lincoln Tunnel. Beyond the trees, the meadows were teeming with bright yellow dandelions. It was like a child's painting, like some kid decided neon yellow was a better color for grass.

The GPS was clearly fucked, or else Google had a twisted sense of humor, because it announced, "You have arrived," just as Will reached an ancient cemetery, where the lichen-covered gravestones were broken and leaning.

He drove a little farther and found the sign for the estate. *Indian Meadows*, it read, because of course it did. Leave it to his mother to find the one property in liberal Vermont that was racist.

The house was massive. His mother claimed it was a refurbished farmhouse, but if any of the original house remained, it was buried deep inside. This place was bigger than the large white barn beside it. It had a wraparound porch, forest green shutters, and baskets of purple flowers hanging between white columns.

Will parked next to James's Toyota 4Runner. It was a good thing the house was huge. Will had no intention of becoming buddies with his mother's newest boy toy. Will was almost thirty, and it was high time he stopped lusting after his mother's boyfriends.

Speaking of which, James jogged down the stone path in a white tank top and silver aviators, looking like a redneck porn star. Fuck Will's life. Maybe he could convince his mother to rename the property *Blue Balls* since that was what the summer had in store for him.

"You made it." James opened Will's door, and Will came face to face with the crotch of James's dusty jeans. "Just in time for dinner. You hungry?"

Was that a trick question? "Not especially."

All the air conditioning escaped from Will's car and was replaced by a warm blanket of humidity. Like any good New Yorker, Will knew better than to breathe through his nose. Yet, he was assaulted by the stench of lilac and something that smelled suspiciously like cum. Was that a plant, or had he already lost his sexually repressed mind?

James leaned against Will's car and took a drink from a can of PBR. "Okay, well, I've got you all set up in the room next to mine. Your stuff is already in there."

"My stuff?" Will's stuff was in garbage bags in the trunk of his car.

"Yeah, your mom left you a bunch of clothes and a credit card." Little tufts of rusty brown hair poked out from under James's tan arms. "And a package arrived this morning from Miles. I think it's a pull-up bar. I put that in your room, too. Oh, and your dad sent over a copy of the script and a call sheet. They're both on your desk."

Jesus Christ. Was Will sweating already?

James gave Will a crooked grin. "You look like you could use a margarita. I noticed it was near the top of your list of prohibited drinks, so I figured you must like 'em. I'm a lousy bartender, but Theo is pretty good in the kitchen. I'm sure you won't be disappointed. He's been marinating the chicken all day, so when you do get hungry, you're in for a real treat. Come on, I'll help you carry your stuff in."

"You don't have to do that." Will didn't need James making fun of his lack of suitcases.

"It's not charity, dude. I'm getting paid."

"To babysit the dog, not me." Will leaned against the hatch to keep James from opening it.

James looked like he wanted to say something, probably that Will's mother was, in fact, paying him extra to babysit Will, but he drank his beer instead.

Will's room was the last one on the left. It had a king-sized bed and a private bathroom with a clawfoot tub and a stand-alone shower. It shared a balcony with the room next door, James's room. Hopefully, James and his mother would keep their fucking contained to his mother's room. Will didn't need to hear that shit.

Will's therapists assured him he wasn't insane, but sane people didn't grow up jacking off to fantasies of their mother's boyfriends or get drunk and try to murder their crushes.

The balcony looked out over a stone patio and a decent sized swimming pool. There was a manicured lawn that sloped down to the lake, where there was a dock and a small boathouse. The lake was narrower than Will expected, not much wider than the Hudson River, and Will could see all the way across to the blue peaks of the Adirondack Mountains on the other side.

A comically tall, lanky boy came out onto the patio with a large bowl of chicken breasts and started putting them on the grill. He wore dark hipster glasses and basketball shorts. He closed the grill, and as he turned to go back inside, he looked up and locked eyes with Will. He jumped about a foot in the air, and then, before Will could say hello, ran inside.

CHAPTER 14
JAMES

James had just about given up on William joining them for dinner when the broody actor came out onto the patio dressed in a baggy T-shirt and ill-fitting khaki shorts. He must have showered because his black hair was clumped together in thick waves.

"Sorry if I scared you earlier," William said to Theo. Man, how many times a day did William Chapman apologize?

"It's okay," Theo replied, handing William a margarita without meeting his gaze.

It was almost eight, and the sun was still high above the mountains. James considered joining them for margaritas, but opted for a beer instead. He was working, after all.

"You'll have to forgive Theo. He's having trouble separating you from your character in *The Beautiful*."

It wasn't true, though Theo had watched William's movie at least half a dozen times, whereas James had yet to sit through the whole thing once. It was way too depressing for James's tastes. Why did every movie about gay men have to end with death and heartbreak? But Theo was far from traumatized. In fact, most of his thoughts revolved around the film's representation of sex work as dirty and desperate, instead of as a viable career option for many people.

"It's fine," William said. "I'm used to people running in the opposite direction when I come into a room. I have a bit of a reputation." He took a cautious sip of his margarita, and then a much larger one. "Wow, this is really good." He looked over at Theo. "You made this?"

"Yeah." Theo pulled the asparagus off the grill and helped himself to a margarita.

William looked at James like he expected him to put a stop to Theo's underaged drinking. But Travis had been the disciplinarian. The last time James had tried to put his foot down, Theo didn't talk to him for a week. It wasn't worth the fight. And kids were going to drink either way. Theo might as well do it at home, where he wouldn't have to drive anywhere.

William took another generous gulp of his margarita and sat down across from Theo at the patio table. "Was that you playing guitar earlier, too?"

"Uh, yeah, sorry. I didn't mean to bother you."

William pulled out a small bottle of hand sanitizer and slathered some on. "You didn't bother me. You're really good. Do you sing, too?"

Theo looked up at William, his cheeks flushed. "Sometimes, but I'm more of a guitar player."

"He's being modest." James ignored the tongs and grabbed a chicken breast off the platter with his fingers. "He's got, like, twenty original songs up on Soundcloud. And he does all the parts himself, singing, drums, piano, bass, backup vocals, you name it. Plus, he made this bread from scratch."

"Wow, impressive. If you're ever in the mood to share, I'd love to hear your work." William bypassed the chicken and went for the salad.

Theo cocked his head to the side. "You actually mean that, don't you?"

A hint of a smile played across William's lips, and James wanted more. He wanted the whole thing, teeth and all. *Just keep going*, he silently urged William's mouth, but to no avail.

"Yeah, of course. Contrary to popular belief, I'm actually a terrible liar."

"So, you really don't remember why you tried to kill Derek Hall?"

James kicked Theo under the table. What the hell was wrong with him? "Forgive my son. He's got a broken filter."

Bringing Theo was a mistake. James's dad would have called him a straight shooter, but he was more like a loose cannon.

William laughed. "It's okay. That's actually one of the reasons I like teaching kindergarten so much. They always give it to me straight. I never have to wonder if there's a zit on my nose or if there's something in my teeth. And no, I don't remember anything from that night."

"Because you were drunk?"

James tried to kick Theo again, but Theo was too fast.

Will lifted his margarita and winced. "Yeah, but I'm not proud of it."

"And it's total bullshit that Derek doesn't remember either, right?"

Wow, this was going great. Five minutes into meeting William, and Theo was already giving him the third degree. Had Esther put him up to this?

William took a sip of his margarita and shrugged. "I wouldn't know. We've exchanged exactly two words in the last ten years—hi and hi."

"Well, he's just down the road, isn't he? Why don't you just go ask him?"

"Enough, Theo," James said, glaring at his nephew. Was it too late to send him to Florida?

To his credit, William was nonplussed. "I can't do that. Everyone already thinks I'm a stalker. If I even look at Derek the wrong way, Tony will have me shot."

"Who's Tony?"

"Derek's manager. The guy hates me, and always has. Like, he hated me even before . . . well, you know."

Theo nodded. "Okay, I see what we're working with here. We can handle this, though."

We? Two seconds ago, Theo had been sure William Chapman was the next Hannibal Lecter. Now they were a *we?*

By the time they were on to dessert, lemon meringue pie, the sun was setting and the peepers were out in full force. So were the mosquitoes.

"I know Ryan's bi, but between you and me, he definitely leans more towards guys, right?" Theo hadn't shut up about Ryan Ashbury all night.

Will wiped the meringue from his lips. "I couldn't tell you. You obviously know far more about Ryan than I do."

"But you're friends, right? I mean, he gave you a ride home."

"No, he's my brother's friend, not mine."

"Yeah, but you could still, like, invite him over, right?"

William shook his head. "Believe me, Ryan doesn't want to hang out with me. He just feels guilty about getting the part."

"So? Invite him over and tell him he doesn't need to feel guilty anymore."

William finished off the pitcher of margaritas. "Thanks for dinner. That was amazing."

"God, that was the most pathetic subject change ever."

James, who'd hardly gotten a word in all evening, glared at Theo. "Why don't you give William a break and go take Atticus for a walk? I'll clean up the dishes."

Theo rolled his eyes and threw his napkin on the table. "Ugh, whatever."

James watched his nephew walk inside and then fell back in his chair. If he smoked a bowl right now, would William tattle?

"Sorry, he can be kinda annoying. He's just starstruck by all this, that's all."

"He's fine. He reminds me of Andy at that age. And he's far too earnest to be annoying."

James thought so, too, at least when they were alone. But out in public, Theo's "earnest" behavior was more obnoxious than anything else.

"Are you going to watch them film the movie?" James asked, hoping William would let him tag along.

William's face fell, and James immediately regretted the question.

"Not if I can avoid it." William drained the last of his margarita and started clearing the table.

"You don't have to do that, William. I've got it."

"Listen, I'm not my mother. I don't want you waiting on me. I mean, dinner was great and all, but seriously, I'd rather just cook for myself. And it's just Will."

"Okay, I'll call you Will then, save myself a syllable." James stood and started helping Will clear the table. "But I should warn you. You're gonna break poor Theo's heart if you insist on cooking for yourself. He's planning to put this on his application to culinary school. Are you really gonna deny him that?"

It wasn't true, but it could be. Maybe culinary school was the compromise they'd been looking for. It wasn't college, but at least Theo would be preparing for his future instead of running from it.

William didn't respond and continued stacking dishes. He did it like a caterer, too, like he knew what he was doing.

He was an odd duck, William Chapman. At first glance, he seemed morose and high strung. Yet, he showed remarkable patience with Theo. He even seemed interested in what Theo had to say. Plus, it was clear he'd been telling the truth all along. He really didn't remember what happened that night. Maybe Esther was right.

Maybe William Chapman wanted to know the truth as much as everyone else.

"Do you have any plans for tomorrow?" James asked, following Will into the kitchen.

"Not really. Just meeting my dad for dinner."

"Great! Why don't we all go riding in the morning? I've been trying to get Theo out of the house for weeks. I bet he'll go if you go."

"I don't ride." Will set his stack of dishes on the counter and rummaged through the cupboards for Tupperware to put the leftover chicken in, proving, once again, he was a Chapman in name only.

"I can teach you. I've been riding almost as long as I've been walking."

"Did my mom put you up to this?" The chill in Will's glance made James's heart skip a beat.

"No, but if you don't go, Theo won't go either. You'd be doing me a favor. Plus, I hear Derek rides most mornings."

Will dropped a chicken leg, and it landed with a splat on the counter. *Well, that did the trick.*

"And there's an amazing view of the lake," James added, like a fisherman setting his hook.

Will recovered and threw the fallen leg in the trash. "I went horseback riding once when I was five and knocked my two front teeth out. It's not for me."

James smacked an engorged mosquito on Will's arm, leaving behind a smear of bright red blood. "Got him."

Will examined the blood and frowned, like it was a tattoo he didn't remember getting. "Her," he said.

"What?"

"Only female mosquitoes bite. The males are harmless." Will wet a paper towel and wiped the blood from his arm.

James couldn't help but smile. The little shit really was a teacher. "I didn't know that."

Will nodded and proceeded to put the leftover chicken in the fridge.

"Hey, grab me one of those beers, will you?" James said, nodding towards a twelve pack of PBR. "You know there's a saying for this very situation, don't you?"

"I do," Will said, not missing a beat. "Fool me once, shame on you. Fool me twice, shame on me."

James couldn't help but laugh. William Chapman was a bit of a smart ass.

"I meant 'get back on the horse.' Come on, it'll be fun. And Theo and I will be with you, so no one is gonna accuse you of stalking Derek."

Will cringed, like every time someone mentioned Derek's name a needle was jabbed into Will's voodoo doll. "I'll think about it."

JAMES FOUND Theo up in his room watching TV, Atticus asleep on the bed next to him. "You done being a little shit yet?"

"Look who's talking."

James shrugged and picked up the photograph on Theo's nightstand. It was a picture of James, Travis, and Theo at Disney World from when Theo was maybe nine or ten. They were smiling awkwardly in front of Cinderella's Castle. Travis was in the middle, and he had one arm around James and one around Theo. His mother had made them pose for the picture, and their expressions didn't say, *this is the happiest place on earth*, so much as, *are you happy now?*

"I like William," Theo said. "He's not phony like most celebrities."

"I like him, too." James set the photo back down. "And just so you know, he prefers to be called Will, not William."

"Then why did you try to ruin his life?" Theo reached over and adjusted the angle of the photo so it was facing him.

"I didn't try to ruin his life." Shit, did Theo know about Esther?

"Yeah," Theo scoffed. "Keep telling yourself that."

James rolled his neck. He was getting too old for this. "Can you maybe not drink so much in front of Will? You're making me look like a bad father."

"You are a bad father." Theo grabbed the remote and turned up the volume.

Well, on that note, it was time for James to go smoke a bowl.

CHAPTER 15
WILL

"Are you seriously telling me you've never even run your hands through his hair?" Theo was appalled. "He's Ryan Ashbury."

"I'm aware." Will stood in the stirrups to let his ass breathe. Applejack had to be the widest horse on the planet, and he was slow as hell, waddling up the mountain like a penguin. How had he let James talk him into this? Oh right, the beard, and eyes, and cocky swagger.

Still, it wasn't that bad. Will had expected to hate horseback riding, but it was a lot easier to stay on as an adult. And he had to admit, the forest was beautiful, all dappled sunlight and birds chirping.

The trail followed a narrow stream up the mountainside, which tumbled over rocks and gurgled like one of the settings on Miles's noise machine.

"Ryan's not only the hottest guy ever. He's also really talented. He's a much better actor than anyone gives him credit for. It's not his fault the writing in *Blood Brothers* is so basic."

"I'll take your word for it."

"Wait, you've never seen *Blood Brothers*?" Theo's jaw dropped. "You better clear your schedule tonight. We're binging the first season."

"I can't. I'm having dinner with my father."

"After, then."

Will had plans after. Well, not plans so much as hopes. Derek was staying at the same inn as Will's father, and Will hoped they might run into each other.

"Do you have a boyfriend or, like, a friend with benefits?"

Jesus, maybe Will should have volunteered to take Atticus to the hospital instead of James. That morning, just as they were about to leave, Atticus had a seizure, and James had to rush him to the vet. But Will wasn't too worried. That dog was indestructible.

"No," Will said, doing his best not to sound bitter.

"Why not?"

"Why do you think?"

"Come on, you're, like, super fit. You could have any guy you wanted. What's your type? Do you like 'em older or younger? Twinks or daddies?"

"I'm not having this conversation with you." They reached a fork in the road. One way continued next to the meandering stream, and the other climbed a steep bank that looked like a landslide waiting to happen. Their guide, naturally, chose the landslide route.

"What's up the other way?" Will asked.

"It's a loop," Beth said. "It's easier on the horses if we go up the steep way and down the switchback."

"Can't we just go up and down the switchback?" Will didn't want Applejack to break a leg. Plus, they were never going to catch up to Derek at the rate they were going. Their only hope was to intercept him on his way back down.

Jesus, Will really was a stalker, wasn't he?

"Sure." Beth changed course, and Will immediately regretted saying anything. Who was he kidding? He wasn't ready to see Derek again.

Theo pulled up alongside Will on his shiny chestnut thoroughbred. "What about my dad? Do you find him attractive?"

Will found all his mom's boyfriends attractive, which wasn't entirely his fault. He'd reached sexual maturity surrounded by shirtless models and rugged handymen who used to toss him in the pool and call him sport and little man. It'd warped his brain. Now, instead of being attracted to intelligence and kindness, Will liked disgusting things like armpits and tattoos and scratchy facial hair.

"I already told you. I'm not having this conversation."

Theo pushed his glasses up the bridge of his nose. "Why, are you, like, a virgin or something?"

"I'm not answering that." Will was a mandated reporter, and he wasn't going to have a sex talk with an eighteen-year-old boy.

Beth stopped at a break in the trees. "There is a nice view here if you want to take some pictures."

It was beautiful, so beautiful Will momentarily stopped thinking about Derek.

The lake was a flat plane of silver below them, and every house, road, and driveway was visible for miles, even the cars parked out front and the dandelions and orange lilies in the yards.

"That must be where they're filming the movie," Theo said.

Will followed the line of Theo's outstretched hand to a small rundown farmhouse with a dilapidated old red barn next to a much larger, much newer barn. All along the twisting drive were film trailers, one after another, like a long white train. In a hollow below the house, there was a small pond with a majestic weeping willow tree hanging over it.

"Will, is that you?"

Will felt the tickle of Derek's deep voice in his balls before the sound reached his ears. Applejack whinnied beneath him, sensing Will's fear.

Will turned, and there he was, coming around the corner on a shiny black stallion. Well, maybe it wasn't a stallion, but it could've been.

"Listen, Will, I want to apologize for Sharron. I was going to say something at the party, but... well, you know."

"It's fine."

Another rider came up behind Derek, and Will almost didn't recognize him without his lustrous blond locks.

"Hey, Will. I didn't know you made it up. You should've called me," Ryan said, looking every bit the Abercrombie model.

At Will's side, both Beth and Theo ogled the young heartthrob, too mesmerized by his beauty to even close their gaping mouths. But Theo wasn't speechless for long.

"You cut your hair," he said.

Ryan ran his hands over his stubbled scalp. "It'll grow back."

The young actor was uncharacteristically self-conscious, but even without all the hair, he was gorgeous. If anything, it just made his supernaturally blue eyes shine that much brighter.

"This must be the boyfriend Tony was telling me about. He's"—Derek looked Theo up and down and swallowed his surprise—"tall."

"He's your boyfriend?" Ryan asked.

Fuck Will's life. This was all Miles's fault. Still, he could salvage this without admitting he was an undateable loser, right? He just had to be vague.

"I'm not dating Theo. He's only eighteen."

Ryan laughed, showing off his pointy incisors.

"You'll have to forgive Ryan," Derek said. "Your father's on a mission to get you two together by the end of the summer. I think he wants to turn all those tabloid rumors into reality. I tried to tell him you already have a boyfriend, but he didn't believe me."

"He does," Theo said. "And they're very serious."

The saliva in Will's throat turned to concrete. What the hell?

"He's dating my dad. They're very happy together. They have sex multiple times a day, every day." Theo must have realized people would wonder why he knew that because he added, "And they're very loud about it. It's disgusting."

What was wrong with this kid? "Theo doesn't know what he's

talking about. We're not—"

Derek held up a hand. "It's none of our business."

"Hey, do you guys wanna come over for dinner this weekend?" Theo asked. "Our house is huge, and there's a pool and a boat. We could all go water skiing."

What the literal fuck?

"Or, if you don't like water skiing, you could always just ride on the tube. It's actually more fun, if you ask me. You have less control, but that's what makes it fun. You just have to kinda hold on and hope for the best."

"Words to live by," Derek said, not taking his eyes off Will.

Jesus, Will wanted to crawl under a rock and die. Maybe he should come clean and tell them the truth, that he hadn't had sex in over two years—forget multiple times a day, every day.

"How about Friday? I can make spanakopita and other vegetarian things for Ryan. And you haven't seen Will in years. You must have a lot to catch up on."

Now it was Derek's turn to look flustered. "Uh, I don't know if Donna would want us bugging her at home."

"She won't mind. She misses having a full house. She said so."

That, at least, was true. Growing up, Will's mom loved it when he and Andy had their friends over. She got a kick out of all the MILF attention.

"I can make an apple pie, too. It's Ryan's favorite. Come on, don't make me spend another Friday night alone listening to my dad and Will go to pound town."

Jesus, this kid was something else.

"I'll run the idea by Donna and see what she thinks," Derek said.

"Okay, but I promise you, she's not gonna care. And what else are you gonna do? It's not like there is anything else going on around here. But don't bring your girlfriend. That was seriously uncool, what she did to Will."

Derek looked momentarily taken aback, and even Ryan did a double take.

"She's back in L.A. now," Derek said, sounding almost ashamed.

"Good. Leave her there. We'll have a boys' night. Do you like mojitos? There's all this fresh mint growing in the herb garden, and I make a really good mojito. But I can make margaritas, too, or basically anything you want."

By the time Derek and Ryan rode away, Will couldn't tell which way was up and which way was down. This was a disaster. How the hell was Will going to get out of this mess? What if Derek accepted Theo's invitation and caught them in the lie?

"What the hell, Theo?" Will asked the moment they were alone in the car.

"I know, I'm a fucking genius, right? Now you can ask Derek what really happened. And he can't accuse you of stalking him because you have a boyfriend. And he's coming to your house. So it's more like he's stalking you."

"But I don't have a boyfriend."

"He doesn't know that. And he already thinks you do, so what's the big deal? My dad's not gonna care."

"I care."

"Why? You don't think my dad's hot enough for you? I know he's starting to get a bit of a dad bod, but I never took you for a fatphobe."

"I'm not. And your dad is plenty hot, but—"

"Great! Then what's the problem?"

Will had taught long enough to know there was no getting through to some kids. Usually, though, they were too angry to reason with, not too happy.

"I can't believe Ryan is coming over to our house. And I'm gonna get to feed him."

Maybe Will's mother would say no. Maybe Derek would invent an excuse not to come. Maybe the monster that lived in the lake would swallow Will whole and this would all be a moot point.

CHAPTER 16

JAMES

James sat up on the couch when he heard the screen door open. Finally, they were back. The trip to the vet had been relatively quick and painless, leaving James hours to stress over Theo telling Will the truth and ruining everything.

Theo burst into the living room like an exploding piñata, only instead of spraying candy all over the place, Theo peppered James with words, so many words. "Guess who's coming to dinner? Ryan Ashbury. And we're gonna go tubing, and I'm making spanakopita and margaritas and mojitos and probably an apple pie, too, because it's Ryan's favorite, though apples aren't in season." Theo did a trust fall over the arm of the couch, and his head landed inches from James's leg. "And even though Ryan shaved his head, he's still super hot, like in that army soldier kinda way."

"What?" Ryan Ashbury was coming to dinner? James peered down at Theo, who looked like he was waiting for the rapture.

"Yeah, I know. I can't believe he shaved it either, but it just shows how committed he is to the work. Oh, and Derek Hall is coming, too, which you'd think Will would be happy about, but he's being a pissy little bitch. He wouldn't even talk to me the whole way home."

"What did you do?"

"Why do you always assume I did something? I didn't do anything. Well, I told everyone you and Will were boyfriends. But I knew you wouldn't mind."

"You what?" Clearly, James had misheard.

"Don't give me that face. I just did you a favor. Think about it. If you're Will's boyfriend, they'll have to let you onto the set. Plus, you'll get to be Will's date to the wedding, which is, like, the social event of the summer. And me, too, because now I'm, like, Will's stepson."

Theo could have lit a thousand light bulbs with the wattage pouring off him. "And I know what you're thinking, but I already asked him, and he said he's not worried about the sex because he's not really a virgin. But, between you and me, he's definitely a virgin. He's just really embarrassed about it, so maybe go slow at first, like just give him a hand job or something."

"I'm not giving William Chapman a hand job."

Theo held up his hands, like James had been the one to go too far. "Whatever you do behind closed doors is your business. But can you drive me to the grocery store later? I gotta pick up supplies for the party."

TEN MINUTES LATER, James found Will sitting alone in his car. "Mind if I join you?"

Will didn't answer.

James slid inside, but kept the door open. It was hot as balls in Will's car.

"Theo filled me in."

Will tightened his grip on the steering wheel, but kept his eyes forward, like he was actually driving.

"Come on, it's not that bad, right? I know I'm no Derek Hall, but you could do worse."

Will dropped his hands from the steering wheel and leveled his dark eyes at James. "You don't need to pretend to date me. I'm just going to tell Derek the truth."

"Okay." James nodded as he considered what to say next.

It wasn't that he wanted to date William Chapman. James didn't date older guys. They were too focused on commitment and forever and finding "the one." Plus, Will was kind of his boss, and if he found out who James really was, James might lose his job at the agency.

But Theo had a point. Pretending to date Will had the potential to open all the right doors. Not only might James get to watch them film, but he might get to hang out with Robert Chapman, too. Maybe he could even give him some pointers, make sure he got his father right.

"But won't Derek trust you more if he thinks you're in a committed relationship?" James asked.

"Probably. But so what? Maybe I don't deserve to know what happened. And it's not like this will be the most embarrassing thing to happen to me this month. Let them all laugh at me. I don't care."

"Don't be like that. I'm more than happy to spare you the embarrassment. It's really not a big deal. And of course you deserve to know what happened."

"Why?"

"Well, it's obvious that night still haunts you. And I get it. How are you supposed to move forward if—"

"No, why would you want to do this for me?"

James met Will's dark, bottomless eyes. "Not everything has a catch, dude. Can't a guy just do something nice for another guy?"

Will didn't say no, but his furrowed brow did.

"Come on, I haven't seen Theo this happy in ages. And it's not like I've got anything else going on. Plus, if people think I'm your boyfriend, maybe they'll let me watch them film the movie. I've always wanted to see how it's done."

"You're not even gay."

"Says who?" James flashed Will his best bedroom eyes.

"You, for one. When I was changing at the party, you told me not to worry because you didn't swing that way."

"No, that's not what I said. I said you weren't my type. And does it matter? We won't actually be dating." That was the best part. Actually dating guys over twenty-five was dangerous. They had too many expectations.

"It'll matter to my mom. I'm pretty sure she has other plans for you." Will pulled his knees up to his chest, fitting his whole body into the driver's seat.

"How many times do I have to tell you? I'm not sleeping with your mother. And we can just tell her the truth. She'll understand. She's your mom."

Will turned to glare at him, like James was the dumbest man on the planet. "No, trust me, she won't." Then, without saying another word, he got out of the car and started for the house.

James caught up with him on the porch. "Listen, it's totally up to you. But don't wreck your plans and embarrass yourself on my account. I'm happy to play along. In fact, I think it will make a funny story. You know, like some cheesy rom-com, only instead of falling in love, you'll get the answers you're looking for, and I'll get a story to tell my grandkids." *Not to mention access to the film set.*

Will stopped with his hand on the front door. "They'll recognize you from the party. They'll know you work for the agency. Everyone is going to think I hired a boyfriend, and then I'll look like even more of a stalker."

Will had a point, and thanks to Esther, Will was back on the paparazzi's radar again. Her one article had inspired at least fifty more. It seemed like every gossip rag in the world was taking a shot at William Chapman these days. If the press put two and two together, it would be all over the news in a heartbeat. But wasn't that James's fault, too? Didn't he owe it to Will to do this? The knot of guilt in his gut was all the answer James needed.

"What if I shave my beard off? No one will even recognize me then."

"Don't do that." Will recoiled in horror, and James couldn't help but smile. Wasn't William Chapman a little old to be a chaser?

"How about I leave the mustache?"

Regaining his composure, Will said, "Do what you want. It's your face."

"So, we're doing this?" James's heart pounded in his chest. This was wild, even for him.

"No, we're not doing this." Will opened the door and stepped into the house.

A minute later, James found him in the kitchen uncorking a bottle of champagne. "Celebrating something?"

"You really want your face plastered across every tabloid in America with captions like *William Chapman Hires Professional Escort* and *William Chapman Fucks His First Cousin?*"

"I'm not your cousin, dude." James couldn't help but laugh. Will was funny when he was pissed. "You know what I think? I think you need this. You've spent the past ten years hiding under a rock, letting everyone think the worst of you, hoping time will fix all your problems. But it won't. And neither will hanging your head in shame. You gotta take action."

"What's that supposed to mean?"

"It means you gotta fake it till you make it, dude. No one's gonna buy a used car that's been sitting on the lot, rusting. They gotta see someone else take it for a spin first."

"And you're, what, going to take me for a spin just so you can watch my dad film some stupid movie? That's ridiculous. I'll get you onto the set if you want. You don't need to degrade yourself by pretending to date me."

"See, that's your problem right there. You've got no self-respect. If you don't believe you're worth something, no one else will either."

Will rolled his eyes and poured champagne into a pint glass. "Jesus, you and your fucking dad talks."

"Fine, would you feel more comfortable if I told you I was only doing this so I could be your date to your brother's wedding? I mean, it'd be nice to attend one of these fancy shindigs for once instead of just working it."

"My mom isn't going to pay you extra. She might even fire you."

"She's not gonna fire me. She likes Theo way too much to fire me." That was the one thing James was certain of. Everything else, not so much. "Now pour me some champagne, and let's make this official, boyfriend."

Will rolled his eyes, and James couldn't fight the smile overtaking his face. This was gonna be fun, and a total win-win. He could make things right with Will and see Travis's project through to the end. Sure, Theo's plan was like something out of a bad Christmas movie, but it felt right, and James knew when to trust his gut.

CHAPTER 17
WILL

His father was at the inn, waiting. He wore dress pants and a light blue collared shirt, with not three but four buttons undone. He had a glass of chardonnay clasped in his slender fingers, and he studied something outside the window. Will shivered at the sight. Other than being too skinny, he looked normal, not at all like a man with only months to live.

"Can I help you?" the hostess asked.

"I'm just meeting my dad." Will nodded toward his father's table. It sat in front of a large stone fireplace, which was probably cozy as hell in the winter. Now, it was dark and cold. The hostess looked confused and disappointed. "I'm the other son, Will."

She flushed red with embarrassment, and Will felt bad for being such a dick.

"Right this way, Mr. Chapman."

As they made their way over, Will steeled his resolve. He had two questions to ask his father—Why Derek and not him? And why give up and not fight?

His father stood. "The prodigal son re—"

"Don't"—Will held up a hand—"it's okay."

His father sat back down, but didn't take his eyes off Will. They stared at each other for a long moment, and then his father's shoulders fell. "I see your mother has ignored my wishes, as always."

"Yeah." Will's shoulders fell, too. He wanted to say more. But what more was there to say?

"And what about Andy? Does he know?"

"No, I don't think so."

"Well, that's something." He poured Will a glass of wine and forced a smile on his face. "How was your drive?"

"Fine. Uneventful."

"That's good. I'm glad you made it safely." He placed the bottle back in the ice bucket. "You're looking well. I see Miles is taking good care of you."

"I take care of myself." The chardonnay tasted like a stick of butter drenched in oak.

"I know." His father leaned back and opened his menu. A moment later, he closed it and set it back down. "This place is fantastic. You can't go wrong. People come here from miles around."

Will looked out the window, where two ravens cawed loudly from a solitary apple tree in the yard. "I guess they'd have to." There were probably more cows than people in this town.

"That's true." His father laughed generously, which Will found off-putting. His father never laughed at his jokes. "I'm glad you're here. You've always been my favorite scene partner."

Rather than point out that that couldn't possibly be true, Will took another gulp of the oaky chardonnay.

"Did you hear we got Amanda Brasel to play Emily, the girlfriend?" His father's gaze darted to Will's glass, which was already half empty. Ever since the bachelor party, Will had been drinking like a fish.

"That's great. She's really good."

"Yeah, she arrived yesterday, same as you." His father stuck his aquiline nose in his glass and inhaled deeply, his way of telling Will to slow down and enjoy it. "She's staying here at the inn."

"Seems like a nice place." Will pulled off a piece of bread and slathered it in herbed butter. Miles wouldn't approve. But if there was any silver lining to the death of Will's comeback dreams, it was not having to live up to Hollywood's unrealistic body standards.

"I'm in the presidential suite. You should come up and check it out after dinner. Maybe we can run Friday's lines."

"Sure, whatever." Will washed down the bread with more chardonnay and left a smear of butter on the rim of his glass.

"More?" His father pulled the bottle from its ice bath. "I'm not drinking myself. It's not allowed. But I still like to have a glass with dinner."

Will wiped his mouth with his napkin. "How are you feeling?"

"Okay. They've got me on some fantastic drugs. Don't tell Enrique, though." He swirled his wine and took another deep inhale.

Will buried his face in his menu. Who was he kidding? He didn't have the balls to ask his father jack shit. What if his father told him the truth? That Will wasn't good enough.

"I hear there's a new man in your life. When do I get to meet him?"

Jesus Christ. Derek didn't waste any time, did he? "Whenever you want."

Will closed his menu. He should've been scared his dad would see through the lie, and yet it wasn't fear that vibrated up his body but pride. James was hot as hell, and soon everyone was going to think they were dating. They were going to think they fucked and told each other secrets and cuddled watching Netflix.

Jesus, who was Will kidding? No one was going to buy that. This was going to blow up in his face, big time.

"You should've invited him to dinner. His son, too. Your mother must be ecstatic. Finally, a grandchild to spoil. I can't imagine Nandi and Andy are in any rush."

"Yeah, probably not."

Andy's fiancée, Nandini Dalal, was a celebrated model and

actress. She was only twenty-two and likely not in any hurry to test the boundaries of her perfect body.

"Derek tells me he's quite the bean pole—the boy, that is."

"Yeah, Theo's tall and skinny."

"Does he like cologne? I've got bottles and bottles of it, and good stuff, too. If I can save one kid from dousing himself in that revolting Axe body spray, I can die a happy man."

Will's face fell. He wanted to smile, but he couldn't bring himself to do it. Apparently, he wasn't into macabre humor. "I don't know. I'll ask him."

After their waiter left, Will's father did away with idle pleasantries and got to work pretending to be helpful. "I'm sorry the meeting with Derek didn't land the way we'd hoped."

"Right." His father acted like Will had been in on the plan.

Outside the window, dark clouds began to gather. The forecast was right. It was going to storm.

"Don't let it get you down, though. Sometimes you have to go backwards to go forwards. And as soon as *Sundowning* comes out, everyone will see that bygones are bygones. And after I'm gone, the offers will come pouring in."

"Because you'll be dead?" Will wasn't trying to be a dick. He was trying to understand. How exactly did his father dying translate to movie offers for him? Was Steven Spielberg going to say, *I'm sorry your dad died. I know what will cheer you up. How would you like to be the next Indiana Jones?* But maybe Will wasn't being fair. If his father needed to pretend Will would be fine after he was gone, who was Will to deny him that?

"No, because you're a gifted and talented actor." His father paused like he'd said something heartfelt and profound and wanted the camera to linger on his face to show just how heartfelt and profound it was.

"It doesn't matter." Will tore off another piece of bread. "How's everything going? You ready to start shooting?"

Will didn't really care about the movie. He just didn't want to talk about his glorious future anymore. And once Robert Chapman started discussing his latest project, he couldn't be stopped.

Will's father lived his movies, every aspect of them from the financing to the cinematography. If he was playing a pilot, he would learn how to fly. If someone in the restaurant needed emergency bypass surgery, Robert was the man for the job because he'd once had a guest spot on ER, which, incidentally, he won an Emmy for. By the time his father rose to go to the bathroom at the end of the meal, Will was an expert on early-onset familial Alzheimer's disease (eFAD), the inner workings of rural Vermont dairy farming, and the glottal stop necessary to produce a proper Vermont accent.

Once his father was out of sight, Will checked to see who'd been blowing up his phone all night. It was probably Miles, pissed Will hadn't sent any nudes yet. But it wasn't. They were all from some unknown number.

How's dinner going
Should I have a few shots ready
Theo is using your pull-up bar
I hope that's okay
He wants to get swole for Ryan
This is James btw your boyfriend
It looks like it might rain
Let me know if you need a ride home
I'll come get you

The fucker ended with a kiss emoji followed by a mustache emoji. What a dick.

Will texted back, *Anything but Tequila*. If he wasn't careful, he'd wind up in rehab again.

WILL's father insisted he get dessert. "The chef doesn't make the pies. The owner's grandmother does, and not even a three-star chef can compete with a grandmother's pies. And don't worry, I won't tell

Miles. Your secret is safe with me. Oh, that reminds me. Does Andy know to give Miles his own invitation? I think we all just assumed he'd be your date."

"I don't know. I'll ask him."

"I can do it. I have to call him tonight anyway. I need to find out what kind of swans he wants for the wetlands photoshoot. Who knew there were so many varieties? There's the mute swan, which is what everyone pictures when they think of swans. But there are also black swans, whooper swans, trumpeter swans, tundra swans, and black-necked swans."

Will ordered the strawberry rhubarb pie, and it arrived with a scoop of vanilla ice cream as the first flashes of lightning lit up the sky. A crack of thunder followed seconds later, and then the deluge came.

"I was right about the pie, wasn't I?" His father helped himself to a small bite. "You should order a few pieces to take home to Theo and . . ."

"James," Will said. "And that's okay. They don't need pie."

"No one needs pie. That's not the point of pie." His father added a bit of ice cream to his spoon.

Will sighed and looked longingly at the empty bottle of chardonnay. All that remained was the piss-warm swill in his father's glass. Would it be rude to drink it?

"This guy you're seeing, James, he must be fairly new on the scene. You've never mentioned him before."

New on the scene was putting it mildly. "Yeah, fairly new."

"Ryan is disappointed, but he's certainly not wanting for suitors. Did you know he has over a hundred million followers on Instagram?" Will did not. Nor did he think Ryan was in any way disappointed. "He's a sweet kid. And if things don't work out with you and James, I'm sure—"

"You don't even want to try?" Will didn't want to talk about Ryan. His father was dying. He was dying, and he was giving up. "It worked last time."

His father's smile vanished, and gone was the movie star. In his place was a man in his early sixties with salt and pepper hair, finely plucked eyebrows, and impeccable posture.

"It's too advanced this time. It's already spread to my liver and lymph nodes. It might buy me a few extra months, but at what cost?" His father didn't attempt to brush away the tears that slid down his cheeks. "I want to spend what little time I have left with my family, doing what I love most: acting."

Will couldn't speak. If he spoke, he might cry, too.

His father set his balled-up napkin on the table. "Do you mind if we run the scenes tomorrow instead? I'm feeling a bit tired tonight."

Will looked up from his half-eaten pie. He'd never wanted to run the scenes in the first place. "Of course. That's fine."

His father forced a smile and set his hand on top of Will's. His skin was cold and damp. "It will mean more if you earn it yourself."

It was the same bullshit as when Will was a kid, when his father didn't want him auditioning under the Chapman name.

"It doesn't matter, Dad. I'm happy teaching." Sure, it was their last chance to star on screen together. But whatever. His father had Ryan and Derek now. And while Will wasn't rich and famous—just infamous—he was doing okay for himself, and without any help from his family, either. But teaching fifth grade was going to be awful.

Another crack of lightning lit up the fields and the muddy dirt road.

"It looks pretty nasty out there. I'll have someone give you a lift back to your mother's."

"That's okay. James is going to pick me up."

Will said goodbye to his father on the stairs and walked straight into the bar.

Derek found him two hours later and pried the glass of whiskey from his fingers. "Let me give you a ride home."

"I can walk." Will attempted to stand, but his legs were sparkling. No, not sparkling. They were asleep. Derek caught him as he collapsed. "I just have to get my sea legs."

"My Jeep's right out front." Derek turned to the bartender. "Put it on my tab, okay?"

They were both drenched by the time Derek hoisted Will into the Jeep and got his seat belt fastened.

"You know about your dad now, don't you?" Derek started the Jeep, but the windshield was too fogged-up to drive.

"You mean about him dying?" Will wasn't sure if he was crying or if it was just the rain.

"I thought so. I could see it in your eyes this morning. How are you doing?"

"I'm fine." How could he be anything but fine? He wasn't dying.

"Your stepson is quite the character. He kind of reminds me of you."

"Why, because he's a stalker?" The words were out before Will could stop them. Whatever. They were true.

"No, because he's fearless."

"Why did I do it?" Will couldn't see the scar because it was on Derek's left eyebrow, but he could picture it, thin and white, and nearly fatal.

Derek put the car in gear and started driving, the wipers going a million miles an hour. "It doesn't matter, Will. You're more than one drunken night. We all are."

The world began to spin, and Will felt like he might puke, so he closed his eyes. When he opened them, Derek was unclipping his seatbelt.

"Let me help you out."

Will pushed his hand away. "I got it."

CHAPTER 18
JAMES

James sat on the porch and watched the lightning flash over the rolling meadow. He held a packed bowl in his hand, which he'd somehow forgotten to smoke. Where was Will? He should've been home hours ago. They needed to get their backstory straight.

Lights appeared at the end of the driveway and climbed the hill towards the house. A shiny red Jeep pulled up and stopped. The passenger side door opened, and Will fell out—like, literally fell out.

"I'm okay," he said, springing back up like one of those orange traffic posts. "Don't get out."

Whose Jeep was that?

James flicked on the porch light and watched Will make his way up the stone path as the Jeep's red brake lights disappeared down the driveway. Will's clothes were soaked, and his knees were muddy. His thick black hair lay plastered across his forehead.

"Who dropped you off?"

"Derek." Will paused on the top step and held onto the railing for support, water pooling around his feet. He was clearly very drunk.

James's stomach tightened. He wasn't jealous, just curious. Did Derek go to dinner, too?

"That was nice of him. Have you guys patched things up? Did he tell you what happened?"

Will didn't answer. He was too busy staring, slack jawed. He let go of the railing and stumbled forward. "Oh my god, what have you done?"

James almost forgot he'd shaved his beard. "You like it?" He ran his fingers down his smooth jaw. It had been at least five years since he'd felt the skin on that part of his face.

"Can I touch it?" Before James could answer, Will's fingers danced across his upper lip. "This is the best mustache I've ever seen."

James grabbed Will's waist to steady him. How could someone made entirely of muscle move like Jell-O? It was hard not to laugh at Will's wide eyes. He was like a kid seeing fireflies for the first time.

"I'm glad you like it."

"I love it." Will smiled, and it almost knocked James over. The guy really was a movie star. "I can't believe you did this for me."

James lowered Will onto the bench before he fell over. "It's just hair, dude."

"It's more than that." Will swayed like a top-heavy sunflower, and James had to sit next to him to prop him up. Maybe now was not the best time to construct their fake relationship backstory.

"Is that marijuana?" Will's face dropped to examine the bowl in James's hand, and James had to push Will back by the shoulders so he didn't fall off the bench.

"It is. Want some?"

"Yes, please."

"Are you sure you can handle it? It's not always a good idea to mix."

"I haven't smoked weed in years. I miss it."

Against his better judgment, James passed Will the bowl and lighter. "Don't forget there's a carb on the side."

"A what?"

"A carb." James pointed to the hole on the side of the bowl. "You gotta plug it or else it won't light. And then release it when you wanna inhale. It's like a vent on a gas can."

"Oh, well, if it's like a vent on a gas can." Will's voice dripped with sarcasm, but he really was fine. He lit the bowl, took a hit, and immediately coughed out a billowing cloud of smoke. "It burns. Make it stop."

James handed Will his can of PBR, and Will drank the whole damn thing like some meathead frat boy.

"That's disgusting. You drink that shit?" Will pounded a burp from his chest.

"Can I have my bowl back, please?" James snatched the bowl from Will's hand.

"I need to lay down." Will lifted his feet onto the bench and rested his head on James's lap. *Well, alright then.*

Will's cold, wet hair soaked through the fabric of James's pants and sent a shiver up James's leg.

James thought Will was joking. But he wasn't. He was actually asleep. It happened faster than putting Theo in his car seat as a baby.

A lock of thick black hair fell over Will's eyes. James brushed it away and tucked it behind Will's ear. A light dusting of black stubble dotted Will's angular chin, and there was that one freckle on his cheek. Up close, it looked almost blue in color, like a rogue fleck of glitter. James ran his thumb over it, and Will sighed at his touch.

James was going to have to put the little shit to bed, wasn't he? James lifted the bowl to his lips. What had he gotten himself into?

CHAPTER 19
WILL

Will woke with a pounding headache, a strong desire to puke, and a memory full of holes. He didn't remember going to bed, plugging in his phone, or putting on his dirty workout shorts. He vaguely remembered Derek driving him home and James smoking him up, but that was about it.

He drank from the faucet and then turned on the shower.

He came downstairs twenty minutes later, hoping everyone had gone for the day, and found Theo sitting in the sunbaked breakfast nook, strumming his guitar.

Theo stopped playing when he saw Will and set his guitar down. "Oh, good, you're up. Do you want an omelet? These frying pans are amazing. Nothing sticks. It's incredible."

Will shielded his eyes from the sun. "I'm all set. Is there coffee, though?"

"Yeah"—Theo jumped up—"I'll make you some."

Will held up a hand. "I can do it." He put the kettle on to boil and emptied the French press into the compost.

"Are you really best friends with a personal trainer?"

Will looked up from the counter, where he'd been lost in the glittering flecks of mica. "Yeah." Jesus, he still had to call Miles and Tiffany and tell them about James. They were going to give him so much shit.

"Do you think he'd help me get in shape? I know we only have a few days before Ryan comes, but aren't there, like, secret insider tricks that only celebrity trainers know?"

Will looked up at the clock. It was a little after ten, which meant Miles was probably home trying to get the cum dingleberries out of his belly hair.

"I can call him right now if you want."

Miles answered after the first ring, and Will could tell by the paisley cock on the wall behind him that he was sitting on the toilet.

"You look like shit. Are you drinking enough water?"

"I'm here with Theo." Will turned the phone to show the gangly teen. "He needs your help. Ryan and Derek are coming over for dinner on Friday, and Theo wants to look his best. Can you help him?" Will knew this would get Miles's juices running. Miles loved deadlines almost as much as he loved teen romance.

"Who's he trying to impress, Ryan or Derek?"

"Ryan, obviously." Theo came and stood behind Will.

"How old are you?" Miles asked.

"Eighteen."

"Step back so I can see all of you."

Theo did as he was told.

Miles tilted his head from side to side like he was examining a piece of modern art. "What are you, six-five, a hundred and fifty-two pounds?"

"Wow, you're amazing. How did you do that?"

"I'm Miles Greene, personal trainer to the stars. And if I'm going to take you on as a client, I'm going to need to test your mettle first. Go run two miles and call me back. Oh, and make a list of everything you ate yesterday, every cracker and glass of water. Don't leave anything out. Write the approximate times down, too."

"Right now?"

"Yes, right now. Now go."

Theo left his guitar in the breakfast nook and tore out of the room.

"I take it that's your new little brother?"

"Actually, he's my new stepson now." Will told Miles everything, and as predicted, Miles gave him shit.

"I fucking called it. I knew he was into you. I just knew it."

"You did no such thing, and I can assure you he's not into me. He's just stuck in the middle of nowhere with nothing better to do. He thinks it will make a funny story. The guy acts just like a five-year-old. Plus, he's straight."

"Perfect. Don't you have, like, a master's degree in five-year-olds? Maybe you're his soulmate. Maybe you're the only one who can truly understand him."

"You're not funny."

Miles propped his phone by the sink and turned on the shower. "So, has Derek told you what happened yet?"

"No, but he did give my drunk ass a ride home last night. So, baby steps."

"Should I come up? I bet I can beat the truth out of him."

"No, I've got it under control. It's all part of my master plan." Apparently, Will's master plan was to act like a total loser until Derek felt bad enough to tell him what had happened.

"Let me see how expensive flights are. Maybe I can come up for the weekend." Miles stood naked, pulling hairs from his nose while the bathroom mirror fogged up.

"That would be awesome. Now stop wasting water and shower if you're going to fucking shower."

JAMES CAME into the kitchen shortly after Miles hung up, and Will almost dropped his phone down the garbage disposal when he saw the mustache. The air caught in his lungs, and his fingers tingled, like they could remember the soft bristle of those rusty brown hairs. Fuck, he'd touched it, hadn't he?

James helped himself to the rest of the coffee in the French press. "Good morning. How did you sleep?"

"In gym shorts." What the hell? In gym shorts? Why did he just say that? Although, it was unusual. He never slept in gym shorts, especially dirty ones.

"You don't say." There was a smirk in James's voice. Jesus, what had Will done? "Any big plans for the day?"

"Not really." Will took a big gulp of his coffee, hoping to scald away the shame.

"Good, because I'm taking you out on the boat."

Will's chest burned with the easy confidence in James's voice. No one was going to believe this guy was his boyfriend.

"Isn't there, like, a sea monster living in the lake?"

"Technically, he's a lake monster, not a sea monster. And his name is Champ. And he's a myth."

Jesus, why did James have to be so fucking hot? And why did he have to keep smiling at Will? "Fine, I'll go out on the boat. But I'm not swimming."

James's smile turned into a smirk. "We'll see."

Two hours later, the three of them were bobbing somewhere out in the middle of Lake Champlain.

"Aren't you going to drop an anchor or something?" Will asked.

"It's a lake, dude, not a river. Now, pick your favorite color." James gestured to the stack of inflatable rafts he probably got on sale at Wal-Mart for $7.99. Then he started to undress like he was alone in his room, or up on the stage. He even did that thing where you cross your arms and grab the hem of your shirt and pull it up and off in one fluid motion.

Christ, he was even sexier with his shirt off. He had the perfect amount of chest hair. It dusted across his collarbone and lightly flecked his pecs before it ran in a thin line down the center of his abs and disappeared into his bathing suit.

Will swallowed and looked at the stack of inflatables. "You don't have my favorite color. My favorite color is orange. And I already told you. I'm not swimming."

James put his aviators and hat back on. "No one's favorite color is orange. Now pick a raft already." He kicked off his sandals and snatched the green one for himself. "Hurry up, we've got work to do."

"Actually, Miles and I already figured everything out," Theo said, opting for the red raft, "so it shouldn't take that long."

Will should've known better than to introduce Theo and Miles. This whole excursion was a waste of time. Sure, he understood the need to come up with a convincing backstory. It was the kind of exhaustive preparation his father was renowned for. But why did they have to do it while floating like breadcrumbs on top of a bottomless lake filled with sea monsters, or lake monsters, or whatever the fuck they were? And why was there no shade on this boat?

James and Theo jumped overboard without any hesitation and climbed onto their rafts, which folded in the middle like tacos. Meanwhile, Will stood in the boat, sweating through one of the shirts his mother had left him, which he only wore because he hadn't dared go to the laundromat before he left the city. The paps were everywhere.

James turned lazily in the water below him. "Come on, Will, what are you waiting for? The water's fine."

"I can talk just as well from up here."

"Get your ass in here. We won't watch you undress, I promise. Theo, turn around. Will's shy."

"Why? He's, like, the fittest person I've ever seen."

"Just do it." James paddled with one hand until his raft was facing the other way. Theo rolled his eyes, but did the same.

Jesus Christ, fine. Will quickly undressed and pulled the yellow raft in front of his body. "Is it cold?"

"No, it's refreshing. Now jump in."

Fuck James and his perfect porn 'stache. Clutching the raft to his chest, Will jumped into the lake, which was not refreshing. It was iceberg-cold. His skin clung to his body like he'd been vacuum sealed.

"Jesus!"

"You'll get used to it."

Will climbed up onto his raft, his teeth chattering.

"Holy shit, is that really your body?" Theo asked. "If I looked like that, I'd never wear a shirt. You have an eight pack, an honest-to-god eight pack. How is that even possible? And look at your v-cup. How long did that take?"

"Theo, check your filter. It's not polite to count someone's abs." James tried to splash his son and missed by about five feet.

"You're the one who told me he had an eight pack. I was only counting to make sure you weren't lying."

How the hell would James know if Will had an eight pack or not? *Shit.* Suddenly, the gym shorts started to make more sense. Had James put him to bed? Had he seen him naked? That was it. Will was never drinking again.

James twirled back around to face Will, and the blue sky and jagged outline of the Adirondack Mountains lit up his aviators like mini TV screens. "Now, why don't we start at the beginning? How did we meet?"

"Miles and I already figured this out, and we decided it's best if we stick as close to the truth as possible," Theo said. "So, you two met at a party and fell in love because you both needed to pee at the same time. One thing led to another, and before you knew it, you were playing swords."

Will smacked his forehead. "What? No. Just no."

"It's not that bad," James said. "We'll just leave out the swords part. And let's back it up a month or two so we seem more established." He lifted his hand from the water and let it rest on his bare chest, causing thin rivulets of water to slide down his tan skin and pool at his navel. "We just have to figure out why you didn't mention me to your family sooner."

That was easy. Why would Will give a boyfriend the opportunity to fanboy over his father, lust over his brother, and call his mother a MILF? "How about because I hate them?"

"You don't hate them. You wouldn't be here if you hated them."

"Fine, we'll just say I didn't want to jinx things."

James smiled. "There you go. That's the spirit."

"Okay, so how does it end?" Will asked. "How do we break up?"

James lowered his sunglasses and glared at him. "That's where your mind goes, to how things end? You don't want to, I don't know, maybe find out my favorite color or if I have any hobbies before you dump me?"

"Oh, I already know how things end." Theo's lips curled into a wicked smile. "Will has a moment of insecurity, and he's not sure if you like him as much as he likes you, so he tests the strength of your relationship by floating the idea of possibly breaking up, secretly hoping you'll be horrified and tell him you never wanna break up. But, because you're you and find it easier to just start again rather than suffer through even the tiniest bit of drama, you don't act remotely horrified. In fact, you just shrug and say, 'Okay, if that's what you want,' which confirms all of Will's worst fears, and then he has no choice but to break up with you for real."

Okay, that was oddly specific.

"Or, because this is Will's first long-term relationship, he thinks to himself, you know, this isn't so bad. I'd give this relationship an eight out of ten. I mean, the sex is decent, and we're ranked first in our bowling league. But I bet I could do better. It's not like anyone gets it right the first time. I better end this now and try for a nine out of ten, maybe a ten out of ten."

Jesus Christ, what was going on? "My favorite color really is orange, and my birthday is December 5th. I'm a Sagittarius. I have no hobbies, but I sometimes write children's songs. My two best songs are my dinosaur song and my community helpers song."

"This is perfect. You both like music. You're gonna fall in love for real. I just know it. And I already came up with your pet names. One of you can be Excalibur and the other can be Fierce Deity. You can decide who's who later. It doesn't really matter to me. And when people ask why you're named after famous swords, you can tell them how you met."

Where did Theo come up with this shit? And what the hell was Fierce Deity? And why did Theo think his father would switch teams for Will? Was James bi?

"My favorite color is green," James said. "My birthday is April 5th, and I'm an Aries. I like playing video games, hiking, camping, playing basketball, skiing, you know, that kinda thing."

Okay, so James wasn't a five-year-old. He was a thirty-eight-year-old middle schooler.

"Oh my god, you're both fire signs, and you both had your golden birthdays when you were five. Mine is when I turn twenty-one, which makes it basically the coolest golden birthday ever. I'm gonna make everyone get wasted on Goldschlager."

Yup, they were fucked. So fucked.

CHAPTER 20
JAMES

After dinner, James found Will on their shared balcony, reading a Jane Austin anthology. He wore baggy sweatpants and a hoodie to ward off mosquitos.

James handed Will a revised call sheet. "Someone dropped this off for you. I thought maybe we could run tomorrow's scenes."

Will used the call sheet as a bookmark and closed his book. "I'm not going to go. But don't worry, I'll still ask my mom if you can watch."

James set a six pack of IPA on the table. Will had said the same thing that afternoon at the quarry. He'd also said he wouldn't jump, and look how that had turned out. Granted, it had taken him twenty minutes to build up the nerve to jump off the lowest cliff, which had been barely ten feet off the water. But he'd done it. And by the time they'd left, he'd been jumping off the thirty-foot cliff like a pro. Will just needed a little encouragement, and James was happy to supply it.

James opened a beer using the edge of the table and handed it to his grumpy fake boyfriend. "I know you were hoping to get the part. But you can't let one setback knock you out of the ring."

"I wasn't hoping to get the part." Will scowled, and a crease formed right between his thick black eyebrows. He really was a terrible liar.

"It will be fun, and I'm from Vermont, so I can help you with the accent. By the time I'm done with you, they're gonna regret not casting you."

Will seemed surprised to find a beer in his hand. "I can't drink this."

James grabbed a beer for himself. "We're gonna show 'em what they're missing. And lesson number one, Vermonters drink beer. Granted, they don't drink craft beer, but they drink beer, usually light beer. In fact, it's customary to carry a cooler in the back of your truck with your favorite beer so you have it with you at all times. I only got you this fancy shit because it was second on your list of forbidden drinks. Plus, after you dissed my PBR the other night, I figured you needed to be eased into redneck culture."

"What are you talking about? I never dissed your PBR."

James figured Will didn't remember passing out in his lap. But James remembered. He'd left Will's briefs on, but he'd taken off the rest of Will's wet clothes before shimmying him into a pair of dry shorts.

"Here"—James set the script between them—"you be Travis, and I'll be Bruce."

"This is pointless."

"No, what's pointless is you sitting around the house all day waiting for life to come to you. You gotta be proactive. You gotta take risks. You can't take no for an answer."

"Like you're doing right now?" Will took a swig of his beer, forgetting he wasn't going to drink it.

James smirked. "Exactly."

Will rolled his eyes. "Fine." He perused the scene for twenty seconds and then announced, "Okay, I'm ready."

"Let's do this." James gave a wink, and then tried to imagine himself as his father, a beer-gutted asshole with the temper of a two-year-old and the fists of a boxer. "Where the fuck are my sunglasses?"

"I don't know, Dad, but you were wearing them this morning when you went riding."

"Did I leave 'em up on the mountain?" James swallowed hard. It was weird, the way he could hear his father's voice in his head as clear as day. "Go get 'em for me."

"I'm not going all the way up the frigging mountain just to get your stupid sunglasses."

"Okay, stop," James said. Will sounded like a second grader pretending to be the sheriff in the school play. "Can you maybe make your voice a little deeper and talk a little slower?"

"Why, so I can sound more like Derek?"

"No, so you can sound more like Travis."

Will rolled his eyes again. "Fine."

"And don't pronounce the t in mountain. It's moun'ain. And no g's either."

"What do you mean no g's?"

"I mean, in Vermont you don't go fishing, you go fishin'. You don't go mudding, you go muddin'."

Will raised an eyebrow. "What the hell is mudding?"

"Muddin'," James corrected.

"Fine. What the hell is muddin'?"

"It's exactly what it sounds like. It's when you take your truck up the old logging roads and look for mud to drive through."

"You're kidding?" Will looked at James like he had a third nipple.

"I'm not kidding."

"I think you mean kiddin'."

"There you go." *Smart ass.* "Now let's start again."

They went again, but it still wasn't right. Will sounded like he was mocking Travis, making him into a cousin-fucking hillbilly. Of course, the point wasn't to get Will not to suck. It was to get him excited about participating so he'd want to go to the set tomorrow.

"When you and Theo went riding, did you meet Howard by any chance?"

"Old guy, one eye, kind of looks like Charles Bronson?"

James tipped his beer at Will. "That's the one. He's got a thick Vermont accent. But don't go that thick, okay? Only ole-timers sound like that. But you get the idea. Do that, only subtler."

"Fine"—Will rolled his eyes again—"whatever."

"Why don't we get this one line sorted out first, and then go back, okay?" James pointed to Travis's line halfway down the page.

"Fine." Will closed his eyes for a moment, took a deep breath, and then said, "I'm not goin' all the way up the friggin' moun'ain just to get your stupid sunglasses."

James couldn't speak. Holy shit! How had Will done that? He not only sounded like a real Vermonter. He sounded like Travis.

"How was that?"

James reached for his beer and took a long, slow pull, trying to chase away the ghost of his dead brother. "It was good." He gripped the bottle tighter, hoping Will didn't notice the way his hand shook. "Okay, let's go from the top."

They read through the scene half a dozen times, and each time Will got better, which didn't seem possible. It was uncanny how much he sounded like Travis. Their voices were different, Will's a little more melodic, but the subtext, the weight behind the words, was exactly the same.

James glanced at the next scene on the call sheet. He knew he shouldn't, but he couldn't help himself. "Let's try this one. I'll be Jimmy."

Will read the first line—"Hey bro, whatcha up to?"—and James was transported back to his tiny apartment in Queens, where he'd ducked out onto the fire escape so no one would hear him lie to his brother.

"Nothin', just chillin'," he said.

"Emily and I were wonderin' if you wanted to come up for the baby shower next weekend."

James pictured Travis standing in the kitchen, the old rotary phone pressed to his ear, the table below him covered in mail and coupons and half-used batteries.

"You know I can't do that." It was a lie. James could've gone. He could've been there for Theo. But he was in love, and he and Alex, his boyfriend at the time, were going bowling that weekend.

"Come the fuck on. Dad doesn't even remember kickin' you out. He fuckin' thinks you still live here. Yesterday, he accused you of eating all his beef jerky." Will took his time saying each line, and it wasn't like he was reading them. It was like he hit play on an old answering machine message. "And I need you." His voice was softer now, embarrassed, desperate. "He's fuckin' killin' me. I can't keep this up."

"I'm sorry. I can't." James closed his eyes and saw Alex through the window, a greasy slice of pizza in his hand. "Alex and I are going to a protest." Another lie.

"What kind of protest?"

"It's for, uh, social justice."

James must have made a face or something because Will set his hand on James's—his skin cold and damp from his beer—and asked, "Are you okay?"

James shook his head. "Sorry, lost in thought." He forced a laugh. "You're a really good actor, you know that?"

Will ignored the compliment and grabbed two more beers from the six-pack. "You're going to have to open these. I can barely do it with an actual opener."

"I'll teach you. Real Vermonters don't need an opener."

After teaching Will how to open a beer like a pro, they finished the scene. This time, James kept his expression neutral. What was wrong with him? He'd helped write the book. Why should reading the script be any different?

"This Jimmy character is a real asshole," Will said. "How much do you want to bet his idea of social justice is bottoming for Asians?"

That startled a laugh out of James. He'd spent the better part of the last ten minutes trying not to cry, and now he was laughing. Man, he needed to smoke a bowl and get his balance back. It wasn't true, of course. Well, the asshole part was. But not the bottoming part. James had only bottomed for one guy before, and that had been a long ass time ago.

"Want to try again?" Will asked, and for a split second, James thought he was talking about bottoming, which made his ass clench like a fist.

James swallowed thickly. "Sure."

By the time they finished another read through, the sun had set, and the sky was a dark amethyst. In the yard below, little blips of fluorescent light flickered over the grass, and James thought about how he and Travis used to smear firefly guts across their faces and clothes and pretend they were ninjas.

Someone hiccupped behind James, and he turned to find Theo standing in the doorway, tears in his eyes.

"Hey, bud," James said.

Theo turned and ran into the house without saying a word.

"Jesus, Miles made him cry, didn't he?" Will said. "I'm going to kick his ass."

"He's fine. But I better go check on him."

JAMES FOUND Theo in his room a few minutes later, holding Atticus like a stuffed animal.

"He sounds just like Dad." Theo wasn't crying anymore, but his face was drained of all expression.

"I know." James walked over and picked up the picture on the nightstand, the one of the three of them at Disney World.

"I didn't know who you were talking to, and—"

"I know." James set the picture back down and turned it to face Theo.

"He should be playing Dad, not Derek Hall. It should be Will." Theo sounded like he was going to cry again.

"I know." James felt like a broken record. But what else could he say? "Can I get you anything? Ice cream, perhaps?" Theo wasn't five anymore, but it was worth a try.

Theo shook his head. "No. Ice cream isn't allowed this close to bedtime."

"Good lord, not you, too?"

CHAPTER 21
WILL

Will's mom was sitting at the kitchen island, drinking coffee with Theo, when Will came downstairs late Friday morning.

"Look who's awake." She left a smear of lipstick on her ceramic mug.

Will had been awake for hours. He'd just been waiting for his mother to leave. Fuck his timing.

When his mother had arrived the night before, Will had expected her to grab James by the dick and snarl, "Mine." But upon finding out about their fake relationship scheme, she'd merely rolled her eyes and shrugged with feigned indifference.

But she wasn't done with the topic. Of that, Will was certain. She was just waiting until they were alone. Then she'd give him hell. She'd tell him the whole thing was going to blow up in his face, ruin his father's last chance to win an Oscar, detract from Andy's wedding, and force her to clean up his mess, yet again.

"And just in time, too. We leave in ten minutes."

Will grunted and headed straight for the last inch of coffee in the French press. "I think I'm just going to hang around here today and finish my book. But James said he'll go with you. Let him run lines with Dad. He's actually from Vermont, so he'll be better anyway. And he's always wanted to see how movies are made."

"You'll have plenty of time to read there. The first day of shooting is always a shit show. And James can't go. It's a closed set. You know that. Oh, and in case it wasn't obvious, I'm not paying him extra for this little stunt of yours." *There it was.* "And your little cry for attention can't interfere with his duties or the wedding. Is that understood?"

"It's not Will's fault," Theo said. "I'm the one who told everyone they were dating, and I'm the one who invited Ryan and Derek over for dinner. Don't be mad at Will."

She laughed like it was all an amusing lark. "Believe me. I'm not mad. In fact, I'm fully on board. This might actually do wonders for William's image, show people his sweet, lovable side."

"I don't have a sweet, lovable side."

His mother smiled into her coffee and didn't argue the point.

"And you don't mind that Derek and Ryan are coming over later?" Theo asked.

"No, of course not. It will be like old times. I miss having a full house."

The front door opened and closed, and James called from the hall, "That's the last of 'em."

"Great. And while we're gone, maybe you can chop some wood or something. That way we can have a fire later."

"Okay." James came into the kitchen drenched in sweat. He looked at Will, and his eyes said, *Did you ask her?* He had sweat stains under his arms and down the center of his chest and back. Was it weird that Will wanted to bury his face in James's armpit and inhale like it was an oxygen mask on a crashing plane? "I can do that. And when I'm done, I can bring you guys lunch."

Will's mother set her mug next to the sink. "Don't worry about that. That's why we have craft services. Plus, as I just told William, it's a closed set. But maybe some other day when we're not hosting a dinner party."

James wiped the sweat from his brow. "That'd be great."

"WHY ARE YOU SMILING?" The dandelions sailed by in a yellow blur as his mother sped down the dirt road.

"Can't a mother be happy for her son? It's not everyone who can pull off having both a fake husband and a fake boyfriend. Although, if I'm being totally honest, I preferred the beard. But I suppose the mustache is cute, too, if you're into that sort of thing."

Will didn't respond, and they rode the rest of the way in silence.

It was strange being on a movie set again. *The Beautiful* had been a small production, nothing like this. He and Derek had had trailers, but they'd been shitty, and everyone had been so worried about going over budget they'd had to shoot everything in five takes or less. Will hadn't been on a proper movie set since he'd been a kid, back when the makeup artists used to give him fake scars and realistic looking tattoos and tell him he should have his own Disney show.

Well, he didn't have his own Disney show, but he did have a role to play today. He had to stroke his father's ego and pretend he didn't care that a teenage vampire twink was living his life. Will looked down the line of trailers. Which one was Derek's?

"It's this way," his mother said. She didn't look back, and her red hair swirled behind her like flames.

Normally, it was customary to shoot some on location and the rest in studios in L.A. and New York. But because of his father's illness and the time crunch, they were filming the entire movie on location and had converted the newer barn into a makeshift studio. They had one stage set up as the interior of a rundown farmhouse. It was hideous, with vertical wood paneling, orange shag carpeting, a torn-up recliner, and a tan couch with tiny log cabins printed all over it.

They found his father in hair and makeup, and his parents immediately started fighting. Will's father and Roger, the cinematographer, wanted beams of sunlight and dust motes. Will's mother thought they could do without. Will left them to it and went for a walk.

He was on his way down to the pond when one of the trailer doors opened and Derek's manager, Tony, stepped out, his gold hoop glinting in the sunlight.

"What are you doing here?" Great, Tony probably thought Will was stalking Derek, skulking around his trailer.

"Well, right now, I'm headed down to that pond to read my book." He lifted his book and waved it in the air, as if that proved he wasn't stalking.

Tony didn't look convinced, lifting his eyebrows until his forehead was creased with lines.

"Will, is that you?" Derek appeared in the doorway behind Tony, and of course, he wasn't wearing a shirt. Will recognized most of Derek's tattoos, but there were a few new ones, including one of an Oscar, as if the actual statue wasn't enough.

Will looked away. He was not a crazy stalker. He was minding his own business. "Nope. Just pretend I'm not here. I'll walk the other way next time." He turned and continued walking.

"Hey, wait. Can you do me a favor?" Derek's deep voice felt like a magnet tugging Will back. "This accent is killing me, and you were always so good at accents. Mind helping me out?"

"I don't think that's a good idea," Tony said, not moving from Derek's trailer door.

"Relax, Tony. You don't always have to be such a papa bear. It's all in the past now, right? Isn't that why we're doing this?"

That was definitely not why Derek was doing this. He was doing this because his last two movies had bombed big time, and he needed Will's father's coattails to salvage his crumbling career. He may have won the Oscar for *The Beautiful*, but that had been ten years ago, and in this business, you were only as good as your last movie.

"Fine. I'll just stick around, then."

Derek laughed. "Get the fuck out of here, Tony. I'll be fine."

"Sorry about that," Derek said after Tony left. He opened his fridge and passed Will a sparkling water. "He's just overprotective."

"It's fine."

Derek's trailer was huge and far nicer than Will's apartment. It had a long white sofa and a giant flat screen TV.

It was unsettling being alone with Derek again after so much time. Yeah, he'd been alone with him earlier that week, but he'd been super drunk then. He wished he was drunk now. Maybe then it wouldn't be so awkward.

"I see you're no worse for wear after the other night." Derek gestured to the sofa. "Sit."

Will sat. "Thanks for giving me a ride home. Sorry I was such a mess. It's been—"

"You don't need to explain. I know how much you worship your dad. This has got to be harder on you than anyone."

The prick of tears came quick and sharp, but Will fought them off. Growing up in the Chapman household, there was nothing more taboo than suppressing one's emotions. But teaching was all about composure, and Will had learned to keep an even keel.

"What's tripping you up about the accent?" he asked, changing the subject.

"I'll show you." Derek passed Will the script, and they read through the same scene he and James had worked on the night before.

It was different reading it with Derek. With James, it had felt personal, like reading someone's diary. But with Derek, it felt easy, trite almost. It was probably because there was almost no distinction between Derek playing Travis and Derek playing Oliver, his character in *The Beautiful*, except now he was ten years older and sounded vaguely southern.

But it worked for Derek. It really did. He was like Sandra Bullock or Brad Pitt that way. You always knew what you were getting with Derek Hall. Watching one of his movies was like hanging out with an old friend for two hours.

Derek rubbed his bare chest, and it released whiffs of his musky cologne, like a scratch and sniff sticker. "What do you think?"

Apparently, Will was going to have to blow smoke up Derek's ass, too. "It was great. But remember, while it's a rural accent, it's not southern."

He tried to show Derek what he meant, but Derek was incapable of playing anyone other than Derek, and if anything, he sounded even more southern after Will's tutelage.

Derek collapsed onto the sofa next to Will. "Whatever, all rednecks sound the same."

He turned on the TV, and for one thrilling second, Will couldn't breathe. Derek had done the same thing ten years ago. "Let's do some research, shall we?" he'd said, as gay porn had appeared on the screen.

This time, it was a low budget movie called *Man with A Plan*.

"This is the best the dialect coach could find for us, and it's completely unwatchable."

This was too weird. Ten years ago, being in the same room with Derek had made Will's whole body buzz with anticipation. Now, all he wanted to do was get the hell out of there.

"You'll figure it out." Will stood and looked out the window at the majestic weeping willow hanging over the pond.

In theory, this was exactly what he'd been hoping for. Derek was opening up to him again, seeking out Will's advice like he used to. Yet, for some reason, Will wanted nothing more than to be down by the pond reading *Persuasion* in quiet solitude.

"You could always go listen to Howard, the guy at the stables. He's got a Vermont accent."

"That's actually a good idea. Thanks, Will." Derek turned the TV off. "So, tell me about this new boyfriend of yours. Is he really hotter than me?"

Will's pulse spiked at the mention of James.

"Wait, don't answer that. I don't want to show up tonight feeling all self-conscious. But I'm happy for you. I really am. When Tony said you'd made up some fake boyfriend to make me jealous, I was worried this whole thing wasn't going to work out. But now that I know he's real, we can show the world that we're just friends and get you back in the game."

Will swallowed a walnut-sized lump in his throat. "Right."

"Do you miss it? Acting?"

Acting had been Will's dream since infancy. While Andy had been out being popular, playing sports and hanging with his friends, Will had been shut away in the library, running scenes with their father.

"Sometimes, yeah."

"We're going to get you back out there, I promise." Derek smiled, but all Will could see was the thin white scar slicing his eyebrow in two.

A NERVOUS ENERGY thrummed through the room as the director, Michelle, called action for the first time. Everyone anticipated greatness, film history in the making, especially after Robert Chapman's rousing speech. But not Will's mother. She expected a disaster. Of course, she didn't appreciate doing her ex-husband a deathbed favor.

There was no reason the movie shouldn't be amazing. Everyone involved was the best in their field, especially Michelle, the director. She'd won the DGA the previous year but had been snubbed at the

Oscars, which meant she was owed an apology nomination, if nothing else. And while Derek wasn't a great actor, he was at least consistent. Besides, he was de-glamming for the role, becoming a mere mortal like the rest of them. And Ryan was so pretty it didn't matter how well he did, not with eyes like those.

But by the third take, Will wondered if his mother knew something he didn't. This was worse than a soap opera readthrough.

His father and Derek had no chemistry. And it wasn't Derek's fault. Sure, his accent was southern, and he talked too fast, but that was nothing compared to the amateur theatrics Will's father was putting on. It was like his father was doing a *Saturday Night Live* spoof of himself. For all his talk of trusting the cameras and the crew, he performed to the back of the theater, every gesture huge, every word a booming proclamation. He made Nicholas Cage look like an understated Helen Mirren.

Michelle kept yelling cut and whispering in his father's ear, but take after take, his father kept giving the same lurid performance. After what must have been the twentieth cut, Will's dad leaned over to Derek and said, "You should definitely remember that accent in case they ever remake *Gone with The Wind*. You sound exactly like Rhett Butler."

Derek's face turned beet red, and he looked like he was about to Kool-Aid Man through the wall.

Before he could, Tony walked up onto the stage and put his arm over Derek's shoulder. "Derek will be in his trailer. Let us know when Robert remembers how to act."

"Take twenty." Michelle pulled off her headset. She was a stoic woman who exuded the kind of calm authority that would've made her an excellent teacher. But she looked like she'd aged about ten years in the last hour.

The room cleared, and Ryan came and sat next to Will. "Is your dad okay?"

"I don't know." Will had never seen his dad perform so poorly before. He hadn't known it was possible.

"Robert told me about the . . ." Ryan made a strange gesture in the air instead of saying the c word. "I can't believe Andy doesn't know yet. How are we supposed to keep this a secret from him?"

"I don't know."

Will knew why his father hadn't told Andy yet, and it had nothing to do with the wedding. He just couldn't bear to make Andy sad. Andy was like their mother in many ways, beautiful and statuesque, but he didn't have her mettle. His heart was as porcelain as his skin.

Ryan ran a hand over his stubbled scalp, his fingers splayed as if he expected to find his golden locks miraculously restored. "Maybe he's in his head too much, this being his final performance and all."

"Yeah, maybe."

Will's father had a tendency to overthink things, but never on set. He always did his freaking out at home. He used to say, "If you do your homework, you never have to feel nervous in front of the camera, because it isn't you anymore. You're not even there. You're just the character now." Maybe that was it. Maybe everything had come together so fast he hadn't gotten a chance to work through his process, to leave the second guessing at home.

When Will had been growing up, the months leading up to a shoot had been an absolute misery for everyone around. Well, everyone except Will, who'd liked being his father's constant companion. He'd pull Will into the library at all hours to run scenes, convinced he was about to ruin his career.

Every time it would be fine, or better than fine, and his father would tell any interviewer who'd listen how terrified he'd been, but how glad he was to still feel that way after all these years because it meant he was giving himself fully to his characters. The day he stopped feeling terrified was the day he'd retire.

Well, he didn't seem terrified now. He sat in his chair, sipping herbal tea with a bemused smile. Maybe he was on too many drugs.

"William"—his mother waved to him from across the room—"a quick word, please."

"Shit, I better go. Your mother scares me." With vampire-like speed, Ryan vanished.

"So, Theo tells me you and James have been rehearsing. According to him, you're way better than Derek and I should replace him this instant."

"Theo said that?"

"What can I say? The boy has taste."

Wait, hold the presses. Was that a compliment?

"And just so we're clear, I'm keeping him. Even after you fuck everything up with James, I'm keeping Theo."

"I'd expect nothing less."

"Anyway, I need you to go run the scene a few times with your father, see if you can get him to dial it back a few million notches."

"He's not going to listen to me." Across the room, his father accepted another cup of herbal tea from a PA.

"Well, don't tell him directly, for fuck's sake. Just lead by example, see if you can bring him down to reality. And hurry up before Derek comes back. The last thing I need is another ego to stroke."

"What, afraid I'm going to make him look bad?"

"Frankly, yes."

Jesus, was that another compliment? What was going on? It wasn't even self-serving, like when *The Beautiful* came out and she'd said *Aren't you glad you got my ass and not your father's?*

"Fine." The room was mostly empty now, except for some of the crew and Roger, the cinematographer, who was watching the playback. Will came and stood beside his father, who smiled up at him.

"You see what I'm saying about the dust motes? We need them."

Will was not going there. "Want to run the scene a few times with me? I'm curious what you think of my Vermont accent. I got a few pointers from an actual Vermonter."

"I thought you'd never ask." His father stood and extended his arm towards the stage, like he was asking Will to dance.

Panic jabbed into Will's gut. "I was thinking maybe we could go back to your trailer. Looks like it might be a minute before you start up again."

"No, this will be better. We'll have Carl and the boys hop behind the cameras for a second. I want to see what it looks like if I try stumbling when I come out of my room, almost like I'm blind without my sunglasses."

Will found it strange to have multiple cameras on a movie set. That was usually a sitcom thing. But it had been ten years since he'd been in this world, and things had changed.

"Do you need a script?" his father asked.

"No, I should be fine." Will had a great memory for lines.

It took his father three tries to get the stumble the way he liked, and in that time, Will was surprised to discover it didn't feel strange being in front of the camera again. It wasn't like riding a bike or putting on an old sweater. But it was familiar in a way that was only mildly unsettling, like a Grindr hookup after a long hiatus.

It was different running the scene with his father. In fact, it didn't feel like doing a scene at all, not like it had with Derek, who made every interaction feel like doing a scene. Maybe it was because his father really was dying, or because acting was the only way they could share authentic emotions with each other. Maybe it was because they'd done this sort of thing a million times before. But whatever the reason, it felt, for lack of a better word, natural. And then it was over.

Will couldn't say if it was good or bad. But he felt sick with longing when his mother called him off the stage.

"William"—her high heels clicked rapidly on the barn floor—"pull the car around. Theo just called. Atticus had another seizure."

And that was that. End scene.

CHAPTER 22
JAMES

James came into the kitchen, hoping to get a beer and a moment's peace before the circus started. He found Theo putting the finishing touches on his citrus sculpture, a pyramid of stacked lemons and limes.

"I talked to my mom today, and I was thinking, if it's alright with you, maybe I could borrow your car and drive up there sometime next week. She says it's only a little more than an hour away."

James's hand jerked inside the refrigerator and knocked over several beer bottles. "Please tell me Emily doesn't know we're here in Vermont?"

"Why, is it a secret or something?" One of the lemons rolled onto the granite counter, and Theo scooped it up.

"Yes, it's a secret. We're literally under cover right now. If I lose my job, we're fucked. We need this money."

Theo produced a bottle opener and handed it to James. "No, you need this money. I have my own money."

James ignored the opener and used the lip of the counter. The cap fell and pinged across the floor. "No."

"No, what?" Theo reached down and picked up the bottle cap.

"No, you can't borrow my car."

"Why not?"

"Well, let's see"—James started counting off the reasons—"you don't have a driver's license, you can't drive a stick, and Emily is only after one thing, and it's not to listen to you go on and on about Ryan Ashbury."

"Why are you like this?"

"Like what? Like someone who cares about you?"

"No, like someone who thinks people can't change, that there aren't relationships worth fighting for."

James set his beer down harder than he'd intended, and it erupted like a volcano onto the counter. "Your mother is the most selfish person I've ever met."

"That's not true."

"She didn't even leave a note, Theo. She just left your dad and me to take care of everything."

James hated the broken look on Theo's face, the tears forming behind his blue eyes. But the kid needed to know the truth. The moment they'd found out Travis carried the gene, Emily was gone. And because there had been a fifty percent chance Theo did, too, she'd left him behind. She'd hated that they wouldn't test a minor. She'd wanted to know for certain whether or not it was safe to love her own son. She hadn't given a shit about what was right for Theo, hadn't thought for a moment that the choice should be his. After all, it was only his life.

"People change." Theo refused to cry, but he was close.

"No, they don't. People don't change. Did you know, when the book was published, she sued for half of the profits, claiming Travis started it while they were still married? That's right, she wanted half of your money."

James's beer was mostly foam, but he took a swig anyway. He knew this was hurting Theo, but it was necessary to prevent Theo from getting hurt by his mother's total disregard for anyone but herself.

"The only reason he wrote the book in the first place was so he could leave you with something. And she wanted half of it. She wanted half of your money so she could piss it away on cigarettes and booze and whatever wife-beating loser she was fucking at the time. Do you know how much it cost us in lawyer fees to keep her at bay?

"She hasn't changed. Believe me. And I know exactly the yarn she'll spin if you let her. Oh, poor Emily. She's suffered so much. Her life has been so hard. Can you just imagine how it was for her, finding out her husband was gonna die young, that her son might, too?

"She expects everyone to see things from her perspective, but she's incapable of doing the same in return. She's the victim. She's always the victim. You could get stabbed in the eye right in front of her, and she'd be the victim for having to watch you go blind. That's just who she is. And it's not gonna change, Theo. In her delusional mind, she thinks your money is her money. Why? I don't know. I honestly don't. But you don't owe her shit, not money, not kindness, not forgiveness, and certainly not your time."

Theo looked like he wanted to say something, but he didn't. He would, though. He'd come up with something. And it would make sense, too. It would be logical and disgustingly optimistic, and James would wind up feeling like a complete asshole. Of course, he already felt like a complete asshole. He'd basically just told Theo his days might be numbered and he shouldn't waste them on his mother.

"I'm sorry, Theo. I didn't mean—"

"Yes, you did." Theo grabbed a dishrag from the sink and started wiping up James's mess.

"Let me do that." James reached for the rag.

"I got it." Theo picked up the beer, wiped off the bottom, and handed it back to James. "Just drink your fucking beer."

LOVE ON THE D-LIST

James was on his way up to shower and dress when he saw Will's bedroom door open.

"How did it go today?" he asked, poking his head inside.

Clearly, someone had dressed Will. Normally, Will looked like the before scene of a makeover montage. Now, he wore distressed jeans, a tight-fitting gray T-shirt, and tan Timberlands. He looked good. He looked really good. He smelled good, too, like soap and something else. Was Will wearing cologne?

Will shrugged, and a lock of his black hair fell across his brow. "It was alright. I got to read the scene between takes, so that was something."

"Really? That's awesome. Did you wow them with your Vermont accent?" James felt a strong desire to brush the lock of hair from Will's face.

"Hardly."

"I'm sure you killed it." Instead of brushing the errant hair away, James stepped across the sea of dirty clothes and sat on the corner of Will's bed. "Anything specific you need from me tonight?"

"What do you mean?" Will tried to shove his hands in his pockets, but they were too tight. He gave up and just hooked his thumbs in instead.

"You know, like PDA and all that." James wasn't sure why he'd let himself get off topic. He was there to find out about the first day of shooting, not Will's views on cuddling. "Like, are we one of those couples who hold hands, or do we just do a lot of leaning?"

"Leaning?"

"Yeah, you know, leaning." James was aware he sounded ridiculous, but leaning was a real thing. He just wasn't explaining it right. "Like this." He got up and approached Will, who recoiled like James was going to hit him. "Hold still."

James grabbed Will by the shoulders and tried to press him into the floor, like a tent stake. Then he leaned his shoulder against Will's, forming the apex of a teepee.

"Or you can do it with the arm, too, kind of a half hug thing."

James threw his arm over Will's shoulder and pulled him into the crook of his armpit. It was kind of alarming how perfectly Will slotted in there, like a nested pair of salt and pepper shakers.

Will relaxed slightly, and James felt the steady pressure of Will's body against his own.

"I guess leaning would be alright. If you feel comfortable with it."

"Yeah, totally comfortable." James liked how solid Will was, like a fire hydrant. Would adding *benefits* to their arrangement be out of the question? Probably. Plus, it was clear Will was still hung up on Derek.

"And maybe we can steal glances at each other all night," James said. "And if that's not selling it, we can make up some excuse about how we both need to get wine from the cellar and then come back ten minutes later all disheveled and without any wine."

Will cast his eyes to the floor, but not before James saw the rosy blush flood Will's cheeks. Man, he was adorable.

When Will looked back up at James, he said, "Fine, but you gotta walk like a bow-legged cowboy so there's no mistakin' who just got fucked."

James wasn't expecting those words to come from Will's sweet mouth, nor was his sphincter, judging by the way it tightened like a Chinese finger trap.

James swallowed hard. "Okay, and should I call you Daddy and sit on your lap, too?" He meant the words to come out playful and teasing, only they came out stilted and breathless instead.

"You can if you want, man. I'll take real good care of you."

It wasn't until Will winked that James realized Will was doing his Vermonter impersonation, and it was fucking phenomenal.

THE BACK YARD looked like the setting of a Mayan sacrifice. There were at least fifty citronella tiki torches burning around the stone patio. Was this a dinner party or the Tribal Council on *Survivor*?

Will lay by the pool in the orange glow with a mojito in his hand. On the other side of the patio, his mother stared at her phone. She wore huge black headphones like a DJ and had changed into a tight-fitting chocolate brown dress cinched at the waist with a matching belt and an off-centered silver belt buckle.

Theo bounced between them, topping off their drinks the moment they took a sip. He must have been wearing one of Will's shirts because James didn't recognize it. It was almost a simple white button down, except it had these strips of fabric hanging down the center.

"They're not here yet." Theo approached James with a tall glass stuffed with mint leaves.

"I can see that." James smiled, determined not to catch the nervous energy hanging in the air like a sneeze on an elevator. He took the cocktail from Theo and tried to strain the liquid through his teeth so he didn't choke on a mint leaf. "Well, that will certainly counteract the Cool Ranch breath."

Earlier, Theo had chewed James out for buying only "white trash" appetizers, claiming rich people didn't eat Doritos. They ate tortilla chips and extremely mild salsa.

Theo refilled James's drink like his life depended on Derek and Ryan finding everyone with completely full glasses. "We're not having Doritos. And you better not embarrass me."

James winked at his nephew, who was too nervous to remember he was mad at James. "How about I go embarrass Will instead?" He took his drink over to Will's lounge chair and nodded. "Scoot over."

Will set his phone down. "Are you serious?"

"Practice makes perfect." Maybe if they got a head start, Derek wouldn't notice how Will folded up like a hedgehog every time James got close enough to touch him.

Will glanced around the patio. "But there are so many chairs."

"Only one with my handsome boyfriend in it."

Will rolled his eyes, a habit James was growing rather fond of. He hadn't enjoyed annoying someone this much in ages, maybe ever.

There wasn't room for two grown men to sit shoulder to shoulder, and instead of looking like two cozy boyfriends, they looked like a Bloody Mary with one too many sticks of celery.

"You don't fit," Will said, listing dramatically to the side.

"I would if you'd lean this way." James lifted his arm to make room for Will under it.

"What's it with you and leaning?" Will held his drink out as he obediently wedged himself in place.

"That's better." James relaxed his arm on Will's shoulder and draped his leg over Will's. "Now, isn't this cozy?"

It really was. The sun was setting over the lake, and the sky was the exact same shade of orange as the flames from the tiki torches. The drink in James's hand was delightfully cold, and Will's body felt like a warm rock that had been sitting in the sun all day.

"You better not spill your drink on me," Will said.

Donna took off her headphones and smiled at them. It was a curious smile, almost wicked, but it softened slightly at the end.

"Theo, hun," she said. "I just got a text. Our guests are pulling up now. Why don't you show them around?"

James gave his nephew an exaggerated thumbs-up and squeezed Will a little tighter. "Our little boy is growing up."

"This is so fucked up. Theo's only eighteen, and Ryan's, like, twenty-five or something."

"Come on, it's not like he's got a shot in hell."

Will shifted, and his bony elbow pressed into James's gut. "Normally, I'd agree with you. But I think you're underestimating Miles's influence, not to mention my mother's."

"Oh, whatever, if they were any good at matchmaking, you wouldn't be stuck with me."

"That's actually a valid point."

James didn't appreciate Will's sass, so he licked his ear. It was right there, after all.

"Did you just lick my ear?"

"You're not supposed to agree with me. Don't you understand how self-deprecation works?"

"Yeah, but you can't just—"

"Fine, I'll lick the other one, too, for balance."

"What? Are you—"

James didn't let Will finish. He snaked his head behind Will's and ran his tongue up the back of Will's ear, making Will squirm like a worm trying to avoid the hook. "Did you know you taste like cookies?"

"I do not. Stop making shit up."

"So you're saying I shouldn't tell Derek and Ryan about the time I fucked you so hard you came in my face and gave me pink eye?"

"Jesus Christ!"

"Shh, here they come."

Theo led their guests out onto the patio, walking backwards like a college tour guide. It was kind of absurd how beautiful Ryan Ashbury and Derek Hall looked side by side—the pretty boy and the rugged man. They resembled before and after pictures of a new testosterone therapy.

"Here's a mojito to start, but I also made margaritas, and there's wine and beer and anything else you want."

Donna rose to greet her guests, kissing them each on the cheek the way rich people did.

"Thanks for inviting us," Derek said. He took a sip from his drink and made a show of looking all around the stone patio before settling his gaze on James and Will, like he hadn't noticed them snuggled up by the pool the second he'd walked around the house.

Derek strode over with his hand outstretched. "You must be the boyfriend I've heard so much about. I'm Derek." Like James didn't know who he was.

"James."

The actor's handshake was comically firm, and James had no choice but to squeeze back with equal force, like it was some kind of dick measuring contest.

"And what do you do, James? Are you a teacher like Will?"

"God, no. I'm not nearly so accomplished." James returned his arm around Will's shoulder and smiled at the way Derek traced its arc. "I'm more of a freelancer, a little of this, a little of that. You know, whatever pays the bills and gets me back to enjoying life."

"Sounds very bohemian."

"I never thought of it that way, but I guess it is."

Derek pulled up a nearby chair and took a seat facing them. "So, what did you think, Will? Is this going to be *Titanic* the movie or *Titanic* the ship?"

Will tensed beneath James's arm. "It was just the first day, and it's not like it was a crucial scene or anything."

"Look at this guy, a regular Honest Abe. Couldn't tell a lie to save his life."

Apparently, the first day of filming hadn't gone very well. James knew they were going to fuck up his movie. Why wouldn't they let him help?

"I need to pee." Will started to scramble to his feet, and his elbow jabbed into James's stomach.

James wrapped his arm around Will and pulled him back down. "Not so fast. You gotta pay the toll first."

"The toll?"

"I'll accept a kiss, a compliment, or cash." James felt Will's whole body go rigid. "Just kidding. But can you grab me a beer while you're in there?"

Will jumped to his feet the moment James released him. "Sure."

"Me, too," Derek said.

Will nodded and raced inside.

"Have you two been together long?" Derek asked, filling the awkward silence left by Will's abrupt departure.

"Not too long, no." It was a warm evening, yet James felt oddly cold without Will pressed against him. "I'm only meeting his family now. I was beginning to think he was embarrassed of me or something."

"Will's not like that." Derek's words were like a whip, and James watched the instant it happened, the instant Derek judged James unworthy. "I'm sure it was the other way around. He was probably embarrassed of his family."

James nodded, feeling like an asshole. Derek was right. Will wasn't like that.

CHAPTER 23

WILL

Theo talked all through dinner. He bombarded Ryan with question after question like he was a prisoner of war. Did Ryan have a type? *He probably did, but wasn't sure what it was yet.* What was his favorite book? *Lonesome Dove.* Who was his favorite actress? *Tilda Swinton.* Why did he decide to become a vegetarian? Was it because of the environment, animal rights, or his own health? *Some of each.* Why a pit bull rescue and not, say, a polar bear rescue? *He had pit bulls growing up, not polar bears.* What was his favorite holiday? *Christmas.* If he could have one superpower, what would it be? *Teleportation.* Would he rather propose to his future husband or wife or be proposed to? *He didn't care, so long as it was heartfelt and not in public.* Did he believe in monogamy? *It depends.* On what? *The relationship.* If he had to die in a natural disaster, what would it be? *Tsunami.* If he got a four-chair turn on *The Voice*, who would he choose? *Kelly.* And what if she was blocked? *John.*

When Theo came up for air, Will pushed his chair back and said, "I'll go get more wine."

"I'll help." James set his hand on Will's hip, and his thumb slipped under Will's shirt and stroked the skin underneath, causing Will's heart to stutter in his chest.

"Actually, James"—Will's mother's voice came out honey sweet, which wasn't a good sign—"I was hoping you could start a fire. And, Theo, while he's doing that, why don't you run up to your room and fetch your guitar? We'll have a sing-along."

James's hand fell away, and Will could breathe again. But Jesus, this was why he didn't like tight pants. He did his best to think of sad things—dead puppies and old ladies in nursing homes—but it wasn't working, so he just turned and walked away, hoping no one noticed the erection tenting his pants.

Will should've known something like this was coming. Not the erection, that was unavoidable, but the sing-along. His mother may have moved behind the camera, but she still loved to be the center of attention.

There wasn't enough wine in the world to make this night okay. Theo was acting more ridiculous than ever. Ryan refused to do or say anything Will could hate him for, even going so far as to claim Will had inspired him to become an actor. Derek kept staring, trying to figure out what a thirst trap like James was doing with a loser like Will. And James kept touching him—his hip, his back, the nape of his neck. Once, he even ran his finger over Will's bottom lip and scooped up a bit of aioli Will had missed with his napkin.

Inside, Will pulled a bottle of chardonnay from the wine fridge and a bottle of pinot from the rack. It wouldn't be enough, but it was a start.

Footsteps approached, and Will turned, expecting to find James grinning at him, proud of himself for his tour de force performance as Will's handsy boyfriend. But it was Derek.

"Oh, hey."

"Your boyfriend seems cool." Derek sat on a barstool at the kitchen island.

Will tightened his grip on the wine. "Yeah, he is."

Derek pulled a lemon from the center of Theo's pyramid, and Will thought the whole thing was going to come tumbling down. But it held. "I just hope he appreciates you, that's all."

"He does." It wasn't a total lie. At least James asked Will to do things with him, like cliff jumping, boating, and ping-pong. That was more than Will could say for anyone else, besides Miles and Tiffany.

"You deserve more than just a pretty face. You know that, right?" Derek set the lemon on top of the pyramid like he was playing a game of Jenga.

"He's not just a pretty face."

And he wasn't. James was funny and sweet. Well, sweet in a cocky, ridiculously sexy sort of way. He was a terrible disciplinarian, but he was a good father. Will had seen his fair share of bad parenting over the years, and the secret was never in the details. It wasn't about rules and schedules and piano lessons. It was about unconditional love. And James had that in spades for Theo, who could be a real pain in the ass sometimes. Most of the time, if Will was being honest.

Derek ran a finger across his eyebrow, as if checking to see if the scar was still there. It was. "I'm glad to hear that. You deserve a prince."

"I deserve prison time."

"That's not true." Derek's deep voice dropped the words like an anvil, but Will still couldn't believe them.

He looked down at Derek's hands and recalled the scene they'd shot where Derek's character, Oliver, sliced his palm open and Will's character, Chase, had to stitch it up without any anesthetic.

"What were we fighting about?"

Derek sighed, like he'd been expecting this question. "It doesn't matter. It's all in the past now."

That was easy for Derek to say. He'd walked away with a scar and an Oscar. But Will still lived in the fallout zone of that drunken night.

"It matters to me."

Derek sighed again and stood. "Can I give you a hug?" He didn't wait for an answer. He just wrapped his strong arms around Will and squeezed. "I need you to trust me on this, Will. You're better off not knowing."

CHAPTER 24

JAMES

Ryan made his escape the moment Theo left to get his guitar, saying he wanted to check out the dock. But James suspected he just didn't want to be alone with Donna.

James was surprised how much he liked the young actor, and not just because he was portraying him in the movie. Normally, James found it annoying when stars like Ryan talked about their childhood dreams and aspirations, like they were unique in their delusions of grandeur, like they were famous now simply because they dreamed hard enough and not because they were born handsome.

But when Ryan said he wanted to be an actor after watching *The Beautiful* and seeing how unapologetically gay Will was, something softened in James's chest. He'd never thought of William Chapman as a pioneer before. But in a way, he was. While there were plenty of gay actors in Hollywood, there weren't a lot of out ones, especially not ten years ago, and almost none in their teens.

James was worried about Will. He'd barely said a word all throughout dinner. And with each drink he'd receded further into his head. And now, Derek was inside making things worse while James was stuck out here building a fire.

"I know." Donna was on her phone again. "I watched what you sent me." She slumped into her Adirondack chair, crossed her legs, and was silent for several minutes. "Well, they're both here now. I'll run the idea by them. But they're not going to like it." She was silent again. "Okay, thanks, Michelle." So she was talking to the director. "I'll call you back later tonight, and whatever you do, don't breathe a word of this to Tony. Leave Tony to me." Donna hung up the phone and only then seemed to realize James was there, listening.

James lit the newspaper and wads of magazine pages before taking a step back. Green and blue flames licked their way up the logs. But as the ink burned away, the flames turned orange.

"There is something I want to make perfectly clear. Now that you're dating my son"—she fell into the word dating like it was a hole in the beach—"you're bound to become privy to some, shall we say, sensitive information. And I just hope, should you ever consider breaking your NDA, that you'll come to me first. I'm certain we can work something out."

"Ouch, yikes." James picked at a bit of pine pitch on his palm. "Is that really something you have to worry about?"

Donna seemed briefly mesmerized by the orange flames. "Every single minute of every single day. Just look at William. He lost his job, and all he did was attend his brother's bachelor party."

"He lost his job?" James's stomach constricted to the size of a walnut. Will had never mentioned losing his job. "But he didn't do anything wrong."

"Of course he did." The firelight flickered in her eyes. "He was born a Chapman."

DONNA WELLS COULD SING, and she did so for close to forty minutes straight, covering everything from showtunes to contemporary pop. It would've been annoying if she wasn't so damn good. Theo was in heaven playing as her accompaniment. Finally, the boy had a real musician to spar with.

Back in the day, Theo had made them form a family band, but Travis and James had been amateur musicians at best, and it had shown.

"I need to use the ladies' room," Donna eventually said, setting her wine glass on the arm of her chair. "William, why don't you take over while I'm gone?"

"Fuck no," Will said, slurring his words. James didn't like to see Will so shit-faced and withdrawn, but at least he was standing up for himself.

"Come on, Will," Derek said. "Sing that old Jewel song you used to sing to me. What was it called?"

"I'm not singing 'Foolish Games.'"

No sooner were the words out of Will's mouth than Theo had the tabs pulled up on his phone. "I'm ready when you are."

Ryan took it upon himself to top off Will's glass, like Will needed more wine. "I didn't know you could sing."

"Will's a great singer. Isn't that right?"

It took James a second to realize Derek was talking to him. Was Will a good singer? James didn't know. "The best," he said, hoping he wasn't wrong.

"Fine, but only through the first chorus." Will set his glass down, and half its contents sloshed into the grass.

Donna had been amazing, a Broadway caliber singer. She had a husky voice, like Stevie Nicks, and an engaging theatricality. But somehow, Will was even better. His voice was textured and full, and it ached with emotion. It hurt James's heart to listen, but in a good way, like the throb of a healing wound.

True to his word, Will stopped after the first chorus, and James was surprised to hear his own voice say, "Keep going."

Will scoffed, but finished the song.

James had been to his fair share of concerts, recitals, and drunken karaoke nights, but Will's private performance was the best thing

James had ever heard. Will's voice could do anything—a delicate, airy falsetto one moment and a gravelly baritone the next. And he was always on key and always in the pocket. James could have listened to Will all night. What would he sound like singing some Chris Stapleton?

When Will was done, James reached over and took his hand. He squeezed, and when Will looked up at him, James watched the reflection of the firelight flicker in Will's black eyes. "You're the world's best kept secret, you know that?"

Will's face turned as red as the wine in his glass, and James wished Ryan and Derek would leave already so they could be alone.

DONNA RETURNED with more wine and decided it was time to put Theo on the spot. "Why don't you play us one of your original songs?" She set her hand on Ryan's arm, and the poor guy practically turned to stone. "Theo is a very talented songwriter." She was wasted, too, though not as wasted as Will.

"I can play guitar, but that's about it. I'm not really a singer."

Ryan flashed his blue eyes at Theo. "Come on. If you sing one of yours, I'll sing one of mine."

Shit, was James going to have to buy a gun and start cleaning it whenever boys came around?

Theo's eyes went wide, and his jaw went slack. Sure, Ryan had been nice to Theo all night, but only in response to Theo's constant pestering. This time, Ryan spoke first. And he asked Theo to sing one of his songs, no less. This was getting out of hand.

"Okay." Theo swallowed, and James knew right away what song Theo was about to perform. *Please, not that song. Any other song.* "I wrote this one with my dad."

Everyone turned to look at James, including Will. "I didn't know you wrote songs."

James didn't write songs. Travis had written songs. Well, he'd tried to, anyway. Theo had ended up doing most of the work.

"What, you think you're the only one in this relationship with hidden talents?" James's heart raced. He really needed to smoke a bowl.

Will's face broke into a wicked smile. "Please tell me there are harmonies."

"Definitely." Theo slid his capo onto the second fret, and James snatched the glass of wine from Will's hand. *Friggin' harmonies.*

"It's called 'Cursed Name.'" Theo strummed the first chord, and James felt his sweat turn cold. He downed the rest of Will's wine and handed the glass back.

The song started simple and grew in depth with each successive verse. It told the story of a family of fathers and sons who shared everything from their brown hair and blue eyes to their quick tempers and stubborn hearts. And it ended the way it always ended: each son watched his father die before his time, knowing he was next.

James hated the song. He'd hated it even before Travis killed himself. But he did his best to sing the harmonies, even though he wasn't Travis.

When they sang the final refrain of the final chorus, Will's hand settled tentatively on James's back. It was the first time Will had initiated physical contact, and James let himself lean into it.

I'll take my life behind closed doors
And give you an end that's only yours
Let me be the one to take the blame
For giving you this cursed name

The final chord rang out in harmony with the peepers and the hum of the pool filter. And after several beats of depressing silence, Ryan spoke.

"You wrote that? That was incredible."

Derek clapped Theo on the back. "You're going to be a famous songwriter one day. I hope you realize that."

Donna beamed, proud enough to cry. "That was beautiful. Didn't I tell you he was a gifted songwriter?"

"Maybe now would be a good time for that apple pie," James said. He needed to get as far away from that song as possible.

"But Ryan hasn't sung yet," Theo said, holding his guitar out to the young movie star.

"I'm not going after that. No fucking way."

"But you promised."

Ryan crossed his arms over his chest and stuck his lower lip out in a childish pout. "How about next time, okay?"

Theo's eyebrows shot up. "Next time?"

James watched it all play out on Theo's face—the menu, the drinks, the entertainment, the goodnight kiss and the promise of another next time and another next time. He wished Travis was here to see this, to see his son fall in love with a movie star. And then to kick Ryan's ass for indulging a teenager's fantasies.

"William, Derek"—Donna picked up a log from the pile James had cut earlier—"hold back a sec. I need to speak to you both in private."

Will looked at his mother and then over at Derek. His hand fell away from James's back, and then, without any warning or explanation, Will sprinted off into the night.

"Where the fuck is he going?" Donna asked, tossing the log on the fire so carelessly James had to jump back to avoid the spray of embers.

JAMES FOUND Will ten minutes later, sitting on the edge of the dock. His socks and shoes were scattered about, and his bare feet dangled over the side.

"I just took the most glorious pee of my life," Will said, not turning around. "There were literally two skies, one above me and one below me. And I peed right inside the moon. You should have seen it. I sent ripples through the universe and time and space and probably reality, too."

"Probably." James came and sat beside Will. He wasn't flexible enough to sit cross-legged so he hugged his knees to his chest.

It was a beautiful night. The water was remarkably still, with only Will's feet sending small waves through the reflection of the stars and moon.

"Are you sure Derek's straight?" All night, Derek had behaved like a jealous ex, staring at James like he was public enemy number one.

"Pretty sure, yeah."

"I don't know. I think he might be in love with you."

Will let out a bitter laugh. "I can assure you, he's not. He tolerates me. I'm like his annoying little cousin, which is fine. I know I'm not the most lovable person."

"That's not true."

Will pulled his feet from the lake, and fat drops of water dimpled the surface. "Yeah, I suppose my kids love me. In fact, they really love me. Sometimes, I think they love me too much. I bet they wouldn't fight all the time if they didn't love me so much, if they weren't always competing for my attention."

James felt his stomach pull in on itself. "I'm sorry you lost your job. You must really miss your students."

Will shrugged. "I don't know. I guess."

There was no need to guess, not with the tears welling behind Will's eyes. James put his arm around Will's shoulder and pulled him close. Then he asked the question he'd been wondering all night. "Do you love him?"

Will wiped the snot from his nose and shrugged. "I don't know. I used to."

It wasn't the answer James had been hoping for, but at least it was honest. "Come on, let's go see what your mom wants."

Will kicked at the water again, and it shattered the moonlit reflection. "You go. I just want to be alone for a minute. She can come down here if she wants to talk to me so badly. Besides, I'm too drunk to be around other people. It's not safe."

"You're ridiculous. You're, like, the gentlest person I've ever met."

"Yeah, well, tell that to Derek's skull."

"Fine, I'll wait with you, then."

"Don't do that. I won't be alone if you're with me."

James didn't want to leave Will on his own, not this drunk. What if he fell in? James strode over to the boathouse and grabbed a life vest. "I'll go, but only if you put this on."

Before Will could object, James took Will's arms and shoved them inside the life vest and zipped it up the front.

Will sighed and hugged the vest to his chest, like James had just given him his varsity jacket. "Just think how differently things would've ended for Ophelia if you'd been Hamlet."

JAMES STOOD JUST outside the halo of torchlight and pulled the bowl from his pocket. He'd been planning to wait until after everyone left to smoke, but that was before he was forced to sing Travis's song.

He packed the bowl and was about to light it when he heard Derek's raised voice.

"I'm not going to do that to Will."

James shoved the bowl back inside his pocket and stepped closer, making sure to stay hidden in the shadows of the cypress trees hemming the yard. Derek was talking with Donna, who stood backlit against the fire.

"Tony won't stand for this." In spite of Derek's deep voice, he sounded like a petulant child.

"This is my movie, not Tony's." Donna's voice was calm and even. "I'm not asking for your permission, Derek. I'm telling you what's happening." She took a step forward and set a hand on Derek's arm. "May I remind you, you need this movie to succeed far more than Robert. You knew what you were signing up for. He can barely stand being in the same room with you. And we need him to do his best work. You need him to do his best work."

"And what about Will? You're just going to use him? This was Robert's plan all along, wasn't it?"

"William is none of your concern. He's my son."

"Yeah, when it's convenient for you." Derek's voice rumbled so low James wasn't sure he heard it so much as felt it, vibrating through the ground.

Donna took a deep breath, and instead of yelling or screaming, she smiled. "Be that as it may, this is what's happening. You can vilify me all you want, but I'm doing this for you just as much as Robert." Donna stepped closer until they were separated by mere inches. "And if you still care about William at all, you'll leave him the fuck alone."

Derek took a step back. "Fuck this. I'm going home."

CHAPTER 25

WILL

Will tried to listen, but he was drunk and predisposed to ignoring his mother anyway.

"And we'll pay you, of course," she said.

"But I won't actually be in the movie?" This was absurd. According to his mother, Michelle loved the scene he'd shot with his father that afternoon and wanted him to do it again, but not because she wanted him in the movie. No, she still wanted Derek. What she wanted in the movie was the performance Will's father gave acting opposite Will.

"They won't be able to use any of the wide shots, but the whole reason we went with multiple cameras in the first place was so we could do most of the work in post-production. All of your father's closeups and all of his audio will come from your takes, so in a sense, you will be in the movie. You'll be the heart and soul of your father's performance. You just won't appear on screen, except for maybe your shoulder every now and then, but—"

"And Dad and Derek are okay with this?"

"Are you kidding me? This was your father's idea." His mother gave him that look, that *It's high time you stop being surprised your father is an asshole* look. "He wants to give you a chance to show Michelle your talent. He wants you to act, to carry on the family legacy."

What the fuck? If his father wanted him to carry on the family legacy so badly, then why had he given Will's part to Ryan? Why hadn't he used his connections to get Will a role in some other movie? Did he honestly think being Derek's understudy was going to do shit for Will's acting career?

"And what about Derek? He can't possibly be okay with this." It was insulting as fuck. How could his father even suggest something so petty? If he didn't want to act opposite Derek, he shouldn't have agreed to do a movie with him.

"Derek needs this movie to succeed as much as anyone." His mother reached out and tried to touch his arm, but he stepped away. "Believe me, if there was any other way, don't you think—"

"Stop, Mom. Just stop."

"William, please. I've had a fucking day from hell, and I don't need this." She lifted her legs in turn like a flamingo and removed her heels. "You're just drunk. This isn't a big deal. Your father needs you. I need you. And frankly, it's the least you could do."

What was that supposed to mean? Will was about to ask that very question when a firm hand settled on his shoulder.

"I'm gonna take Will up to bed." It was James. Where had he come from? "This isn't what he needs right now."

"I don't care what he needs right now."

"That much is obvious." James's hand fell to Will's waist, and the scent of pot filled Will's nostrils.

Will expected his mother to fire James on the spot, but she didn't. Instead, she did something she never did. She apologized.

"You're probably right. I'm sorry, William. It's been a long day. We'll continue this conversation in the morning."

CHAPTER 26

JAMES

James wasn't sure if he should be concerned or amused. Will was having a hell of a time getting his pants off. He'd already fallen over three times. And on the third time, he didn't get up again. Instead, he tried to wriggle out of his painted-on jeans from the floor.

"Need help with that?"

"It doesn't matter." Will stopped struggling. "I'll just take them off in the morning."

James bent down and grabbed the cuff of Will's pants. He eased the fabric over Will's heels and pulled. Will's legs weren't very hairy, but they were toned and muscular. James got the first pant leg off and then set to work on the second.

Meanwhile, Will lay back in a sea of dirty clothes and tried to explain what his mother wanted. But it didn't make any sense. How could Will shoot all of Travis's scenes and not be in the movie? Sure, they could do a lot with camera angles and editing tricks, but this? Will, however, wasn't concerned with logistics. He just wanted to get his metaphor right.

"Derek is the presentable wife you bring to dinner parties and church. And I'm the mistress, the other woman, the one you're ashamed of but keep around because I'll lick your ass and tickle your balls."

James pushed Will into a sitting position so he could remove his shirt, propping him up with his knee. "You're so talented. I had no idea you could sing like that. Screw acting. You should just be a singer."

"Whatever. Do you have any idea how many voice lessons I've had in my life?"

James managed to get Will's shirt off and tried not to notice the burn of Will's bare skin beneath his fingertips. It was so soft and smooth, and yet even the slightest pressure revealed the steel underneath. "This might be a good opportunity for you. Michelle is a very influential director, and you never know who's watching. Some cameraman or something could pass your name along. It's not ideal, I get that. But it's something."

"Derek will hate me."

There it was. Will didn't want to do it because he was still in love with Derek.

"Don't give up a great opportunity just because you're afraid you're gonna hurt someone's feelings. Derek is a big boy. He can handle it." James offered Will his hand to pull him up, but Will started shaking it instead.

"Thank you," he said.

"For what?"

"I don't know." Will closed his eyes and yawned. "Everything."

James couldn't very well leave Will on the floor, so he scooped him up.

"You're like a firefighter"—Will threw his arm around James's neck—"and you smell nice."

"Oh, yeah?" James set Will on the bed. "What do I smell like?"

"Like campfire and pot and apples."

"Apples?" James grabbed the sheet and pulled it up to Will's chin. "Must be the pie."

"No, it's not the pie."

"Sorry about licking your ear earlier. I was just trying to get into character."

"It's okay. I kind of liked it. But don't tell anyone."

James's pulse quickened. "Okay, your secret is safe with me." Will wasn't going to remember any of this, was he?

"I wish you were my real boyfriend. I thought my mother was going to fire you."

So did James. In hindsight, criticizing his boss's parenting skills probably wasn't his best move.

"I wish I could kiss you." Will rolled over on his side and sighed.

"What's stopping you?" James's heart felt like a pheasant in the bush.

"Because I'm not a stalker, and I'm not a pathetic fuckboy." Will curled into a fetal position. He looked so small like that, like a bristly little hedgehog. "I know it's just pretend."

"Yeah, right, just pretend." James reached over and clicked off the light.

CHAPTER 27
WILL

Will knocked on Derek's trailer door, feeling as nervous as the first day of school, and not his first day as a student, when it was perfectly acceptable to cry and cling to his nanny's leg. No, he was as nervous as his first day as a teacher, when he'd had to convince a room full of petrified kids he knew what he was doing.

The door opened and Derek stood before him. This time, he was fully clothed. He wore his costume, a red flannel shirt, wrangler jeans, and a scuffed up Red Sox baseball cap. Behind him stood Tony.

"I'll come back." Will cast his eyes to the metal step to avoid Tony's menacing glare.

"That's okay. Tony was just leaving." Derek stepped aside to let Will in.

"William." Tony nodded curtly before exiting the trailer.

"The last time I saw you, you were sprinting off into the night," Derek said. "I assume there was a damsel in distress you needed to rescue?"

"Yeah, something like that." Will shoved his hands in his pockets and rocked back and forth on his heels. "I just wanted to come and—"

"I know why you're here. You want to know what I think about your father's plan to pit us against each other."

That wasn't how Will would have put it, but yeah, that.

"I think it's stupid. I think it's unfair to you and me."

Will nodded, afraid to look up.

"But I'm not mad at you, Will. I know this has nothing to do with you."

"I'll tell them no." Will meant it, too. Even if this was likely the closest he'd ever come to acting again, he'd turn it down for Derek.

"I think you should do it." Derek lifted Will's chin until their eyes met. "Show Michelle and the studio what you're made of. I'm well aware you're going to make me look bad. But that's okay. If it gets you back in the game, it's a price I'm willing to pay. Maybe we can talk someone into making a sequel to *The Beautiful*. Chase can be on the run from some sex traffickers and crash on Oliver's couch and befriend his wife and kids. But this time we'll give them the happy ending they deserve."

Chase was dying of AIDS when the credits rolled, but that wasn't the point. "Are you sure?"

"I'm positive. Now, let's watch some *Man with A Plan* and figure out this stupid fucking accent."

WILL HAD a lot to process after his first day of filming in over a decade, so as soon as he got home, he put on his running shorts and set off.

That morning, they'd filmed the dead dog scene, which had been surprisingly difficult. Ryan had performed his part—unbridled outrage at their father shooting the family dog—expertly. And Will's father had found the perfect balance of spite, indifference, and contempt.

"Sounds like a personal problem to me," he'd said.

But Derek and Will had been tasked with conveying Travis's rage, grief, and astonishment through a mask of stoic resignation, which had been a tricky needle to thread.

It had taken Derek several hours and countless takes to get something passable. He'd been so exhausted afterward, he'd gone and taken a nap. Though he might as well have stayed and watched Will film his version of the scene because Michelle had wanted to move on after only three takes, reminding Will that they didn't need perfection from him, just his warm body for his father to play off of. Or so he'd assumed.

Later that day, when they'd been on a break, Michelle had called Will over to watch his version of the scene, and for the first time in over a decade, something akin to pride and validation had flooded Will's nervous system.

"This is some very impressive work, William," Michelle had said. "There's not even a trace of you in this performance. And the camera is catching it all, every internal emotion. It's really quite remarkable."

Will's phone chimed in his ear, cutting off his running music and pulling him from his musings. It was Tiffany.

"Hey, what's up?"

"I can't believe you didn't tell me you have a new boyfriend. I had to hear it from Miles, and now I don't know what to believe."

"He's not my boyfriend. We're just pretending so James can go to Andy's wedding."

"You know you're allowed to bring someone you're not fucking, right? Someone like me."

Will loved this part of his run, gliding under the canopy of giant oak trees. "We're definitely not fucking."

"Then explain yourself. What does this James guy have that I don't?"

"Well, a killer mustache, for one." The neighbors must have recently mowed their lawn because the air smelled like fresh-cut grass. "And it's not just so he can go to the wedding."

Will explained how Theo had made the whole thing up and had tried to play it off like he'd done Will a huge favor.

"I think Theo actually thought Ryan was interested in me and got jealous."

"I get the Ryan part," Tiffany said. "He's so fucking hot, it's no wonder the kid lost his mind. But please tell me you see the irony in pretending to have a boyfriend just so people won't think you're pretending to have a boyfriend."

"I don't know what you're talking about. This all seems totally normal to me. And it's working. Derek is talking to me again." The oaks ended, and Will was immersed in sunlight.

"Can you hold on a sec?" Tiffany must have cupped her hand over the phone because her shouts caused only mild hearing loss. "Sorry about that. Jennifer thinks I'm playing with her. She's got her door locked and her music blaring. I'm strongly considering removing her doorknobs."

"Should I let you go?" Will ran around the flattened body of a dead garter snake.

"Yeah, maybe. Can I call you later?"

"I won't be around later. James is taking me to play miniature golf, and then we're going to go get creemees."

"What the fuck are creemees? Is this some kind of gay sex thing?"

"No, it's just what they call soft serve ice cream up here. Apparently, you haven't lived until you've had a maple creemee. Don't tell Miles."

"So, your fake boyfriend is taking you out on a date? Remind me which part of this is fake again."

"The part where we're not sleeping together and the only displays of affection I get are public displays of affection." Will told her about the dinner party and how convincing James had been. "And it's not a date. We just like to hang out, that's all. Yesterday, we played horseshoes for, like, four hours. James said it was important to fully understand my character. I tried to tell him that he's not my character, but James doesn't take no for an answer."

"So, let me get this straight, you're acting in the movie, but you're not actually in it?"

"Yeah, exactly. They shoot it several times with Derek and then several times with me, and I don't know about the rest. That's what the editing team is for. I guess they just cut me out and put Derek in." Will could barely work the copy machine at school. How the hell would he know how they edit footage together?

"So, when are you going to make your move on James?"

Fields of corn spread out on either side of Will, framed by ancient stone walls. "Uh, never."

"Why not? You obviously like him. Every other word out of your mouth is James this and James that."

"Don't be ridiculous." Will could never make a move on James. What if James got mad and broke up with him? What if he punched Will in the face? What if he told the tabloids what a pathetic loser Will was, making up a fake boyfriend just so Derek wouldn't think Will was stalking him? "We've got a good thing going on. It's fine the way it is."

"You're fine just palling around? You don't wish you could snuggle up and watch a movie together?"

"I didn't say that." Watching a movie with James would be heaven, James's breath in his ear, the scratch of his facial hair on Will's neck, and . . .

"So you do want more. What are you going to do about it? What's your plan? You can't just throw a dinner party every time you want a little physical intimacy."

That wasn't a terrible idea. Will's father had been asking to meet James all week. Was it wrong to use dinner with his dying father as an excuse to get James to touch him?

There was a loud crashing sound on Tiffany's end of the line. "Shit, I gotta go," she said. "Tell James you've never played mini golf before and need him to show you how to hold the club, and then back that ass up."

"I'll call you tomorrow." Will hung up.

Normally, Will turned right and ran past the inn. But today, he turned left. If he cut through the cemetery, he could finish his run in front of the house, where James liked to sit on the porch in the evenings.

With that thought in mind, Will did something he never did. He took off his shirt and stuffed it into the waistband of his shorts.

WILL FINISHED his run as planned, but he didn't see James out front. Instead, he saw something far more puzzling. Someone was driving his rental car.

Will tried to head them off, but he'd run close to ten miles already and was out of juice. As the car sped away, there was no mistaking the tall, lanky frame behind the wheel.

"I think Theo just stole my car."

James was in the pool, floating on a neon green noodle. "You're kidding."

The noodle shot out from under James as he hoisted himself out of the water. He didn't bother putting on a shirt or dry pants. He didn't even lace his shoes. He just grabbed his keys and ran out the door.

"I'll come with you."

"No, I'll handle this."

"Don't be ridiculous. He stole my car. And if we manage to catch up with him, someone will have to drive it back."

"Fine." James climbed into his 4Runner, and Will made his way over to the passenger side. He didn't even have time to shut his door before James tore down the driveway, kicking up enough dust to blot out the house receding behind them.

Will put on his seatbelt and his sweat-soaked skin clung to the leather seats. "Where's he going? And why would he steal my car?"

"Because I told him he couldn't borrow mine."

It wasn't the most illuminating answer, but the set of James's jaw told Will not to push for more.

They drove in silence for several minutes, and Will searched for something reassuring to say. They turned onto the paved road, and Will rolled down his window to let the breeze cool the sweat on his skin.

"Andy used to do shit like this all the time. Once, he and his buddies stole a fucking yacht."

James grunted. Shit, Will was using dismissive empathy, wasn't he?

"I'm sorry. You must be really worried. I am, too. But Theo's smart, and this is Vermont. There's hardly any traffic. And he has his permit, right? So, it's not like he has no driving experience."

James kept his eyes on the road and his hands on the wheel. He'd gotten a sunburn recently, and the skin on his shoulders was starting to peel.

They came to a fork in the road, and James turned right without hesitating.

"Do you know where he's going?"

"Maybe."

Will let his arm dangle out the window. "I could call him, or do you think that might distract him while he's driving?"

"No, go for it."

Will tried several times, but Theo didn't pick up. "I could have Ryan call him. Then he'd definitely answer."

James slid through a stop sign at forty miles an hour. "Except he doesn't have Ryan's number saved in his phone and won't know who's calling."

Will hadn't thought of that. Then, another idea occurred to him. "I'll have Miles call."

Miles was better than any therapist or bartender when it came to building a rapport with his clients. People trusted him. They confided in him. They told him all their dirty secrets.

Ten minutes later, Miles called back. "He's okay," he said. "But your rental car is fucked."

They found Theo and the car two miles away. He'd run off the road and into someone's yard. He'd smashed through their log fence and trampled their orange lilies. According to Miles, Theo had accidentally pulled the emergency brake thinking it was the lever to move the seat back, and the car had spun out of control. Luckily, no one had been home.

"Theo, what were you thinking? You could've been killed."

Will had never seen James so angry before. Every part of his body looked tight enough to snap.

Theo was on the verge of tears, his shoulders shaking.

"Will, take Theo home. I'll take care of this." James walked over to examine the tire tracks cutting across the yard.

Will left Theo by the 4Runner and caught up with James. "Why don't you go with Theo?" He leaned in so only James could hear him. "I have every type of insurance possible, so as long as they think I was driving, it should be covered."

"I can't let you do that."

"Yes, you can. Now go give your son a hug. He's scared out of his mind. You can yell at him tomorrow. Believe me, nothing good will come from yelling at him now."

James gave Will a strange look, like Will was on fire or something. "I'm gonna make this up to you."

Will took a chance and set his hand on James's bare shoulder, where his sunburned skin was hot and dry. "You already have. And what else are fake boyfriends for?"

CHAPTER 28
JAMES

When Donna had mentioned someone was coming to the house to take their measurements for their wedding attire, James had pictured the men from *Queer Eye* and had braced himself for a lecture on his lack of style and class. Instead, it was a blue-haired, tatted-up young woman named Autumn who wanted them to stand naked on a rotating pedestal while she took their measurements using her iPad.

Theo volunteered to go first, not because he was eager to get naked in front of a lady but because, in his mind, this might as well be his and Ryan's wedding. As a result, Will and James were alone for the first time in days.

Will spent very little time at the house anymore. When he wasn't filming, he was off rehearsing with his father. But every night, as Will poured his bedtime bourbon, James did his best to get a play-by-play of the day's shooting. Of course, Theo was always on hand to usurp the conversation, trying to get the latest Ryan anecdote or to get Will to record vocals on one of his songs. They barely even had time for ping-pong anymore.

James knew their relationship was fake and he shouldn't feel cast aside and ignored like a 1950s housewife. But he did. Of course, he was probably just jealous that Will got to be part of Travis's movie and he didn't.

That wasn't to say James didn't miss Will in his own right when he was gone. He did. Sure, Will always said no to everything before he said yes, but once he said yes, he fully committed. He was even getting pretty good at horseshoes. And it was fun to take Will out, to show him new things, like when they'd hiked out to the old beaver pond, or when they'd taken the boat up to Burlington and watched the fireworks from out on the lake. Even just drinking a beer on the porch was way more fun when Will was around.

James still couldn't get over what Will had done for him. To think, he'd once written William Chapman off as a spoiled brat who'd sink someone else's dreams just so he didn't have to drown alone. But that wasn't Will at all.

Will was loyal to people who didn't deserve his loyalty, James included. After Theo's accident, Will had told the police he'd seen a deer and panicked. And when he'd finally returned home, hours later, still in his running shorts, the first words out of his mouth hadn't been about how hungry he was or how it had taken forever for the tow truck to arrive, but, "How's Theo?"

James had promised Will he'd make Theo pay for the damage. He'd even take away Theo's computer and guitar. But Will had told him that was pointless, that Theo had already experienced the only consequence likely to make a difference, a natural consequence: he'd crashed the car.

Will had explained that kids rarely learn anything or change their behavior because you take away the things they love. Instead, when they should be reflecting on their actions, they spend the whole time blaming you for being unfair. It had sounded like horseshit to James, but he started to think about his own father and how the only lesson he'd ever learned from him was how to not get caught. So, instead of punishing Theo, like he'd wanted to, he'd taken Will's advice and given Theo driving lessons.

James snatched an orange from the fruit bowl, tossed it in the air, and caught it. "How are things going with the movie?"

"Good."

"Just good?"

Will shrugged and sat on a stool at the kitchen island. The skylight overhead made Will's skin glow. Even though he wore copious amounts of sunscreen, William Chapman was starting to get a tan. "It's been a little awkward lately, to be honest."

"Is Derek giving you shit? Is it Tony?" James's hackles started to rise.

"No, nothing like that. I don't know. I'm just being weird. It's just that, ever since I was a little boy, I've wanted to be in a movie with my dad. And now I am. And that part's actually pretty awesome. Only, when it's all said and done, I won't be in the movie. It won't be me. It will be Derek. And I know that shouldn't matter because it's the journey and not the destination, but. . ." Will stared out the window, his eyes tracing the back and forth of the weathervane atop the barn. "I don't know. I'm probably just being selfish."

"I don't think you're being selfish." James set his half-peeled orange on the counter. "Every artist and performer needs an audience to feel complete. Anyone who says otherwise is lying. Even people who never show their work to anyone fantasize about being the next Emily Dickinson, about someone going into their basement and picking up their cat portraits and saying, 'If only we'd known.' That's just human nature. And what you do is amazing. It should be seen."

James thought of Travis and how he'd never get the chance to watch his own movie.

"My brother spent years writing a book, and he wouldn't show it to anyone, draft after draft. I told him books are supposed to be read, not just written, and he said, 'I know that. It will be.'"

Why was James doing this? He never talked about Travis, not if he could avoid it. And Travis had eventually shown it to someone, just not James. He'd hired a private editor, and she hadn't been kind, though she had provided a lot of suggestions along with her criticism. But Travis had already started getting sick at that point.

"But this is different," James said. "All of your work is gonna end up on the cutting room floor. No one will ever be able to see it, even if you want them to."

Will shrugged and forced a smile. "Did your brother ever publish his book?"

Of all the stories James could've told. "Yeah, eventually."

"Was it any good?"

"It was alright." James picked up his orange and finished peeling it.

"He's the pee shy one, right?"

James couldn't believe Will remembered that. Man, James used to give Travis so much shit for being pee shy. He used to stand right outside the bathroom door and say obnoxious things like, "Have you started yet?" and "Hurry up, other people live here, too," and "You call that a stream? Come on, let her rip."

"What's he do now?" Will asked. "Is he a famous novelist or something? Are you James King, brother of Stephen King?"

James shoved an orange segment in his mouth and drained every last drop of juice before swallowing. "He died, actually. Killed himself."

Will's smile vanished. "Jesus, I'm so sorry. I can't even imagine."

"It's okay. These things happen."

Normally, when James told people about Travis's death, he fed them the easy lie that Travis had drowned in a boating accident. Will was the only person, other than Esther, James had ever admitted the truth to.

Will didn't seem to know what to say, but his silence was oddly comforting. He met James's gaze, and his dark eyes seemed to whisper, *You can pretend you're okay if you want to, but you don't need to.*

"How long ago?" Will asked.

"About a year and a half." James knew he should stop there, that saying more would risk revealing his secret, but for some reason he kept talking. "I should've seen it coming, but I didn't. He was my best friend, you know? He was my best friend and my big brother, and I still didn't know. I mean, fuck, how oblivious can you get? We were even living together at the time."

"I don't think you're oblivious. But I hear what you're saying. It's easier to blame yourself for missing the signs than it is to give your brother credit for being able to keep a secret."

Will wasn't wrong. Travis had been able to keep a secret. But James should've known. "I was supposed to be in charge. I was supposed to be the one with a clear head. But I was fucking high and, I don't know, just too preoccupied with my own shit, I guess."

Will inhaled deeply, as if taking a hit off James's guilt and heartache. But he didn't cough or stumble. He remained centered and stable. "I'd tell you not to blame yourself, that it's not your fault, but I know you probably won't believe me. I think that's the saddest thing about getting older. You realize everyone is just faking it, even the so-called experts. And eventually, there is no one left to tell you what to think or how to feel, no one you trust anyway. Christ, we don't even have Oprah anymore, not really. And when all you have left is yourself, there's no more objectivity. It's all just doubts and fears and delusions."

The truth of Will's words hit like an arrow. James had been on his own ever since his father had kicked him out of the house at sixteen. That had been twenty-two years ago, and in that time, James had not only lost his idols, but also half his capacity to love.

James knew how to love as an uncle, as a caretaker. James loved Theo more than anything in the world. Theo needed him. James was responsible for him. And James got Theo's love in return, and it was the best kind of love. It was the kind of love a son gives his father. And Theo had always given it to James, even when Travis had been alive.

But the other half of love, the kind you accept from a parent or a partner, the love you get when you let someone else take care of you, that no longer existed in James's life.

"I think your advice about Theo is paying off," James said, trying to bring them back to less tragic ground before he gave in and told Will everything. "He seems genuinely remorseful. At least, he's taking our driving lessons a lot more seriously these days. So, thank you. You're obviously an amazing teacher."

"I'm really not." The sincerity in Will's voice was heartbreaking. "You can read all the books and do all the things they recommend, but to be effective you need to be superhuman. You have to have infinite patience and boundless composure. You can't let them see you sweat, and I sweat all the time."

James handed Will an orange segment. "Yeah, but you're a terrible judge of your own talent. Like, seriously, the fucking worst. So, forgive me if I don't believe you." That earned James a genuine smile, and it felt like he'd won the lottery.

"Yeah, well, I'm pretty sure my principal would back me up on this one."

"Then fuck her."

"Nah, she's alright. She's just doing her job. It's not her fault I've got a target on my back. That's all on me. Besides, it's actually kind of nice to have someone hate me for something other than what I did to Derek. It makes me feel more well-rounded."

"I'm sure she doesn't hate you. There's no way anyone could know you and hate you."

"You'd be surprised. Christ, my own mother can barely stand me."

"That's not true. Your mom's an intimidating woman, and she's not exactly warm. But, trust me, she loves you."

Will shrugged, not letting James's words sink in.

"I don't mean to change the subject," Will said. "But my dad was wondering if you and Theo wanted to come to dinner tonight. I told him you guys like to do your own thing, but I thought I'd ask just in—"

"You're ridiculous." James couldn't help but laugh. "Of course I wanna meet your father, and not just because he's Robert Chapman, either. I wanna meet him because he's your dad. I wanna see the prototype."

"Okay, thanks." Will's shoulders relaxed, and he tossed the orange segment in his mouth. He didn't even sanitize first. They were making progress.

They were ten minutes late to dinner because Theo had refused to leave the house until Miles gave him the thumbs-up on his outfit. After all, what if Ryan popped downstairs for a night cap? Robert was already there waiting for them, and it wasn't until he smiled that James saw the family resemblance.

Robert Chapman was delicate and aquiline, impeccably groomed and very distinguished. Will was none of those things. He was trim like his father, but solid as stone, and James wasn't sure it was possible to tame Will's thick black hair. And yet, they both had smiles that made you second guess every assumption you'd ever made about them.

On an impulse, James pulled Will's chair out for him like a gentleman, and Will rolled his eyes so spectacularly James decided he'd have to do that from now on, whether they had an audience or not.

"Ryan tells me you're quite the songwriter," Robert said to Theo after the waiter left with their dinner orders.

"I don't know about that." Theo blushed and helped himself to more bread.

"How is the movie coming along?" James set his hand on Will's and laced their fingers together. Even from the top, Will's hand was sweaty. "Is Will, here, behaving himself?"

Robert smiled at his son. "Oh, yes. I think William has surprised everyone, even himself. It's one thing to be eighteen and innocent and play eighteen and innocent. It's another thing to play such a sober, masculine part that's far more internal than external."

Will yanked his hand out from under James's and reached for his wine glass. What kind of backhanded compliment was that? Was Robert really suggesting Will hadn't been acting in *The Beautiful*, that he'd merely been playing a version of himself? That was ridiculous. Will was nothing like Chase. Chase was fragile, an open wound, all crocodile tears and sensuality. Will, on the other hand, was stoic and solid. His heart was anywhere but on his sleeve.

A couple of nights ago, when Will was off with his father, James had decided to watch *The Beautiful* all the way through. Normally, depressing art house movies weren't his thing, but as Will's fake boyfriend, he'd figured he should probably watch Will's movie in case it came up in conversation. And maybe, if he was being honest with himself, he'd missed having Will around, and this had been the next best thing.

Two hours after hitting play, James's stomach had been in knots, and his eyes had burned with the threat of tears. No wonder Will had won the Golden Globe over Derek. Will was astonishing. There wasn't a false note in his heartbreaking performance.

"I suppose they don't let gay guys play straight roles very often," James said, his skin prickling with annoyance. Like himself, Will wasn't particularly feminine. And even if he was, the guy was an empty vessel. Watching Will transform into Travis had been one of the creepiest, most amazing things James had ever seen.

Robert continued swirling his wine, which he wielded more like a prop, never once drinking it. "They should. But it's rare."

The meal was phenomenal, and Robert got a kick out of discussing the subtlety of flavors with Theo. Robert had played a murderous French chef once and knew all about preparing fine cuisine. At the end of the meal, he insisted Theo go up to his suite and bring down the very knife he'd used in the film. Apparently, he took a souvenir from every project. The fact that he brought them with him on location was odd, but everything about Robert Chapman was odd.

He was impossibly thin, and even though he was a good-looking man, it was hard to imagine him with the buxom bombshell, Donna Wells. She was powerful and domineering while he was delicate and soft spoken. You had to lean in to hear what he was saying, which was probably the point. He commanded your full attention through subtle manipulation.

Robert pulled a key from his pocket and gave it to his son. "William can show you where to find it. You know where I keep my souvenirs, right?"

"Now?"

"If it's not too much trouble."

"Jesus Christ, fine." Will was not excited to go on a vanity errand for his father, but he went anyway and left James alone with the acting legend.

The second they were out of the dining room, everything about Robert Chapman changed. It was like someone swapped out the soundtrack. He steepled his long fingers and stared at James with such coldness James felt his skin tighten. "Tell me, when did you stop going by Jimmy and start going by James?"

Shit. James met Robert Chapman's cold stare as panic sizzled in his veins. He was going to get fired, wasn't he? He'd probably lose his job at the agency, too.

"We don't have much time before they come back," Robert said, letting his steepled fingers knit together. "So let me cut to the chase. I know who you are. I know you snuck Esther Kim into my son's bachelor party. I know you worked as a paparazzo yourself once upon a time, among other things. And I know to what lengths you're willing to go to see your late brother's work succeed." Robert nodded his head towards Will's empty chair when he said the word *lengths*.

James didn't know what to say, but he had to say something. It wasn't like that with Will. "I—"

Robert silenced him with a raised hand. "Don't interrupt. I'm not finished. The reason you weren't invited to participate in the filming is because I have cancer. I'm dying. This is my final movie, and I don't have long. I probably won't even be around to see the final cut." The actor's face sobered, and the mask of anger he wore was replaced by one of fear. He was dying? "We wanted to keep my illness under wraps for as long as possible, at least until after the wedding."

"Does Will know?"

Robert looked momentarily taken aback, as if he hadn't been expecting James to ask that question. But he recovered quickly. "He does, but I'm not planning to tell Andy until after the wedding."

"I'm so sor—"

"Here's what I propose." Robert's eyes darted to check the doorway before settling back on James, his expression one of angry efficiency. "I'll keep my mouth shut and allow you to join us on the set. And in exchange, you'll do me a favor."

THERE WAS a reason James had given up his career as a private investigator. Sure, it had paid more than being a paparazzo, but not nearly as much as stripping.

James had had many jobs over the years—waiter, farm hand, plumber's assistant—and had despised them all. He'd briefly considered becoming a cop or a firefighter, but he hadn't wanted to give up smoking weed, so he'd followed his best friend, Esther, into the paparazzi business.

The money had been decent—well, sometimes—but then there had been long stretches when he'd had to subsist on rice and beans and brief stints as a stripper. So, he'd tried his hand at being a P.I., figuring it was basically the same skill set as being a paparazzo without the social stigma. And he hadn't been entirely wrong. Instead of everyone dismissing him as an immoral slimeball, he'd been regarded as a vigilante badass. But it hadn't been worth the ulcers.

So, he'd started stripping full time. He'd worked on a few Magic Mike type shows for a while, and then he'd gotten hired to strip at a celebrity bachelorette party. It was there he'd met Aiden, who'd successfully parlayed his stripping gig into one working for a domestic staffing agency. James, knowing he couldn't strip forever, had followed in Aiden's footsteps.

Now, he was right back where he'd started, his hands sweating in a pair of rubber gloves and his stomach churning with acid.

He slipped out of Tony Wallingford's room at the inn and down the long hallway to the stairs. He'd installed two different monitoring devices, a voice-activated pen recorder and a USB charger with a hidden camera.

Robert wouldn't tell James what he was after, but he'd promised to fill him in, should he unearth something incriminating against Derek Hall's manager.

Spying on Tony Wallingford wasn't the only string attached to Robert Chapman's little deal, which felt far more like blackmail than a mutually beneficial arrangement. He also wanted James to break up with Will the moment filming wrapped.

"I know what people think of my son, that he deserves every bit of bad luck that comes his way just because of one drunken mistake. But I will not allow you to break his heart just to satisfy your own curiosity."

James could've told Robert the truth, that breaking up at the end of the summer had been the plan all along, that he hadn't seduced Will just to get onto the movie set. But he hadn't wanted Robert to ask for something else instead, and he hadn't wanted to embarrass Will in front of his father, so he'd kept his mouth shut and agreed.

He'd tried to tell Robert that he was a shitty P.I., which was why he'd become a stripper, hoping to convince the old man to hire a professional instead. But Robert had been undaunted.

"No, I need someone I can trust, someone who can be both on and off the set with his eyes and ears open, someone who won't raise suspicion."

"Why though? What's Tony done?"

"That's what I'm trying to figure out." Robert wanted to keep everything on a need-to-know basis. "And if you do, I'll make sure you're generously compensated."

James sat in his car and checked the feed on his phone. It was working. The USB plug he'd swapped out was near the ground by the bed, so he wouldn't get much footage beyond Tony's feet, but he'd still get decent audio. The pen recorder, James's backup, didn't have a transmitter, so he'd have to collect it periodically and download the audio files.

Okay. James exhaled and pulled the bowl from his pocket. He was going to need to buy more weed soon at the rate he was going, but, on the bright side, today marked a whole week of watching them film Travis's movie.

CHAPTER 29
WILL

James was hands down the best fake boyfriend ever, and not just owing to his unparalleled leaning skills. Now that he was coming to the set every day, their little boyfriend act had been upgraded from an occasional cocktail hour cabaret to a full on Broadway run. And it was awesome.

James was ridiculously sweet and supportive. Whenever Will would finish filming a scene, James would pull him aside and press their foreheads together and whisper unbearably saccharine things like, "Holy shit, you're incredible," and "How did you just do that?" and "You're a better Vermonter than I am."

Over the past couple of weeks, they'd gotten so used to playing their parts that it no longer felt awkward or forced when James rested his chin on Will's shoulder, or when he wrapped his arms around Will's waist. It was just another way to stand, the best way in Will's opinion.

Plus, they would talk about it. Driving home every night, James would ask Will what he thought about this or that fake boyfriend move. "Did you like it when I smacked your ass?" and "That was pretty cool, right, when I reached over and yanked that nose hair right out of your nose? Did you see the look on Derek's face?"

Will would do his best not to melt like a crayon left in the sun. And instead of saying, "You can do whatever the fuck you want to me," he would respond the way someone might if they had an ounce of self-respect. "Maybe don't smack so hard next time," and "Don't you ever do that again. Nose hairs are an important part of the immune system."

Occasionally, they'd continue the charade even when no one was looking, like the time they'd been shooting late at night and James had lain down with his head on Will's lap. Will had sat there for five excruciating minutes debating whether or not to run his fingers through James's hair. When he'd finally gotten up the courage, he'd started tentatively, just brushing a single lock of hair behind James's ear with a single finger.

But James had responded like Will had touched some magic button, leaning into Will's touch like a purring cat. "Mmm, that feels nice. Keep going."

For ten minutes, Will's fingers had combed, raked, and slid through James's hair, and it had only seemed surreal for the first eight minutes. The last two minutes had been spent wondering what it would feel like to kiss James. Maybe one of these times James pressed their foreheads together Will would. He'd lift James's chin, look him straight in the eye, and kiss him.

That fantasy, among others, lived rent free in Will's head. He'd yet to act on it, but as the makeup team added the final flourish to his costume—deer piss—he wondered if maybe today was the day.

"You know I'm not actually in the movie, right?" Will said to Carmen, the head of the makeup team. "And, contrary to popular belief, cameras don't actually record odors, no matter how foul said odors might be?"

Carmen shrugged. "Don't you want to make your father happy?"

They were going to cut Will out of the movie, so it was pointless to put him in full costume and makeup, especially deer piss makeup.

But Will's father had insisted, claiming he needed to see—and, apparently, smell—Travis opposite him, not William.

It wasn't the deer piss alone making Will wish he'd stayed home. In a few minutes, they were going to make him sit on a tiny seat twenty feet above the ground, holding a deadly weapon. Will didn't like standing on a chair to change a light bulb. Plus, he looked ridiculous. He was dressed head to toe in camouflage, including camouflage face paint. He looked like he was ready for the jungles of 'Nam, not stalking Bambi.

But James liked it when Will did ridiculous country boy things, like going muddin' and artificially inseminating cows. And for some reason, he was more excited about this scene than any other. Therefore, Will was determined to act the shit out of it.

James was hands down Will's biggest fan. His only fan, really. His eyes would light up the moment Will stepped out in some new costume. And while Will was filming, James would stare at him with rapt attention. As a teacher, Will was used to being ignored, so this was a welcome change of pace. And it was helpful. Will could tell, just from the look in James's eyes, whether he'd hit the emotional core of a scene or not.

"I can't get over how sexy you look right now," James said. "I'm gonna go ask if they'll let you wear your costume home tonight."

"I look like the scuzz they pull out of clogged storm drains. And I smell even worse."

James smiled and rested his hands on his hips. He was really leaning into the whole erotic '70s mustache vibe. Over the past couple of weeks, he'd started wearing paisley button downs and three-quarter sleeve T-shirts. It was torture.

"Show me your packing skills." James nodded towards Will's pocket.

Will rolled his eyes, but did as he was told. He took out the Skoal can and thwacked it three times in rapid succession with a loose index finger the way James had shown him. "Happy?"

"I can't believe how good you are at that. It took me most of seventh grade to get a sound that loud."

"I don't know if you know this or not," Will said, "but I was recently recruited into this new hipster mariachi band. Instead of castanets, I'm going to thwack Skoal cans. It's going to be awesome."

"Ooh, can I be your groupie?" James took the can from Will and gave it a few good thwacks. "Or better yet, I can be your manager. I'll make them give you double the free drink coupons."

"Okay, let's reset and go from the top with Will," Michelle said.

Derek, who'd made it safely down from the tree stand, headed over in his equally ridiculous camouflage hunting attire. "You're up, Will," he said. He stopped three feet away and then took a step back. "What's that smell?"

"It's buck urine," James said. And then, instead of calling Derek a pansy to his face, James wrapped his arm around Will's shoulder and kissed his cheek, which earned him a lecture from the makeup team.

"That was phenomenal, Derek," Tony said, sneaking up behind them. The middle-aged man looked totally out of place in the woods. He wore a light gray two-piece suit that set off his artificially silver hair. "I need you to sign this, and then we can go."

Tony pulled a pen from his briefcase, along with a stack of papers, and handed them to Derek.

"Ow, stop," Will said, shrugging out of James's death grip. "I don't need a deep tissue massage right now."

It was pretty obvious James didn't like Derek. At first, Will had assumed James was just getting into character as the jealous boyfriend. But one night, James had let his jealousy follow them home.

"Why did Derek touch you like that?" he'd asked. "I know this is a fake relationship and all, but Derek doesn't know that. What kind of asshole macks on another dude's man right in front of him?"

Derek hadn't "macked" on Will. He'd merely touched Will's knee. "Trust me. Derek is not putting the moves on me. First of all, he's straight. Second of all, he's a theater kid. All theater kids are like that. They have no physical boundaries."

"How come he's not like that with Ryan or your dad, then?"

"My dad hates Derek, and I don't know about Ryan. For all I know, they go home and fuck like rabbits every night."

"I thought you said Derek was straight."

"He is. I'm just . . . Whatever. It's not important."

Derek didn't stick around to see Will film his version of the scene. He never did.

"You should have a beer can," James said as Will was halfway up the ladder. "Real hunters would never spit their chew directly on the ground. The deer would smell it."

"Get William a can," Will's father said from ten feet above him. "James is right."

Will's father was a perfectionist, and the moment he'd found out Will's fake boyfriend was born and raised in Vermont, he'd started treating everything James said like gospel. According to James, no Vermonter in their right mind had a key bowl or a key rack in their house. They just left their keys in the ignition. So, that was how they'd filmed the driving scene.

The scene they were shooting that afternoon was an important one. In it, Bruce and Travis are bow hunting, sitting in neighboring trees. Bruce sees a flash of white and thinks it's a deer tail running away. He draws his bow and aims. He's just about to let his arrow fly when Travis realizes it's not a deer tail but a child wearing white gloves. He jumps to his feet and yells at his father, who startles and misses the girl by only a few inches. It's this incident that leads to the Alzheimer's diagnosis.

"It's kind of beautiful up here, isn't it?" his father said as Will made his way up to the tiny platform.

"Uh huh." Will wasn't sure what was scarier, looking down or not looking down.

"Your ass looks incredible from down here," James called from below. "Michelle, you're gonna wanna get that on film."

They had hooked Will to a harness for safety, but he didn't trust it, and the first few takes didn't go very well. He was supposed to jump to his feet and yell. And he tried. He really did. But his body refused to cooperate, and instead of looking like a spry young man, he moved like a pregnant woman in her third trimester.

"It's just like jumping off the quarry," James called from Michelle's side. "You're gonna be fine, I promise."

Okay, Will could do this. He wasn't William Chapman, pathetic, weak loser. He was Travis Young, confident, strong hunter. He liked muddin' and fishin' and jumpin' off cliffs. Standing up quickly was no big deal. Letting his father murder a little girl? Now that was a big deal.

What if it was one of Will's students? What if it was Awa? He pictured the little girl with her tight braids and radiant smile. Some mornings, Will would get off the subway and find her walking to school by herself. She always wore a *don't fuck with me* grimace on her face, but the moment she saw Will, her eyes would light up and she'd run over and take his hand. Then, instead of making photocopies when he got to school, like he'd planned, Will would report the incident to the state central registry like a good mandated reporter.

"Yer gonna scare the deer away," his father said.

"Nah, they'll just think it's a woodpecker," Will's Travis replied. He took a pinch of freshly packed dip and shoved it into his bottom lip. It was real dip, too. Derek used the fake shit, but Will's dad insisted he not take any shortcuts. It tasted alright, but it made Will extremely lightheaded.

"That shit's gonna kill you," his father said.

"Probably."

After a beat of silence, "Did the check clear yet?"

"Yeah, Dad, we already talked about this. It cleared yesterday."

"Right"—his father nodded—"right. I just forgot."

"Yeah, well, who's scarin' the fuckin' deer away now?"

This time, when his father rose to take the shot, Will didn't hesitate. He screamed so desperately his father really did flinch. "Dad, Dad, no!"

Will leapt to his feet like he'd sat on a cactus. The arrow flew from his father's bow, and Will was so focused on its trajectory, willing it to hit anything but Awa, he stepped right off the platform.

Green and brown streaked past him, and his stomach rose to his chest. The harness yanked tight around him, and chewing tobacco spewed from his mouth as he bit down hard on his tongue. The bow fell from his hands and smashed onto the stone wall below.

Will opened his eyes and found himself suspended ten feet above the ground.

"Are you okay?" Michelle asked.

"Oh, fuck, sorry. Did I ruin the take?"

As crew members scrambled to get Will down, his father looked over the edge of his tree stand and asked Michelle the same question, "Was that the one? Did we get it?"

"I think so." Michelle headed over to watch the playback on the monitor. "We got it," she said a moment later, and everyone cheered.

James was there to receive Will the second he was safely back on solid ground. He didn't even seem to care that Will was covered in paint and smelled like deer piss. He pressed their foreheads together the way he always did. "That was incredible." His sweaty brow melded with Will's. "You're incredible."

Now was Will's chance. He should just do it. He should just kiss James. That was what a real boyfriend would do. And if James got mad, he could just tell him it was for show. Then again, maybe that was a terrible idea. Will probably tasted like chewing tobacco, and there was blood in his mouth from biting his tongue.

"Thanks," Will said.

"I can't believe you fell. What were you thinking? I don't think I've ever met anyone as fearless as you."

"You're kidding me, right?" Will's eyes traced the hem of James's shirt, which just barely covered the silver of his belt buckle. "I'm scared of my own shadow."

"Yes, but you always get over it. You always go for it in the end."

Not always, Will thought. *Not with you.*

CHAPTER 30

JAMES

Will's lips were right there. All James had to do was tip Will's head up a few degrees and . . . But then Will pulled away.

It was strange being attracted to the man playing his brother. But it wasn't all the time. When Will was in character, it wasn't attraction James felt but a bittersweet cocktail of grief and nostalgia. Unlike Derek, who never stopped being Derek, Will's version of James's brother was so spot on, it was like watching an old home movie.

But the moment the scene was over, and Will was back to being a quiet city boy in redneck attire, James's attraction would come rushing back. His heart would swell with more gratitude and awe than he knew what to do with. Will's portrayal of Travis was a gift, a monument to Travis's life and sacrifice, and James loved Will for that, even though Will's version would never be seen.

It wasn't like James could act on his desires, though. This was all going to end in a month, and seeing the pen recorder in Tony's hand earlier had been another painful reminder of that. Even if James tried to make Will his actual boyfriend, Will's dad would put a stop to it.

He'd tell Will the truth about what James and Esther had done, and Will would never forgive James.

James was better off focusing on work. He had a job to do. He needed to get that pen recorder back. He'd stashed it where he'd thought Tony and the cleaning crew wouldn't see it. But obviously, he'd fucked up, because now Tony was carrying it around in his briefcase. It was voice activated, so it shut itself off when no one was talking. But the battery would need to be recharged soon and the files downloaded. If Tony lost the pen or gave it away, everything it had recorded would be lost, too.

The camera in Tony's room wasn't picking up shit. The only interesting thing James had gotten so far was a Grindr hookup with some Middlebury student who was unidentifiable and probably of legal age anyway.

After Will's epic fall, they sat on the stone wall, drinking coffee, waiting for Will's dad to finish talking to Michelle. While they sat there, Heather, the crane operator, came over in cutoff jeans and a white tank top. "Hey, boys, come on, we're going out for drinks. It's Friday night, and thanks to your man, here, we get to knock off early."

Will looked down into his cup. "You guys go. I probably shouldn't."

Heather scowled. "Go put a wig on or something. No one's gonna recognize you."

"It's not that—"

"Awesome. We'll meet you at the Starlight in an hour, then. It's right on Route 7. You can't miss it."

James liked Heather, especially the way she had zero tolerance for Will's constant hedging.

Will looked sexy as fuck all decked out in camo, so it was with reluctance that James said, "Go shower and change. We don't have to stay long."

James hadn't been to the Starlight in years. It was the bar he used to suggest when he met guys from Burlington. It was far enough away from his hometown that he wouldn't have to run into anyone he knew and close enough that he wouldn't have to spend all night driving just to meet some loser with ten-year-old profile pictures.

It wasn't a gay bar. Those didn't exist in Vermont. But it was about as close as you could get. Did Kay still run karaoke every Friday and Saturday night?

"You'll have more fun without me."

"No, I won't." James leveled his eyes at Will and winked. Will was a sucker for a wink.

"Fine. Jesus Christ."

THEY WALKED into the bar an hour later. Heather was already there with some of the crew members. Their table was littered with pitchers of beer and baskets of french fries. Up on the stage, in a little booth, sat a short, round woman with more makeup than Tammy Faye. Kay looked exactly the same.

"Come here. There's someone I want you to meet." James grabbed Will by the hand and dragged him towards the stage.

It was a ballsy move, introducing Will to someone from his old life, but Kay was harmless. She only knew important things about James, like which songs he liked to sing and how much reverb he required.

James rested his elbow on Kay's booth. "Remember me?"

Kay's eyes searched his face for several seconds, and then she jumped up and almost knocked over her Diet Pepsi.

"Honey, I thought you'd left us for good." She came around and gave James a perfumed hug. "What are you doing here?"

"I'm in town on a job. This is my boyfriend, Will. Will, this is Kay, the best KJ in Vermont."

Kay looked Will up and down, and for one terrifying moment, James thought she recognized him. But then she smiled and said, "He's too handsome for you."

"I know, right?" James draped his arm over Will's shoulder. "Let's hope he doesn't catch on."

"It's nice to meet you." Will tried to shake Kay's hand, but she was already going in for the hug.

Most Vermonters didn't hug. Kay was the exception. "He's strong, too." She squeezed Will's biceps as she pulled away.

She reached behind the booth and turned down the volume on the drunk couple butchering "Picture" by Kid Rock and Sheryl Crow. "I saw Michael the other day. I asked him about you, but he said you don't keep in touch."

"We don't." James shifted his weight from one foot to the other. Maybe this wasn't such a good idea. He turned to Will. "Why don't you go join the others? I'll get us a pitcher."

He waited until Will was out of earshot and then asked, "Can you do me a huge favor?" As far as James could tell, the world was unaware William Chapman could sing better than Freddie Mercury. What Will needed more than anything was good publicity, a positive viral moment, one that didn't involve Derek Hall. "Can we skaraoke Will? He's way too shy to come up on his own."

"What did you have in mind?" Kay asked with a grin.

"Something big, like Whitney or Celine."

"Better do Celine. Paula just did Whitney."

"Great, perfect." James pulled out his phone and tried to hand it to Kay. "And can you record him, too? But it's gotta be in secret."

"Oh, honey, you don't want me to do it. I'll just get the back of his head. And my hands"—Kay held up her quivering, arthritic hands—"shake too much. Let's ask Megan."

Kay called over a tall woman with curly black hair, and James gave her his phone. He told her to be discreet. His boyfriend hated being recorded and would flip out if he realized.

Five minutes later, James set a fresh pitcher of Budweiser on the table in front of Will, whose cheeks were as red as an apple.

"You're the best thing about this whole fucking movie," Heather was saying. "And that goes for your father, too. I hope they're paying you well."

"They're not." Will looked at James like he needed saving.

"Diane overheard Michelle talking to your mother, and they're gonna use your takes for Ryan, too. Apparently, your dad isn't the only one who does his best work when you're around."

"I'm sure that's not true."

Heather took it upon herself to pour Will a beer. "It is. And come to think of it, *The Beautiful* is the only movie Derek doesn't suck ass in. Now I know why."

Will hid his face inside his beer. The guy could not take a compliment.

Heather was James's favorite of the crew members. She operated the cranes for all the aerial shots, and like James, she wasn't impressed by fame and reputation. For her, Robert Chapman was a pompous windbag and Derek Hall a talentless hack.

Heather would've kept on embarrassing Will, but it was her turn to sing. The whole table got up to support her on the dance floor, and James and Will were left alone with a fresh order of mozzarella sticks.

"So, tell me about Michael." Will eyed the mozzarella sticks, but didn't take one.

James had a feeling Will wouldn't let that go. Will had a habit of asking a bunch of insightful questions every time James slipped up and revealed something personal about himself, like the time he'd told Will about accidentally zipping Theo's penis up in his pajamas as a toddler. Will had cringed and then asked how James had become a father in the first place. James had had to lie and say he didn't want to talk about it, that he'd been young and confused.

"Michael's just a guy I used to date."

Will leaned in close, so close James could see his reflection in Will's black eyes. "We're not actually dating. You don't have to protect my ego by downplaying the significance of your past relationships."

James poured himself a beer. "I'm not. It wasn't a big deal. I thought we were in love. He didn't. He was in law school at the time and needed someone to pay the rent, simple as that."

Will pushed the mozzarella sticks farther away. "How long were you two together?"

"Three or four years, I guess."

"You guess?"

"Well, it took him six months to move out after we broke up. So, it was three years until I realized we were just roommates who fucked and four years until we stopped being roommates who fucked."

Will winced and reached for his Budweiser. "I bet you're wrong."

"About what?"

"I bet he loved you back. How could he not?"

James used to think Michael was a heartless monster who only let the relationship carry on because it was financially convenient for him. But he understood Michael better now. He was him.

Love wasn't always a big deal. James had loved Brice in his own way. Brice was a good person, and he was hot. James would've happily stayed with Brice forever. And yet now, only a few months later, Brice hardly ever crossed his mind.

"There are a lot of things you don't know about me. Things you wouldn't like very much." James took a mozzarella stick from the basket and handed it to Will.

Will grimaced, but took the mozzarella stick. He took a bite and a long string of melted cheese stretched from his fingers to his lips. "Please tell me you got drunk one night and tried to kill someone. Right now, I'm the only one in the support group, and it's exhausting always having to talk at meetings."

James leaned in and pressed his forehead against Will's, the way he did after every scene. It had started as a way to stop Will from looking so sheepish and embarrassed, like a dog who'd just shat on the floor. But now it was just something they did.

"You're a good guy, Will. I didn't think you would be. I thought you'd be a spoiled brat, but you're not. You're—" Will pulled back, and their eyes locked. James saw the moment it happened; the moment Will finally got up the courage to kiss him.

Will's eyes darted to James's mouth. James only had a second to react, a second to save them both.

"You're a good friend." His face raced past Will's and landed on his shoulder. He hugged him, and it was the most awkward hug in the history of hugs.

"Now it's time for some skaraoke." Kay's voice boomed from the speakers behind them. "In case you're not familiar with skaraoke, it's when we force some poor sap to sing a song they didn't choose and probably hate. According to his boyfriend, our next victim is extremely shy and is gonna need a lot of encouragement. I've got a shot of whiskey ready, but you're gonna have to do the rest. So, let's give a big round of applause to Will."

Will's face went chalk white. "You didn't."

James smirked and shrugged. "Who, me?"

The crew members ran off the dance floor and dragged Will up on the stage, where Kay was waiting with a shot of whiskey and a microphone. Will looked up at the monitor and gave what had to be the biggest, most adorable eye roll of all time.

"Celine Dion? You've got to be kidding me." The first dramatic piano chords of "It's All Coming Back to Me Now" reverberated through the bar.

James glanced over at Megan, who held James's phone inconspicuously in her lap, the camera pointed at Will.

"Jesus Christ." Will downed the shot and rolled his shoulders like he was about to attempt a deadlift.

James had given minimal thought to the song choice, but judging by the way the whole bar went silent and every drunk redneck in the place turned to watch the moment Will sang the first line, he'd chosen well.

Power ballads were tricky with karaoke. Drunk people liked songs they could sing to, songs they could dance to, songs they knew so well it didn't matter if the loser on stage made up his own melody or was nowhere near the beat. People went to karaoke to sing karaoke, not to listen to it. When someone sang a power ballad you either had to suffer through it or go smoke in the parking lot.

No one got up to smoke a cigarette. In fact, the smokers started coming in to listen.

Like every time Will performed, James couldn't take his eyes off him, and he wasn't the only one. Will belonged on a stage. Sure, he was probably an amazing kindergarten teacher, too, but a talent like his was wasted on a room full of snot-nosed kids who thought "Twinkle, Twinkle Little Star" was good music.

The performance ended too soon, and with it, Will's confidence. He ducked his head and ran off the stage even though there was more applause than the Starlight had ever heard before.

"What the fuck, Will?" Heather cupped Will's face in her hands so he couldn't look away. "You can sing?"

Through squished cheeks, Will said, "Everyone can sing."

An old man with a neon blue cocktail set a paint-stained hand on Will's shoulder. "That was amazing. You should go on *American Idol*."

"James," Kay said into the microphone for all to hear, "if you don't marry that boy, I'm gonna."

Later, after the adulation had died down and the room was once again immersed in off-key versions of "Friends in Low Places" and "Sweet Caroline," Will said, "This was what you were talking about earlier, wasn't it, the thing I wouldn't like very much? You make all your friends embarrass themselves in public."

James hated the way the word *friends* slipped from Will's lips, even though he'd been the one to put it there. "You could never embarrass yourself." James took Will's hand under the table and squeezed.

CHAPTER 31

WILL

The night of the rehearsal dinner in Montreal, James strode from the bathroom of their luxury suite wearing a steel gray jacket over a thin gray sweater that stretched across his chest. The look, paired with his new haircut, which left just enough length to curl above his ears, was more than Will could handle. Plus, the fucking mustache and five o'clock shadow weren't helping.

"How do I look?" The cocky smirk on James's face proved he knew exactly how he looked.

"It's a good fit." Will slipped on his loafers. James was just a friend, and the sooner Will accepted that, the better off he'd be. Besides, friends were great. Will needed more friends.

"Are you kidding? I look better than I did when I was your age."

"Don't pull that daddy shit on me. You're nine years older. In gay years, that's nothing. NASA lands lunar rovers with greater margins of error than that."

"Doesn't mean you can't call me Daddy." James brushed a lock of Will's hair from his face. Jesus, why did James have to say shit like that?

"Should I come back in five minutes?" Theo stood in the doorway of their adjoining suites.

James cocked an eyebrow. "Is that enough time for you? I can be fast if necessary, though fifteen would be preferable."

Will, who was about ten seconds away from coming in his pants, managed an eye roll and a little "humph" before turning to hide his blush. Unfortunately, he turned to face the bed, the bed he and James would, in theory, be sharing that night. Of course, they did have two rooms. Maybe James was planning to sleep in Theo's room.

"How do you guys want to handle the whole bed situation?" That sounded casual, right?

"Well, I'm certainly not sharing with him." Theo hooked a thumb at James. "He snores."

"Only when I drink too much."

Theo plopped down on the sofa. "Is Miles here yet? And are we taking the limo to the restaurant or walking?"

That didn't answer Will's question. *Fuck.* "I don't know."

Jesus, this night was going to be a disaster. It was one thing to parade a fake boyfriend through a closed set. But tonight, there were going to be photographers, a lot of photographers.

The attention from the bachelor party fiasco had dissipated some, but now Will had the karaoke video to deal with. Some woman named Megan had recorded him at the bar and posted the video online. It had a million views and counting.

Derek had seen it and suggested Will consider a Vegas residency. His parents, on the other hand, had taken turns berating him. His father had accused him of doing it on purpose. He'd told Will if he wanted to be taken seriously as an actor, he couldn't play amateur games like some Kardashian. His mother had accused him of trying to steal Andy's thunder. *Stop trying to upstage your brother. You'll only make a fool of yourself.*

Will had been so preoccupied with the bed situation, he hadn't noticed Theo in his new suit. "Uh oh, you better keep your eye on Ryan tonight."

Theo wore a brown suit bordering on burnt orange, with a charcoal gray button down and shiny black shoes. He looked far older than eighteen, the suit hiding his gangly arms and legs.

"What happens in Canada stays in Canada," Theo said, a hopeful glint in his eye.

"I think you mean Vegas," James said.

The rehearsal dinner was in Montreal. Nandi was fine with the small-town wedding. She was even onboard with the floating reception. But for the rehearsal dinner, she wanted to be in a real city with fancy restaurants and adoring fans.

Will's father was putting everyone up at the Four Seasons and treating them to dinner at Maison Boulud. Afterward, the plan was for the old people to go to bed and the young people to go clubbing, which was going to suck balls. At least Miles would be there. Maybe he'd stop Will from getting drunk and throwing himself at James.

There was a knock at the door. "Room service."

Will glared at James.

"Don't look at me."

Will opened the door, and the entire wedding party—Enrique, Andy, Ryan, Nandi, and three gorgeous models—charged into the room.

"We come bearing edibles"—Enrique tossed a white paper bag at Will—"and this." He produced a bottle of booze from behind his back. "This bad boy is one of only two hundred and fifty bottles ever made, and we're not leaving this room until it's empty."

Enrique took in his surroundings. Somehow, his man bun had grown three inches taller since the bachelor party. He saw James standing by the bed and headed straight for him. "You must be James. I'm Enrique."

"Nice to meet you." James was unfazed by the sudden influx of movie stars and runway models because James was unfazed by everything, one of the many perks of being perfect.

Enrique thrust the bottle at James, not recognizing him from the bachelor party—thank God. "Have you heard of this vodka before?

It's made from an ancient Russian czar's recipe. It's distilled through solid gold pipes and infused with diamonds."

Two thoughts popped into Will's head. *What were they all doing in his room? And why would anyone want to drink diamonds?*

Andy and Ryan started rounding up glasses while Will stood there with his hand on the doorknob. Nandi stopped beside him and kissed his cheeks.

"Will, you are looking handsome. Is this your boyfriend?" She walked over and kissed James on the cheek and left a smear of maroon lipstick, which she wiped off with a finger. "I'm so happy to meet you. Will has told me absolutely nothing about you, so we have a lot to catch up on."

"Theo, is this your room over here?" Ryan disappeared into the adjoining suite before Theo could answer.

"James"—Enrique took the bag of edibles from Will—"mind if I manhandle Will for a sec?"

James didn't look up from the bottle. "By all means."

"He doesn't get to give you permis—"

Enrique lifted Will off the ground in a giant bear hug. "Andy, come feel how hard your brother's body is. He's like a little marble statue."

Will wriggled free and smoothed his rumpled shirt. "I'm five fucking ten. I'm not little."

"You're five eight, don't lie." Andy wrapped a long, freckled arm around Will's shoulder. "Nandi, take a picture of us."

Nandi spent the next several minutes making them pose. Fucking models.

Ryan returned with his fingers stuffed inside half a dozen glasses. "This should be enough."

"Awesome, there is no way we're surviving tonight sober." Andy released Will with a pinch at the back of his neck. "I don't know how you've lasted a whole month with Mom and Dad in the same state, let alone on the same movie set. Remember that time they tried to do that Super Bowl ad together?"

Will was surprised Andy remembered. He'd only been four at the time. It had been three days of constant screaming. His mother had only had one line, "It's the breast," which she had said in a yellow bikini holding a chicken leg. His father had been livid because she'd said it with too much irony instead of complete sincerity, which he'd insisted was the whole point of the joke.

"Who's the stud?" Enrique made his way towards Theo, who stood in the glass-encased living room too stunned to talk or move, his eyes darting about the place like some haunted medieval painting.

"Hand's off, Enrique," Ryan said. "He's only eighteen. And you do realize that's his dad right there, don't you?"

Enrique looked from Theo to James and then back to Theo again. "No, shit? Fuck yeah, Will, landed yourself a legit daddy."

"Wait, that's Mom's new grandson?" Andy could have walked around the bed, but he opted to roll across it like he was doing a stunt. "It's so nice to meet you. I'm Uncle Andy."

Jesus Christ. Will felt like he was standing in the center of Time Square on New Year's Eve in the middle of a bomb threat. "What are you all doing here? Get out."

"Slow your roll, Will." Enrique took the bottle back from James. "We're not leaving here until this bad boy is empty."

Andy glared at Will. "And you have no right to make demands. I'm fucking pissed at you. I get you not telling Mom and Dad about James, but you could've told me." Andy offered his hand to James. "I'm Will's brother, Andy. Will and I used to be close, but now we're just mild acquaintances who can't even be bothered to mention our new boyfriends."

"I know who you are. I'm a huge fan." James shook Andy's outstretched hand.

Of course James was a huge fan. Will dated three types of guys: guys into his mom, guys into his dad, and guys into his brother. Although, he wasn't actually dating James, so whatever.

"Tell me, James"—Nandi grabbed James's hand and led him into the living room—"what's Will like in bed? Is he a biter like Andy?"

This was too much sensory input. "Enrique, hurry up and open that fucking bottle."

"Diamonds, Will." Enrique's voice was irreverent. "It's infused with diamonds. We're not just chugging it. We need to give toasts and shit."

The model in the champagne dress flitted over. "Ohhh, I'm great at giving toasts. Hi, William. I'm Monika. I loved you in *The Beautiful*. How come you don't act anymore? Did you really quit to become a kindergarten teacher?" She didn't wait for a reply. "That's so amazing. You must be, like, a Zen master. Oh, Andy showed us your video. You're, like, the best singer I've ever met, and I've met a lot of singers, including every Jonas Brother."

Ryan thrust a glass into Will's hand. "I didn't get a chance to say anything yesterday, but damn, Will, that was amazing. I think that's going to be the best scene in the whole movie. I felt like I was having an out-of-body experience, like I wasn't in my body. There just wasn't any of me left. It was all Jimmy. That's never happened to me before."

"I know the feeling," Monika said. "I once slept with this chubby guy from the Peace Corp, and at first I thought I peed myself, but no, I squirted. That'd never happened to me before either."

Jesus Christ, was this really happening? Will tried to catch James's eye, but Nandi had him in her clutches, and she was touching his mustache, Will's mustache. Well, not Will's mustache. But still, hands off.

Enrique leaned in and asked, "What's the teenaged hottie's name again? Can he have some, too?"

"No," Will said.

Theo finally found his voice. "I'm Theo, and I love vodka." He said it like he was attending his first AA meeting. "Plus, the legal drinking age in Montreal is eighteen."

Enrique pulled a red hair from Will's shirt. "Should I ask his papi first?"

"In my country, we let the kids drink." The tall French model in the yellow dress with the plunging V-neck came and stood beside Theo. "I'm Noel. We should be photographed together tonight. We will look amazing."

She had a point. She was at least as tall as James, and considerably taller in her heels. But next to Theo, she looked dainty.

"Daddy"—Enrique made a pouty face at James—"can my future husband have some vodka? It's infused with diamonds."

"Just one glass because it's a special occasion."

Will rolled his eyes. Like James didn't let Theo drink whenever the fuck he wanted to.

"Alright," Enrique announced. "I'm going to open it."

There was another knock at the door. "Room service."

This time, Will recognized the voice and threw open the door. "Thank God you're here. Enrique is making us drink diamonds."

"What? That's incredible." Miles stepped into the room, and Will's mouth dropped to the floor.

There, hiding behind Miles, was Tiffany. "Oh my god, what are you doing here? Are you Miles's date? How did you talk him into that?"

Tiffany returned Will's hug. "I have my ways."

"You look amazing, and you're wearing a dress." Tiffany never wore dresses.

"Anthony let me borrow it." Tiffany spun around to show off the form-fitting dress, with its bold pink print and wide belt. Anthony taught third grade and moonlighted as a drag queen on weekends, specializing in Michelle Obama.

"I'm giving the first toast," Monika said after introductions were made and Ryan scrounged up two more glasses. She stood in the living room with the Montreal skyline sparkling behind her.

"I'm so excited to be here, with old friends and new, to celebrate the marriage of Nandi and Andy. I've known this day would come ever since I saw Nandi and Andy making out at Elton John's Oscar party. As many of you know, I am blessed with a superpower. I can watch any two people kiss and tell you exactly how long their relationship will last. And when I watched Nandi and Andy kiss for the first time, I thought, yes, they will be together all through their reproductive years, and they will have very cute babies."

Will was surprised when James's hand found his. It was as if James knew Will needed something to squeeze, which he did. This woman was ridiculous.

"Long ago," Monika continued, "countries would strengthen their alliances by marrying their children. Henry VIII, King of England, married Catherine of Aragon, a princess of Spain, and to this day, the two countries are very close, at least geographically. And while we've entered an era where nationalism is only appropriate during the Olympics and Eurovision, there are other divides we must bridge.

"I think you all know what I'm talking about, the divide between meat eaters and vegetarians. Andy eats meat. In his lifetime, he will consume roughly 7,000 animals: 11 cows, 27 pigs, 2,400 chickens, 80 turkeys, 30 sheep, and 4,500 fish.

"Nandi is a principled vegetarian. And sure, she could guilt trip Andy at every meal and make him get his own refrigerator. But she doesn't. She loves him, murder and all. And Andy could become defensive about his questionable morals. But he doesn't. He recognizes Nandi's superiority and worships her all the more for it." Monika lifted her glass. "To Nandi, Andy, and true bipartisanship."

The vodka tasted, surprise, surprise, like vodka, although Enrique and Miles swore they could taste the diamonds, like anyone knew what the fuck diamonds tasted like.

Andy caught the bag of edibles Enrique tossed him and selected a red gummy. "How much do you want to bet Dad's toast tonight is going to be all about him?"

"Oh, without a doubt." Will glanced over at Miles, who was

whispering something to Theo. This couldn't be good. They both smiled and waved Monika over. Definitely not good.

"So, Ryan filled me in on everything. Are you really okay with this? Sounds like a lot of work for nothing." Andy offered Will the bag of edibles, and Will passed it directly to Noel. The last thing he needed was to get high.

"It's alright." Great, now Monika was smiling, too.

"Hey, apparently, they're casting Wes Anderson's new movie. My agent wants me to audition, but I don't think I will. I don't have that dry wit thing he likes. But you should totally go out for it."

"Uh huh." Fuck, now they were coming this way.

Miles put his hands on James's shoulders and steered him across the room like he was starting a conga line.

"Good news, Will." Miles had an evil glint in his eyes. "Monika has agreed to use her superpowers on you and James."

It took Will a moment to catch on, and when he did, time stopped. *I'm going to get to kiss James?* That thought was quickly supplanted by *While everyone watches and analyzes?* This was not good. James didn't want to kiss Will. He'd made that perfectly clear at the karaoke bar. As far as James was concerned, they were friends, and friends didn't kiss. They hugged. They cuddled. They leaned and held hands. They pressed their foreheads together and whispered tender endearments. But they didn't kiss.

"Absolutely not." Will took a step back.

"Wait, what's going on?" Enrique fished another edible out of the bag and popped it in his mouth like popcorn.

Miles deposited James right in front of Will. "Will and James are going to make out and Monika is going to tell me if I need to get a divorce lawyer."

James's eyebrows shot up. "What's he talking about?"

Nandi clapped her hands together. "Oh, this is perfect. I love watching two men kiss. And Monika is the real deal. Not only did she call Kim and Kanye, but Bill and Melinda, too."

Noel, the French model, asked, "Is it still working if they are knowing you are watching?"

"It's not ideal"—Monika waved a paper-thin hand through the air—"but it should still work."

"No, just no," Will said, taking another step back. He was up against the wall now with nowhere else to go.

"Kiss, kiss, kiss, kiss," Enrique chanted, and everyone joined in, including Miles, Tiffany, and Theo, who should've known better. "Kiss, kiss, kiss, kiss..."

Jesus fucking Christ. Will met James's gaze and could see he was enjoying this, because of course he was. It was easy to kiss a friend. Anyone could kiss a friend. But Will wouldn't be kissing a friend. He'd be kissing the guy he'd been jacking off to three times a day all summer, the guy he might very well be in love with.

"Kiss, kiss, kiss." Their voices grew in volume until they were as loud as the heart spasming in Will's chest.

James smiled down at him, and Will thought he saw James's lip twitch. Jesus Christ, fine. Will rose to his toes and kissed the smirk off James's face.

James's full lips were wet and warm and smelled like vodka. And the contrast of their pillowy softness against the bristle of James's mustache sent a wave of goosebumps over Will's skin. It was quite possibly the most thrilling half-second of his life.

"There, happy?"

The chanting dropped off a cliff, and you would've thought Will had stepped on a baby the way everyone stared at him.

"Oh, come on, papi," Enrique said. "He's your daddy, not your grandma."

"He's got a point." James shrugged his shoulders. His grin was definitely not kissed away. In fact, it was now ten times bigger.

Fine, if they wanted a show, Will would give them a fucking show.

He grabbed James by the back of the head and fisted his fingers into James's hair. He pulled James down to his level and pressed their lips together. With his free hand, he grabbed James by the belt and pulled his body flush, until they were pressed crotch to crotch. He forced James's lips open and slid his tongue over the sharp ridge of James's teeth and into the warm cave of his mouth.

Will was fairly certain he hadn't taken an edible, but he felt high as hell. Was this really happening? He'd been expecting the heat. He'd been expecting the wet. He'd been expecting the swell of his dick. But he hadn't been expecting to feel James grow hard through his pants. He hadn't been expecting James to taste like berries and copper and minty toothpaste. And he certainly hadn't been expecting James to kiss him back, to grip his shirt so tightly it came untucked.

"Well, fuck," Andy said the moment Will pulled away. "Is it weird that I'm super turned on right now?"

Will stood there dazed, like he'd just run through a glass door.

Enrique put his arm around Andy. "Of course not. Incest is the best. And your brother's hot."

"So," Nandi said, totally immune to her fiancé's fucked-up sense of humor, "what's the verdict?"

Monika held her hands to her chest like she was praying, and her face grew redder and redder by the second until she exploded like a volcano. "It's true love."

Everyone cheered like they were at a basketball game. Everyone but Will and James, that is. They knew the truth. It was just pretend.

MONIKA HUNG UP THE PHONE. "Okay, they're ready for us."

Will could've used another moment to collect himself. But this wasn't a big deal. So what if he hadn't been photographed publicly in over a decade? No one was going to pay any attention to him, not with actual movie stars and models around. The big story was probably going to be Ryan's shaved head.

A steady hand settled on Will's back. "You okay?" James asked.

"Yeah, I'm good." Will wanted to puke.

Enrique and Monika led the charge across the narrow expanse of ground between the hotel doors and the waiting limos. Andy and Nandi came next, followed by Noel and Theo. Those six made up the first limo.

The camera flashes were blinding, but as Will suspected, the barrage of questions were not directed at him.

"Nandini, who are you wearing?"

"Enrique, is it true you're going on the honeymoon?"

"Ryan, what can you tell us about your new movie? Are you playing a war hero?"

Andy and his friends made it look easy. They smiled and glided through the press like they were being carried by a swift and delicate breeze. The models posed for photographs. Enrique signed autographs. Andy and Nandi looked lovingly at each other as if they were the only two people in the world. The only one who looked the way Will felt was Theo, who blinked furiously at the camera flashes and didn't know where to put his hands.

A man jumped in front of Will, and Will had to take a step back to avoid getting hit by the man's camera.

"William, what was it like seeing Derek again? Has your memory come back? What is your response to Sharron Moore saying you should be glad she threw wine on you and not acid?"

Will tried to walk around the man, but the mention of Will's name brought more reporters until there was a wall of press between him and the limo.

"What is your response to the article just released by *TMZ* that you were fired for physically abusing your students?"

What? Will's throat started to close.

"William, is it true that Michelle Liu wanted you, but your father convinced her to cast Ryan Ashbury instead?"

The camera flashes turned to white tracers across Will's vision, and his lungs constricted. He couldn't breathe. Why couldn't he breathe?

"William, is it true Robert is not your real father, that your mother had an affair with her massage therapist? Is that why he didn't want you in the movie?"

"William, what do you say to the accusations that you're a racist? Is that why you abuse your students?"

The questions kept coming, but Will could no longer differentiate them. It was too hot, and he couldn't breathe, and he couldn't make his legs move.

Strong arms came around him and pushed him forward, and a faraway voice—James's voice—said, "No comment," on repeat.

The voice was joined by another—Miles's voice. "Get the fuck out of the way, or I'm going to shove that fucking camera up your fucking dick."

The world went dark and cold, and a hand pushed Will's head between his knees. "Just breathe," James said. "There you go. You're okay. We're in the limo now. You're safe."

Was he having a panic attack? Pathetic. He should be used to this by now.

"What just happened?" Tiffany sounded unsure, and Tiffany never sounded unsure. "How can they just make up stuff like that? Will doesn't abuse his students. If anything, he's way too nice."

"Yeah, that wasn't normal," Ryan said.

Will lifted his head and stared at all the concerned faces. Well, concerned and pissed. Tiffany and Ryan were concerned. Miles was pissed. He couldn't see James, but he could feel his arms holding him up. As they approached the restaurant, James lowered the divider and spoke to the chauffeur.

"Hey, drive around for a bit," he said. "We haven't finished the champagne yet."

Will glanced at the wood paneled bar, where bottles of champagne poked out of buckets of ice.

"I'm alright. I just thought . . ." What had he thought? That ten years was long enough? That next to four models and three movie stars, he'd be invisible? That being a teacher made him safe? But it was worse than ever. Now they were dragging his students into it.

"Seriously, what the fuck was that?" Miles asked.

"I'm going to call Principal King as soon as we get there," Tiffany said. "We'll fix this."

Ryan squeezed his hands between his knees. "I think I might know what's going on, but I don't want to start any rumors."

"Here's what we're gonna do," James said. "Will and I are gonna get out a few blocks from the restaurant and walk. You four go through the front entrance and see if you can find a way to let us in the back. Ryan, maybe you can stay out front a little longer and sign some autographs, keep them distracted."

CHAPTER 32
JAMES

James pulled Ryan into a corner of the banquet room. "What do you know?"

He felt guilty leaving Will's side, but Will was in good hands with Miles and Tiffany. Well, Tiffany, at least. Miles was still mad as hell. Purple veins coiled down his forearms like rope as he clenched and unclenched his fists. Will, on the other hand, was fine, or so he claimed. But how could he be fine? Someone had just slandered the shit out of him.

It was calculated, too, timed perfectly with Will's first public appearance in ten years. And it was cruel. It made Will out to be a child abuser. Accusations like that didn't just go away, either. Even if you could disprove them, they still left a permanent stain.

Before pulling Ryan aside, James had typed Will's name into a Google search. There were two new articles, one in *Entertainment Weekly* and one in *TMZ*. *Entertainment Weekly* reported Will was set to co-star alongside his father and Derek, when his father, believing Will not up to the task, convinced the director to go with Ryan Ashbury instead. The story in *TMZ* was even worse. It cited someone "close to William" who wondered if his erratic temper and use of physical intimidation forced him to leave his teaching position early.

"Nothing for certain," Ryan said. "But the other day, when you guys were filming in the woods, Derek's manager, Tony, came back to the farm, and I overheard him talking to someone on the phone. I don't think he realized I was there. I didn't hear much, just Will's name and something about excessive force."

James nodded. This was all his fault, wasn't it? Anyone with half a brain could see through Robert's plan. He didn't just want Will to show off in front of an influential director. He wanted him to take over Derek's part. There was almost no chance that would happen, but the karaoke video must've made Tony nervous.

And maybe Tony wasn't totally off base. The video was divisive, certainly, but those that liked it really liked it. For the first few nights after the video was posted, James would sit on the corner of Will's bed and read all of the positive comments to him.

"@ForeverTwentyNine says you're hot AF when you sing. And @BroadwayBitch69 says you should play the Phantom in *The Phantom of the Opera*, and that comment has over two hundred likes."

"Ryan"—Robert stood ten feet away, holding the hand of a small child—"our esteemed flower girl, here, has a very important question to ask you."

Ryan smiled and waved at the little girl before turning back to James. "Sorry, I should probably go."

James's heart jumped in his chest. What if Tony had had the pen on him when he'd leaked those stories? Maybe this was what Robert was looking for, proof Tony was intentionally sabotaging Will. Maybe Tony had even put Sharron Moore up to the whole wine incident. James needed to get that pen back.

James grabbed a glass of champagne off a passing tray and took in the warmly lit banquet room for the first time.

There weren't any windows, which, for once, was a good thing. Crystal chandeliers hung over two long tables with high-backed upholstered chairs, and swaths of brown and gold textured fabrics hung from the walls. In the center of the room stood a life-sized swan carved out of ice, which Enrique was making alterations to with a butter knife.

And there was Will, sandwiched between Miles and Tiffany, right where James had left him, only now he had an empty glass dangling from his fingertips.

"KING ISN'T PICKING UP, but I left a bunch of messages," Tiffany was saying as James rejoined them. "We're going to fix this."

"It's fine." Will's eyes found James's, and he smiled. The color had returned to his cheeks, and he was talking again, even if every other word out of his mouth was *fine*.

"No, dude, it's not fine," Miles said, and James wished he could lock Miles in a room with Tony. It would be like a fox in a hen house. "That was fucked up. They can't do that. Someone's going to pay for this."

James agreed. Someone was going to pay for this. He just had to get that pen back.

Donna broke free from a huddle of Nandi's relatives and made her way over. Great, just what they needed.

"Miles, dear"—Donna placed a ring-clad hand on Miles's massive arm—"your devotion to William is appreciated. But threatening the paps never makes things better. You can't let them get you riled up like that. William is a big boy. He can handle himself."

No, he can't. If Will could handle himself, he wouldn't be melting into the walls with shame and resignation. He'd be fighting back.

"YOU DON'T HAVE to keep doing this," Will said the moment they were alone. Tiffany was in the bathroom, and Theo and Miles were in line for Enrique's ice luge. Enrique had somehow managed to carve a groove in the swan's neck without snapping it off, and now he was pouring shots of Cristal down it. "This isn't what you signed up for, and you don't need them—"

"Stop." James turned to face Will, and their eyes locked. "I'm not going anywhere."

"They won't stop—ever." Finally, there was a thread of anger in Will's voice. "They never stop. It's only a matter of time before they go after you and Theo."

James ran his thumb over Will's lips to shush him. "I don't care. I wanna be here with you. I wanna be seen with you. I don't care what anyone says. I'm proud of you, and I'm proud to be with you." Then, before Will could say *But you're not with me*, James kissed him.

It wasn't the hungry kiss from the hotel room. James didn't feel like he had to fight to keep his body solid, to keep from turning into a puddle on the floor. But the same burn was there. It radiated up the sides of his face and bloomed in his chest.

At first, Will didn't kiss him back. But then he did, just a little, his lips returning the pressure and parting slightly to let James inside. Will didn't take charge, not like he had in the hotel room, forcing James to either keep up or be consumed.

This time, his movements were minimal, just enough to give consent. His hand came up to rest on James's chest, and he let out a soft guttural groan at the back of his throat. *I'll follow your lead*, his body seemed to say, and it gave James ideas, filthy, obscene ideas.

A piece of lettuce struck James in the face. He turned, and there was Andy, smiling. "Stop making out and come over here. You have to try the ice luge."

James wiped his cheek and smiled down at Will, who still had his hand on James's chest. He leaned into it, forcing Will to hold him up. "Shall we?"

Will nodded, though he looked skeptical. "Okay."

James stood up straight, easing the pressure from Will's palm. He wanted his entire body on Will, wanted to feel him squirm and writhe in pleasure beneath him. But there were children present, including Theo, who was watching them with a big smile stretched across his face.

"Oh, great, here he goes again." Donna's mother was a silver-haired woman in her early eighties. "I still haven't recovered from the last time. Your father's wedding vows were twenty minutes long. I'm not kidding. It was insufferable." She topped off her champagne glass and then James's and Will's, too. "My offer still stands. If you want to emancipate and come live with me, you're more than welcome. You too, James."

James liked Will's grandmother. She reminded him of a sassy Angela Lansbury.

Robert tapped his glass to get everyone's attention and waited a full minute for the room to fall silent, including the waitstaff.

"Thank you all for coming. It's a remarkable thing when two families join as one, especially two families with such complimentary bone structures."

He paused, cuing obligatory laughter.

"Nandi, you are a striking woman, both inside and out. And the Chapman family is honored to call you daughter, wife, and sister." Robert smiled warmly at Nandi and then up into the chandelier, as if searching for the rest of his toast in the glowing crystals.

"I'm currently shooting a movie where I play a man dying of Alzheimer's, a man whose life is slipping away from him memory by memory, and it's forced me to reflect on my own life. I always assumed my legacy would be my filmography. I considered myself blessed because, unlike my character, who fades into obscurity with each lost memory, my life is preserved in celluloid and digital for generations to see, for Nandi and Andy to say, should they choose to have children, that's your grandpa." Robert took a moment to savor the image before continuing.

"William, I hope you'll forgive me for addressing the elephant in the room. But it's important I say this, not only to you, but to everyone here, so my words will be remembered. Ten years ago, our family suffered a publicity nightmare so big it would be pointless to describe it now. At the time, I remember thinking, ah, so this is my legacy. I will be remembered as William Chapman's father. My decades-long acting career will be relegated to a footnote in the margins of film history."

Every eye turned to look at Will, whose body grew more rigid with each passing second. James found Will's clammy hand under the table and squeezed. But Will didn't squeeze back.

"Most parents intuitively know that their legacy lives in their children. They think, I will die one day, but my kids will live on, and their kids after them. It's biological. We die, but our genes survive. Yet, for whatever reason, that thought never occurred to me." Robert lifted his glass of champagne, like his rambling toast might end there. But instead of drinking, he swirled the honey gold liquid, inhaled it like a drug, and then set it back down.

"I played a linguist once. This was many years ago, and the details have grown fuzzy now. But in my research for the role, I came across a very fascinating scientific paper. It described a group of missionaries, or maybe they were colonizers, I forget. But anyway, they found themselves marooned with a group of natives. In order to communicate and trade, they created a sort of pidgin, a combination of the two languages.

"And here's where the story gets interesting. According to linguists, the language they created didn't actually qualify as a language, even though they meticulously built it from the ground up. Think Esperanto. It didn't have proper syntax or grammatical structures, all the stuff that makes a language a language. But interestingly, their children, the children who grew up speaking the pidgin, miraculously transformed their parents' best academic efforts into a real language, a natural language. That's because a child's brain is primed for language acquisition. These children instinctively added all the necessary grammatical structures."

Robert stopped and looked down, as if his point had migrated from the crystal chandelier above him into the golden beads in his champagne.

"I've spent my entire life learning the craft of acting, finding ways to make Robert Chapman disappear and my characters come to life. But it's always been work. It's always been a product of choice after choice after choice. Nothing has ever come easily to me." A tear slid from Robert's eye. "But over the past few weeks, I've watched my son, William, do something I've never seen before, something I've only ever dreamed of. I've watched him effortlessly, organically, naturally, call it what you will, become consumed by his character. And, perhaps more importantly, I've watched him drag everyone in the scene with him, myself included.

"My own father never shared his acting process with me, but William has been watching me for years. Donna used to say I did my best work acting opposite William. When he was a baby, I'd carry him around on my chest, skin to skin, and we'd run scenes together. I was playing Macbeth in Central Park at the time, and William used to fall asleep to the cadence of tomorrow and tomorrow and tomorrow. And as soon as he could talk, we'd run lines together. Before Meryl famously played Charlotte Reid, William occupied the role. Before there was Julia and Angelina, before there was Anthony and Diane, before there was Glenn and Helen, there was William."

Will's hand was still ice in James's, but, like a coma patient regaining consciousness, he began to squeeze back.

"Just like those children who created an actual language out of their parents' best academic attempts, William has turned a lifetime of watching me labor over the craft of acting into an instinct, an artform. And finally, I get it, what every parent seems to figure out naturally. My legacy isn't my career. It's my family. It's my son, Andy, with his effortless charm and charisma, not to mention his big, generous heart. It's William, who is quite possibly the most versatile, naturalistic actor of his generation. It's the time we got to spend together and the lessons we learned along the way."

Will's hand was now cutting off James's circulation, but James didn't pull away. He wanted Will to fight back, even if Will was fighting him.

"We all die." Robert paused to let his words sink in. "And that's scary. But it doesn't need to be. We can take comfort in knowing we're just one link in a long chain that gets stronger and stronger with each generation. We are not our accomplishments. Those are finite. They are shelved and forgotten. We are our families. We are the time we spend with each other.

"In two days, Andy and Nandi will start a new act in the same movie we're filming right now, a movie that started production long before they were born and will continue long after they die. Their storylines will intertwine, and the chains that bind us will grow stronger and stronger until the last syllable of recorded time."

Robert Chapman didn't drink his champagne. He didn't say, "Here's to love," or "May you have a long and happy marriage," and no one knew what to do. Was the toast over?

Robert could've achieved a similar reaction by performing a tender saxophone solo in the nude.

The awkward silence might have gone on indefinitely had Enrique not lifted his glass and cried, "And all our yesterdays have lighted fools the way to dusty death."

James didn't know what that meant, but it seemed to do the trick. Glasses were raised, emptied, and promptly refilled.

CHAPTER 33
WILL

James had kissed him. He'd kissed him. And no one had put him up to it either. He'd just done it.

James lifted his arm from around Will's shoulder and snatched two glasses of champagne from a passing tray. Will felt untethered without James's arm holding him down, like a hot air balloon after its sandbags have been cut. James handed him one of the glasses and put his arm back in place.

Will's head was a tangle of emotions. It was like he felt everything and nothing all at once, like his emotions were heightened, and yet so opposing they balanced, his dreams and nightmares staring eye to eye on a level teeter-totter. He'd waited his whole life for his father to be proud of him. And now he was. Yet, inexplicably, it was his father who'd slammed the door on his dreams.

Will lifted the glass of champagne to his lips, the same lips James had kissed unprompted, and for a moment it didn't matter. The past was just backstory.

Will had enough privilege, oceans of it compared to his students, to indulge in hopelessness for the rest of his life if he wanted to. But he had enough perspective to see it for what it was, a wasted luxury. James had kissed him, and the rest could wait.

It was going to be okay. Tiffany was deep in conversation with a runway model, and she was drunker than Will had seen her in ages. Miles and Theo were doing wall sits while they waited in line for the bathroom. And James had kissed him.

Maybe it was just for show. Maybe later he'd say, "How about that time you were freaking out and I kissed you in front of your entire family? That was pretty badass, right? That'll fool 'em." But maybe it wasn't. Maybe James had wanted to kiss him.

"James, mind if I borrow my brother for a sec?" Andy asked.

Will followed Andy into the hallway outside the banquet room and leaned against the wall. Andy didn't say anything, so Will filled the silence. "I can't believe you're getting married in two days."

"I know." Andy smiled, and it was a wonder his freckles didn't come rolling down his laugh lines. "Is Dad okay? Is he having a midlife crisis or something?"

The air caught in Will's lungs. Did Andy suspect? "Or something." Will took a breath and looked up at his little brother. Will had been sixteen when Andy first started growing taller than him. "I'm sorry he did that."

"Whatever, it's fine." Andy ran a hand down his freckled face and wiped off his smile. "How are you doing?"

"I'm fine." Andy gave him that look, that *bullshit* look, so Will added, "Or I will be, anyway."

"I'm sorry, Will. I feel like this is all my fault. I keep dragging you out and this shit keeps happening."

Will forced a smile. "It's not your fault. It's my fault. I did this to myself. And it's fine. I'm used to it."

"Are you still coming out to the club?" Andy flashed Will his *please* face, the one Will had helped him perfect twenty years ago when they'd wanted their dad to install a slide in the pool.

How could Will say no to that? "Yeah, for a little bit."

LOVE ON THE D-LIST

THE NIGHTCLUB WAS LOUD, packed, and perfect. Finally, Will was invisible. Shouts over the music filtered through the crowd, but not about him. He was the guy standing between Andy Chapman and Enrique Navarro, the guy holding Nandini Dalal's drink.

Enrique opened his palm and revealed an assortment of colored pills, like a fistful of Lucky Charms. "I scored us some Molly."

"Boys"—Tiffany grabbed Will and James by the wrists and steered them away from the drugs—"it's time to dance."

James looked down at Tiffany's hand on his arm. "I don't dance. But I'll watch."

"Come on, Will and I are teachers. We'll teach you."

"Oh, I *can* dance," James said, pulling his arm away. "I just don't."

"Fine, we'll just talk about you behind your back, then."

"Okay, but just so you know, I'm an excellent lip reader."

It had been ages since Will had danced outside his classroom. Could he even still do it if there weren't freeze breaks? The crowd made room for them, and it was just what Will needed. He'd forgotten how sobering it was to move his body, to sweat and jump, to not think about anything other than the beat.

"Something's different about you." Tiffany twirled around, and the pink ruff of her dress lifted into the air.

"What do you mean?" There was nothing different about Will. He was the same walking disaster as always.

"I don't know. I haven't figured it out yet. Maybe less defeated." She danced in place as she looked at Will with growing curiosity. "Or less like a victim, maybe, if that makes any sense."

"It doesn't." Will wiped the sweat from his brow. "I'm pretty sure I'm still the poster child for the world's biggest loser. I'm probably going to have to change my name and move to Antarctica."

Tiffany draped her arms around Will's neck and rested her head on his shoulder. At least someone was shorter than him.

"See, that's what I'm talking about. You're already coming up with contingency plans."

"I was joking."

"And joking about them." Tiffany lifted her head and met Will's gaze. "That's not like you. Normally, you sulk for a week and then pretend nothing happened."

"You're drunk."

"Yeah, and you're in love."

Will leaned in and whispered, "Did you take some Molly when I wasn't looking?"

"No, I just figured it out. It's James. That's what's different." Tiffany turned and backed up against Will, her ass pressing into his crotch. "You've never had a real boyfriend before. It suits you."

"I don't have a real boyfriend now. This is all fake, remember?" They sank to the ground, going low, low, low.

"Then why has he been staring at you this whole time? He likes you, Will. It's obvious to everyone but you."

"I know he likes me. We're friends. Friends like each other."

"Trust me"—Tiffany removed her ass from Will's crotch—"he doesn't just like you like a friend."

Will wanted to believe her. And he was almost drunk enough to let himself. But ultimately, it didn't matter. Even if James did like him, it wasn't right to force him and Theo to keep Will company at the bottom of the barrel. Theo was too young for that, only one year younger than Will had been when his life imploded. And it did things to you, being hated by everyone. Maybe James could take it, but Will would never do that to Theo.

Will knew what he had to do. After the wedding, he'd thank James for his help and friendship and go back to the city. They wouldn't let him keep filming the movie now anyway.

But Will had options. He would just have to swallow his pride and ask his parents for money. Maybe he could become a doctor or get a PhD in something impossible, like chemical engineering. That would kill a lot of time, right? Maybe he could get several PhDs and try to set some kind of record.

"You look thirsty." James offered Will his beer.

Will pushed the bottle away. "I think I'm done drinking for the night."

James nodded and handed Will a glass of water instead. "I know I shouldn't be surprised, since you're basically good at everything you do, but you're a really good dancer."

Will rolled his eyes. He wished he could have this. He wished he deserved it. But he couldn't. And he didn't. He'd made his bed a long time ago, and it was a single bed.

Will slumped into the black sofa and looked around for Miles. He spotted his broad back and curly hair across the VIP balcony. He couldn't see the guy hidden beneath him, but he was sure he was there.

James sat down beside Will. "You hungry? They've got tapas here."

Will closed his eyes and wished he was sitting in a dive bar in rural Vermont with his forehead pressed against James's. "I'm okay."

James set his beer down. "Come on, let's go home. You've done your duty for the night."

Will opened his eyes. "I can't. Miles and Tiffany are having a good time, and—"

"Good, I wasn't gonna invite them." James winked, and Will's skin started to burn.

"Why? Are you not having a good time?"

James stood. "Wait here. I'll go make our excuses. The hotel's not far. The limo can drive us home and be back in plenty of time to pick up the others."

CHAPTER 34
JAMES

It was eerily quiet inside the limo after the thrum of the nightclub, and it took James's pulse a while to settle back down to a comfortable pace. He wished he could call Esther and ask her if these feelings were normal. Maybe he was having some sort of midlife crisis. Maybe Enrique had spiked his drink.

James understood wanting to fuck Will. Will was hot, and James was horny. But it wasn't just that. He also wanted to snuggle up with him and watch a movie. He wanted to confess all his sins and let Will tell him it wasn't his fault. He wanted to sit with Will on the front porch in the morning and drink coffee. He wanted to go on a long road trip with him and take turns reading cheesy romance novels from the passenger's seat. He wanted to introduce Will to Esther and his other friends. Worst of all, he wanted to protect Will, to save him from every abuse, including all the obscene things James, himself, wanted to do to him. What was James supposed to do with that?

It had never been like this with Brice or the others. Sure, James had enjoyed spending time with them, but he'd always been equally content on his own. That wasn't the case with Will. When Will was gone, even just to go take a shower, James missed him. For the past few weeks, they'd been spending practically all day, every day together, and it still wasn't enough. James always wanted more.

"Why are you staring at me?" Will asked. "Do I have glitter on my face?"

James didn't realize he was staring. "I can't help myself, I guess." Great, now he was being honest. "Here, I'll put some music on." Picking a playlist would be the perfect distraction.

Of course, that turned out to be impossible. James had to lean over Will to get the AUX cord. He could smell the sweat on Will's skin, musky and sweet, and he could feel the heat radiating off Will's body, a body that was tight and hard and right there.

He chose one of Theo's obscure playlists at random and then glanced out the window. Shit, the hotel was only a few blocks away.

James lowered the divider. "Hey, change of plans. Can you drive us somewhere outside the city, somewhere where we can see the stars?" James closed the divider. "Is that okay?"

Will shrugged. "Sure. I assume you want your nightly bowl in the country?"

"Yeah, something like that." James helped himself to some of the leftover champagne. Why was he so nervous? He was never nervous with boys. But Will wasn't a boy. He was Will. "About the kiss, I—"

"It's fine." Will waved his hand dismissively. "I think you really sold it. But I meant what I said earlier. You don't need to keep doing this. I get that you're all confident and self-assured and don't care what others think about you, but Theo is only eighteen. Kids are fragile, especially teenagers. What's stopping them from writing a story about how I molest my boyfriend's teenage son while he's at work?"

"No." James shook his head.

"No, what?"

James wasn't sure. But no. Just no. This wasn't Will's fault. It was James's. If he hadn't released the karaoke video, none of this would've happened. If he hadn't invited Esther to Andy's bachelor party... He couldn't think about that now.

"No, I didn't kiss you because I thought people were watching. I kissed you because I wanted to, because I meant what I said. I don't care about the tabloids."

"But Theo—"

"Theo is having the time of his life, and it's all because of you."

A tear threatened to slide from Will's eye. "But it'll get worse. It always gets worse."

James reached up and cupped Will's face. "Not this time. This time, it's gonna get better. I promise." And then, because he couldn't bear to see Will cry, he kissed him again. And this time, Will couldn't doubt James's intentions. This time, they were alone. There was no one to put on a show for. This time, the kiss was for them.

As soon as they were back in Vermont, James was going to get his pen recorder back and expose Tony for the snake he was. He was going to make this right if it was the last thing he did.

James kept his lips on Will's, salty and sweet with alcohol. Like before, Will acquiesced. His body twisted to meet James's, and his head tilted back. James broke the kiss, but only barely, just enough to slide his mouth past Will's chin and kiss the stubbled skin on his neck. Will let out a sigh that turned into a purr.

James slid his tongue from the hollow below Will's jaw up to the soft cushion of his earlobe. He blew a steady stream of air over the trail of his saliva, and Will shivered.

James breathed hot air into Will's ear. "You're amazing," he said, and Will's purr became a growl.

For a moment, James forgot to be gentle. He grabbed Will's leg and yanked it across his lap so they were facing each other. But Will was off balance with one leg on the floor and the other on the seat.

James liked having Will at his mercy. He pushed him down onto the leather seat and towered over him. He pushed Will's legs open wider with his knees and slid between them. Their bodies pressed together, and James's erection strained painfully against the confines of his pants.

Will's face took on the colorful shades of the outside world—

streetlights, brake lights, and neon signs. Light and shadow danced across his skin, but one thing remained constant, his dark eyes following James's every move.

His lips looked fuller than before. Swollen. James kissed them and bit them softly. He pushed into Will, chest to chest. His dick ached inside his pants, and he pressed it against Will's ass, as if he hoped he could pierce through the fabric.

When James couldn't take it any longer, he sat up. "Take your shirt off."

Will bit his lip and shook his head, his dark hair swishing across the leather seat. "No, you do it." Then he smiled so brightly, James felt like his chest might explode.

Fine, if that's how Will wanted to play this. James started with the top button, careful not to rip the shirt. After all, it cost more than he made in a month. Button after button, James revealed fresh tracks of smooth skin. When he was finally done, he pushed the fabric aside and bent to lick the small indent at Will's sternum, the bit of bone between his sculpted pecs.

"Remind me to write Miles a thank you note for all this. Your body is incredible." James teased Will's taut little nipples with his teeth. The dark rings around them were small, barely the size of a penny.

"You talk a lot." Will huffed out a breath, and it ruffled the hair on James's forehead.

James lifted his head and found Will smiling at him again, a mischievous glint in his eye. Will reached out and trailed a finger across James's mustache, like he'd done at the beginning of the summer. But this time, James didn't freeze in surprise. This time, he tried to kiss Will's finger.

Will attempted to pull his finger away, but James grabbed it before he could. Then he took Will's finger into his mouth and hummed softly as his lips slid over each knuckle.

"Oh, Jesus." Will closed his eyes and let his head fall back onto the leather seat.

James gave equal attention to each of Will's fingers as he fumbled to unbuckle Will's belt with his other hand. Once the belt was off, James bit the fleshy part of Will's palm at the base of his thumb. He pushed Will's hands and arms up over his head and forced his torso to stretch and lengthen until his ribs showed and his abs relaxed.

James snaked a hand under the small of Will's back, and Will arched in response without any prompting so James could slide his pants off. James didn't get very far, though. The moment he saw the pre-cum soaking through Will's tight black briefs, he stopped and left Will's pants bunched around his knees. He ducked his head inside and hooked Will's legs over his shoulders like the yoke of a saddle.

He touched the wet spot on Will's briefs with his finger and brought it to his nose. Will smelled sweet, like pineapple. James licked his fingertip, and it was salty and bitter.

He pulled the damp fabric over Will's erection, and Will's dick sprang forth. A fresh pearl of pre-cum glistened on the tip. James already knew Will was packing from putting him to bed at the beginning of the summer. But his cock looked even bigger out of the confines of his underwear, the skin stretched as tight as a drum.

He wasn't bigger than James, although it was close. Will certainly looked bigger, though. That dick belonged on a lumberjack, not a scrappy little kindergarten teacher. Either way, James couldn't wait to swallow every inch of it.

James had seen Will act. He'd seen the way Will didn't just deliver his lines and wait for his next turn. He reacted. He played off the other characters' words and actions with pinpoint precision and authenticity. And apparently, his responsiveness carried over to the bedroom, too.

Every touch and caress from James elicited a noise or a movement from Will. Just the brush of James's lips across the glistening slit of Will's cock made Will shudder. The pressure of James's hand on Will's chest made him groan.

James smiled at the effect he was having on Will and lapped up the bead of pre-cum. When he took Will to the back of his throat, Will gasped in pleasure, and his thighs squeezed James's shoulders like a vice.

"Fuck, you've done this before, haven't you?" Will's hands fisted into James's hair, though he didn't try to take control. He let his hands rise and fall with James's bobbing head, let his fingers run through James's hair and massage his scalp.

James wasn't sure how long he sucked Will off for, but not nearly long enough. He could tell Will was close, and he couldn't wait to taste all of him, to swallow every last drop. But then the little shit pulled James's head away. James resisted, and his lips made an obscene smacking sound as they left Will's glistening cock.

"Too close," Will said, breathless.

James smiled up at him, and he ran his stubbled chin over the pale white skin of Will's inner thigh, not breaking eye contact. "Can I fuck you?"

Will flashed him a wry smile. "I don't know. Can you?"

James bit Will's leg, and Will yelped.

"Let me rephrase that. May I fuck you?"

"Hmm, let me think about it." Will rolled back and lifted his legs over James's head, offering himself up to James. Or so James thought before Will pulled his pants the rest of the way off and set his legs down on the other side of James.

Will lay back and placed his hands behind his head. "How about you strip for me, and then I'll let you know?"

What a little shit. Fine. It was only fair, right?

James stood, and his head and back pressed against the roof of the limo. James knew how to strip—he'd made a lot of money stripping—but he was far too revved up to draw this out. He'd been wanting to do this for weeks, and here Will was, naked and beautiful, and his, all his. James couldn't wait to be inside Will, to make him moan, to prove to him there was absolutely nothing fake about the way James felt.

James shuffled out of his jacket and tugged off his sweater and undershirt. He kicked off his shoes, but left his socks on. Who had time to worry about socks? He sat down to take off his pants and figured he might as well take his underwear off, too, while he was at it. Screw suspense. James just needed to feel Will's skin against his own.

"Jesus, you're such a stereotypical guy. You call that a striptease?" Will's smirk was mocking, but his hands betrayed him. One was stroking himself and the other was between his legs, his fingers massaging his entrance.

James stood, and Will rocked his head from side to side, making a show of examining the merchandise, which was bone hard and standing at attention.

"I don't know. It looks pretty big. Do you think it'll fit?" Will pulled the hand from between his legs and flipped over onto his stomach. He rested his chin in his palms and kicked his legs up behind him, like he was watching a movie on the floor.

Will's ass was a work of art. It was not a bubble butt. It was too hard for that. But it was round and perky, smooth and unblemished, and James just wanted to bite into it like it was an apple.

"I think there's only one way to find out."

Lights from the passing cars flickered across Will's perfect ass and the taut muscles of his upper back. They danced over the two little dimples where his spine gave way to his hips. James wished he could take a picture, not that it was necessary. There was no way this image—Will ass up on the leather seat, legs kicking, head turned over his shoulder to give James a taunting smirk—would ever leave James's mind.

James didn't remember stepping closer, but there he was, hovering over Will. He wanted to push Will's head into the seat and take him, enough with the games already. But he held back, determined to take his time, to savor this.

A rumble sounded at the back of James's throat, and he lowered himself onto Will's naked body. He let his dick slot into the crease between Will's clenched ass cheeks, parting the skin in a gentle thrust that sent a wave of pleasure up James's body. He lowered his arms so his chest pressed against Will's back, where the skin was as hot as a fever.

"Who knew you were such a cocktease?" James said, mouthing the nape of Will's neck.

"I'm not a cocktease. I'm just being realistic. Big cock. Small hole. You do the math."

"Trust me, it's gonna fit." James would make it fit.

He sat up and snaked his arm under Will's stomach so he could lift his ass into the air. "I hope you like getting your ass eaten, because it's happening."

Will didn't reply verbally, but he dropped his head from his hands so his fingers could grip the edge of the minibar. Then he let out a soft moan.

James buried his face in Will's crack and spread him open, running his tongue around Will's hole several times before diving in.

"Okay, yeah, you might be right. It might fit. Let's find out, like, now. Like, right fucking now." Will's words came out more air than sound.

"Flip back over. I wanna see your face when I make you come."

Will did as he was told, but instead of lying down, he sat up and rested his head against the window. He set his feet on the opposite seat and spread his legs. James had never been so horned up in his life.

He fished a condom and some lube from his jacket pocket. "Oh, and remind me to write Miles a thank you note for these, too."

The limo pulled off the interstate, and James had to steady himself with a hand on the roof to keep from falling over. *Shit, how much time did they have?* He wouldn't need much, and judging by the way Will kept pulling his hand away from his twitching cock, he was close, too.

James lifted Will's leg like it was a gate and shuffled inside. He got his fingers slick with lube and slid one inside Will, where the skin was as smooth as velvet.

Will's back arched, and he let out a puff of air. He lifted his hand from the seat and cupped James's chin. "Just give me the real thing."

Will was so tight James could hardly get his finger out. There was no way Will was ready for the real thing. James went for two fingers, but Will caught him by the wrist.

"James."

That was all Will said, just James's name. But he said it like James was in trouble, like he was a naughty little boy, and it made James's temperature rise. It made him want to rebel. Maybe that had been the point.

James pulled his hand free and rolled on the condom. He coated himself in lube and almost came from his own touch. Will's tight little hole was right there. He inched forward and rose so his knees were off the ground. He had one hand on the seat for balance and one gripping his cock.

He pressed against Will's entrance, firm and steady, and the tip disappeared as Will's skin stretched around it. James pressed harder, but slowed when Will closed his eyes and started to breathe heavily. He waited for Will's breath to grow steady again and then pushed in farther. Damn, he was tight. Holy shit.

Will's head lolled back against the window and made a loud thud. The sound of it, both hard and soft, made James want to rail into him. He wanted to hear that sound over and over again as he fucked Will into oblivion. But he went slowly. He was a gentleman, after all.

Or at least he was until Will's hands gripped his ass and pulled him all the way inside, like he was sheathing a sword. James had to close his eyes to keep from coming. It was so soft and warm inside Will, and there was this pressure all around James, steady and strong.

"Holy shit, you're big," Will said, and there it was again, the sound of Will's thick black hair thudding against the window. James was already all the way inside, but he kept pushing, lifting Will up off the seat.

He pulled out slowly, and then thrust back in. Holy shit. This wasn't going to last long.

Will must have realized this, too, because he said, "I'm sorry, but I'm about to come. You have less than two minutes to show me what you've got. And you better not be gentle."

Then, as if to drive his point home, Will's dick lifted a full inch off his stomach without him even touching it, like it was doing sit-ups.

The caretaker in James wanted to tell Will to relax and take it slow, but the animal in him just wanted to fuck, and so that's what he did. He fucked Will hard, harder than he'd ever fucked anyone before. He fucked Will until Will's toes curled. He fucked Will until he got the sound he wanted, the sound of Will's head thudding against the window. He fucked Will until the music faded and there was nothing left but that thud, thud, thud.

Will let out a low moan, followed by an, "Oh, fuck," and then his ass clenched around James's dick and thick white ribbons squirted from his rigid cock. The first spurt hit his chin and dribbled into the hollow at the base of his neck. The next spurt missed his torso completely and hit James's arm.

Sweat dripped from James's face. He probably should've slowed down and let Will have his moment, but he couldn't stop, not now, not when he was this close.

He pounded Will until every last drop was milked from Will's body. James locked eyes with Will, and that was all it took. Every muscle convulsed like he'd touched an electric fence, and then his climax overpowered him. Pleasure shot through his body like fireworks. But he didn't slow his rhythm. He didn't let his tired arm buckle. He plowed into Will until he, too, was spent, until the condom was full and the world was nothing but a blissed-out, throbbing numbness.

He collapsed onto Will's hard, sticky body and buried his face in Will's neck, letting Will's dark hair fall over his face like a curtain.

Neither of them spoke for a long time, but the moment James's brain came back online, he lifted his head and stared down at Will. Will's expression was unreadable, but James could tell he was already starting to overthink everything, so he said, "Just for the record, that wasn't fake sex. That was real sex. And it was really fucking hot."

Will laughed, and James kissed him again, long and slow and deep.

CHAPTER 35
WILL

Will pried his eyes open when it became clear the knocking wasn't going away. "Can you go see what they want?" he asked James.

James didn't answer, so Will flung his arm behind him, hoping to smack James across the face. He hit cold sheets instead. Will rolled over and stared across the wide, empty expanse. Had he dreamt the whole thing?

"Hold on." He got out of bed and pulled on one of the white robes from the bathroom.

When he opened the door, Miles barged into the room. "Where is he? I'm going to kick his ass. Doesn't he know you're a married man?"

Tiffany followed Miles into the room. "Good morning, sunshine. Where's James?"

"How should I know?" Will closed the door and headed for the coffee maker. "How was the rest of the night?"

Miles bent to examine the sheets for signs of coitus. "Fuck that. What happened after you left? Did you use the condoms and lube I gave James?"

"It doesn't matter." Will tightened his robe and ran his tongue across his teeth. He could still taste the joint he and James had shared in the shower at three in the morning.

Tiffany picked up and studied the empty bottle of diamond-infused vodka from the night before. "Did he go sleep in Theo's room?"

"I don't know. He was here when I fell asleep." Will gave up on the coffee and crawled back into bed.

"When you fell asleep naked and covered in jizz, right?"

Will rolled his eyes, but he told them everything. Well, almost everything. He refused to indulge Miles's request to sketch an accurate picture of James's dick like it was on *America's Most Wanted*. And he didn't tell them how unbelievable James felt inside him, how the sweat fell from his brow, and how his green eyes blazed with this animal intensity. Oh, and his rhythm. James fucked like a sweaty drummer in some punk band, fast and hard and relentless.

"I knew this would happen," Will said. "Sex ruins everything."

"Why? Was it bad sex?" Miles hopped off the bed and headed for the bathroom.

No, it had been amazing sex, maybe too amazing. Maybe it had been so amazing James thought Will hooked up all the time, that he really was the fuckboy Derek had accused him of being. "I don't think so. It doesn't matter, though. It was never going to last anyway."

"His toothbrush is still here," Miles said.

Tiffany lay next to Will on the bed. "Why do you say that? He's obviously into you, and he's not another Derek. He's not too worried about his own image to admit he likes you."

"He could be, and that was never Derek's problem."

Tiffany called bullshit with her eyes. "If you say so."

"It doesn't matter. And it's for the best. It was only a matter of time before the paps started in on Theo. The kid has no filter. They'd have a fucking field day with him. James was right to run away."

Miles leapt onto the mattress and sent Will and Tiffany bouncing into the air. "I don't think he ran away," Miles said. "His suitcase is still here. His toothbrush, too. He probably just went to buy more condoms."

"Why are you two even here?" It was the question Will should've asked the moment they barged into his room. Miles never woke up before ten, not if he could avoid it.

"Okay." Tiffany exhaled, and Will knew he wasn't going to like this. "We found out something last night. After you left, Ryan got really drunk and let it slip that it was Derek who leaked those stories about you."

"Don't be ridiculous. Derek would never do that."

Miles and Tiffany exchanged looks, like they'd been expecting Will to say that. "Maybe not," Miles said, "but Tony sure as hell would."

"Ryan thinks Tony saw your karaoke video and assumed you were going after Derek's part," Tiffany said.

"What? That's ridiculous. I'm not trying to take Derek's part. I had no idea anyone was even filming. And it doesn't have that many views. Derek gets more views than that standing in line at Starbucks."

"Yeah, but after your dad's little speech last—"

"No." Will shook his head. This was absurd. "My dad is not trying to replace Derek with me. If he wanted me in the movie, I'd be in the movie." Will hopped out of bed and looked around for his pants. "Where's my phone?"

"Why?" Tiffany's eyes darted over to the arm of the sofa, where Will's phone sat charging. James must have plugged it in for him before running away. Or maybe Miles was right. Maybe James really was just getting more condoms.

Will yanked the cord out and tossed it aside. "Because I'm going to call Derek and tell him he needs to fire that asshole."

Tiffany sat up in bed. "Maybe you should wait a minute and think this through."

No, if Will thought this through, he wouldn't call. It was now or never.

Derek answered, and his deep, cool voice was the antithesis of the screaming tea kettle in Will's brain. "So, you did save my number. Guess where I am right now?"

Will felt his temperature drop, which wasn't good. He needed his anger. Without it, he had nothing. "I don't know. Where are you?"

"I'm up on the mountain, riding. It's beautiful up here. There's all this fog. I feel like I'm King Arthur riding through the mists of Avalon."

Jesus, how was Will supposed to yell at Derek when he was being all tranquil and reverent? "Okay, I don't want to disturb you. I was just wondering if you saw the new articles about me."

There was a beat of silence, and Will wasn't sure if the huff he heard came from Derek or his horse. "I did. I'm so sorry, Will."

Okay, time to rip off the band-aid while there was still enough rage left inside him to overpower his good sense. "Did Tony leak those stories?"

"What?" Derek tried to sound surprised, but he really wasn't a very good actor. "Why would Tony do that?"

"That's what I want to know. You know I'm not trying to take your part from you, right? I didn't even want to do this in the first place."

"I know that." Derek tried to hide the defensiveness in his tone, but it was still there. "I'm glad you're doing it. I like seeing you every day."

"Yeah, and what about Tony? Does he know that?"

"I'll talk to him, okay?"

He'll talk to him? Was that supposed to be comforting? Tony had just fucking destroyed both of Will's careers, and Derek was going to talk to him?

Will gripped his phone tighter to keep himself from throwing it at the wall. "And what if he admits it was him? What will you do then?"

"I know you don't like Tony. But he's like family to me. He's been my manager since I was sixteen years old."

"Yeah, and did he run his hand up your leg and tell you how pretty you are?" Will could tell by the way Tiffany's eyes bulged that he'd gone too far, but he didn't care.

"What's that supposed to mean?"

"It means he's in love with you." Will switched the phone to his other ear, hoping it was less sweaty.

"Yeah, he does love me, but not like that."

"Why, because you're old enough to grow a beard or because you're straight? You think that matters? You think being straight stops guys from falling in love with you? It doesn't. In fact, a lot of guys get off on that shit."

"Will, I promise you, it's not like that." Even though his voice was as deep and melodic as ever, Will could tell Derek was getting flustered. "And you of all people should know that no one is a hundred percent anything, straight or gay."

At that, Miles did a double take and started pantomiming giving a blowjob.

"Why should I, of all people, know that?" Jesus, he was letting Derek distract him.

"I kissed a guy once," Derek said, "and not for a movie either."

Jesus, why was Derek telling him this? Was he trying to make Will jealous? "So what? You want a medal?"

"You're so dense sometimes, you know that?"

That was it. Fuck this. "I have to go, Derek. I'll see you at the wedding." Will hung up the phone before Derek could respond. And then, for good measure, he shut his phone off.

No one said anything for a long time, and then Will's stomach grumbled. "My dad's paying. Let's order some fucking lobster and mimosas."

CHAPTER 36
JAMES

On his way to buy coffee and donuts—a surprise for Will—James stopped to check in on Theo.

"You're not gonna believe what I discovered last night," Theo said, sitting up in bed. "Donna was giving me voice lessons, and apparently, I really do have a tendency to sing behind the beat, just like Will said, but it's not because I don't have rhythm. It's because I don't trust myself. I'm holding all of my shorter notes too long because I'm constantly checking to make sure I'm hitting all the right pitches, which is throwing everything—"

"That's great, bud, but I just—"

"I'm getting to the good part, chill."

James glanced at the clock. It was almost nine, and he wanted to get back before Will woke up. "Go on."

Theo was like a riptide. The only hope for survival was to go with the flow and try to angle your way out slowly.

Theo grabbed his glasses off the nightstand. "Okay, as I was saying, Donna was giving me voice lessons, but then she passed out, which is not surprising. She drank a lot at dinner and then another whole bottle at the hotel. I think we might need to have an intervention for Donna and Will.

"Anyway, someone was blowing up her phone big time, and I was worried. I was like, what if it's about Will? What if there's another story? So I looked. Her phone was locked, but she told me the passcode a couple weeks ago when she wanted me to download Soundcloud so she could listen to my music. And I remembered it. I'm clearly a genius. And guess who she was texting all night?"

James was not in the mood to play guessing games, and Theo must've realized that because he didn't give his usual six beats of wait time.

"Derek's manager, Tony. She accused him of leaking those stories about Will and said if he pulled anything like that again, she'd fire Derek."

Donna knew? Was she in on Robert's plan?

"And that's not all." Theo reached over and grabbed his phone off the nightstand. "Check out the video Tony sent her in response."

Theo opened his photos app and clicked on the most recent video.

"I thought about forwarding the message to myself, but then I got scared, thinking Donna might be able to trace it, so I just took a video with my phone. The quality isn't the greatest, but it's really about the audio anyway. And I know what you're thinking, but don't worry, I didn't open any of the new messages, even though I really wanted to. And they were right there. But they were all from Michelle and Robert, so I figured they were probably just boring stuff about the movie. Still, you should be proud of me."

James wanted to point out that only half spying on someone, someone who'd only ever done nice things for Theo, was not something to be proud of. But he was too taken aback by what he saw to speak.

The video was of a fancy hotel hallway, and when James looked at the time stamp from ten years earlier, the hairs on his arms stood on end. Was this what he thought it was? Was this the missing security footage from the night of the Golden Globes?

He heard Will's voice, only not. It was slightly higher in pitch, and there was a frenetic energy James had never heard in Will's tone before.

"You fucked my mother? No, you're just making this up because you're mad I won. Is this some kind of sick joke?"

Derek's voice could be heard next, deep and resonant. "I ended it months ago. And it didn't mean anything. You have to understand. I had her poster on my wall growing up. I used to beat off to her like twice a—"

"Shut up. You're talking about my fucking mother. How could you do that and then kiss me?"

The video ended and started again. James watched it seven times before pulling his eyes from the screen. "Holy shit."

Theo nodded, wide eyed. "I know, right?"

HALF AN HOUR LATER, James stepped into Robert Chapman's palatial suite.

"Was it you? Did you sell William out to your little friend in the fishnets?" Robert asked. Somehow, his room was even nicer than theirs. It was a whole friggin' apartment.

"I would never do that."

"Except you already did."

After watching Robert embody his father, it was hard not to recoil at his sharp words. Of course, if he'd been James's real father, he'd have struck with his fists along with his words.

But James was not a little boy anymore, and he didn't need to put up with this shit, especially from a man who'd sidelined his own son for ten years because he was afraid Will's reputation would spoil his chances to win an Oscar.

James strode over to the sitting area and made himself comfortable on the small loveseat. "Did you know Donna and Derek were having an affair?"

There was no denying Robert Chapman was a great actor, but even he couldn't have pulled off the look of genuine shock that froze his features and dilated his pupils unless he was truly surprised.

"What?"

"Yes, ten years ago. Be straight with me. What's really going on with Tony? Is he blackmailing Donna? Is he blackmailing you? Is that why you threw Will over for Derek and Ryan?"

Robert didn't speak, and James recognized the way the old man's eyebrows pinched in concentration. Will's eyebrows did the same thing.

"Are you sure?" Robert asked a minute later. "How did you come by this information?"

James couldn't think of a lie fast enough, so he told the truth. Maybe if he was straight with Robert, Robert would be straight with him.

"Theo broke into Donna's phone last night and opened a text Tony sent her. Tony leaked those stories about Will, not me. Donna must've figured it out because she threatened to fire Derek if Tony pulled anything like that again. His response was to send her this video."

James took his phone from his pocket and pulled up the video.

Just like James, Robert watched the video several times before speaking. "And this was all he sent?"

"As far as I know. Why? Do you think there's more?"

"Oh, I know there's more."

Robert shuffled over to the window overlooking the Montreal skyline and didn't move from that spot for several minutes, leaving James to stare awkwardly around the opulent suite. Then he spun around with surprising agility, especially for a man in poor health.

"Isn't there some kind of spyware you can install on Tony's phone? You know, like they did with Brittany, something that will allow you to read all of his messages and open all of his files? I need to see the rest of that video."

"Yeah, but installing it would be next to impossible. Tony has an iPhone with facial recognition. I'd need access to his phone, and it would have to be unlocked, which means he'd have to stare into the screen for several seconds with his eyes open."

Robert snorted like a bull. But like his son, he didn't fall apart at the first setback. Instead, he grew quiet and contemplative.

"We'll do it at the wedding," he said a few moments later. "Everyone has to turn in their phones anyway. That will give you a few hours to do it."

"Yeah, and how do you propose I open it?"

Robert shook his head. "I haven't figured that part out yet."

James knew what he was about to say wouldn't go over well, but he said it anyway. "I have a friend who might be able to help, if you're willing to pay."

Esther answered on the third ring. "What up, bitch?"

James slumped against the brick wall outside Tim Hortons. "I have a job for you, and it pays really well."

"How many laws will I have to break?" Esther was nothing if not to the point.

"Check your email. There's an NDA for you to DocuSign before I say anything else."

The rapid click of computer keys sounded on the other line. "Ooh, from Robert Chapman, your new father-in-law. Don't think I didn't recognize you lurking in the background. Nice mustache, by the way."

"Are you gonna sign the NDA or not?"

"Already did. What's up?"

After checking back with Robert that she had, in fact, signed the NDA, James told her what he needed.

"Don't worry, I got you. I'm gonna need a flight to Vermont—first class, of course—and a hotel suite with a balcony and a couch. I hate watching TV in bed. Oh, and a job as one of the wedding photographers."

Getting Esther involved was almost certainly a mistake, especially since the video they were trying to steal proved Will had a motive to attack Derek. And Esther had a way of making every situation worse. Yet, for the first time since he'd seen the video, James felt a pang of hope. Maybe there was a way out of this.

CHAPTER 37
WILL

They were just polishing off the first bottle of champagne when the door to Theo's suite opened and James backed into the room, his hands full. "Don't tell Miles, but I got you—"

"Those better not be fucking donuts," Miles said.

James fumbled the box from Tim Hortons, but managed to save it by trapping it against the doorframe.

Will couldn't believe his eyes, nor could he pull back the grin spreading across his face. James was back, with donuts no less. And were those coffees?

"Of course not." James set the box on the table. "These are rice cakes and kale chips." He set the coffees next to the donuts. "And these are definitely not mochas. They're distilled water, I think."

James eyed them suspiciously. They must have made quite the sight, the three of them in bed together, a picnic of lobster, champagne, and orange juice laid out before them.

"You're talking about me, aren't you?"

Will shrugged, and his heart skipped a beat when James flopped down onto the mattress next to him and plucked the mimosa from his fingers.

"You know you're supposed to put more than just a drop of orange juice in here, right? It's not just for color."

James handed the glass back and reached down to remove the pad of hotel stationary under his ass. His eyes went wide when he saw the first sketch. But he took it in stride and examined each penis in turn.

"The fifth one is probably the closest." He tossed the pad to Miles. Of course James knew what he was looking at.

Miles removed the pencil from behind his ear and circled the fifth picture. "Interesting. And when was the last time you bottomed?"

"Jesus." Will tried to smack Miles without spilling any of their mimosas.

"I must be drunker than I thought," Tiffany said. "For some reason, I'm not finding this the least bit awkward."

Will gave in to his racing heart and leaned against James. The press of James's shoulder both calmed and excited him. "Don't answer him. It's like feeding a bear."

"Fine." Miles closed the pad. "You don't have to answer now. But I'm going to ask you again in two days, and if you don't say something like, 'Last night,' or 'Two days ago,' I'm going to kick your fucking ass. You hear me? Will's vers. You got that?"

Tiffany's long, manicured nails clinked on her glass. "Okay, I changed my mind. This is actually super awkward."

She wasn't wrong, yet Will had never been happier. Did it get better than this? He was drinking in bed with his two best friends and James, who fit in perfectly, like their trio was always meant to be a quartet.

"Well, maybe if you guys got the fuck out of our bed, we could get to work on that," James said and helped himself to more of Will's mimosa.

"Good answer." Miles got up and offered Tiffany his hand. "Go easy on him, Will, okay? Just not too easy."

The moment the door clicked shut, James removed the mimosa from Will's hands and set it on the nightstand. "You thought I ran away, didn't you?"

"No."

James took Will's arms and pinned them behind his head. "Don't lie." James teased his tongue up Will's neck. *Damn, that felt good.*

"I might have considered the possibility." Will groaned as James slid down his body and used his teeth to pull back the folds of Will's robe.

"I've only bottomed for one guy before." James grabbed Will's dick with both hands and tugged, like he was pulling weeds. "And that was ages ago. Plus, he wasn't quite so well endowed."

"You don't have to." Will meant it, too. Sure, he'd love to fuck James, but not because Miles guilted him into it.

James lowered his head and gently kissed the tip of Will's dick, his mustache tickling the sensitive skin. It was sweet and oddly chaste. "I know. But what if I wanted to?"

"Then I'd say, when you're ready. There's no rush."

James jumped off the bed and headed for the bathroom. "Give me fifteen minutes."

THIRTY MINUTES LATER, James was on all fours on the bed, covered in a sheen of sweat. "I can do this, I swear. Just shove it in there."

"I don't want to hurt you," Will said, catching James's gaze in the reflection of the mirror.

"It will only hurt for a sec. You just gotta break me in, that's all."

"That's not how this works."

James lowered his head to the mattress, and every muscle in his back rippled in response. "Let's try missionary again."

"I have a better idea." Will slid the condom off and tossed it aside. He wrapped his arms around James's naked, sweaty body and pulled him down onto the mattress. "Let's talk instead."

"No, I wanna do this. I probably just need to smoke a bowl or something."

Will couldn't help but laugh. Confident James was hot as hell, but flustered James was even hotter. "Actually, I have a better idea, one that doesn't involve any talking whatsoever."

"Blowjobs?"

"Close, but no. And yes, later." Will pushed the pillows aside and sat cross-legged on the bed. "We're going to stare at each other for five minutes straight without talking."

James's eyebrows shot up. "You wanna have a staring competition?"

"No, not exactly. You can blink all you want. You just can't talk. And you can't look away."

"Can I eat a donut?"

Will shook his head. "Nope, no eating or drinking."

"Maybe we can ask Miles for poppers. Those help, right?"

Will was close to bursting at the seams from all the adorableness. James was like an awkward teenager. "No poppers. This will be better, trust me. I read it on the internet."

"Oh, well, in that case."

James closed his eyes and took a deep breath. He tried to sit cross-legged like Will, but his knees were practically pointing straight up. Will tried to push them down, but they just popped back up again.

"You don't have to sit cross-legged. We can practice stretching some other time. Right now, just get comfortable. This is going to be the longest five minutes of your life."

"Wow"—James switched to a kneeling position—"you're really selling this."

Biting back his smile, Will copied James's kneeling position and set the timer on his phone. "Okay, so no talking and no looking away until the timer goes off. Got it?"

"Yes, master."

See, that was James's problem right there. He viewed bottoming as an act of subservience instead of one of trust and pleasure. It wasn't about giving up control, but about sharing it.

Will would've said as much, but he'd already hit start on the timer, and James's eyes were just so beautiful. At first glance, they appeared moss green, but upon closer examination, they became so much more. There was a rim of gold around the iris, though it wasn't uniform. It was thicker and darker at the top and fell away at the bottom. And there were striated lines of light, like the ripples at the bottom of a swimming pool.

After thirty seconds, James's eyes started to water, and then he started to laugh. Will wanted to censure him, but he didn't. He kept his gaze steady until James found his way back. James blinked a lot at first, and every ten seconds or so he let out an exasperated puff of air. But after about two minutes, he settled down.

Will really had gotten the idea from the internet, some clickbait article on how to fall in love in thirty-six questions. Will couldn't remember a single one of the questions, but he remembered this part, the staring into each other's eyes part.

Will thought it might be a nice icebreaker to get James to laugh at himself and relax, but this was ridiculously intense. It was like taking mushrooms. There was this strange energy field building between them that washed back and forth, like waves in a bathtub. It was green and gold, and there were streaks of light, just like James's eyes.

Will was reminded of something he'd read in college about the brains of small children, how they experience the world differently because they've yet to build up the same efficiencies. The brain is constantly inundated with sensory input, sights, sounds, tastes, touches, and smells. Adult brains are masters at categorizing everything. *This is a potential threat. This is a potential reward. Ignore all that.* And it happens in a snap, without us even knowing it.

We think it's reality, but it's a personalized reality, a filtered reality. Kids, on the other hand, don't have the same filters, and they see the world more accurately, even if more chaotically.

That was how Will felt now, like his filters had been peeled away. The world he found himself in was not his own. This world was scary and magical and overwhelming. But it was truer. Will could sense that. Maybe that was how this whole falling in love thing worked. Because what was love if not scary, magical, and overwhelming?

You're just a pathetic fuckboy. The thought popped into Will's head unbidden, and he had to scold it away.

The timer went off, the same timer Will used every day at center time, and before he could stop himself, he yelled, "Rotate."

"What?" James shook his head and squeezed his eyes shut, like he'd been staring at the sun.

"Sorry, ignore me."

James frowned, and the corners of his mouth drew his mustache down. "You're crying."

"No, I'm not." Will reached up to feel his cheeks, and sure enough, they were wet with tears. Jesus Christ. He pressed his palms to his eyes to stem the flow. "I'm sorry. I have terrible ideas."

James pulled Will's hands from his face. "No, you don't. And it's okay to cry."

"Right, because who doesn't love a weepy top?"

James laughed, but not unkindly. It rolled out of him in gentle waves. And it was infectious. Will couldn't help but laugh, too.

"That was really intense." James sank back down onto his ass. "Like, seriously, what was that? Did you know that would happen?"

Will shrugged, and this time the tears he wiped away were mostly from laughter. "No, not really."

James stood and offered Will his hand. "Come on. I'm gonna suck you off in the shower. And when we get home later, after I've done some exhaustive research on bottoming, that big boy is going inside me, all the way inside me."

CHAPTER 38

JAMES

Sometimes, you don't realize how cold you are until you put on a hoodie. Sometimes, you don't realize how hungry you are until you smell bacon frying in the pan. Sometimes, you don't realize how lonely you are until you stare into someone's eyes for five minutes straight.

The whole time, James had felt his body blush with embarrassment, certain Will could see right through him, could see James was making everything up as he went along, that he didn't know shit about anything, and never had. Travis had been the one with his head on his shoulders. James was the fuck-up, and he was fucking up now.

He should've told Will the truth about who he really was before he kissed him, before they fucked, before he let himself get lost in whatever this was. But there was too much going on behind the scenes, too much Will didn't know about.

After watching the video, Robert had assumed Will had been keeping Donna and Derek's secret all these years, but James had assured him that wasn't the case. James was positive Will didn't know about his mother and Derek, that he had no memory whatsoever of the argument he and Derek had that night.

Will had a right to know, of course. But what good would telling him do now? It would just make him hate his mother, and Derek, too. More importantly, it would make him hate himself. And between the two of them, they had enough self-loathing to last a lifetime.

Seriously, why couldn't James bottom? Will had no problem bottoming, neither did Brice or any of the other guys James had been with. So why couldn't James? It was frustrating as hell.

"What the fuck is wrong with me?" James buried his face in the pillow. He'd managed to get two fingers inside himself when they'd gotten back from Montreal, but apparently, Will's dick was way bigger than two fingers.

"Nothing. You're perfect." Will slid off James's back and laid his head on the pillow beside James's, their noses touching. "And you'll get there. I know you will. And when you do, you're going to be so fucking tight. I can't wait. Did you know you've starred in every one of my masturbation fantasies since the bachelor party?"

That got James's attention. "Oh, yeah?"

"Uh huh. Do you want to hear one of them now? Maybe we can make it come true."

That was how James ended up fucking Will out on the boat in the middle of the lake shortly after lunch and then again in the barn just before dinner.

James loved Will's sexual candor, and after a day of reenacting Will's sexual fantasies, James decided it was time Will returned the favor. "Wanna try one of mine?"

The fantasy James had in mind wasn't as exciting as any of the ones Will had shared. Nothing from James's imagination could ever top the thrill of seeing Will's toned arms grip the railing of the boat while James held his legs and fucked up into him, or fucking Will from behind amongst all the garden tools hanging in the barn, Will's pants spooled around his ankles, his palms pressed into the rough, untreated wood of the barn wall. But sex didn't always have to be rough and hard. It could be slow and sensual, too. And some fantasies didn't involve sex at all.

James wasn't as kinky as Will. Will got off on quickies in semi-private places where there was a chance of getting caught, like on a boat, or in a barn, or in the coat closet of a crowded party. James was a little more sentimental.

James told Will his fantasy, the one he'd jacked off to the night Ryan and Derek had come over for dinner, expecting Will to laugh. But Will didn't laugh. He blushed and said, "I'm game."

Will looked hot as fuck in James's flannel shirt and baseball cap, and he sounded amazing singing country songs. He had James's hat pulled low on his head, which hid his eyes and accentuated his jawline. He added a smokey tone to his voice and a slight hitch in his step that made the fifteen-year-old boy in James, the one who used to jack off to fantasies of his brother's best friends, grow hard as a rock. Fucking an actor was great. Fucking a great actor was amazing.

They didn't leave Will's room. They didn't need to. Instead, James lit some candles and sat back on the bed while Will, dressed like a proper redneck, sang song after song to him. Will only knew the most popular ones, but that suited James just fine, and Will made every word believable.

It was embarrassing. James felt like a teenage boy at a One Direction concert, but Will didn't judge. In fact, it seemed to turn him on.

Most guys wanted James to be their daddy, and James was good at it. He liked it, even. But Will was different. Sure, Will liked that part, too. But mostly, he wanted James to be himself, and James was terrible at that. Will may have been the professional actor, but James had been acting for as long as he could remember.

At first, it had been about hiding his sexuality, about being one of the boys, hunting and fishing and saying shit like, "Show us your tits." Then, after he'd come out, it had been about hiding his anger and guilt—anger at being rejected and left behind, and guilt for surviving. Now, it was about hiding his fear, about making Theo feel safe and taken care of, like James had it all under control, which was the biggest lie of all.

"Get over here and fuck me," James said when he couldn't take it any longer.

Will switched the music from karaoke to some country playlist he found on Spotify. Not breaking character, he told James exactly what he wanted him to do. It shouldn't have turned James on so much, but it did.

"Go into the bathroom, face the mirror, and push your pants down to your ankles."

James was starting to understand why most guys preferred bottoming. It felt nice to give up control, to be the object of someone else's desire, and not because of what you could do to them, but because of what they could do to you.

James knew why Will wanted to fuck him in the bathroom. He was doing it for James, knowing James was a bit of a voyeur. The bathroom was full of mirrors—one above the sink, one on the wall, and one on the shower door. James was going to get to watch Will fuck him from every angle.

As soon as James complied with Will's orders, Will turned his baseball cap backwards and sank to his knees. He spread James open and tongued his hole.

Will had tried to rim James before, but James had refused. This time, Will didn't ask. And holy shit did it feel amazing. James always assumed guys were putting on a show when he ate them out, but holy shit, nope. This was unreal.

Will stopped, but only long enough to spit in his hand and reach around and jack James off. The combination of Will's tongue in his ass and Will's slick hand sliding up and down his shaft was too much.

"Stop, you're gonna make me come."

Will stopped, and in a low, husky voice said, "That's the idea."

"But I want you to fuck me." James hated how desperate he sounded.

"Babe"—Will stared at James through the mirror, and he must have seen the way the word *babe* made James blush because his mouth twisted into a crooked grin—"I will, when you're ready."

Will's voice carried such authority, such cool confidence, James was compelled to bite back the lie on the tip of his tongue—*but I am ready*. He closed his eyes instead.

He opened them when he heard Will bring up another wad of spit and closed them again when Will's tongue sank back into him. Ultimately, it didn't matter. Either way, eyes open or eyes shut, he was undone.

His legs buckled, and he had to use the counter to hold himself up as Will emptied him, his cum splattering against the cabinet doors. James started to turn around so he could return the favor, but Will caught his eye in the mirror and shook his head.

Will took his cock out, and James thought he'd changed his mind and was going to fuck him, after all. But he didn't, not technically anyway. Instead, he ran his dick up the seam of James's crack, fucking past his hole, but not into it. It was hot as shit, especially the way Will pulled up the bottom of his flannel shirt so he could watch his cock slide through the white groove of James's ass, exposing his chiseled abs and v-cup in the process. It was even hotter when he took his length in hand and finished on James's ass and lower back.

Will took his hat off and placed it back on James's head. "You did good," he said, half in character and half chuckling.

James flushed with pride and something else. What was it? It wasn't embarrassment, though it probably should've been. It was more like a warm, sticky relief, like when your fever breaks after a night of cold sweats and you can finally sleep.

"Tomorrow, all the way in. You hear me? This time, I'm serious."

"Tomorrow's the wedding," Will said.

It was time for another shower, so James started unbuttoning Will's flannel shirt. Well, James's flannel shirt. Though maybe he'd give it to Will. It looked better on him anyway.

"I'm sure they've got a closet or two at the church."

Now it was Will's turn to flush red. James could get used to this, this whole being himself and taking turns thing.

JAMES'S PHONE rang early the next morning, and he sent it to voicemail, or so he thought.

"James, you there?" Brice said.

Shit. James rolled out of bed, careful not to wake Will, and darted into the bathroom. He would've shut the door, but Will's pull-up bar was hanging in the doorway.

"Hey, sorry. I was asleep and didn't realize I answered."

"Oh, sorry, dude, didn't mean to wake you." Brice sounded two bong rips into his morning, and rap music boomed in the background. "I just couldn't believe it when I saw the pictures. Was that really Theo with Noel Jameson? He hasn't gone over to the dark side, has he?"

"No, nothing like that."

"And was that really you? When did you shave your beard? Are you really dating William Chapman? I never took you for the bad boy type." Brice sounded like he was joking, but James could hear the jealousy in his voice.

"He's not a bad boy."

"When did you meet him? Is it serious?"

James looked in the mirror and fingered the tender red mark on his neck and smiled. At least Will had the good sense to leave his brand below the collar line.

"I don't know. It's all pretty new. But listen, I can't really talk right now. Can I call you in a few days?"

"Okay, I'll call Theo. He must be going out of his mind. I saw Ryan—"

"Please don't call Theo." James's heart quickened.

"Why not? He didn't decide to get the test, did he?"

"No, nothing like that." Theo was only eighteen, and while he was eligible to get the test, there was no good reason to do it now. Sure, finding out might bring him peace of mind, but it also might extinguish all hope, not to mention screw up any chance of ever getting affordable health and life insurance. It was one of those questions with no easy answer. "Theo's great. He's on cloud nine, actually. It's just not a good time, and he's sure to break his NDA if he talks to you."

"Wait, like a non-disclosure agreement?"

"Exactly."

"Wow! That's so badass."

"Listen, I'll call you in a couple days, okay? But can you do me a favor and not mention this to anyone?"

There was a beat of silence on the other line, and then the bubble of a bong. "Sure, no problem. Who would I tell anyway?"

"Thanks, Brice. I'll call you in a couple days." James hung up and turned to find Will standing naked in the doorway.

A playful smile curled up Will's lips. "Ex-boyfriend?"

"Yes, actually." James set his phone on the counter. "He saw the photos online, and—"

"I'm sorry." Will wrapped his arms around James's waist and placed his head on James's chest. "I really won't be offended if you want to take separate cars."

James pushed Will away so he could look him in the eye. "I already told you. I don't care about any of that shit. I wanna be there with you. Someone's gotta keep you out of trouble."

"True, but my husband is basically a gladiator, so . . ." Will held up his hands like the scales of a balance.

"I still can't believe you're married to Miles." James could absolutely believe Will was married to Miles. Those two were ridiculous.

Will softly bit James's neck. "Only legally. It's not a real marriage."

"Except that you live together and he controls everything you eat, drink, and do with your body."

"Gosh, when you put it that way, it sounds almost traditional."

Will laughed and buried his face in James's chest. James wanted to argue the point, but Will played dirty. "Since we're both up anyway, there is this one fantasy I haven't told you about yet. We're going to need a blindfold, a rope, an eggbeater, and the wine cellar."

WILL WORE A DARK TEAL TUX, which should've looked hideous, but didn't for some reason. Will tried to explain Nandi's wedding aesthetic to James as they waited on the porch for the limo, but Will was an even worse fashion gay than James. The best he could come up with was, "I think I'm supposed to be the blue fairy from *Sleeping Beauty*."

Theo looked good, too, though too mature. His finely tailored tux hid his gangly arms and legs, and it gave him an imposing Bond look that was sure to make James's life harder. Theo was already starting to trend on Twitter, even though no one knew his name. Things were getting out of hand, and fast.

Donna joined them, looking like she had something to prove. She wore a form-fitting, asymmetrical saffron yellow dress that was impossible not to stare at. One arm was covered in a long, flowing sleeve and the other was totally bare, aside from a silver cuff she wore around her wrist.

"Here." She handed James a slip of paper with a phone number on it. "Call Rebecca. She's an amazing yoga teacher. She did wonders for my pelvic floor after I gave birth to Andy."

James was confused, and it wasn't until Theo snickered that he figured out what was going on. James's cheeks flushed.

James made a point to never discuss his sex life with Theo. Theo made a point to discuss James's sex life whenever possible.

The night before, when James had gone to grab a beer, Theo had said, "Miles tells me you're gonna start bottoming. How's that going?"

James had frozen, his fingernail paused under the tab of his beer. "I'm not discussing this with you."

"Why? Is it difficult? I heard you have to practice a lot and really work up to it. Is that true?"

"I don't know, bud. I'm not the one you should be having this conversation with."

"Then who should I be having it with?"

James had given this some thought, and when the best he could come up with was Miles, he'd said, "We'll get you a therapist or something."

"You don't know, do you? Oh, no. What if it's hereditary? What if I've inherited Dad's Alzheimer's and your tiny asshole?"

"I don't have a tiny asshole," James had said before storming upstairs, feeling like a terrible bottom and a terrible uncle.

And now Theo had gone and told Donna.

"There's nothing to be embarrassed about," Donna said. "It's perfectly normal, especially for someone your age." She looked at James like she was twenty years his junior.

Theo rocked back on his heels and changed the subject. "Maybe we should just drive ourselves. If we get really drunk, we can always take an Uber back."

Donna looked down at her phone. "We might have to."

Just then, a cloud of dust rose at the end of the driveway.

"Hold that thought," James said.

The cloud of dust grew and spread out over the fields of dandelions, which had grown long and white in the midsummer. But the car that crested the knoll was not a limousine. It was a beat-up old Subaru.

"Who's that?" Donna raised her diamond-studded clutch to shade her eyes. "Jesus fucking Christ."

The car pulled into the drive and parked next to Will's new rental. The door opened, and James's heart fell to the pit of his stomach.

"Mom? What are you doing here?" Theo stepped into the sunlight.

Panic struck James like a lightning bolt, knocking the wind from his lungs.

Emily walked up the path in patterned leggings and an oversized T-shirt. Her round, sallow face was framed by severe bangs, probably something she did herself. She looked old, far older than forty. A lifetime of cigarettes, booze, and God knows what else hadn't been kind to her.

"I saw you on TV and had to come say hi. I had to see my baby." She jogged up the steps and wrapped Theo in a hug, like she hadn't abandoned him as an infant.

"Wow." Will turned to James. "This is quite the day for your exes, huh?"

"Exes?" Emily released Theo, who stared down at this strange woman like she was a ghost. "I'm not Jimmy's ex. I'm his sister-in-law." She struck a pose. "I'm in the movie."

CHAPTER 39
WILL

Will had always written James's insights off as a Vermont thing, like all Vermonters were the same. But that wasn't it, was it? Jesus, how could Will have been so oblivious?

"You're Jimmy, aren't you?"

"Will, I can explain." James set a hand on Will's shoulder, but Will took a step back, and the hand fell away.

Will had known this was too good to be true. James wasn't interested in him. He was just interested in Will's proximity to the movie. What had James said to him when they'd first decided to do the whole fake relationship thing? Wasn't it something about getting to tag along and watch them film?

"You didn't know?" The woman had dark circles under her eyes and looked nothing like Theo.

"This is all very fascinating, but our ride is here, and we're late." Will's mother stepped into the sunlight and shaded her eyes with her purse.

"I'm sorry. I just had to see my baby." The woman reached up and smoothed the lapel of Theo's tux. "Look how handsome you are. You get that from me, you know?"

Will's mom, who'd never been affectionate a day in her life, reached over and manually closed Will's mouth. "Perhaps next time you could call first." She turned to Theo. "Theo, hun, run in and grab another bottle of champagne from the fridge. I think we're going to need it."

Theo did as he was told, and the second he was inside, James moved on the woman, towering over her. The raw anger in his eyes was terrifying.

"You shouldn't be here."

The woman met James's anger with her own, not backing down. "He's my son."

"He's not your son. And you're not getting a cent of his money."

"I don't want his money."

"Yeah, right." James balled his hands into fists. *Was he going to hit her?* "And I'm supposed to believe that, that it's all just a coincidence, that you just happen to suddenly care, that it has nothing to do with them turning Travis's book into a movie?"

The woman started to cry, and this time, she did take a step back. "I know I fucked up. But I'm better now. I've been clean for over a year. And Tommy is a good man, a good father. Theo has a little brother."

"I don't give a shit. You had your chance. You had eighteen years of chances. You don't get another one now just because Theo finally has something you want."

Fuck, he really was Jimmy. Will could see it now, the anger, the quick temper hidden just below the surface.

Last week, they'd filmed the scene where Jimmy punches his fist through a stained glass window at church after being asked to change out of his "faggy" clothes.

Tears slid down the dark grooves of the woman's face. "What was I supposed to do? Was I supposed to just sit around and watch my husband die? Was I supposed to raise our son and pretend he wasn't next?"

"Yes." James swung his fist, but instead of punching the woman, he punched the porch column, sending the baskets of purple flowers swaying on their hooks. "That's exactly what you were supposed to do. You were supposed to think about someone other than yourself for a change."

"Oh, like you're innocent, like you didn't run off to Florida the second Bruce got sick. You left me and Travis to take care of everything."

"I didn't run off. He kicked me out. I was sixteen, and he kicked me out. And that was years before he got sick." James's knuckles were bleeding, but he didn't seem to notice.

There was a stifled sob in the doorway, and Will turned to find Theo in tears. In the shock of it all, Will hadn't considered who Theo was in all of this. He was Travis's son, not James's. That meant he—

Will's chest constricted. *No, not Theo.*

"William, please escort Theo to the limo," Donna said. "James and I will be right behind you."

Will did as he was told, but even with the limo doors closed, he could hear his mother's voice. She wasn't yelling. She never yelled. She didn't need to.

"I don't claim to know what's going on right now, but I do know this is not the time or the place. By the sounds of it, you've had eighteen years to be a mother to that boy. Waiting a few more days won't hurt you."

"Stay out of this. This is none of your business." The woman's voice filtered into the limo in muffled tones. Theo stared at the floor and pretended not to hear.

"You're standing on my porch, making me late for my son's wedding, so yes, this is my business. More importantly, I care for that boy. And, unfortunately for you, I happen to be disgustingly rich. I sincerely hope your intentions are honorable. I really do. But honorable or not, you will never see a single penny of that boy's money. So let's take that off the table right now."

"You can't do that."

"I know, it doesn't seem fair. Frankly, it's not. But this is America, and I have scores of lawyers and deep, deep reservoirs of spite. So, like it or not, I can do whatever the fuck I want. And right now, I want to get drunk, watch my son get married, and try to bed a Hemsworth. So, if you'll excuse me." His mother pushed past the woman, and her stiletto heels clapped down the steps. "James, lock the door and get your virgin ass in the limo."

Theo kept his eyes on the floor, and Will wished there was something he could say. Will should've been furious with Theo. He was the one who'd orchestrated the whole fake relationship in the first place.

But Will wasn't mad, not even a little bit. All he wanted to do was hold Theo and tell him it was going to be okay. Will's mother would take care of everything. If he did carry the gene, she'd find a doctor, the best one money could buy, and they'd find a cure. It would be different for Theo. They'd stop the cycle. They had to. There was no other way.

The limo doors opened, and his mother and James slid inside. No one looked at anyone else, and no one spoke. They all sat in silence as the chauffeur made his way around.

"Do you have a first-aid kit by any chance?" his mother asked the chauffeur as he got behind the wheel.

"Yes, ma'am." The chauffeur climbed out again and retrieved the first-aid kit from the trunk.

He gave it to James, who looked down at it in total confusion, like he'd just been handed a small baby possum. He met Will's gaze, and the pain in James's eyes looked far worse than the cuts on his knuckles.

Will had no idea what he should do. But after a second of staring into James's green eyes, he knew what he would do. He'd bandage James's hand and figure out the rest later.

"Give it to me." Will took the first-aid kit and pulled out the disinfecting wipes. As a kindergarten teacher, he was no stranger to cuts and scrapes.

His mother took the bottle of champagne from Theo. "I'm putting you in charge of the travel playlist. Play something upbeat. We're going to a wedding." She opened the champagne slowly, and the cork sighed from the bottle and released an apple, sweet mist into the cabin. "It's a good thing you two are only pretending to date. Otherwise, this would be very awkward."

CHAPTER 40
JAMES

Will finished bandaging James's hand and accepted a flute of champagne from Donna, who promptly transitioned from mothering Will to mothering Theo—if mothering is what you could call it.

"We don't get to choose our parents. Just ask William. But we do get to choose our therapists, and I know some great ones. I'll make some calls in the morning."

Only an inch separated James from Will, but the air felt like it was lined with lead. What was Will thinking? Was it over?

"Do you have your toast prepared?" Donna asked.

"I wrote it months ago." Will, who was capable of making his voice sound like anything he wanted, any accent, any emotion, any shade of humor or irony, spoke in an unreadable monotone.

"That's good." Donna topped off Will's glass and smiled at Theo. "I couldn't get you seated next to Ryan because he's in the wedding party, but you'll be with Miles and Tiffany and that Spider-Man kid, what's his name, Tom something?"

Theo's eyes went wide. "I'm sitting with Tom Holland? Is Zendaya coming, too?"

The limo drove through the security perimeter and pulled up to the front steps of the cathedral. Donna and Theo got out, but James grabbed Will by the wrist and held him back.

"Can we talk for a sec?"

"I should probably go. Andy is going to be freaking out, and—"

"Please, just for a sec." James let his grip slip from Will's wrist, not wanting to force him.

"Okay." Will closed the door, and they were alone.

James wanted to hold Will. He wanted to stare into his eyes and press their foreheads together. He wanted to make Will remember how happy they'd been just an hour ago, when they were bumping shoulders and jockeying for control of the bathroom mirror. But he didn't dare.

"I really like you, Will, more than I've liked anyone in a long time, maybe ever, and—"

"When you were encouraging me to read the part"—Will spoke to the white bandages wrapped around James's fingers—"when you kept going on and on about how talented I was, was that just so you could go with me to the set every day?"

"No, Will, no." James tried to make Will meet his eyes, but he wouldn't. He kept staring at James's throbbing hand. "You can't think like that. You are talented. You're the most talented person I've ever met, and you—"

"Okay." Will nodded, but he still wouldn't lift his gaze. "I should probably go."

"Don't do this. This doesn't have to change anything." James lowered his head and tried to find Will's eyes behind the curtain of his black hair. "It's not important how we met, just that we met. What's important is how we feel right now."

"I honestly don't know how I feel right now."

"Well, I do. I feel scared and sorry. So friggin' sorry. I should've told you. I wanted to, but—"

"It's fine." Will's voice was colorless. "It is what it is."

"No, it's not fine. And it's not what it is. It's what we make of it." James was tired of waiting for Will to look at him, so he grabbed Will's face and forced it up. "And I think we can make something pretty damn awesome if we give this a chance."

Will tried to look away, but James wouldn't let him. "That's not what I meant. I just meant it will be fine. I just need a minute to process, that's all."

"Okay." James let go of Will's face. "That makes sense." And it did. Of course Will needed a minute. He probably needed days, or even weeks. "Can I kiss you, though, before you go?"

Will didn't look away, and though the smile that played on his face was heavy, it was still a smile. James closed the gap between them and pulled Will into a kiss.

Will's lips were dry and cracked, and James was determined to kiss them until they were soft and supple once more. But there was a knock at the window.

"You're late." The wedding planner tapped her cream-colored heels on the pavement.

"Sorry about that." Will climbed from the limo, and just when James was certain he was going to walk away without saying goodbye, he ducked his head back inside. "Just so we're clear, I'm never calling you Jimmy. You got that?"

James was so relieved he wanted to run laps around the parking lot like a dog let off its leash, but he pulled Will in for another kiss instead. "I can work with that. And tonight, all the way in. I mean it."

JAMES HADN'T PARTAKEN of the champagne on the ride up, but he reached for it now. It seemed a shame to let it go to waste. He had one glass to steady his nerves and helped himself to some of the Advil in the first-aid kit.

When that did nothing to dull the pain of his throbbing hand, he snuck back behind the old brick cathedral and pulled out the joint he'd rolled that morning, the one he'd promised Will they'd smoke at sunset from the deck of the ship.

He held the unlit joint between his lips and sighed. Maybe this was a good thing. No more secrets. Well, except for one. But James didn't want to think about his role in getting Will fired.

James would tell Robert the deal was off. After tonight, James was done spying. Robert could get a real professional, or just let Esther take care of it all. And there was no way in hell James was going to dump Will now. Screw that. James hadn't felt this swimmy feeling in ages, maybe ever. Will made James's whole body feel like a lava lamp—psychedelic, messy, beautiful, and constantly in motion.

Yes, it was agony to have such a tenuous grasp on something you wanted so badly, but it was also thrilling because, tenuous or not, a grasp was still a grasp, it was still a thread of hope connecting desire and fulfillment.

James was old enough to know that chances like these, connections like the one he felt with Will, were like comets. They didn't come around very often, and if it was cloudy, or if you were watching TV, you'd miss it. James wasn't going to make that mistake.

James felt better having a new plan, and he checked to see if Esther had texted. It was his last chance before going inside and surrendering his phone. Sure enough, there was a new message.

Got the phone. Now, it's time for phase 2.

James breathed a huge sigh of relief and let his head fall back against the old oak tree. He looked around to make sure no one was watching and then lit the joint. It was almost over, and then he'd be done with all the lies and backroom deals. He could tell Will the truth. He could tell him everything.

Phase two was simple, at least the way Esther described it. And James's part was especially easy. Esther had a custom-designed phone case that fit backwards on an iPhone and made the front look like the back. There was an opening at the top for the front facing camera. Now, all she had to do was put Tony's phone inside, pretend to take his picture at the wedding, and voila, she'd be in. Then she'd give the phone to James, and he'd install the necessary spyware.

The joint went out after one long pull, and James was about to relight it when he saw movement out of the corner of his eye. He peered around the large oak tree he was leaning against and saw Robert and Derek heading towards a white clapboard outbuilding behind the old cathedral.

What was Robert up to now? Their plan was working. Why couldn't he just chill? Of course, Robert had a lot of plans, and he wasn't big on sharing them with James. But that was fine. James wanted no part of them anyway. Well, except for helping Will. He did want to do that.

After Robert had agreed to bring Esther on board, James had asked Robert again if Tony was blackmailing him. He'd asked if Robert had intentionally blown his scenes with Derek to get Will involved. Was he hoping Derek would get fired and Will would take over? Had he been planning to get Derek booted? Was that why he'd asked James to spy on Tony? But Robert had stayed closemouthed, not betraying so much as a smile or a shrug to let James know if he was on the right track.

James felt the familiar knot of guilt twist in his gut. What if Robert's plan had been working and James had ruined it by posting that karaoke video?

James slid the joint back into his breast pocket and, against his better judgment, followed Robert and Derek across the lawn.

He stopped outside the white outbuilding and peeked through the window. The place was dimly lit and littered with children's books and toddler crafts. There were tissue paper stained glass windows and flowers made from tiny handprints. But Robert and Derek were nowhere in sight. James was going to have to go inside.

He tiptoed through the empty Sunday school classroom and followed the sound of voices down a dark hallway. Light spilled from the last room on the left, and James sank into a shadowy doorway across the hall. He tested the door behind him and was relieved to find it unlocked. *Good*. He'd be able to slip inside if Robert and Derek tried to make a hasty exit.

"She told you?" Derek was saying, and though his voice was still deep, it was higher pitched than normal.

"It doesn't matter how I know. What were you thinking, Derek? You knew William was head over heels for you. And he was just a boy. How could you get his hopes up like that and then tell him you'd been fucking his mother? What did you think would happen?"

"I didn't want to lie to him anymore. I wanted us to—"

"You wanted to make him suffer because you were suffering. He ruined your big night, so you ruined his."

"That's not true. I—"

"You had plenty of opportunities to tell William the truth before that night. But you waited until he was riding high, and then you brought him down because you're jealous and petty and—"

"This is fucking rich coming from you. You never wanted Will to be in *The Beautiful*. You were terrified he'd outshine you, and then he did, and you couldn't handle it."

"That's not true."

"Isn't it? Isn't that why you kept telling him that he wasn't really acting, that he was just playing a version of himself, that people just felt sorry for his character? Admit it. You're afraid of your own son, afraid he's going to upstage you. That's why you didn't want him in *Sundowning* either."

"I've never been afraid of my son. It was the wrong part. There was too much nudity. Plus, I knew if he played gay right off the bat, he'd never be taken seriously as an actor. He'd spend his whole life as some rom-com twit's best friend." Robert spoke the words with conviction, but they were edged with doubt, like he'd said them so often they'd worn a rut just south of the truth. "Donna is the one who went behind my back. She's the one who got him the part. And look what happened."

"He was brilliant. That's what happened."

There was a long moment of silence, and James could hear the shuffle of footsteps. He considered slipping into the room behind him, but then Robert spoke again.

"Do you want to know the real reason William's not in the movie and you are? Because, believe me, you were never supposed to be part of this. This was William's movie. I picked it out just for him." Robert paused, and though James couldn't see him, he knew Robert was crying by the slight hitch in his breath. "I wanted my last movie to be with my son."

"Then why did you give his part to Ryan? The whole reason I agreed to do this in the first place was because I thought Will was going to be playing Jimmy."

"Are you really this profoundly stupid? Do you honestly not see that this is all Tony's doing? He's the one who got William replaced. He told the studio you'd agree to play Travis, but only if William wasn't part of the movie."

"That's not true."

"He's the one who leaked those stories about William to the tabloids."

"What? Why would he do that?"

"I don't know, Derek. But he's made it his mission to destroy my son's life, and you've helped him every step of the way. He's your manager. He acts in your best interests. And that makes you responsible."

"I'll talk to Tony, and if he's the one who leaked the stories, I'll—"

"It's too late now. The damage is done. If you really want to help William, you'll quit the movie and give him a shot. He just needs one role to—"

"I can't do that."

"Why? Because Tony won't let you? You're his boss, Derek. He works for you. Oh, he'll talk you out of it alright. He'll deny it, and you'll believe every word, just like you always do because you don't care about the truth, not really. You'll accept any reality Tony feeds you so long as you come out on top. If you had any self-respect, you'd fire Tony this instant. He's a terrible manager. And while you're at it, you should fire your agent, too. I mean, come on, a Michael Phelps biopic? Who wants to watch a movie about an overgrown frat boy who wins all the time?"

"You're being unreasonable."

"Oh, am I?" James had never heard Robert get this riled up before, and he'd watched him play his father, a man who'd lived in a constant state of agitation. "What's stopping me from going to the tabloids and telling them the truth, that you practically goaded Will into attacking you? You really think anyone's going to want to cast you after they find out you were fucking William and Donna at the same time?"

"That's not true. Will and I nev—"

"Oh, because the tabloids really care about the truth. Think about it, Derek. What do I have to lose? I'm dying. And thanks to you and Tony, William's acting career is over; his teaching career, too. The statute of limitations is up on assault, so it's not like they can touch him legally. We have nothing left to lose. But you, you stand to lose everything. I've got a reporter on the premises right now who can get this story out before you even—"

"What's going on in here?"

James froze as the hallway flooded with bright, fluorescent light and Tony stepped forward. *Shit.* James had been so busy eavesdropping that he hadn't heard Tony come in.

"I take it this is your man on the inside?" Tony grabbed James by the arm and yanked him out of the shadows.

All the color drained from Robert's face, and James knew he'd fucked up.

"He's not even William's real boyfriend, is he?" He studied James. "I knew I recognized you. You were at the bachelor party, too, weren't you? Only, you had a beard then. Let me guess, Robert planted you there to capture the start of William's epic comeback?" Tony turned to sneer at the dying man. "Didn't turn out exactly the way you'd planned, did it? He's probably the one who wrote all those nasty things about William, too. That poor kid. With parents like you and Donna, it's no wonder he turned out to be such a mess."

James wanted to defend himself, to defend Will, but something in Robert's cold stare told him to keep his mouth shut. Maybe Robert was right. Maybe he shouldn't show a single card. What was that line Es said all the time? *The moment you show your cards, they know you're playing the game.*

"Why don't you two head back inside?" Tony said. "Robert and I need to have a little chat."

"Does Will know?" Derek fell in step beside James as he made his way across the lawn to the front entrance of the cathedral.

"Know what? That you fucked his mother? No, he doesn't remember anything from that night."

"No, that you're a pap. I've seen the way he looks at you. He's in love with you. How could you use him like that?"

James picked up the pace. "Robert was right. You really are profoundly stupid."

"What's that supposed to mean?"

James stopped and turned to face Derek. He was about the same height as James, but he had at least twenty pounds of brawn on him. "It means I didn't leak those stories. Tony did. And you know it."

"Oh, and I should believe you?"

"Whatever. You're gonna believe what you wanna believe. But the truth is still the truth even if it's not convenient for you." James started walking again. He was done with this asshole.

But Derek wasn't finished. "I'm going to tell him, you know. I'm going to tell Will."

James hadn't punched anyone in the face in a long time, not since he'd socked Travis in the jaw. He rounded on the Academy Award winning actor, and his bandages stretched as he balled his hand into a fist.

"Will is not a violent person. He's not even hot-tempered, not like me. What did you do to him, besides get him drunk and fuck his mother? The Will I know wouldn't hurt a fly. There has to be more."

Derek didn't respond, but the shame in his eyes was all the answer James needed.

"Why did you tell him?" James asked. "Did you really just wanna hurt him?"

Derek still didn't answer, but he cast his eyes to the ground, and the scar cutting across his eyebrow twitched. As much as James wanted to hate him—as much as he did hate him—he was starting to see what was really going on.

"You liked him, didn't you? Is that why you told him? You wanted to come clean before—" James couldn't finish the sentence. The idea of Derek and Will together made his blood boil. But that had been Derek's plan, hadn't it? He hadn't wanted to hurt Will. He'd wanted to love him, the right way, without secrets.

"What do you care? Are you going to put it in your next story? You don't even like him. This is all just a paycheck to you."

"Of course I friggin' like him. I love him." The words were out before James could stop them. It was too soon to think about love, let alone say the word.

"Then tell him the truth, or I will." Derek took a few steps away and then turned back. "And when you do, word of advice, make sure there aren't any blunt objects nearby."

As Derek disappeared across the lawn, James stared up at the giant white steeple on top of the old brick cathedral. What was he supposed to do now? He couldn't tell Will at his brother's wedding. Will had a toast to give, and there might be directors and producers there willing to give him a chance. Besides, Esther needed more time to open the phone.

Shit. Derek had better keep his friggin' mouth shut, at least for the rest of the day.

What James really needed was that fucking pen recorder. Maybe if he had proof that Tony was the leak, Derek would do the right thing: fire Tony and quit the movie.

CHAPTER 41
WILL

Andy tossed the tabloid onto the hard leather sofa. His face was so pale his freckles looked like a child's splatter painting. He usually did a good job of ignoring the trash written about him, but today he was particularly vulnerable.

"What if it's right? What if the real reason I'm marrying Nandi is because she's the only woman in the world hotter than Mom?"

"This article is bullshit." Enrique pushed Will out of the way and adjusted his bowtie in the mirror. Enrique wore a mint green tuxedo, and instead of his usual man bun, his hair was down. "Your mom's still pretty hot, and she's old. It's like comparing apples and old apples. We're going to have to level the playing field somehow to really get to the bottom of this."

He stepped away from the mirror and realized he'd left his champagne on the other side of the room. "I know, maybe we can compare magazine covers from when they were both the same age. We'll spread them out and ask a random sampling of a hundred men and lesbians to rate them. Or, to avoid bias, because they're both so well known, we can ask your dad to tell us where to find that tribe in the

Amazon he was talking about, the one where only the kids are allowed to talk."

Will stared at Enrique, who looked like a shamrock shake with muscles, and reminded himself that his brother's best friend was actually a great guy. He gave more than half of his money to charity, and he was always there for Andy when he needed him, like when Andy's ex-girlfriend cheated on him with her backup dancer. And he was the only one of Andy's friends who didn't make a point of staying as far away from Will as humanly possible whenever photographers were around. In fact, at the first *Hollow Point* premier, Enrique had tried to force Will to walk the red carpet with them.

Still, Will didn't have time for Enrique's nonsense. He had more important things to think about, like how James had lied to him, and for no good reason. Did James really think Will would've cared? The movie was based on his dead brother's memoir; of course James wanted to be there for filming. Fuck, if Will had known, he'd have snuck James onto the set himself.

Ryan, who was probably going to give Theo a heart attack in his rose-colored tux, jumped up to intervene, and for a brief moment Will thought he could sit this one out. But he was wrong.

"You're still going to run into the problem of generational bias," Ryan said. "The hair, the makeup, the editing capabilities, they're all going to skew the results. Like, did they even have airbrushing and photoshop back then?"

"Jesus Christ, who gives a shit who's hotter?" Will handed Andy his untouched glass of champagne. "Nandi is funny and smart and kind, and for some reason she loves you. Stop being an asshole."

Great, now Will was second guessing his wedding toast, which he'd written on the power of positive intent after attending a teaching workshop on the topic. But Andy didn't need advice on how to stay married, especially from Will. Andy needed validation.

There was a knock at the door, followed by their mother's voice. "Are you decent?"

"Yeah, Mom," Andy said. "The circle jerk isn't until later."

The door opened and their mother entered with the photographer on her heels. "We're just going to snap a few candids before the ceremony," she said. "Pay no attention to us."

Well, so much for giving Andy a pep-talk before the ceremony. Although, maybe their mother was onto something. Maybe smiling for the camera was exactly the distraction Andy needed to get him to the starting line. He always was a ham for the camera.

The moment the photographer left, the wedding planner entered with her team of assistants. "It's go time, boys." She went down the line, making sure they were all picture perfect. "Andy, you go with Teresa into the church. You groomsmen"—she wagged a long, bony finger at them—"you follow me."

Enrique clapped Andy on the back. "You got this, man. Just try not to pop wood when you see Nandi in her dress."

Panic flashed across Andy's eyes, and he looked down at his crotch.

"And if you do," Ryan said, "I recommend covering it with a three ring binder. It used to work wonders for me in middle school." He turned to one of the assistants. "Do you have any three ring binders handy by any chance?"

"Jesus Christ, you're not going to get a boner in church, stop." Will locked eyes with his little brother and took a series of deep breaths until Andy did the same. "This is the coolest thing you've ever done, and that's saying something. Remember that time you jacked off while skydiving? Just enjoy it, okay?"

Andy swallowed a brick of saliva. "Okay."

They parted ways, and Andy looked far more likely to puke than pop wood. But there was nothing Will could do about that. Right now, he had his own problems to deal with. He was about to walk through a crowd of people who despised him.

"Holy shit." Enrique's tongue lolled out of his mouth as they met up with the bridal party in their corresponding teal, mint, and rose gowns.

A throat cleared, and they all turned to behold Nandi, who stood apart from the others. Normally, Will didn't care for wedding dresses. They all looked the same to him, beaded and lacy and irresponsibly expensive. But this one wasn't bad. It was simple, modest even. Knowing Nandi, it was probably made from the bleached bones of ivory poachers and would make a bigger splash than Gaga's meat dress, but it looked good, especially with her hair cascading over her shoulders in ebony waves. Of course, Nandi could make a Snuggie look good.

Enrique dramatically clapped his hands over his crotch. "Holy fucking shit. Ryan, get me a three ring binder, *stat*."

"We go in two minutes," the planner said and started arranging everyone. Will in teal and Monika in rose were positioned last, right before the bride. When Nandi had described the aesthetic to him, he'd thought it sounded messy. But now that he saw it for himself, he had to admit, it really was stunning.

Of course, the second they were lined up and ready to go, the ring bearer had to pee. The moment he left, the flower girl started crying.

Will assumed the wedding planner would have some skills with kids, this being her job and all, but telling a six-year-old to stop crying or she'd ruin her makeup was not best practice.

Will intervened and led the wedding party in a rousing version of "The Wheels on the Bus." By the time the ring bearer returned, Enrique had taken over and the drag queens on the bus were going queef, queef, queef, which made no fucking sense.

The great hall of the old cathedral was awe inspiring. The red-carpeted aisle, now littered with rose, teal, and mint flower petals, led through rows of hard wooden pews. Holding up the domed ceiling, with its ornate golden designs, were tall columns of white marble. Lamps on long golden chains hung between the columns, and sharp beams of summer light fell through the long windows, lighting up motes of dust that would've made Roger, the cinematographer, come in his pants.

Will wasn't a religious man, yet he felt humbled by the majesty of the great room, which seemed to have a similar effect on everyone in attendance, putting them all on their best behavior.

Heads turned to watch the procession, and the wedding goers gushed over the little flower girl, who'd rebounded spectacularly from her tears and was now tossing flower petals like beads in a Mardi Gras parade. They snickered and pointed at the little ring bearer, who'd forgotten to zip up his fly. And surprisingly, no one said anything disparaging about Will. He heard a few people whisper, "Is that William Chapman?" but no one threw rotten tomatoes at him or made the sign of the cross.

Will found James in the second row, and he was bowled over by the sudden wave of tenderness he felt for him. Back in the limo, James had said he was scared, and now he looked it. He looked like he was at a funeral, not a wedding. No one had ever cared enough about Will to be scared of losing him, except for maybe his students. To everyone else, Will was either a sure thing or disposable.

Will caught James's eye and flashed his best *this could be us one day* smile, and James did his best to smile back, though it was clear he was going to need more reassurance. Where was a closet when you needed one?

CHAPTER 42

JAMES

James tried to find Will after the ceremony, but by the time he made it through the crowd, the wedding party was already headed to an undisclosed location to take pictures. So, he went outside to look for Theo and Donna instead. He found them on the front steps, talking to Robert.

"Oh, good, there you are," Robert said. "Donna, do you mind if I steal James for the ride over? I need to run a few ideas by our resident Vermont expert."

Donna stared at her ex-husband with thinly veiled disdain. "Of course. Although, would it kill you to stop working for one day? It is our son's wedding, after all."

A wicked smile spread across Robert's face. "You know, it just might."

Once they were alone in Robert's frigid limo, the man's fragile façade crumbled. He pulled a bottle of pills from his pocket and swallowed several with a pained sip of water.

"Are you okay?" James asked, but Robert didn't reply. James knew the drive to the waterfront was short, so he pressed on. "I'm sorry. I shouldn't have followed you. But Es got the phone, and I didn't want—"

"I've come up with a new plan." Robert took another pained sip of water. "But before I tell you, I need to ask you something."

James swallowed hard. "Okay."

"Is it all a performance, or do you actually care for my son?"

The air conditioning was on full blast, and it chilled the film of nervous sweat on James's skin. He thought of Will, of staring into his dark eyes and seeing nothing but vibrant color. Will had been scarred by life, but any bitterness he harbored was only skin deep. The real Will, the one few people got to see, was full of so much goodness. He'd do anything for the people he cared about—brave the scrutiny of the press for his brother, swallow his pride and dignity to support his pompous father. Hell, he'd even committed insurance fraud for his fake boyfriend's fake son.

"It's not a performance." James wanted to tell Robert the rest, that he was done doing things behind Will's back. But Robert spoke before he got the chance.

"I didn't think so. And that's why I'm going to take a chance on you and pray I'm not putting my faith in the wrong person. Though, at this point, I don't know what other choice I have. You're William's last hope."

Robert took another pill from the bottle, and James tried to tamp down the bubble of anxiety growing in his gut. What did Robert mean by last hope?

"That video clip you found on Donna's phone was only a small snippet of the security footage Tony stole from the hotel that night. Ten years ago, I saw a different clip, one showing Donna knocking on Derek's door and William emerging hysterical, the bloody statue in his hand."

A flood of emotions washed over James—jealousy, fear, disappointment. He understood feeling jealous. The idea of Will in Derek's hotel room made James's skin crawl. And he understood the fear. If this got out, Will would be destroyed. But why should James feel disappointed? Had he really been holding out hope that it hadn't been Will who'd attacked Derek? Why should that matter?

"It cost us ten million dollars to silence Tony. He told Derek to lie to the police. He said if anyone knew William was in his room at that hour, they'd get the wrong idea. And since Derek didn't want to get William in trouble, he agreed."

"But it wasn't the wrong idea, was it?"

Robert frowned and shook his head. "I didn't know Derek felt that way about William. And I certainly didn't know about him and Donna. Although, perhaps I should've. I just assumed they were fighting over the award and William's obsession and—" Robert broke off and hung his head in his hands.

"And you've never told Will any of this?"

"Of course not. Do you really want him to live the rest of his life with this on his conscience, hating his mother?"

"Isn't it already on his conscience?" *And doesn't he already hate his mother?* Although that wasn't entirely true, was it? Will had a complicated relationship with his mother, sure. But, for better or worse, he still viewed her as his safety net. And with his father dying, he was going to need her more than ever.

Robert had no reply, other than to close his eyes and wait for the pills to take effect.

When he opened his eyes again, James asked, "Okay, so what's this new plan of yours, and how do I fit in?"

Robert didn't want to abandon their original plan. He still wanted James to recover the rest of the security footage from Tony's phone. Maybe there'd be proof Derek had it coming, or a case to be made that it was self-defense. But Robert wasn't counting on that, which was why he'd come up with a backup plan.

Robert wanted the same spyware they were installing on Tony's phone installed on his phone, too. That way, when Robert paid Tony an additional five million dollars for his continued silence, James would have proof of the extortion, a crime that came with up to twenty-five years in prison. With that proof, James could blackmail Tony into handing the five million dollars over to him.

"You'll walk away from this a millionaire," Robert said. "I don't want the money back. I don't need it. But you and Theo do. And all you have to do is beat Tony at his own game."

There was one major catch to Robert's plan, a catch that made it the worst friggin' plan ever. In order to sell the threat and ensure Tony didn't release the video, Robert wanted James to sell himself as some kind of double agent.

"We'll make Tony think you're also blackmailing me and Donna, that William is just a means to an end, your way of getting close to us," Robert explained. "And because you want to keep on blackmailing us, you need Tony to promise not to release the video. Does that make sense?"

No, that did not make sense. What the hell?

"Look at it this way," Robert said, reading the confusion on James's face. "At the end of the day, the information you and Tony have is valuable. If this got out, not only would it destroy William, but Donna and I as well, not to mention Derek. Tony is either going to continue milking us for all we're worth until he dies, or he's going to sell that video to the highest bidder the moment Derek stops being his number one cash cow. But if my plan works, you'll have the power to stop him, the power to prove he's been blackmailing us this whole time, the power to send him to prison if he doesn't do what you ask.

"But your leverage over him is worthless if he thinks your feelings for William are genuine. Then you'll be no better than Donna or I. Tony can't know that you care about William or else he'll call your bluff. You have to make him think you want in on the action, that, from now on, you're going to be the only one blackmailing us, not him, that you don't care one way or the other if that video is released. You just want to get paid. And since Tony's already gotten ten million out of the deal and likely doesn't want to spend the rest of his life in prison for extortion, not to mention risk destroying

Derek's career, he'll agree. I know he will. He's greedy, but he's not stupid."

"So you're saying you want me to pretend to be some kind of criminal mastermind, just fucking and blackmailing everyone and anyone I can?"

"Well, yeah, more or less."

"But what about Will? This will destroy him. If he thinks I've just been using him to—"

"It will hurt him, yes, but he'll get over it. And he'll finally be able to act again. It's all he's ever wanted to do. And you've only been dating for a short while, right? Come on, you're a handsome man. Surely, you'll find someone else soon enough. And don't forget, you'll be a millionaire. You'll have your pick of any guy you want."

Not any guy. Not Will.

"Think about Theo and what he needs," Robert continued. "Imagine, no more worrying about rent or college tuition or Theo's medical bills, should he test positive for the gene. In fact, I'm going to set up an anonymous trust in Theo's name for another five million. So, that's ten million in total."

James stared back at the frail man in utter disbelief. Was he doing this for Will's sake or his own? Was this all just so he could safeguard his precious legacy and not be remembered as the man who'd tried to cover up his son's crime?

"Just think about it. But don't think too long. We're running out of time."

Robert opened the pill bottle again, and James knew what he really meant. *We* weren't running out of time. Robert was.

"I know you haven't agreed yet, and that this is all a lot to consider. But I trust you. And I know you'll do the right thing for William, and for you and Theo, too." Robert unlocked his phone and passed it to James. "You can still say no, but why don't you just install what you need to install now, just in case?"

James closed his eyes and took the phone from Robert, his stomach roiling. When he was done installing the spyware, he asked

Robert the question that had been bugging him ever since he'd overheard Robert and Derek arguing behind the cathedral.

"Why is Tony doing this? I mean, I get the whole blackmail thing, but why didn't he want Will in the movie if Derek did? Is he jealous of Will and Derek?"

Robert sighed as he took back his phone. "Derek didn't win the Oscar. William lost it. Derek's career is in free fall right now because good looks can only get you so far in this business. The moment William finds an audience again, Derek loses the only thing he has going for him, sympathy."

"You've gotta be fucking kidding me."

"I'm not. Tony swooped in the second he heard the rumors William was starring in my next film. He thought he could kill two birds with one stone, hitch Derek's tanking career to my coattails and prevent William from making a comeback."

The chauffeur opened the door, and a humid wave of hot air washed over James. "I'm not saying yes. But I will think about it."

"Oh my god, did you see the way Ryan's blue eyes sparkled? He needs to wear pink more often."

Theo monologued from the prow of the ship, pausing occasionally to snarf a stuffed mushroom or bacon-wrapped date. But James wasn't listening. He was still reeling from Robert's offer.

Ten million dollars was a lot of money, especially to them. Theo would never have to work a day in his life. He could travel and make music. And Will would get his career back, his passion.

The choice was obvious. So, why hadn't James told Robert yes? What was he waiting for?

A hand settled on James's shoulder, and he lifted his eyes from the trail of sunlight cutting across the lake and blinked away the sunspots dotting his vision.

"So, what do you think?" Theo asked.

"About what?"

"Oh my fucking god. You're the worst. Are you really that worried about bottoming? Why don't you just get one of those dilator sets? You start small and build your way up."

James grabbed a stuffed mushroom off Theo's plate. "I'm not worried about bottoming."

Theo dropped his voice to a whisper. "Don't look now, but here comes Es."

James saw her out of the corner of his eye. She wore all black, and her hair was pulled into a severe ponytail. She looked every bit the unassuming photographer. She had one camera in her hand and another dangling around her neck.

"I'll be right back."

James met Esther outside the men's room. Once he had Tony's phone in hand, he ducked inside, locked himself in a stall, and got to work.

HOLDEN RIVERS, Robert's longtime friend and frequent collaborator, was the emcee for the evening, and he announced the arrival of the wedding party to raucous applause. The moment James spotted Will, a teal streak running hand in hand with Monika, all his certainty vanished. Was he really going to go through with this?

The dining room was lushly decorated. Each table sat under a veritable rainforest of hanging plants. Derek sat two rows back, between Tony and some new blonde model. Apparently, he'd moved on from Sharron Moore.

Derek must've felt James's gaze on him because he turned and raised his glass in salute. *You tell him, or I will.*

Will came and sat next to James at the long table reserved for the wedding party and their dates. He placed his hand in James's and squeezed. His palm was slick with sweat.

"I missed you," James said, accidentally letting the truth slip out.

Will smiled, and James's heart somersaulted in his chest.

"I missed you, too." Will's breath was a hundred proof. "Jesus, I'm so fucking drunk right now. I just spent the past two hours rewriting my entire toast, and now it's all one big jumble in my head because Enrique made me drink tequila. There was a fucking scorpion in the bottle."

"Why did you change your toast? I'm sure the one you wrote is perfect. Trust yourself." James pulled their joined hands onto his lap.

The music changed to some upbeat Bollywood tune, and everyone stood as Holden introduced Andy and Nandi for the first time as husband and wife.

Nandi had changed into a dark cranberry gown overlain with bronze lace flowers. Her hair was pulled back and showed off her long, slender neck. A pair of ruby earrings the size of strawberries dangled from her ears.

Nandi flashed the crowd a radiant smile. "Thank you all for coming. Andy and I are touched you made the journey up here, and we're honored to share this day with you."

"Indeed," Andy added. "Now, let's eat." He rubbed his belly, and a wave of laughter rippled through the room.

The boat pushed off from the dock, and the music changed to something quiet and conversational, all violins and cellos. Evening sunlight poured through the windows and over the hanging plants, sending fern shaped shadows across the tables.

James's stomach lurched, even though he wasn't prone to seasickness. The food was probably delicious, petite crab cakes, white asparagus soup, balsamic poached fig with lemon truffle cherry vinaigrette, but James didn't notice. It could've been dog food for all he cared. How could he go through with this? How could he not?

"Now, it's time to hear from the best man, the groom's brother, Mr. William Chapman."

Will headed up to the podium, and the room fell into an eerie silence. James clenched his fists, ready to fight anyone who so much as shot Will a nasty look. James hadn't felt this nervous on someone else's behalf since Theo's middle school recital.

Will stared out over the crowd and placed a hand on either side of the podium. "You know that part in romantic comedies where the heroine throws out her prepared speech and speaks from the heart instead, and it's, like, a million times sweeter?"

Will mostly succeeded in not slurring his words, though he swayed back and forth with the motion of the boat. This was going to be bad. Not a single fork scraped a single dish. Even the children, who must've sensed the thrum of anxiety, stopped fidgeting in their chairs.

"This is not that." Will gripped the podium tighter for support. He caught James's eye and smiled. "Although, you never know, right? Life is full of surprises."

Will turned and gave his smile to Nandi and Andy next.

"People are always praising women for transforming men, but I want to thank Nandi for leaving Andy alone. He's already perfect, and he's the best brother ever."

Man, Will was wasted. He sounded like all the drunks at closing time at the Starlight, swaying arm in arm back to their cars.

"Andy and I used to share a room when we were little. The nursery, we called it. But then our parents decided we were too codependent and made us get separate rooms. I was a little sad, but Andy was devastated. He was only four at the time, but he held that sledgehammer like it weighed nothing and started knocking down the wall between our new rooms. When Mom asked him what he was doing, he lied and told her we wanted to play full court basketball on our laundry hoops."

"True story," Andy said, and another wave of laughter rippled through the room. The laughter seemed to loosen the set of Will's shoulders and set free his real smile, the one that made James want to find the nearest closet.

"Man, Mom was pissed." Will spoke to Andy like they were the only two people in the room. "Of course, she got over it when Antonio, the contractor, showed up. Damn, he was so hot."

"Speaking of people who are hot. I remember the first time I met Nandi. I was so nervous because Andy had a habit of dumping girls who were mean to me, and I didn't want to ruin this for him. So, when I walked into his house, I tried to make myself as small and unthreatening as possible. I thought maybe if she didn't notice me, she wouldn't accidentally say or do something to upset Andy."

Pressure built in James's chest, and his heart tripped over the truth of Will's words. That was it, wasn't it? Will had spent the last decade trying to be as small and unthreatening as possible. No wonder he'd become a kindergarten teacher.

Will ran a hand through his black hair, and now he looked as drunk as he sounded.

"I needn't have worried, though. The moment I stepped into the room, she smiled and said, 'Can I give you a hug?' And it was a really good hug, too."

Will exhaled slowly, and it physically hurt James to imagine never hugging Will again.

"The best man is supposed to tell an embarrassing story about the groom. And I'm told if you do it right, no one will ever ask you to be best man again, not that I have to worry about that. But I'll do it anyway.

"The most embarrassing story I can think of is the time we threw Mom and Grandma a Mother's Day barbeque and Andy was in charge of the playlist."

"You cannot tell this story," Andy said, his face chalk white.

"It's too late now. I already started." Will forgot he was supposed to wait until the end of his toast to drink and took a swig of champagne. "Anyway, Andy was in charge of the playlist and had his computer hooked up to the Bluetooth on the patio. He must've forgotten to disconnect because, later that night, when we were all asleep, it sounded like some guy with validation issues had broken into our back yard. He kept asking over and over again, in this husky voice, about the size of his . . . well, let's just go with heart. 'Do you like that big heart? Tell me you like that big heart.' But no one would answer him, not the seals clapping in the background—at least, I assume they were seals—or the woman with the leg cramp—at least, I assume she had a leg cramp. She seemed to be in a lot of pain."

The smile on Donna's face in the front row was meme worthy. She looked like she was trying to take a shit while marshaling a parade. But Will had the rest of the crowd in stitches, and James wondered why he'd ever doubted him. Will was magnetic when given the chance, even drunk.

"Mom and I arrived on the scene at the same time, both of us eager to see the size of the heart on the man with the husky voice. But, wouldn't you know it? Grandma Chapman had already beat us there and scared the man, the woman with the leg cramp, and all of the seals away.

"The next morning, over breakfast, Andy told everyone, with a completely straight face, mind you, that he was studying to become a marine biologist and had been watching nature documentaries all night. We all nodded, and Grandma, not wanting to shame her grandson, got him an internship at the San Diego Zoo. So, now you all know why Andy has so many fish tanks."

Will turned to his brother. "Actually, I get why you didn't want me to tell that story now. You're hardly in it, and it really falls apart in the third act."

Will was about to drink his champagne again, but this time he caught himself.

"Anyway, I should probably quote some Shakespeare and get serious now, right?" Will's face took on a look of somber intensity. "Love is not love which alters when its alteration finds, or bends with the remover to remove. Oh no! It is an ever-fixed mark that looks on tempests and is never shaken." His lips curled into a wry smile. "I can't remember the rest, but you get the idea. And it's true, isn't it? Love is indestructible.

"But love is not the same as marriage. Marriage—all relationships, really—are just flimsy containers we try to stuff love inside, not realizing love is so much bigger than commitment. Don't get me wrong. I hope you beat the odds and your marriage lasts forever. But what I'm in awe of right now is not your commitment, but your love. I mean, think about it, you two have the kind of love where you can pop each other's ass zits with impunity. How awesome is that?"

Nandi smacked Andy's shoulder. "I can't believe you told your brother about that."

"I didn't," Andy said, laughing, "I swear."

"Yeah, Nandi, it's called a metaphor. But thanks for sharing."

Will looked down at his champagne, and his desire to drink seemed to overpower his desire to keep talking.

"Anyway, in summary, here are your three big takeaways." Will held up a closed fist and started counting off on his fingers. He could be such a teacher sometimes. "One: Your marriage may or may not last, but your love is forever. Two: Everyone gets butt acne, even absurdly pretty people who give amazing hugs. Three: Always disconnect from the Bluetooth before watching nature documentaries late at night. And four—I know I said there were only three, but I just thought of another one—and four: Andy, you're the best brother ever, and I love you so fucking much."

"To marine biology," Enrique shouted, which pretty much summed up Will's rambling toast. Man, Will was more like his father than James realized.

Holden took back the microphone and said, "And that, my friends, is why we turned in our phones and signed NDAs."

Will found James's hand under the table, and James decided there had to be another way, an option C, something he just hadn't thought of yet.

THE SUN WAS SETTING when the party moved upstairs to the dance floor. For the first several dances, James managed to keep hidden on the perimeter, but then Will started dancing with Nandi, and Andy got it in his head that he and James should dance, too.

Andy draped his lanky, freckled arms over James's shoulders, and James held Andy's hips like they were at a middle school dance. Meanwhile, Will and Nandi looked like they were competing on *Dancing with The Stars.*

"Thanks for bringing my brother back," Andy said. He wore a warm smile, and his pale blue eyes were blissed out and misty.

"What do you mean?"

"You know"—Andy looked at James like he should be able to read his mind—"for bringing Will's sass back. Will used to be the king of sass. He never used to give a shit if he pissed people off. But after everything, he became super cautious and shit, like it'd be the end of the world if he offended someone. But that toast was classic Will."

Andy was still smiling, but now he was crying, too. Apparently, Donna was the only one in Will's family who didn't cry several times a day.

"I missed my brother. I didn't realize how much until tonight. And you brought him back. So thanks."

"I can't take credit for that."

Andy shrugged and rested his head on James's shoulder. People were staring and laughing, and the real photographer was having a field day, but Andy didn't seem to notice or care.

When the song was over, Andy pulled back and said, "Oh, I almost forgot. I did some research today, and I think I've solved your problem. You just need to get Botox on your sphincter. It'll loosen it right up."

James should've been embarrassed, and he was, but it had been a long time since he'd been the butt of a family joke, and it made him miss his brother, and, in a way, his father, too.

"Okay, I'll get right on that."

CHAPTER 43
WILL

"Theo looks happy." Will's mother came and stood beside him at the bar. The band was on a break, and Theo and Ryan were up on the stage covering some obscure song only they knew. It was somewhat atonal, but Will was so drunk he rather liked it.

"He does," Will agreed. Life had dealt Theo a terrible hand, yet he remained spirited and optimistic.

"How are things with you and James?"

"Fine."

"Don't be too hard on him, okay? Sometimes it's not about you."

Will clenched his jaw. When was it ever about him? Even before the Golden Globes fiasco, it wasn't about him. It was about how he might beat his father to the Oscar podium right out of the gate.

"Did you know about James?" Will asked. His mother hadn't seemed surprised when Emily showed up, just annoyed.

"Not when I hired him, no."

Will rolled his eyes. "And after?"

His mother shrugged and took a sip of her wine. "I mean, I had my suspicions, but I didn't think it mattered. Does it?"

The bartender set two Manhattans before Will. "I should probably go bring James his drink."

Will found James, Miles, and Tiffany smoking a joint just outside the strobing lights of the dance floor. Beyond them, the moon cut a silver trail across the lake.

"I thought you were saving that for me," Will said, passing James his Manhattan.

That morning, James had stuffed a joint in his pocket and announced, "We're gonna smoke this on the prow of the ship later tonight, just like Jack and Rose." To which Will had replied, "I think you're misremembering the plot of *Titanic*."

"This one's mine," Tiffany said. "Monika gave it to me. She's taking me to Fashion Week next month."

Will cocked an eyebrow. "Really? Look at you, making friends with models."

"You might make friends with models, too, if you stopped referring to them as models. People are not just their jobs, Will."

"That's a relief, seeing as I don't have one anymore. I'd hate to be a nobody." Will leaned against James, who went briefly rigid before returning the pressure.

"You're going to get your job back," Miles said. "Don't you worry. This is all going to blow over."

Will doubted that, but it didn't matter. With James at his side, Will felt like he could handle anything, even saying goodbye to all the little rugrats who'd given his life meaning for the past five years.

"Can you hold this for a minute?" Will said, handing James his drink. "I have to use the restroom."

"Sure."

Before leaving, Will leaned in and brushed his lips against James's ear. "When I come back, what do you say we go look for a closet somewhere?"

"I heard that," Miles said. "And I already know the perfect one. It's on the bottom floor, near the back of the ship."

Will made his way across the upper deck and headed downstairs to the bathrooms. When he reached the second floor, a deep, booming voice bellowed his name.

"Will, come have a drink with me." Derek sat at the bar in the virtually empty dining room. Derek's date, an Irish model Nandi hated because she wore real fur, was nowhere in sight.

"I have to pee."

"Just have a quick shot, then."

Will hadn't seen Derek this drunk in ages, maybe ever. He'd removed his jacket and pushed his white sleeves up his thick forearms.

"Come on, we never hang out anymore. You're always with what's-his-face."

Will was tempted to point out that what's-his-face's name was James and that they didn't hang out anymore because, until recently, Derek had a court order forbidding it. But instead, he ordered a shot of bourbon.

Derek pointed at his empty glass, and the bartender refilled it with Southern Comfort. "I liked your toast. I love how even when you don't make sense, you make sense."

Will smiled even though he had no clue what Derek was talking about. His toast had been terrible.

"I talked to Tony, and he swears he didn't leak those stories."

Will didn't want to talk about Tony. He knew, in Derek's eyes, Tony was irreproachable. It had been pointless to confront Derek about him in the first place.

"I was thinking maybe I could help somehow," Derek said. "Maybe after the movie is done filming, we can go on *Celebrity Jeopardy* or something. You know, like we did before. I'll even let you win this time."

"I won the last time, and it wasn't even close."

"Yeah, but this time I'll let you win."

Will finished his shot of bourbon and set it on the bar. Ugh, that was the last thing he needed. The room was already starting to spin. "I really have to pee."

"Okay, but there's something I need to tell you first, and you're not going to like it."

Will froze. Was this it? Was Derek finally going to tell him what had gone down in that hotel room ten years ago?

Derek leveled his unfocused eyes at Will. "James is not who he says he is. He's a pap, Will. He was at Andy's bachelor party, only you don't recognize him because he had a beard then. He's the one who wrote the story about you and Sharron, and probably the others, too. It wasn't Tony. It was James. He's been playing you, Will."

Derek was obviously confused. James had a secret, it was true, but he wasn't a pap. He was the real Jimmy Young.

"I think maybe you've had one too many—"

"I know it's hard to believe. But your dad hired him thinking he could control the narrative, only now James knows too much. We're so fucked, Will. He's going to ruin us both."

This was absurd. Derek was obviously high or wasted, or both. Tony was probably filling his head with paranoid bullshit again.

"There you are. I've been looking all over for you." The devil himself, Tony, stepped into the dining room and set his hand on Will's shoulder. He squeezed gently, like he was giving a massage. "William, hilarious toast. Love the adolescent humor."

Will shrunk out of Tony's grip. "I'm going to go."

As Will stepped away, Derek caught him by the wrist. "He's not right for you, Will. He's a liar. At least I told you the truth. And it didn't mean anything. I just had her poster on my wall growing up, and it—"

Tony clapped a hand over Derek's mouth. "You'll have to forgive Derek. He doesn't know what he's saying. He's had a bit too much to drink tonight."

Will turned to leave, but stopped when he saw James standing in the doorway, looking like he'd seen a ghost.

Derek pushed Tony's hand away. "I told you I'd tell him. But you didn't believe me, did you? You thought I'd keep my mouth shut. But I'm not like you. I'm better than you. I tell the truth, even when it hurts. Ask him, Will. Ask him if he's a pap."

Beside Will, Tony started to laugh. "Wait, you didn't know? This is too funny. Talk about déjà vu. Seriously, what is wrong with your family? Do they never tell you anything?"

Tony's words wiped all the color from James's face, and even James's eyes seemed a duller shade of green.

"Yes, your *boyfriend* here moonlights as an entertainment journalist. He's also a stripper, or is that not the right term anymore? I can't keep up with PC culture. Do you prefer exotic dancer? Male escort? Whatever. Point is, the guy will do just about anything for money. Even you, it seems."

This was ridiculous. James didn't even know how to dance. And the agency wouldn't let a pap work for them. *Tell them, James. Tell them you're really just Jimmy.*

But James didn't say a word. He didn't even blink. He just continued starring, like a zombie.

"See, your problem, William, is that you let your parents run your life and career. But they're only looking out for their own best interests, not yours. If you had signed with me when you had the chance, you'd be living in a mansion in Beverly Hills right now, using your Oscars as bookends."

Why wasn't James telling them they had it all wrong? James wasn't capable of something like this.

"Nothing to say for yourself?" Tony asked James. "What, are you just going to plead the fifth? Don't you think poor William, here, deserves an explanation, or at least an excuse? After all, you are fucking him, aren't you? It seems like you owe him at least that much."

Was that panic in James's eyes? Will knew that look. He saw it every day when he caught one of his students doing something they shouldn't, the quick flash of guilt that was replaced almost immediately by fear, anger, or defiance. Or, in some cases, a bottomless void. It wasn't always fight or flight. Some students froze.

"That's not possible," Will said, speaking for James. "He wasn't even in the room when Sharron threw the wine at me. He couldn't have taken the picture."

"No, but his partner could've. Isn't that right, Jimmy? Who is he? Is he here with you now?"

Wait, Tony knew that James was really Jimmy, too? Had Will been the last one to find out?

"I assume you heard the rumors William would be playing you in the movie and went to the bachelor party hell-bent on making sure that didn't happen. Am I right? Of course, you needn't have worried. Once William's father learned he was dying, that this would be his last chance to win an Oscar, he had no trouble throwing William over for Ryan."

Will's mind raced to make sense of Tony's accusations, to come up with a plausible explanation for James's silence. But his body had already begun to believe Tony. His stomach swooped, and his pulse quickened.

James was only using him. None of it was real.

Will's heart hitched in his chest, and his lungs constricted. Panic and despair clawed their way up his throat. "Say something," he begged. "Tell them they're lying."

CHAPTER 44

JAMES

The moment you show your cards, they know you're playing the game. James couldn't move. He couldn't speak. All he could do was stand there and watch Will dissolve from the inside out.

Tony had called it déjà vu, and he was right. It was just like when Will had learned he wasn't getting the part, only this time, it was James who'd put that hurt in Will's eyes. It was James who'd drained all the color from Will's face.

"Please say it's not true," Will pleaded.

James needed to explain, to tell Will everything. Maybe Will could be in on the plan. He was a better actor than anyone. They could just pretend to break up and then keep seeing each other in secret.

Although, that would never work, would it? Nothing about Will's life would ever stay secret, not for long. And then Will would be at Tony's mercy again. He might even turn himself in if he knew the truth.

And when Robert died, who would look out for Will then? Andy was just a baby in a man's body. And while Miles was a true friend,

Will's problems weren't going away with diet and exercise. And forget about Donna. She cared more about getting off than her own son.

If James didn't protect Will, who would?

James watched the moment it happened, the moment Will realized James wasn't going to deny the accusations. Will didn't yell or scream or throw his glass at James's face. He didn't even cry. He just took slow, measured breaths, each one like a dagger to James's heart.

"It's fine. I should've seen this coming. I mean, come on, look at you, and look at me."

James had followed Tony down here, desperate to stop this very thing from happening. But he was too late. Now, he had a choice to make: break Will's heart and keep the upper hand, or tell him the truth and let Tony win.

Both scenarios were too unfathomable to stomach, so he did nothing. He just stood there as every good feeling in his body, every hope for a future with Will, disintegrated like a sandcastle in the tide. Worse still, he watched the same erosion play out in Will's eyes.

Every fiber of James's soul screamed at him to run to Will, to pull him into his arms and tell him he could explain everything, that, yes, he had gone to the party to screw Will over, but that he'd been wrong. They'd all been wrong, the whole fucking world, including Will. Will needed to stop believing all the shit they wrote about him. He wasn't an entitled little rich kid who thought he was owed fame and fortune. He was smart, and kind, and handsome, and he deserved happiness, and he deserved love.

Derek stood and put his arm around Will's shoulder. "It's okay, Will. Fuck him. He's just a pap. You can do better."

Fuck this. James was going to beat the living shit out of Derek, screw the consequences.

But before he got the chance, Miles ran into the dining room. "Will, come quick. It's your dad. He's collapsed."

James wanted to reach for Will as he ran past, but he couldn't even bring himself to look Will in the eye, let alone make his arms move. Shame and anger coursed through his veins. He was going to fucking kill Tony for this.

Derek ran after Will, but stopped just long enough to gloat. "I always knew you were a liar."

Tony stayed behind and regarded James with curiosity and amusement. The ceiling above them hung with ferns and vines, and the world felt upside down. James feared if he took a step or said a word, gravity would realize its mistake and he'd fall.

"Want a drink?" Tony asked, patting the barstool beside him. "I've been sober twenty years, myself, but you look like you could use one. Plus, we have some business to discuss."

James's temper flared, and it was all he could do not to strangle Tony and throw his lifeless body overboard. He was going to destroy him. And Derek, too. Just not tonight.

"You don't know the half of it," he said, surprised by the venom in his own voice. "But not now. I'll be in touch."

He left Tony at the bar and headed below deck. He considered locking himself in a bathroom stall, but opted for a room full of stacked chairs and unused tables instead. He kicked the wall, and then turned and slumped against it.

He considered smoking the rest of the joint in his pocket, but he had to keep his head on straight. Will needed him. So did Theo.

James thought that by staying silent he hadn't made a choice. But he had. His silence was his choice, a choice to finish what Robert had started and take care of Will, to finish what Travis had started and set Theo up for life. It didn't matter what James wanted. He'd given up that right the moment he'd let Esther loose on a harmless kindergarten teacher.

James felt when the ship docked, though they couldn't possibly be back. They must've stopped in Charlotte or Shelburne to get Robert to an ambulance. Only it wasn't sirens James heard ten minutes later but the thrum of a helicopter.

Shit. It was serious, wasn't it? What if Robert died tonight?

THEO AND ESTHER found him shortly after the helicopter flew away and the ship began its long slog back to Burlington.

"What are you doing in here?" Theo asked. "Why didn't you go with Will?"

"He knows." James stared at the patterned blue carpet through his knees. "He knows everything."

"What do you mean everything?"

James lifted his head. "I fucked up."

It was a long time before Theo spoke. "Does this mean we have to go home?"

James bit his lip and nodded.

"Theo, go see if you can scrounge up some of those macarons," Esther said. "I need to have a quick word alone with your uncle. And get the pink ones."

Theo left without protest, and Esther slid down the wall and sat beside James.

"You shouldn't have come down here with him. What if someone saw you two together?"

Esther shrugged. "He was worried. No one could find you. And relax, no one saw us. They were too busy talking about Robert and what happened to Derek Hall."

"What happened to Derek?"

"You'll get a kick out of this. Apparently, Derek's new girlfriend called William a crybaby, and Derek told her to fuck off and go eat some celery, which was a pretty weak insult, though it did the trick, assuming he wanted to piss off an Irish model with three-inch nails. She got him good, too. Almost scratched his eye out. Seriously, that man needs to find himself one of those passive-aggressive southern belles. You know, the kind who channels all her negative emotions into hating other women." Esther probably expected James to laugh, and when he didn't, her tone grew serious again. "Did you get it installed?"

James nodded.

"Does William know about me?"

James shook his head.

"So he doesn't know everything. He doesn't even know you're working with his father to take down Tony Wallingford, does he? What does Tony have on Robert anyway? He's blackmailing him, isn't he?"

James didn't respond. Esther was like a shark. She could smell a single drop of blood from an ocean away.

"It's about William, isn't it? Is it proof that he did it?"

Esther must've seen the outline of the joint in his pocket because she reached in and pulled it out. She fished a lighter from her own pocket.

She took a drag and passed the joint to James. "You actually like this one, don't you? He's got one hell of an ass on him, that's for sure."

James hit the joint, not because he wanted to, but because it was in his hand.

"Talk to me, Jimmy. I promise, I'm not gonna say a word. Trust me, that was a beast of an NDA, and I know who butters my bread. Robert was very generous. Hell, I'd fucking shoot Wallingford myself for what he's paying me."

"He wants me to blackmail Tony, and he wants Tony to think I'm blackmailing him and Donna, too."

Esther took the joint back, and because she was the smartest person James knew, she understood immediately. "So now you have to pretend you were only fucking William to screw him over. That's brutal, babe. But don't worry, I've got you. We'll nail that fucker's balls to the wall, and then you can go right back to tapping that fine ass."

"It's not gonna be that easy, not if Robert dies tonight." And even if Will knew everything, would he forgive James? James had cost him his job. No, not just his job, his whole friggin' career.

"Trust me, I know men like Tony Wallingford. I bet he's got a lot of secrets on his phone. I hear he's a regular Harvey Weinstein when it comes to recruiting new talent, especially with the young ones."

"Was Will okay?" James already knew the answer, but he had to ask.

"Are you kidding me? He's fine. It was Andy Chapman who fell apart. I think I get why you like William so much. He's just like you, thinks he has to be strong and take care of everyone else."

James filled his lungs to capacity and only exhaled because he was about to pass out. "I can't do this."

"Yes, you can. And I'm gonna help you."

CHAPTER 45
WILL

It was late morning and Will was alone in the waiting room when the doctor came out and said his father was asking for him.

Will's mother was away dealing with the dog, and Andy and Nandi were back at their hotel getting a change of clothes. Miles was down in the cafeteria getting Will another scone. That was how Will knew things were serious. Miles was even buttering them for him.

The air caught in Will's lungs when he saw his father in the hospital bed. Growing up, his father had seemed larger than life, a giant of the big screen. Now, he was small and pale, his skin the blueish gray of death. But he smiled when he saw Will.

"I was doing some thinking"—his speech was only slightly slurred from his mild stroke—"and if we shoot the death scene now and rewrite the script to focus more on the brothers, we can still salvage the movie."

"Would you just forget the fucking movie already? It doesn't matter."

"They need to see it. They need to see you. Once the studio sees . .

." His father lost his train of thought, and his eyes followed a shadow on the wall like a cat chasing a laser.

Will let every molecule of air slip from his lungs before he took another breath. "I'm not in the movie, Dad, and they've already decided to postpone the shoot for a while. You're in the hospital, and Derek has to wear an eyepatch for the next six weeks."

"What? No." His father's voice was hoarse. "We don't need Derek. It's you. It's always been you."

Will set his hand on top of his father's. "No, Dad, it's never been me, and I'm okay with that. I know you had all these hopes for me, and I appreciate that. I really do. But you're the movie star. You're the legend. You and Mom and Andy. And that's good enough for me." Will reached up and wiped the drool from his father's mouth. He knew his father would be inconsolable about the movie, knew how much he wanted to die believing he was going to win a posthumous Oscar. "And you don't need an Academy Award for everyone to know how great you are."

Tears slid down his father's chalky face. "You deserved better. Better than me. Better than your mother. I shouldn't have stood. I don't know why I stood."

Will didn't know what his father was talking about, but the doctor had warned him he might be muddled and confused. "It's okay." Will tried to sound soothing, like he was talking to one of his students. "It doesn't matter."

"I should've fought harder. I should've found another way. I should've made your mother tell me everything. But I just let it happen. I just let her take care of everything."

Will squeezed his father's hand gently. "It doesn't matter."

With considerable effort, his father turned his head away from Will. "You have every right to hate me."

"I don't hate you, Dad. Why would you think that? I don't hate anyone. This isn't your fault. My fucked-up life isn't your fault."

Will closed his eyes and forced himself to practice the power of positive intent, like he did with his students. It was easier to cope with the world if you focused on the outcome people were hoping to achieve instead of the harm they caused along the way. Julian didn't pull Brianna's hair because he wanted to make her scream. He only wanted the blue chair she was sitting in.

James hadn't set out to destroy Will's life. He and Theo had just needed the money. That had been all. Stories about Will paid well, and since James had wanted to be there when they filmed his brother's movie, Will had been an obvious target.

It had been the same with Will's father. He hadn't been trying to squelch Will's comeback. He'd just been trying to achieve his dream of winning an Oscar.

Will hadn't been the subject of some coordinated offensive. He'd been collateral damage. If Will hadn't been the only other gay man around for miles, James never would've even given him the time of day. It had been the same with his father. If Will hadn't sullied the Chapman name, his dad never would've been put in a position where he had to choose between his legacy and his son's acting career. None of this had been personal.

Once, when Will was very young, his nanny had let him stay up late and watch TV because he had a bad cough and couldn't sleep. A nature documentary had come on about a mother tiger and her two cubs. One had been born blind, and though the mother had carried him around for a while, she'd eventually given up and left him to die. His cries, little chirps like a bird, had been pathetic and heartbreaking.

Will had run past his sleeping nanny and into his father's room. He'd been expecting his father, who knew everything about movies, to tell him that one of the cameramen had probably taken the cub to the zoo after the director yelled cut. But his father had refused to listen to him. He'd held Will at arm's length and told him he was having a bad dream. Then he'd called for the nanny and reminded her he had a very important scene to shoot in the morning and couldn't afford to get sick.

"Why does Derek have to wear an eyepatch?" his father asked, his eyelids drooping.

"His girlfriend tried to claw his eyes out."

"Really? Wow, he certainly has a type, doesn't he? No wonder he was screwing your mother."

His father slipped into unconsciousness, leaving Will reeling. His mother and Derek? What? No way. His father was clearly out of his fucking mind.

Or was he?

The truth began to settle in Will's body like a virus as the pieces knit themselves together. All these memories came flooding back. The time Derek had shown up at their house unexpectedly to rehearse and his mother had run upstairs to remove her face peel and change out of her lounge pants, cursing the whole way. The time his mother had left her phone on the edge of the hot tub and Will had spotted three missed calls from Derek.

Will pictured his mother and Derek lying naked in bed together, laughing at how pathetic and scrawny and ugly Will was. Was that why he'd done it? Had he found out and been so disgusted and traumatized that he'd tried to kill Derek?

Will swallowed the bile rising in his throat. He closed his eyes and tried to breathe through the revulsion, despair, and betrayal poisoning his blood. He didn't want to feel like this. He didn't want to be like this.

Miles was sitting in the waiting room when Will returned. He stood and offered Will a scone that was not only buttered but drenched in strawberry jam. "How's he doing?"

Will shrugged and took the scone. Part of him wanted to tell Miles about Derek and his mother, but it was too humiliating. Miles was one of the few people who thought Will was worth something, and Will couldn't bear to show him how truly pathetic he was, how even his own mother laughed at him behind his back.

"He still wants to finish the movie. I told him they're postponing the shoot. I didn't have the heart to tell him it's over."

The studio was going to recast his father's part and try again when Derek recovered.

"Can they do that? What if he's totally fine by tomorrow, or in, like, a week?"

"They can do whatever they want."

"So that's it, then, no more movie?"

Will felt something wet on his cheek and tried to wipe it away, thinking it was butter or jam. But it wasn't. He was crying again.

Miles wrapped him in a hug, and all at once Will no longer had the strength to stand. Miles had to hold him up. Will was exhausted. He hadn't slept much in days, or exercised. Was it possible for muscle to atrophy overnight?

"I don't want to do this anymore."

"Do what?"

Will pinched his eyes closed to stem the flow of tears. "I'm not trying to be dramatic. I just don't want to do this anymore. I just . . . I don't know."

Miles squeezed tighter. "It's going to be okay."

"I just want to be enough for someone, anyone."

"You're enough for me."

"No, I'm not"—Will buried his face deeper into Miles's armpit and breathed in the familiar smell of his Old Spice deodorant—"and you'll fuck anything."

"You're my best friend. You're my brother. I love you way too much to ever fuck you. But if you want to fuck, let's go fuck. If it will make you feel better, let's do it. We are married."

Will was powerless to stop the flow of tears, and they burned like acid. "He didn't say anything. He just stood there. He didn't try to deny it or apologize. He just fucking stood there."

"And he still hasn't called or texted?"

Will shook his head and wiped the snot from his nose, leaving a long shiny smear on his teal sleeve.

Miles hugged him again. "Here's what we're going to do. I'm going to take you back to the house and put you to bed. Then, when you get up, we're going to go for a run, a really long one. We're going to run all the way around the lake."

Will reached for a tissue. "I don't think that's possible. It's a very big lake."

"You say impossible. I say impignorate."

"That doesn't make any sense. I don't know what that word means, but I'm sure it's not what you think."

CHAPTER 46
JAMES

James glanced at the clock. Theo would be home soon from the movies. He should really put his bong away and light some candles. But the video looped again, and James was powerless to look away.

He couldn't find the uncut security footage on Tony's phone, but he'd unearthed more clips, including a longer version of the one Tony had sent Donna in Montreal. But that wasn't the clip he kept watching on repeat.

No, he was transfixed by a far more mundane clip, one of Will and Derek getting off the elevator and going into Derek's room.

They didn't speak, hold hands, or even laugh. But so much transpired in the thirty seconds it took them to walk the hall.

They exchanged a glance as they got off the elevator, just a quick check-in, no more than a second long. But Will's eyes seemed to ask, *is this really happening?* And Derek's smile seemed to answer, *yes, I think so.*

But then Derek stepped ahead of Will, and his expression transformed from one of playful reassurance to one of heavy fatigue, like he could sleep for a week.

Will's face, meanwhile, became more animated, not less. He watched Derek's broad back and long strides with such unbridled love and admiration it made James's stomach shrink to the size of a marble. Will looked at Derek like he hung the moon.

Derek opened the door, and Will stumbled inside. There was a second when it looked like Derek might put his hand on Will's back and guide him over the threshold, but he didn't. Then the door closed, and the clip ended.

Footsteps sounded on the stairs outside the apartment door, and James slammed his laptop closed. There wasn't time to put the bong back in his room, so he stashed it behind the couch instead.

The door opened, and Theo dropped his keys on the table. "It smells like ass in here. Open a fucking window."

James reached for his beer. "How was the movie?"

"Boring."

James got up off the couch and followed Theo into the kitchen. "How's Brice? How come he didn't come up and say hi?"

Theo paused with his head in the fridge. "Not everyone wants to be besties with their ex, you know."

James hoisted himself up onto the counter and ran a hand down his face. He hadn't shaved in a week, and his new beard was coarse and itchy.

He sat there, pretending not to be drunk and stoned, and watched his nephew make himself a cheese and lettuce sandwich.

"Donna called me," Theo said.

"Really? What did she want?"

Someone must have told her by now that James knew all about her and Derek. In fact, he was surprised he hadn't heard from her yet. What was it she'd said to him over the summer, something about going to her first if he ever came upon any "sensitive" information?

"Nothing. She just wanted to know if I'd heard from Will. Apparently, he won't return any of her calls or texts."

James's heart spasmed in his chest. Did Will know, too? Had his father told him? Had Derek? "And have you? Has Will texted or called?"

James realized how pathetic he sounded, like one of those divorcees who pumps their kids for information on their ex.

"Why would Will call me? He probably hates me, too, thanks to you."

James wished he could explain everything to Theo, let him know why he'd let Will go without a fight, why he'd let Will think the worst.

"He doesn't hate you," James said. "Will's not like that."

"He should. I knew you were a terrible boyfriend, and I set you two up anyway."

Theo wasn't wrong, though his words were like a sucker punch to the gut. James didn't mean to be so ambivalent about relationships. He always entered them hoping he'd fall in love. It had just never happened, not until Will.

But that was over now.

"There's one more beer in the fridge, if you want it," James said.

"Why are you doing this? I bet if you just told him the truth, he'd understand. And it wasn't even you. It was Es who wrote the story. Why don't you just blame her?"

Because James was an adult, and he didn't blame others for his mistakes. Besides, there was no turning back now. He already had all the evidence he needed to blackmail Tony waiting in his computer bag. All he had to do now was pull the trigger, and he and Theo would be millionaires.

"It was never real, Theo. And besides, you and I, we don't belong in that world. We're just the hired help."

"Will doesn't care about any of that. He doesn't care about money."

"That's because he doesn't have to."

"Wow, you can be a real asshole sometimes, you know that?" Theo grabbed his sandwich and went to his room.

James drained the rest of his beer, hopped off the counter, and grabbed the last can of PBR from the fridge. When he closed the door, a picture of Travis holding up the head of a twelve-point buck stared back at him.

"I know, I never should've brought the little shit with me to Vermont in the first place. I should've just sent him to Florida with Mom."

James went into the living room and opened up his laptop again. This time, he clicked on the second video, the one of Derek and Will arguing.

The hallway was empty, but there was Will's voice, screaming at Derek.

If only Will had screamed at James that way, maybe James wouldn't be haunted by the look of resignation and acceptance on Will's face, like Will deserved James's betrayal, like he had it coming.

"No, you're just making this up because you're mad I won. Is this some kind of sick joke?"

"I ended it months ago. And it didn't mean anything. You have to understand. I had her poster on my wall growing up. I used to beat off to her like twice a—"

"Shut up. You're talking about my fucking mother. How could you do that and then kiss me?"

"I'm sorry, I shouldn't have done that. But it didn't mean anything. It was just sex, and I ended it. And you have to understand the position I'm in. I'm not like you. I don't come from acting royalty."

"What's that supposed to mean? Did you need to fuck my mother for work or something? What, are you looking for a role in her next Hallmark movie?"

"You don't get it because you were born famous. You were born with a built-in fan base. Why do you think you won? None of this is about the performances. It's all about the narrative, and right now the narrative is about how the Academy's favorite bridesmaid is about to be shown up by his own son. Tony was right. You're just like your father. You just do whatever the fuck you want because you're untouchable. You can be gay and it's cute. But me, I'll lose everything."

"I feel dizzy. I need to lie down."

"Are you kidding me right now? What are you doing?"

A minute of silence passed, and James assumed Derek must've gone to take a leak or something because when he spoke again, he sounded surprised, like he'd just walked back into the room.

"What the fuck? Get out of my bed. This was a mistake. This whole thing was a mistake. I never should've invited you up here."

Will might have said something, but it was too soft to make out.

And then, there they were, the elderly couple who'd overheard Will and Derek arguing. They got off the elevator and made their way down the hall. The woman, who was considerably younger than the man, a spry sixty to his brittle eighty, stuck her keycard in the lock.

"Look at you. You're just a pathetic fuckboy," Derek said. "You're so fucking entitled you think you deserve everything, even me. But I'm not yours, Will. I don't belong to anyone but myself. Now get the fuck out of my bed."

The woman helped the octogenarian into the room and shut the door. The video clip ended there.

CHAPTER 47
WILL

Will's alarm went off at 6 AM, and for a fraction of a second, he thought it was a school day. But it wasn't. It was a Tuesday in August. Although, he did have to go to school today. He was meeting Principal King at 8:30.

He got out of bed and headed for the shower. He dressed and made himself two eggs over easy and a single piece of buttered toast, which he ate while listening to NPR. He liked NPR. They covered real news, not his father's stroke or Derek's eyepatch.

Will took the train up to the Bronx and got off at Cypress Ave. A few people waved and said hi, the fathers, aunts, and cousins of some of his students. It was a dangerous part of the city, perhaps the most dangerous. But Will wasn't afraid. They knew him here. They knew he worked at the school, that their kids spent hours every night coloring pictures for him. In a way, he felt safer here than in Manhattan.

He was early for his meeting, so he walked down the hall to his classroom. All the furniture had been pushed into the center of the room. The floors had been waxed and the walls painted. His classroom had been colorful before. High up, above the bulletin boards, there had been a border of painted shapes circling the room, green triangles, blue circles, orange squares, etc. Now, everything was seafoam green.

"Hi, papi." Jamie, the custodian, poked his head in. "What do you think of the paint job?"

Will didn't care if the research supported calm, soothing colors. He liked it better when it was bright and fun. "It's nice."

The school was so different without students. It was quiet and smelled of grime and floor wax. The bulletin boards were bare, and the hallways seemed twice as long.

Will stepped into the office and found Mary standing behind the counter.

"Mr. Chapman, how are you? How's your dad?"

"Better. He's out of the hospital." Will glanced at King's door, which was open. A faint whiff of cigarette smoke drifted out. When students weren't in the building, King smoked right in her office.

"I hope you know that no one here believes those things they said about you. We all know you wouldn't hurt a fly."

"I know. Thanks, Mary."

"King, she doesn't believe them either. You should have heard her on the phone with the superintendent. She gave her a piece of her mind, I'll tell you."

"William," King's husky voice barked from her office, "is that you?"

"Yeah, it's me." Will gave Mary his usual *okay, here I go* nod and stepped into King's office. He took off his backpack and sat in his usual chair across from his boss. The blinds were open, and the sun was hot on his face and neck. Theodore Roosevelt was there, reminding Will that *People don't care how much you know until they know how much you care.*

King rose and turned on her electric tea kettle. "I've given the matter a lot of thought, and I've decided not to move you up to fifth grade next year, after all. You have such a nice voice, and I think you'd be a great music teacher."

"I'm resigning." Will opened his backpack and pulled out the letter he'd written.

He'd imagined this moment countless times before. In his fantasies, it was righteous and dramatic. But in reality, he felt nothing but shame, like he was surrendering his dog to the pound.

"You don't have to. I'm going to ask the teachers to take their preps in their rooms next year, so you'll never be alone with students. I've already cleared it with the superintendent."

"I appreciate that," Will said, handing her the letter. "I really do. But I think it's best for everyone if I just disappear for a while."

King pulled a cigarette from the pack on her desk. She lit it and sat back in her chair. Smoke curled up towards the cracked ceiling. She looked exhausted.

"You're going to be okay, William. I hope you know that. Those kids put you through hell, and you never gave up on them. So don't give up on yourself, okay?" She pushed her auburn hair behind her ear, and Will was surprised to see her gray roots showing. "Are you a hugger, William? Because I'm a hugger." King set her cigarette on the corner of her ashtray and stood.

"Uh, sure." Will let Principal King hug him, and he was surprised to find she was soft and squishy and barely came up to his shoulder.

"And if you ever need anything, a letter of recommendation, or anything like that, don't hesitate to ask, okay?"

"Okay." Will stepped away from the hug and retrieved his backpack. "I should probably go. I have to meet my mom for brunch."

King sat on the edge of her desk. "Okay. You won't forget us now, will you?"

"Never." And he wouldn't.

"Mr. Chapman," Mary said as he walked back through the office, "will you sign this before you go?"

She unrolled a poster, and Will stopped short when he saw his eighteen-year-old self staring back at him. A single tear was running down his face, and the words *The Beautiful* were etched in elegant print across the top. Where had Mary found this? He hadn't seen it in years.

"I was going to ask you later, but I overheard, and—"

"Sure, of course."

Will's mother was at the restaurant when he got there, and she'd already gone ahead and ordered him a coffee. "Thanks for coming."

"Sure." Will sat down and got to work turning his coffee into a calorie bomb. He added three sugars and enough cream to turn the black liquid a pale beige.

"Your father's feeling better. He keeps calling me to make sure we haven't struck the sets yet. That man doesn't know when to quit."

Will was aware of that. His father had been hounding him non-stop about rewriting the script and filming a few key scenes before he was no longer able to.

"This might be a blessing in disguise," his father had told him. "If the studio knows what's good for them, they'll take what we're giving them. My death will be far better marketing than anything they can build around Derek or whoever they try to replace me with. And with Derek out of commission for the next month, if they want me, they'll have to take you, too."

His father was overestimating how much the studio cared about him winning an Oscar. His father was an awards magnet, sure, but he hadn't been a serious box-office draw in decades. Moreover, he was also grossly underestimating how much everyone hated Will.

If his mother had called him there to push his father's far-fetched agenda, she was wasting her time.

"What do you want, Mom?"

"You haven't returned any of my calls. I was worried about you. What's wrong? I didn't know about James, you know. I had no idea. I was just as surprised as you."

"I don't care about that."

It was a lie, of course, but Will wasn't a foolish teenager anymore. Part of him had always known James was too good to be true. And he'd been right. But for a few days, it had seemed real, more real than anything Will had ever experienced in his life.

"He liked you, William. I know he did. I think he just wasn't ready for all the—"

"Are you seriously defending him right now? Jesus, Mom, you're fucking ridiculous."

"Don't get mad at me."

"Why shouldn't I? You could've told me, you know, saved me the embarrassment. How hard would it have been to say, 'William, hun, you're barking up the wrong tree. Derek likes vaginas, especially mine?' I feel like such a fool. And when this leaks, do you know what they're going to do to me?"

"Jesus, William, I'm—"

"Save it, Mom. Derek was never mine. You didn't steal my boyfriend."

Missing the point entirely, she asked, "Did James tell you?"

Jesus Christ. Of course James knew, too.

"No, James didn't tell me." Will took a sip of his coffee, and it was disgusting. But he drank it anyway. "Well, I haven't seen it in the papers yet, so I assume, what, you paid him off?"

"Your father took care of it."

"Of course he did. Well, it's been fun, Mom. I'll see you at the funeral." Will stood and threw five dollars on the table for the coffee.

"Wait, William, come back. Let's talk about this."

Will didn't look back. He just walked out of the restaurant.

WILL WAS in Barnes & Noble buying GRE books when he got a text from Theo asking to meet up. Theo wouldn't say why, just that it was important. That was how, an hour after walking out on his mom like a bratty toddler, Will found himself sitting on the rim of Bethesda Fountain next to a lanky, blue-eyed teen.

Theo pushed his glasses up the bridge of his nose. "Hey, Will. Thanks for meeting me. I know you must hate me. I'm sorry I—"

"I don't hate you, Theo. Jesus."

If Will hated anyone, it was himself for thinking James might pop out of the bushes, that this was all just an elaborate trick to get Will alone. When was Will going to learn his lesson? James was probably at home right now, balls deep in his new boyfriend, having a laugh at Will's expense.

"I'm sorry I lied to you and made you pretend to be—"

"Seriously, it's not necessary. And, let's be honest, if you had to do it over again, would you really do anything differently? Would you really go behind your uncle's back and—"

"I don't know, but—"

"You're a good kid, Theo, and I'm not mad at you. I'm not even mad at James."

"You should be."

"Yeah, well, I'm not. Maybe I'm just a forgiving person."

Theo leaned back and crossed his legs at the ankles. "I don't think that's true. I think you're probably the least forgiving person I know. You and Uncle James are the same. You both think you're fooling people, but you're not. You both think pretending things don't matter will make them not matter. But it doesn't work that way, not when it comes to forgiveness, especially when it comes to forgiving yourself. I know all about that." Theo reached back and dipped his hand into the fountain, as if trying to wash away his greeting card platitudes. "He did it for me, you know, my dad. I'm the reason he killed himself."

"That's not true." Will tried to catch Theo's eye, but Theo was too busy watching his fingers chase ripples across the water's surface.

"No, it is." Theo said it so matter-of-factly, Will didn't dare object. "He didn't want me to have to watch him get sick and die the way he had to watch his dad. Uncle James won't admit it, but come on, who goes canoeing in February alone?"

"Jesus, Theo, you can't blame yourself for that."

"I should've known. It was right there in the song." Theo's hands danced in the fountain as he sang, "*I'll take my life behind closed doors and give you an end that's only yours. Let me be the one to take the blame for giving you this cursed name.*"

Theo pulled his hand from the water and fat drops plopped onto the concrete rim.

"He thought if I didn't see him die then I wouldn't spend the rest of my life wondering if that's how I was gonna die, too."

"Your father was just trying to protect you. That's what fathers do. And you can't blame yourself for being born."

Theo met Will's gaze. "I get that in theory. But I still do. It's the same as you and what happened with Derek."

Will did a double take. Was Theo being serious? "It's not remotely the same. I got blackout drunk and tried to kill someone. You were born to a man who loved you more than his own life. Our situations couldn't possibly be more different."

"Do you remember hitting Derek? Do you remember wanting to kill him, or even wanting to hurt him?"

"No, but—"

"Exactly, so they are the same. I don't remember being born either."

Jesus, and Will thought arguing with five-year-olds was nonsensical.

"Don't laugh," Theo said. "I'm making a good point. You just don't realize it yet. In school, we talk a lot about intention and impact, like how you might not intend to hurt someone, but you're still responsible if you do. You're still responsible for your impact. For example, when you say, 'That's so gay,' you don't just get a free pass because you 'didn't mean it like that.' You gotta realize it's hurtful and stop saying it.

"And I think that's your problem. You act like you're blaming yourself for your impact, but I don't think you are, not anymore. Derek's fine. He's better than fine. He got a fucking Oscar out of it. He's not mad either, not as far as I can tell. So, if it's not about Derek, then it's about you. And if it's not about impact, then it's about intention. So, that means you're blaming yourself for your intentions, which is ridiculous because you can't even remember your intentions. You just said so. It could've been an accident for all you know."

"It wasn't an accident."

"You don't know that, not for sure. You're just assuming. What if you'd been crying? What if your hands were covered in snot and tears and they were slippery? Personally, I think that's just as likely. So, why can't you just believe that instead?"

"Why does it matter? Who cares if I forgive myself or not?"

"Because maybe then you'll finish the movie." Theo wiped his hands on his legs and left dark smears across his jeans. "I don't want Derek playing my dad. I want you to do it."

So, that's what this was about. Will sighed and closed his eyes. "I have no control over that, Theo. You realize that, don't you?" Will opened his eyes and followed the rippled path of a happy couple rowing out on the pond. "They want Derek. He's the big movie star. He's the one who's going to put asses in seats, not me. And maybe they'll get someone cool to replace my dad, someone like George Clooney. That would be pretty awesome, right?"

"That won't be awesome. It'll be stupid." Theo stood and turned to face Will. His tall, lanky frame cast an even taller, lankier shadow across the water. "I don't understand why you don't just keep going. Your mom says your dad doesn't wanna give up."

"It's not up to me, Theo. It's not up to my dad either. It's not even up to my mom."

"Maybe not, but you could at least try, right? Once they see the footage, they'll see. I know they will. Uncle James told me. He told me how amazing you are. And if you don't hurry up, your dad will be—"

"Dead." Will couldn't bear to hear that word on Theo's lips, so he beat him to it. "I know. But he's had a long and prosperous career. He doesn't need an Oscar." Will stood, too. "And I'm not some victim you need to feel sorry for. I'm just some guy serving his time, and that's what life is. Sometimes, Theo, no matter how hard you try, you still lose."

Theo jumped up onto the rim of the fountain and blocked the sun. "I know that. But your problem is, you don't even try."

WILL CONSIDERED Theo's words as he walked the long way home through the park. Did he try? Did he forgive? Or did he just pretend?

What if he wasn't okay? What if he wasn't fine? What if he hadn't been in a long time?

Will never saw the point in throwing his pain back at those who'd inflicted it. Why would he want to give them any more power? Even if he succeeded in making them feel guilty, how would that serve him? It was better to learn from his mistakes in private and move on, find better people to trust, or no one at all.

But maybe that was foolish. Maybe there were no shortcuts. Maybe there was a definitive sequence. Maybe you needed to fight to find forgiveness. Maybe you needed total failure to claim you'd tried.

But what would trying even look like? They weren't going to throw Derek over for Will. And it wasn't even what Will wanted. He didn't want his comeback to come at Derek's expense.

Will looked up from the path and found himself at the pond at the base of Belvedere Castle. A turtle paddled lazily across the algae-green water, and a thought popped in Will's head.

His father's plan was hopeless, but maybe they should do it anyway. His father was dying, after all. It wasn't important if their version of the film made it into theaters. His father would never live long enough to find out either way. For him, all that mattered was believing he might win. It was slipping from this world imagining the echoes of his name ringing out over the Dolby Theater and the standing ovation that was sure to follow.

His father didn't need certainty. He needed hope. And maybe Will could give him that, if nothing else.

Will turned and started heading in the other direction, towards Grand Central Station. If he hurried, he could be at his father's house by lunchtime.

CHAPTER 48
JAMES

The place Tony suggested was one of those two-story gay bars in the village. James knew it, though he hadn't been there in years.

The basement bar was dark and windowless. There were platforms for the go-go dancers and a dozen small, round tabletops. But it was early afternoon, so no one was dancing, and the bar was mostly empty. The upstairs portion, where they held drag shows, wasn't even open.

Tony sat at a table in the back corner with a young man who looked a few years shy of legal drinking age.

"You found it," Tony said, removing his hand from the boy's lap. "Christian, can you go buy my friend, here, a beer? We need to have a little chat in private."

Instead of the *hello, Daddy* look most twinks gave James, Christian eyed him with suspicion, like James was competition.

"I don't need a beer. I won't be staying long."

Tony's jailbait sauntered away in his cranberry-colored skinny jeans and sat at the far end of the bar.

"So, let's get down to business, shall we?" Tony said. "How much do you think you'll get for a hearsay story without any proof to back it up?"

Seeing no reason to draw this out, or engage in pointless negotiations, James pulled a manilla envelope from his bag and slid it across the table to Tony. He thought he'd be nervous, given that he'd never blackmailed anyone before. But James found, as Tony opened the envelope and pulled out the photocopies, he was kind of enjoying himself.

It was gratifying to witness Tony's patronizing smirk melt from his face. James only wished he'd thought to record their conversation so he could use the wounded little sigh Tony let out as his ringtone.

"What do you want?" Tony asked, sliding the papers back into the envelope. "Twenty thousand?"

"All of it."

"What do you mean, all of it?"

"I want the five-million Robert paid you. And of course, I think it goes without saying, that little video you sent Donna—thanks for that, by the way—stays in the vault, at least for now."

"How much are they paying you?"

James leaned back in his chair and smiled. "I don't like to talk about money. It's vulgar. So, do we have an understanding?"

Tony sat back in his chair, mirroring James's posture. He was dressed casually, in white shorts and a blue polo, like he was on his way to go play tennis. "No."

"No, what?" Staring at the cocky smirk growing on Tony's face made James feel like a naive child, like he was missing something obvious.

"Derek seems to think you've developed genuine feelings for William in the process of your little scheme, and, while I can't fathom why, I'm inclined to agree. I mean, I'd understand if it were Andy. But William? He's so ordinary looking. He's got a nice enough body, I suppose. And while there's nothing obviously wrong with his face, there's also nothing noteworthy about it either."

"Just because Derek has a thing for Will, doesn't—"

"Save the acting for the professionals. I've already made up my mind. I'm not giving you a dime. If I'm wrong, I'll happily live out the rest of my days abroad. But I don't think I am. And if it's any comfort to you, I have no desire to expose William and Donna. Their secret is safe with me. At least for now."

"You're that confident, are you?"

"You don't get where I am without knowing how to take a few calculated risks."

James stood. There was nothing left to discuss. Tony had him by the balls. But James wasn't about to admit defeat. Maybe this was a test. Maybe in an hour, Tony would be singing a different tune. "Okay, but don't say I didn't warn you."

Tony laughed as he beckoned his young boy back over. "I would never. In fact, part of me hopes you'll prove me wrong. I could use an excuse to retire early."

"Well, you have my number when you change your mind. Don't wait too long, though."

Robert took the news of the botched shakedown with surprising grace when James called to tell him. James expected him to be furious, to pop some pain pills and show how disappointed he was with a stretch of unbearable silence.

Instead, he let out a little *humph* and asked, "Do you think you and Theo could make it out to the Hamptons tonight? I want to see everything you have on Tony so far. I'd come to you, but I have company arriving soon."

"I don't know. That's a long drive."

"Stay the night. Theo can sleep in Andy's old room. He'll love it. It has its own balcony, and the ensuite has a tub carved from a giant quartz crystal."

"A what?"

"Yeah, Andy was really into geology for a while. Oh, and I have a present to give Theo anyway."

"A present?" Robert had already set Theo up with a five-million-dollar trust fund. He didn't need any more presents.

"Is there any chance you could get here before six?"

James looked at the dashboard clock. "Maybe if I grab Theo right now."

Forty-five minutes later, Theo slid into the passenger's seat. "You seriously need to go fucking shopping. All of your clothes are hideous."

"Did you remember my toothbrush?"

"Uh huh." Theo pulled the cord from James's phone and plugged in his own. Great, three hours of Theo's music: an eclectic mix of classical, hip-hop, and pop. Maybe James could talk Theo into a podcast.

James had worked several jobs in the Hamptons before, so he wasn't surprised by the circular driveway with room for fifty cars or the gorgeous swimming pool with the ornate pergola. But Theo was awestruck.

"Holy shit," he said as they drove up the tree-lined drive with Beyonce's "Lemonade" blaring. "And this is just his summer house?"

Robert's mansion was a shingle style home with more roofs, balconies, and porches than James could count. The enormous lawn was neon green and sloped to a wooden staircase that, by the looks of it, led down to the beach.

"I think so."

Robert's butler showed James into the library. Meanwhile, the housekeeper took Theo up to his room.

When Will had mentioned running lines with his father in the library, James had pictured a stuffy room full of old books and leather arm chairs. But this was like one of those libraries you see on a college campus or in some British period piece. It was huge.

Books lined every wall, and a spiral staircase led up to a wrap-around balcony, where there were three more walls of books. A chandelier dangled from the coffered ceiling, and behind the desk, a giant, two-story window looked out over a manicured English garden.

There were so many comfy looking couches and chairs, James was surprised to find Robert sitting in a simple office chair behind a shiny mahogany desk.

Robert stood and shuffled over to a side table where there was a crystal decanter of bourbon and several glass tumblers. It reminded James of when he used to get off the bus and watch *General Hospital* with his mother after school. There was always bourbon at the Quartermaine mansion.

"I'm sorry I couldn't get the money," James said, sitting down on the other side of Robert's desk, which was as big as a queen-sized mattress.

Robert passed James a drink he didn't ask for and sat back down. "Let's not worry about the money right now. Chess isn't won in a single move. What's important is that Tony knows you have proof. That will have to be enough for now. But tell me, what else did you find on his phone?"

James sniffed the amber liquid and took a cautious sip. Unlike Will, James didn't consume expensive bourbon like it was iced tea. Was this where Will's love of bourbon had started?

"Well, as I said, there are the video clips, as well as those emails Tony sent to the casting director. It's nothing incriminating, but I bet if we show them to Derek, let him see who Tony really is, he'll—"

"Derek already knows who Tony really is. He just doesn't care. Besides, it's not Derek we need to convince anymore. It's the studio."

"What do you mean?"

"They haven't struck the sets yet, but they will soon, so we have a narrow window to finish shooting my scenes. And with Derek out of commission, if the studio wants me in the movie, they're going to have to take William, too."

James's skepticism must have been visible on his face because Robert said, "Don't look at me like that. I'm well aware this is going to be a hard sell, which is why we're not going to tell them. We're just going to do it. We're going to make a movie so fucking good they have no choice but to finish it."

"But what about Tony?" How could Robert just let this go? What about Will? Tony could send him to prison. There might be a statute of limitations on assault, but what if Tony tried to go after Will for attempted murder?

"Forget about Tony. At least for now. He may have called our bluff today, but trust me, we've got him running scared."

"I don't think we do."

"I'm not saying this isn't a major setback. It is. But Tony's not going to chop off his nose to spite his face. While Derek still has a career, William is safe."

"Yeah, and what happens when Derek doesn't have a career anymore? You said yourself, he's only hanging on by a thread. What happens then?"

"That's why you're going to keep looking. Prove the rumors true. One of these boys of Tony's is bound to be underage. And don't worry about the money. I'll make sure you're compensated."

James forgot the glass in his hand was bourbon and swallowed a mouthful that sent him into a coughing fit. When he finally recovered, Robert was staring at him with amusement. How could he be smiling at a time like this?

"And if Tony doesn't change his mind, there is at least one bright side. You and William can resume seeing each other."

James's heart stuttered in his chest. Was Robert being serious right now? How could he ask James to give Will up one day and the next be like, *Actually, let's not worry about that*? What really mattered to Robert? Was it protecting Will? Or was it keeping the secret hidden long enough so he could win an Oscar?

"Are you gonna tell him the truth?" James asked. "He's not gonna be able to move on from this until you do."

The panic in Robert's eyes was short-lived. "What William needs is his career back. He needs a dream to chase. He doesn't need to wallow in his past mistakes. He needs to plan for his future. Let's just finish the movie, and we'll go from there."

James had been a fool for thinking he had a partner in Robert. Robert only cared about one thing, himself.

But maybe, if James showed him the video clips, Robert would remember what was really at stake here. James queued up the first clip and slid his phone across the shiny surface of the desk, but Robert pushed it away.

"I do want to see those, but later. There's another reason I asked you here tonight. A group of us are meeting to discuss changes to the script, and I want you there. I want your input. I know your brother was the writer in the family, but this is as much your movie as anyone's."

The nerve Robert had to sit there and edit James's life like it was nothing more than words on a page, and then to go and act like he was doing James a favor by letting him participate. How many times was James going to let this man yank him around?

But he was providing for Theo, and James couldn't forget that.

"Is Will gonna be there?"

Robert smiled. "Yes. He's upstairs now with Miles and Tiffany."

CHAPTER 49
WILL

Tiffany gathered bubbles around her like a feather boa. "Aren't you supposed to be downstairs now?"

"Probably." Will closed his eyes and let his head loll back against the hot tub wall.

"I still can't believe it never occurred to you to invite me to your father's mansion in the Hamptons before."

"Sorry." Will wasn't sorry, though. It took forever to get out here, and his family's wealth made him uncomfortable. It served as a constant reminder that he was nothing without them. He'd tried to make his own way in the world. He'd put himself through college and gotten a job. But his family's gravity was inescapable.

Miles's muscular leg fell against Will's under the water. "I'll go for you if you want. I'm probably great at writing screenplays. I watch movies all the time."

"Do it." Will was boiled like a lobster, yet he couldn't find the strength to move, even to pull himself out of the water and into the cool breeze.

"Is there room for one more?" Behind a cloud of steam, Theo stood with a towel draped over his shoulder.

What was Theo doing here? Was James here, too? Jesus Christ, his father must have asked James to help with the rewrites. Was the movie all that mattered to him? Did Will's broken heart mean nothing? Whatever. This wasn't about Will. This was about fulfilling his father's lifelong dream to win an Oscar. Will couldn't be selfish.

Miles shifted over. "Get on in here. Will was just leaving."

Will stood and let the late summer air cool his pickled flesh. "Hey, Theo."

"Is this where you grew up?" Theo peered over the edge of the balcony at the koi pond in the garden below. "This place is ridiculous."

It was ridiculous, and it was only one of his father's many houses. "Some of the time, yeah." Will grabbed a towel and started drying off.

"I heard you guys are meeting tonight to revise the script, and I had this great idea to make your dad's part smaller," Theo said. "Make my mom's part bigger. She's hardly in it now, and that doesn't make any sense. I think my dad just didn't wanna think about her because she left him. It's like how Uncle James gets all quiet whenever I mention your name. You know, avoidance and all that. But isn't that the point of art, to stick your finger in the wound and wiggle it around?"

Will wasn't sure what the point of art was. He wasn't sure what the point of anything was right now.

THEY MET around his father's dining room table. There were ten of them in all. Michelle, the director. Arjun, the assistant director. Roger, the cinematographer. His mom, the executive producer. Vivian, the production manager. Annabeth, the screenwriter. Will, his father, and Ryan. And, of course, James.

Apparently, James hadn't lost his voice or taken a vow of silence.

He still had all his fingers, and they seemed to move just fine, certainly well enough to dial a phone or type out a text message.

Will sat three chairs down from James on the same side of the table so he didn't have to look at him. But he still had to listen to him, to that same gravelly voice that used to whisper words of encouragement in his ear.

Annabeth had a million questions for the real Jimmy Young, and James rattled off a million answers like it was no big deal, like Will wasn't in the same room absorbing every word like anthrax.

"I think we should leave Jimmy alone," Annabeth said an hour into the meeting. "It will muddy the story too much if we go into all of his romantic entanglements. And I like the relationship between the brothers the way it is now. There is already a good balance of drama and fraternity. If anything, I think we should make Jimmy's part a little smaller and add more before he arrives. Maybe we don't even bring him in until the second act." She looked across the table at James and Ryan. "No offense. I just think the story will be stronger if we make Travis the primary point of view character."

"I agree," Will's father said, and Will could hardly believe his ears. His father wanted to make Travis the lead character? Why would he do that? That would mean his father would have to drop down to supporting. He never took supporting roles. Was this some kind of joke?

"That's not a bad idea," Michelle said. "It is based on his memoir."

Someone had to put a stop to this, and Will was about to speak up when his mother beat him to it. "I agree that would make a better movie. But the studio will never go for it." What his mother wasn't saying, what she didn't need to say, was that the studio would never go for Will in the lead role.

"Fuck the studio," his father said. "Let's just make a great movie. Maybe they'll let us buy the rights from them. I'll leave enough money in my will so you can finance the rest independently."

"They'll never go for it," his mother said. "Alan lost his mother to Alzheimer's. This movie is his pet."

Ignoring his mother, Michelle turned to Annabeth. "How do you propose we add more to the first act without adding more of Robert's character?"

"Well, we could cast someone as the younger version of Bruce and do a bunch of flashbacks from the boys' childhood," Annabeth suggested.

Michelle frowned, not enamored with the idea.

"Theo thinks you should make Emily a more pivotal character," Will said, speaking for the first time all evening. "Maybe if we make her a little more three dimensional, humanize her a bit, it will show why Travis loved her in the first place and make it more impactful when she eventually leaves."

"That's actually a great idea," Annabeth said. She closed her eyes, and it was like she was already rewriting the script.

"I agree," Michelle said and flashed Will a rare smile.

AFTER THE MEETING, Will made a beeline for the bathroom and locked himself inside. He didn't care if everyone thought he was constipated or jacking off. There was no way in hell he was exchanging awkward pleasantries with James like nothing had ever happened. His mom and dad might be able to sweep it all under the rug for the sake of the movie, but Will wasn't there yet.

Some time later, after Will figured everyone had gone, he opened the door. He jumped when he saw James leaning against the wall.

"Hey," James said.

Will's heart raced in his chest, and his temperature spiked. "There are other bathrooms, you know."

"Can we talk?"

"Why? I thought we'd already said everything there was to say." *Which was nothing. Absolutely fucking nothing.*

"Because you deserve to know what really happened between you and Derek ten years ago."

Will's blood ran cold.

"Is there somewhere private we can go?" James asked, taking a step towards Will, his green eyes unbearably bright.

Will took a step back, hating how James's presence still made his body buzz with longing. He considered telling James to fuck off. But instead, he walked down the hall and opened the doors to the library. If James knew more about that night, Will had to hear him out.

The library was Will's favorite room in the house. How many hours had he spent within these book-lined walls, running scenes with his father?

"You can sit wherever." Will headed for the bourbon and poured himself a generous helping. He was going to need it. As an afterthought, he grabbed another glass and asked, "Do you want one?"

"I was spying on Tony, not you. That was how I came upon the videos."

"I take it that's a no on the bourbon, then?" Will sipped his overfilled glass before turning around to face James. What videos was he talking about?

James still had the mustache, but his beard was starting to grow back. It was already half the length it had been, which was somehow even hotter. It was the best of both worlds: the look of a mustache, but with the scruff of a beard. On top of that, Will could see the outline of his nipples through the threadbare fabric of his faded blue T-shirt.

"Tony stole the security footage from the Beverly Hilton Hotel, and he's been using it to blackmail your parents for years."

It was clear James expected a big reaction, but Will only nodded, like this made perfect sense. In a way, it did. It made far more sense than Will's mother orchestrating the coverup to protect him. There was nothing Tony wouldn't do for Derek. Will's mother, on the other hand, couldn't even be bothered not to fuck Will's crush.

"I have copies if you wanna see." James held his phone out to Will.

Will stepped just close enough to grab James's phone. Then he retreated over to the chaise by the window and hit play with a trembling finger. Was this really happening? Was he really about to find out the truth firsthand?

It was like a punch in the gut, watching his teenage self trail after Derek like a lovesick puppy. Anyone with eyes could see Derek wasn't into him. Will watched the video several times before moving onto the next one.

The second video was even worse than the first, and Will couldn't hold back his tears any longer. James had seen this, too, hadn't he? He'd seen how desperate and pathetic Will was, how he'd thrown himself at Derek, how he'd ignored Derek's persistent demands to leave, how he'd crawled into Derek's bed like . . . well, like a pathetic fuckboy. No wonder James had never bothered with excuses or explanations.

Still, Will brushed his tears aside and hit play on the third video, which was the most damning of all. Now, Will couldn't even hate his mother. She didn't care that he was in her lover's hotel room, or that he was holding a bloody statue screaming, "He's dead, Mom. He's dead." She took in the scene in an instant and pushed Will inside, away from any prying eyes. A few minutes later, she emerged with Will's arm slung over her shoulder because he was too drunk to walk. The bloody statue was nowhere in sight, probably because his mother had stashed it in her purse.

Will let the video loop a third time, like he had with the others, though he wasn't sure why. He could barely see the screen through the blur of tears.

He jumped when he felt James's hand on his shoulder. "Where are the others?" he asked, rising from the chaise and moving out of arm's reach.

"There are no others."

"No, where is the moment it happens, the moment I try to kill him? Show it to me."

James took a step closer. "I don't have that part."

"What do you mean, you don't have that part? Why the fuck wouldn't you have that part? That's the most important part."

Once again, James just stood there, mute.

"What the fuck is wrong with you? Why can't you fucking talk? Where is the rest of it?"

"I don't know, Will. If I had it, I'd show it to you. Your father didn't want me to show you this much, but I thought—"

"I don't give a fuck what you thought."

James took another step closer. "I never meant to hurt you, Will. I—"

"Then why the fuck did you sneak a pap into my brother's bachelor party?"

James stopped short, and instead of speaking, he closed his eyes and hung his head.

"Yeah, that's what I thought. And you didn't just punish me, you know? My students, they needed me. They counted on me. Julian wasn't even there that day. And do you know how many people he trusts? Two. Just two. Me and his grandma. And I went and disappeared on him without even saying goodbye."

Will didn't dare step within arm's reach of James, so he set James's phone down on the desk and walked to the far side of the room, where the glass doors opened out into the garden.

"I'm so sorry, Will. I really am. I wish I could fix this. I'm trying to."

Will closed his eyes and breathed. James couldn't have known about Julian or his other students. And Will had no right to act like an angry ex-boyfriend. None of it had been real. It had all been staged for mutually beneficial reasons.

Besides, Julian was going to have a hell of a time transitioning to first grade next year anyway. The loss may have come sooner than expected, but it had been inevitable, right?

"Listen, thanks for showing me. I know you didn't have to. But, if it's alright with you, I just want to be alone for a while."

Will stared out at the garden, at the long shadows cast by the topiary, and waited for James to leave. But he didn't.

"I couldn't say anything at the wedding because I wanted Tony to think I'd been playing you for information. He still doesn't know I got it from him. He thinks I got it from your mom. I thought I could use what I knew about him blackmailing your parents to blackmail him back, to get him to stop sabotaging you, to make him get rid of those videos once and for all."

For one thrilling second, Will believed James. Then his brain caught up to his heart, which, even after everything, still reserved every tenth beat for hope. *Pathetic.* If there was any truth to what James was saying, then why hadn't he called or texted? Why hadn't he once tried to explain himself before now?

"And who put you up to that? Who asked you to blackmail Tony? Was it my dad?" When James didn't immediately answer, Will turned to face him.

"Yeah, but it's not what you think."

"How much is he paying you?"

James started to walk towards Will, but stopped when Will retreated. "It killed me not to say anything, to just stand there and let you think you didn't matter, that I was just doing this for a paycheck, but—"

"Weren't you, though? Isn't that what this all comes down to? My father paid you for a job, and you chose the job over me, right?"

"I wouldn't put it quite like that."

"I'm sure you wouldn't, but that doesn't make it any less true."

James chewed his lip as he queued up his next pathetic excuse. "The reason I wasn't able to blackmail Tony is because he called my bluff. He knew I had feelings for you and would never use what I know to hurt you."

"Won't you, though, if the price is right? I mean, at least with Tony, I know the video is safe. He doesn't want the world to know Derek slummed it by kissing me, or that Derek fucked my mom. But there's nothing stopping you from cashing in."

"I would never do that. I did this for you, Will. I was trying to protect you."

Will let his head thud back against the glass door. "I believe you believe that. And I have no doubt my parents will do whatever it takes to buy your silence. And I'm happy for you. I really am. I know this money will make a huge difference for you and Theo. And after all you've both been through, you deserve it."

"I don't care about the money, Will. I care about you. Why can't you believe that?"

Was James serious? Jesus, it was like asking Will why he couldn't believe in Santa Claus.

James moved closer, his green eyes blazing in the warm light of the chandelier. "My dad kicked me out when I was sixteen years old, and I never went to college. I barely even finished high school. I'm a fuck-up and always have been. But this summer with you and Theo, I don't know, but I felt like I was finally doing something right, like I was finally making something that could last, something that didn't depend solely on me not fucking up. It's not just that I like you Will, though I do. I like you so fucking much. You're so friggin' talented and sexy and smart, and you make me laugh. But, more than that, I trust you. I can't even get over how much I trust you, like more than I've ever trusted anyone.

"Before you, I don't think I fully realized how lonely I was, how isolated I felt being the last thread keeping my family together. When we stared into each other's eyes that time, that was when it clicked for me, when I knew. I just knew. I was like, 'Holy shit, I don't have to be alone anymore, not if this works, not if Will stays. And if something happens to me, that'll be okay, too, because Will will be there to take care of Theo, and he'll probably do a better job anyway. And maybe, for once—'"

"Jesus, what do you expect when you date guys fresh out of high school? You expect a 401K and a pension?"

"No, Will, you're missing the point."

"No, I'm not. I'm really not. I get that you've spent most of your life living paycheck to paycheck, and I'm not going to stand here and pretend I know what that's like, because I don't. I have Miles and Andy, and if I get desperate enough, my mom and dad. Christ, I'm sure Enrique would lend me a quick million if I asked him to. The whole world may hate me, but I'm never going to starve. I'm never not going to have a roof over my head.

"And I don't fault you for wanting that, too. Why wouldn't you? Everyone deserves to have that kind of security in their lives. But you don't need me for that, not anymore. Knowing what you know, my parents will set you up for life, and Theo, too. And if you want another father figure for Theo, there are plenty of hot guys out there old enough to rent a car."

"Goddamn it, Will! You're not listening. It's not about the fucking money. It's about you. You as a person, not your money. I like you, William Chapman, even though it pisses me off the way you treat yourself. I think we're great together. Don't you think we're great together?"

Will didn't trust himself not to cave, so he didn't say anything.

"I know it won't be easy and that you've got a target on your back, but I don't care about that. I really don't. I think we can make this work, like for real this time. Can't we at least try?"

Will wanted to believe James, probably even more than James wanted to believe himself. But James didn't want Will back, not really. He just felt guilty.

He was probably getting used to living in big houses and fancy hotel suites, to drinking diamond infused vodka with supermodels and movie stars. But that wasn't Will's life. That was Andy's life. That was Will's mother's life.

The Will James had come to tolerate wasn't even the real Will. The real Will lived in a tiny apartment with his personal trainer. He went to trivia on Thursday nights. He went to the gym six days a week. He watched porn before bed every night. He worked all the fucking time. That was the real Will.

Was James going to be happy sorting through Will's mail, sussing out which death threats were credible? Were they going to go out to dinner and ignore all of the people staring and pointing? And what about when the paps got Theo in their crosshairs? What would James do then?

He'd do the only thing he could do. He'd walk away. Will wasn't worth the hassle.

"How much did you get, by the way? How much is fucking me over worth? Actually, don't answer that. If it's not very much, I'll feel even worse. And if it's a lot, I'll sympathize with you, and I don't want to sympathize with you, not right now. I mean, for all I know, the only reason you're doing this is because it just occurred to you that I'm about to inherit all this." Will gestured around the cavernous library. "Well, half of it, anyway."

"I don't want your money, Will. I wish you could believe that."

The tears were back in Will's eyes before he could stop them. "Yeah, so do I. But I can't. Now, please go, and let me drink in peace."

CHAPTER 50

JAMES

James didn't move. He had to make Will understand. Just because James didn't have the luxury to pretend money didn't matter, didn't mean it was all that mattered.

James knew exactly what Will was doing. He'd done the same thing to Michael. Rather than believe Michael loved him in his own way, it had been easier to accuse him of only staying because it was financially convenient for him. It was all or nothing, black or white. But that wasn't how life worked. Life was gray, all gray, and if you wanted color, you had to fight for it. No one was just going to give it to you.

"You're stressed out and hurt. And you have every right to be. I know how much you love your father, even if you pretend you don't. And I know I'm partially, if not mostly, responsible for the way you feel right now. I just dropped a major bomb on you, too, and at the worst possible time. But you deserved to know, and I hated keeping this from you.

"And I'm not stupid. I know it took you all summer to let your guard down and trust me. And I know the moment you did, I betrayed that trust, or at least it seemed that way to you. But I really did do this for you. And, yeah, I'm not gonna lie, I also did it for Theo. I thought I could give him the life Travis wanted for him. But I also wanted to give you the life you deserve. You are a movie star, Will. And one day the world is gonna realize that. I'm sure of it. I just thought maybe, if I took care of Tony, that day could be now.

"I know how easy it is when everything goes to shit to try and make sense of it all by putting it into neat little boxes, like *he was only doing it for the money*, but trust me, it's not gonna help. You're just gonna wind up putting yourself into a box you don't belong in. You can't see it now, but you're in a prison of your own making. You keep waiting around for someone to let you out, but no one's coming. It doesn't matter how much you punish yourself or how small and unthreatening you try to make yourself. There is no time off for good behavior. If you want out, you're gonna have to—"

"Are you seriously giving me another fucking dad talk right now? Jesus, get over yourself. I don't need your fucking advice on how to handle my emotions. Handling emotions is literally what I do all fucking day, my own and everyone else's. So fuck off. Go find yourself another twenty-two-year-old skater boy who thinks you're old and wise. I'm not interested."

James held up his hands and took a step back. "Okay, I'm gonna give you some space. But will you please go find Miles and Tiffany? I don't want you to be alone right now."

"Fuck you." Will grabbed the crystal decanter of bourbon and left through the glass doors leading out into the garden.

James watched him cross the yard towards the beach and disappear into the darkness. He wasn't sure how long he stood there, staring out the glass doors, but long enough for the sky to fill with stars. And then his phone rang.

"Hey, Es."

"Where are you? Theo just posted a Snap of himself in a bathtub carved from a giant quartz crystal."

"We're at Robert's mansion in the Hamptons."

"Really? Does this mean you patched things up with Mr. Fine Ass?"

James sighed and stepped away from the doors. "No, the opposite, actually. It's over. He hates me, and I don't blame him."

"He doesn't hate you. He hates himself. There's a difference."

"Is there?"

"Definitely, but that's not why I'm calling. I've been doing some more digging into our friend, Tony, and guess who owns a house in Morocco and just applied for a Golden Visa?"

"What's a Golden Visa?"

"It's citizenship by investment, which basically boils down to buying yourself a passport in another country so it'll be harder to be extradited."

Shit, maybe Robert was right. Maybe Tony was getting scared. "How did you find this out?"

"I'm not telling you my trade secrets."

They were in the middle of filming when James entered, so he stayed by the door and hid in the shadows. From his hiding spot, he watched a younger version of himself in cutoff jeans and a tank top attempt to check his father's diaper. But Robert, Bruce, wasn't having it.

"Why are you dressed like a queer?" Robert did a near perfect impression of James's father.

Ryan pushed Robert forward and tried to pull back the elastic of his sweatpants at the back. "Because I am queer, Dad. We've already been over this. You just don't remember."

"Take that fuckin' shit off before your mother sees."

"Mom's in Florida." Ryan gave up trying to see if the diaper was full and shoved his hand in instead.

"Get your fuckin' hands off of me. Maggie? Maggie?"

"I told you, Mom's gone." Ryan pulled his hand out, and the tips of his fingers were covered in shit. "She left your sorry ass." Ryan cleaned his hands with a wet wipe. "Now lay down, so I can change you."

Robert's body started to shake as his eyes glazed over and drool slid from the corner of his mouth. James thought he might be having another stroke until he started screaming homophobic obscenities.

Will ran into the frame, his boots covered in shit and hay, as if he'd been mucking out the stalls. "What are you doin'?" He surveyed the scene. "Why are you dressed like that?" Even as Will seethed with anger, he looked bone weary. "Would you just fuckin' leave Dad alone for five minutes. You're gay, we get it. Now give it a rest."

"Fuck you," Ryan said. James held his breath. He knew what happened next, yet it still caught him off guard when Ryan punched Will in the face.

"Cut," Michelle yelled, and James looked down, where his fists were clenched at his sides.

James wasn't ready for this. The set was like a finely curated exhibit of the worst parts of his life: all of his mistakes on display for everyone to see. Why had he tortured his father like that? It had only hurt them both as he'd come out over and over again, each time hoping for a different result, and each time getting the same hate and loathing.

And there was Will and Travis, together in one. He'd tried to help them both, but he just wound up making things worse, a million times worse. What if Tony flew to Morocco tomorrow and leaked the videos from there?

Robert finally noticed James and waved him over. "Oh, good, you made it. What did you think?"

James swallowed down his shame and stepped into the light. "It was good."

As they reset for the next take, James stepped outside to clear his head. He walked across the drive and sat on the bench overlooking the pond and the weeping willow tree. It was a cool day, at least for August, and a few of the maples edging the property had already started to turn red.

Feet crunched on the gravel behind him, and he turned to find Donna striding across the driveway in jeans, knee high boots, and a white blouse that was mostly cleavage. She had a large Dunkin' Donuts latte in her hand, which was no doubt the best she could do without craft services. She came around the bench and sat uncomfortably close to James.

"Where's Theo?" she asked.

"He's at the motel." Theo had wanted to come. But they were filming the death scene today, and James didn't want Theo to see that.

"You're not staying at the house with the rest of us? I was really counting on one of Theo's homemade meals."

Yeah, right, more like one of his homemade cocktails. "I don't think Will would appreciate that."

Donna seemed to give the matter careful consideration, but when she spoke, it was about something else entirely.

"I always knew William was different, special. All mothers think that, I know, but some of us are actually right." She pulled her blouse tighter against the wind, but it only made her boobs try to escape more. "Andy was a mama's boy, but not William. He worshiped his father. Why? I don't know. Robert was always working. Even when he did spend time with William, it was never to build a tower or to draw pictures. It was always to rehearse. I think maybe he thought if he could keep the attention of a toddler that meant he was doing something right."

She took a sip of her latte, and the smell of hazelnut reminded James of his own mother, who always got that flavor whenever pumpkin spice wasn't in season.

"He must've been three, maybe four, when I found him in the

nursery one day, reciting a monologue from that Tarantino film Robert did. The nanny was passed out in the rocking chair, and William had propped Andy up between two stuffed animals, making a sort of audience for himself. Andy couldn't have been more than one or two at the time. 'You say fuck one more time and I'll show you how to fuck a motherfucking motherfucker up the motherfucking ass,' William shouted at his baby brother. Andy wasn't scared, though. He thought it was hilarious. It was actually his laughter that brought me to the nursery in the first place."

Donna paused to swallow another sip of her latte. "I hid in the doorway and watched as word for word, emotion for emotion, William recited the entire monologue perfectly. When I stopped laughing, I remember thinking, *What have we done to this poor child?* And not because of the cursing either. I've never cared about that."

The wind whipped over the surface of the pond and left a trail of mottled gray ripples in its wake. James wasn't sure what she expected him to say. Was he supposed to agree that she and Robert were shitty parents? He said nothing.

"It's going to be hard for him, watching his father die, as I'm sure it was for you. He's spent his whole life trying to make that arrogant bastard notice him." Donna smoothed out a crease in her jeans. "I think the main thing parents want for their kids, what you probably want for Theo, is just for someone else to see them the way we do, someone else to realize just how amazing they are and to love them for it."

Donna pushed away a lock of red hair that had blown across her lips. "In a way, I was a single parent long before Robert and I ever got divorced. I just hated that he wouldn't even look at him. William would go to such lengths, too. He'd sing his father songs, and he and his best friend, Ariel, would do these elaborate dance routines. Don't get me wrong, Robert would be polite. He was nothing like your father. He was never verbally or physically abusive. He was even generally positive. He'd always point out the parts he liked the most.

"But he never let William get to him, not emotionally anyway. He was never impressed, and I could never figure out why. I always felt like maybe I was crazy or something. But I knew. I knew William was special. I knew he had a gift. And I was right, too."

Donna picked up her latte and took a long sip, as if she were rewarding herself. "It wasn't easy getting him that role in *The Beautiful*. They thought he was too young, too green, too average looking. But I knew he'd be perfect. I never told anyone this, but I financed most of *The Beautiful* myself, anonymously, of course. I made a huge profit, too."

James wasn't looking at her, but he could hear the fragile smile in her voice.

"Finally, the whole world saw what I saw. The director even called me after the first day of shooting and said, 'That boy of yours is going to win an Oscar one day.'" Donna laughed softly, almost bitterly. "Derek hated William at first. He said he was obnoxious. But even he came to like him in the end, maybe even love him.

"But Robert, no. Robert was unmovable. There is no telling that man 'I told you so.' He wouldn't admit that William earned every bit of buzz he got. To Robert, it was just the role, not William. He said he was like Hillary Swank in *Boys Don't Cry* and *Million Dollar Baby*, that people just felt sorry for his character. Then he claimed that half the success of the film was due to the narrative that William might actually beat him, the great Robert Chapman, to the Oscar podium."

James wasn't sure why Donna was telling him this, but he wondered if maybe this, too, had more to do with her than Will. It was no secret Robert had never taken Donna seriously as an actress.

"Even after I figured out who you really were, I didn't say anything because I could tell you saw it, too. I could tell by the way you looked at him, by the way you always found an excuse to be close to him, to touch him, to step into his line of sight, or to find a way to keep him in yours."

"You knew?" James looked up from the pond.

"Not that you were working with Esther Kim. I didn't see that coming. But I figured out you were Jimmy a couple days after you started coming to the set. It wasn't just that you seemed to have this bizarre insight into all the characters either. It was how, when William was filming, you would stare at him like you were seeing a ghost."

"And you didn't say anything?"

Donna shook her head. "I liked seeing William happy for a change." She uncrossed her legs and stood. "Just don't give up on him, okay? He's going to need a friend. And while I love Miles like he's my own son, I don't think diet and exercise are going to cut it this time." She turned her back to the wind, and her long red hair whipped furiously about her face. "Come on, it's almost time to shoot the death scene."

CHAPTER 51

WILL

"It's kinda weird, huh?" Ryan came and stood beside Will as the crew set up for the big death scene, the climax of the movie. "Doing this in front of James now that we know who he really is."

Will put his phone away. "That's definitely one way to put it."

"He hates my performance, doesn't he? It's too feminine, right?"

"It's definitely not too feminine." Will rubbed his jaw, which still smarted from Ryan's sucker punch.

"Sorry again for actually punching you. I just get so caught up, and—"

"It's fine."

Michelle walked them through the scene, which, tonally, was a real minefield. It was meant to be sad, funny, and somewhat callous. The idea was to subvert expectations of the usual deathbed epiphanies and heartfelt monologues, while still being emotionally affecting. So, no pressure.

"Places," Michelle said.

Will sat in the chair next to his father, who took a long, pained breath from his hospital bed. "Why don't you take something? Just think how many drugs Bruce must have been on." Will tried to appeal to his father's sense of craft. "It doesn't get any more method than that."

"I'm fine." His father's breathy whisper sounded anything but fine.

"Action," Michelle said.

Acting was like breathing or blinking. It was involuntary most of the time, but you could wrestle control if you wanted to. The trick was, his father used to say, to find the right balance between going with the flow and being in control of it.

Will preferred to go with the flow. So it was Travis who said, "Jimmy will be here in a minute."

His father coughed, and though the sound effects wouldn't be added until later, Will could already hear the rattle of phlegm.

"Owen's sitter was late again."

When Travis had written the book, he'd kept all the names the same, all except for Theo's.

His father's eyes stared back at him, glassy and confused.

"Your grandson." Will showed his father the background on his phone's home screen, which was a picture of Owen on his bike.

"Jimmy?" There was a lucid twinkle in his father's eye.

"No, Dad, that's Owen, your grandson."

His father coughed, closed his eyes, and drifted off to sleep, the word, "Jimmy," a whisper on his lips. Will stood and walked to the window.

The door opened a moment later, and Ryan rushed in wearing an orange beanie. "Is he . . . ?"

"No." Will turned from the window. "Not yet, anyway. Not that it matters. He's not in there anymore. Although, maybe we should check. Maybe you should remind him how much you like suckin' dick and see what he does." He swiped the Jell-O from his father's tray. "I just wish somethin' would happen. This is boring." He gestured about the room with the cup of Jell-O. "I thought death was supposed to be exciting. I mean, it's not like I expected to weep at his bedside or anything. But I thought, I don't know, maybe I'd feel guilty or somethin'. Or relieved. Or guilty that I feel relieved. But I don't feel anything other than boredom. Did you bring any weed?"

"Owen shit his pants at school today," Ryan said. "You forgot to pack a change of clothes, so they sent him home in a pair of Hello Kitty sweatpants. I think he likes 'em, though."

Will took two bites of Jell-O and set the cup back on the tray. "I envy you. At least you hate him. I just don't feel anything. It's weird, right? I mean"—he looked down at the frame wasting away under the white hospital sheet—"that's gonna be me in a few years. And in forty or fifty years, that might be Owen, too. Shouldn't that cause some kind of existential crisis or something?"

"I don't hate him." Ryan took over the chair by the bedside.

"Could've fooled me, paradin' around him like a fudge packer all the time. I mean, I get it." Will picked up the Jell-O again and started pacing about the room. "He was a dick. I'd never do that to Owen, even if he liked fuckin' sheep."

Ryan pulled off his beanie and ran a hand over his stubbled scalp. "I met someone. His name is Michael. He's in law school. He's gonna be a lawyer."

"Impressive. Maybe you should invite him to the wake." Will scraped out the last of the Jell-O and licked the spoon.

"Maybe I will."

His father's eyes opened, and he started to choke. Will and Ryan stared at each other, and a silent agreement seemed to pass between them. *Let it play out. Let it end.* But Ryan broke the contract and yelled for help.

"Cut." They didn't have anyone to play the nurses and doctors, so they couldn't film the rest of the scene.

"Good," Michelle said, "that was really good."

Michelle was rarely effusive in her praise, but her words didn't quite match her tone, and Will couldn't help but sense that she was unsatisfied with the take.

"Fuck, Will." Ryan clapped him on the back. "That was amazing."

"Thanks, you too." Will looked out into the small audience. He didn't mean to make eye contact with James. It just happened.

"Let's reset and go again," Michelle said. "Ryan, when you say, 'I met someone. His name is Michael,' I want you to take a moment and picture someone from your own life. Don't tell me who it is. I want it to be a private moment. Travis thinks it's just another hookup, but I want you to let your entire future with this man flash before your eyes, Christmas dinners, meeting his parents, taking him to your high school reunion, watching *Drag Race* together with all your friends. Do you see what I'm saying?"

Ryan nodded. "Yeah, I can do that."

"And Will, I loved what you did with the Jell-O spoon. Keep that. It was perfect."

Will nodded, but he wasn't listening. He was too busy staring at his father. He hadn't betrayed any sense of pain while the cameras were rolling, but now his face was white with it.

"Can someone please get my dad something, morphine or whatever?"

"I don't need it." His father waved away the hospice nurse. "James, can you come here please?"

Jesus Christ. Will started to walk away, but his father wouldn't let him. "No, stay. I don't know how many more takes I have left in me today. We need to figure this out before it's too late."

"It was fine, Dad."

"You're right. It was fine. But we need better than fine."

Will's temperature spiked as James approached.

"That was incredible." James wore an old baseball tee with a Counting Crows logo on the front that said, in scribbled cursive, *August and Everything After*.

"But we're missing something," Will's father said, "aren't we?"

"No, that was great." James pulled his eyes from Will and looked at his father.

"What really happened?" His father reached for James's hand, and to Will's astonishment, James gave it to him. "I don't care if it's mundane and boring. It doesn't need to be cinematic. It just needs to be real."

Will was used to his father acting like he was this intuitive genius who understood his characters better than they understood themselves. He expected James to shrug and say, "Nope, that was pretty much how it went down," but James didn't answer at all. He looked down at Will's father's hand in his and then closed his eyes.

CHAPTER 52

JAMES

This was Will's father, not his. James pulled his hand back, but his skin still remembered Robert's cold touch.

"Well, Travis took some artistic liberties. I mean, he didn't actually die that night. It took another few days. He'd been in the nursing home for about five months at that point, and I guess his body forgot how to swallow or something. He got food in his lungs, which led to, I can't remember the name of it, some kind of pneumonia."

"Aspiration pneumonia," Robert said. "It's very common in Alzheimer's patients."

James nodded. "Yeah, that." It was at least ten degrees hotter under the stage lights, and James started to sweat. "And that's when they brought him to the hospital. Anyway, none of what you guys did actually happened, at least not like that. Travis just combined several different days and conversations into one scene for convenience."

Actually, James had done that. It had been one of the editor's suggestions.

"That afternoon, when he almost choked to death, he wasn't

asleep. In fact, he was very much awake. He kept going on and on about airplanes crashing into little Mexican kids and destroying Christmas. My dad never stopped talking. A lot of Alzheimer's patients become non-verbal by the end, but we weren't so lucky. He just stopped making sense. And when he did make sense, it was nothing but hate. I know this is probably a shitty thing to say, but for my dad, the disease destroyed the best parts first."

Robert squinted up into the bright lights. "Thank you, James. I can't imagine it's easy for you to relive all this. But if you remember anything else, anything at all, please let us know."

James didn't want to remember. He wanted to smoke a bowl. "Well, if it's any help, we found out a week after he died that the whole rant about airplanes and Mexican kids was based on a *Desperate Housewives* episode he thought was real."

Robert's eyes perked up. "Really? Which episode?"

James shrugged. "I don't know. I assume the one where an airplane crashes?"

"That's okay. Donna is good friends with Teri. She'll know." Robert closed his eyes in pain, and James backed away to let the nurse through.

"I have to take a phone call," Michelle said. "We'll go again in thirty."

Will turned and walked away, but James caught up to him a second later, grasping the back of his arm. "Can we talk? You ran away so fast the other night I didn't—"

"Fine, I'm sorry." Will pulled his arm free. "I didn't mean to be so dramatic. Let's just go back to being casual acquaintances. How was the drive? Did you bring Theo?"

"I don't want to be your 'casual acquaintance.'"

Will's posture slumped, and he cast his eyes to the floor. He reminded James of one of those sad dogs at the pound that no longer lifts its head when a family walks past.

"Let's go for a walk down by the pond. I'll tell you what really happened the day my dad died."

"Don't tell me. Tell my dad. Or, better yet, tell Annabeth. She's the screenwriter."

"Please, Will. It's something I've never told anyone else before, something I can barely even admit to myself."

Will closed his eyes and took three deep breaths. "Okay, fine."

It had rained the night before, and the path down to the pond was muddy and dotted with puddles. Neither of them spoke until Will parted the long, spindly leaves of the willow tree and sat down on the bench beneath its canopy. In the process, he startled a frog, which jumped into the water and resurfaced five feet out.

"I changed the ending of my brother's book to make myself look better. He sent it to an editor, and she wasn't very impressed. In fact, she gave him so many suggestions he was gonna have to basically rewrite the whole thing. He would've, too. But there wasn't time. He was already getting sick at that point, and, well, you know."

James sat down on the bench, but left a comfortable space between himself and Will. He knew he was stalling. But he couldn't help himself.

"Anyway, I had to work on the revisions myself. At first, I was just gonna fix all the typos and try to publish it the way it was, even if it wasn't perfect. I figured, just because one editor didn't like it didn't mean it wouldn't sell. But then things got out of hand, and I started to think of it as my book, and I started rewriting whole sections and adding new ones. And when I got to the end, I changed it."

"What do you mean, you changed it?" Will kicked at the ground and dislodged a pebble that rolled into the water.

"I didn't want anyone to know what I said, especially Theo. But I don't wanna keep this secret anymore. I want you to put it back the way it was, the way Travis had it."

"Okay. How did Travis have it?"

James couldn't bring himself to look at Will, so he found the frog's amber eyes out in the pond and spoke to him.

"I'm the one who put the idea in his head, the idea to make it look like an accident. I didn't mean it, though. I was just so mad at him. He kept going on and on about how he wasn't gonna put Theo through this shit, how he'd kill himself first. I tried to be supportive, you know. I was like, we'll cross that bridge when we get there, and who knows, maybe they'll find a cure by then. But he wouldn't let it go, and finally, I just snapped. 'Fine,' I said, 'if you're so hell-bent on killing yourself, do it. Just be sure to make it look like an accident. That way we can still collect the insurance money.'"

James reached down and picked up a rock. He considered tossing it out into the pond, but he didn't want to scare the frog.

Will didn't say anything, but James could feel his eyes on him, waiting for the rest.

"And that's exactly what he did," James said, turning the stone over in his hand. "He didn't say goodbye or leave a note. He was in the shower when Theo left for school that morning. That should've been my first clue. He never took long showers. He was in there so long, I eventually just barged in and took a shit. I didn't flush, though. Courteous, right?"

"I'm sorry, James, that's awful. But it's not your fault. He made his own choice, and I'm not sure I would've made a different one if I were—"

"Just because you're playing my brother in some stupid movie doesn't mean you know shit about him."

"I'm sorry. You're right. I didn't mean—"

"No, I'm sorry. I didn't mean to snap at you. I know you're just trying to help. And you can, by fixing the ending."

"I'm not going to do that to you and Theo." The calm in Will's voice made James want to rip every branch off the willow tree. "What if the insurance company wants their money back?"

"They won't. The suicide clause expired after two years." James felt the prick of tears behind his eyes, but there was no way in hell he was letting Will see him cry. "And if you really care about Theo, you'll finish the movie the right way. You won't let Derek Hall anywhere near it."

Then, even though all James wanted to do was collapse in Will's arms and bawl like a baby, he stood and walked to the edge of the pond so Will couldn't see his face.

"We can find another way."

"I don't want another way. I want the truth. You get that, right? I know you do. We're more alike than you realize. The only difference is, I actually succeeded in killing someone."

When James returned to the motel, Theo was on the phone, clearly talking to Es.

"No, he just walked in, and he's definitely not drunk or decapitated."

James must've forgotten to turn his phone back on after watching them film all afternoon. "Tell her I'll call her back in, like, half an hour."

"Fifteen," Es yelled through the phone.

"Fine, fifteen."

Theo hung up and immediately reached for his guitar. "I wrote a new song today. Wanna hear it?"

Most teenagers forced to spend the day alone in a motel with an out of commission pool and only network television to watch would be bored and restless. But not Theo.

"I do wanna hear it, but can we have a little chat first? There's something I need to tell you."

"Okay." Theo set down his guitar, and his expression sobered. They weren't the types who had *talks*.

"You probably don't remember this, but when your dad started getting sick, I sorta took over writing the book for him. I mean, he'd already finished it, of course, but there were all these changes the editor wanted, and . . . Well, I made the changes. And I shouldn't have, but I changed the end, too. I was ashamed because—" James's throat started to close, and he knew if he didn't force the words out now, they might never see the light of day. "I'm sorry, Theo. Your dad and I had an argument, and I said some things I didn't mean. It's my fault Travis—"

"Stop. I already know what you're gonna say."

James lifted his head and stared past Theo to the painting on the wall of a sugar shack in the woods surrounded by piles of melting snow and patches of bare brown earth. "No, I don't think you do."

"You know I can read, right? I read Dad's book like four times. And I know you changed the ending, that you took out the argument you two had. But you made it better. You made it way better. And I know why. You did it for me, so I could go on pretending it was just an accident. But I know he didn't just fall out of the canoe."

"You knew?"

"Why does everyone think I'm just some stupid kid? I know why he killed himself, and it wasn't because you told him to. When did Dad ever do anything you told him to? He did it because he didn't want me to watch him lose his mind."

"That's not true."

"It is true, and you know it. That whole nursing home plan was bullshit. He was never gonna let that happen."

That had been the plan, though it was clear when the book didn't sell as well as they'd hoped that Travis's medical bills were going to wipe them out financially. But they would've figured it out.

"I'm sorry, Theo. I never should've put the idea in his head."

"You didn't put the idea in his head. You don't find out you're going to lose your mind and forget everything and everyone without wondering if maybe you should just quit while you're ahead."

"Theo, please don't ever—"

"I'm not gonna, relax. I already promised Dad."

James pulled at a thread on the thin floral bedspread. "I wasn't going to say anything, but you should probably know. Robert gave you something."

"He told you?"

"Wait, you already know about the money?"

Theo's face scrunched in confusion. "What money?"

"Robert set you up with a trust fund, a fucking huge one, too. You won't ever have to work if you don't want to. You can just travel and make music. Or, you can go to college. It's up to you. There's probably even enough to open your own recording studio, if you want. The point is, you'll have options. You can have the life your father always wanted for you."

"Really? He did that for me? Why?"

"I don't know. But the man gets so into character, he probably thinks you're his real grandson. What did you think I was talking about?"

"Oh, nothing, just the cologne."

Theo looked away, and James knew he was hiding something. Robert had given Theo all his old bottles of expensive cologne, but James already knew that.

"I wanna watch them film tomorrow," Theo said. "I know you think I can't handle it, but I can. I'm gonna watch the movie anyway, so what's the difference?"

James closed his eyes and sighed, listening to the whir and tick of the air conditioner. "The difference is they film it over and over again. It's not just once. They do it from every angle. And these are professionals, Theo. Will and his dad, even Ryan, they make it look so real. It's not like watching *Blood Brothers*."

"I know that. But I have a right to be there."

"Travis didn't want you to see—"

"Yeah, well, he's dead, so excuse me if I don't put his wants above my own."

"Don't be an asshole."

"You're calling me an asshole? You didn't say anything. You just stood there and let Will think the worst, and now we're stuck in this crappy motel while everyone else is back at the house having fun."

James knew this wasn't about Will or being forced to sleep in a shitty motel, but it was easier to pretend it was. "I tried to apologize, I—"

"Yeah, I'm sure you did." Theo dropped his voice an octave and pretended to be James. "'Hey, Will, just wanted to say I'm sorry. Do you wanna, I don't know, maybe get back together? No? Oh, okay. Well, I'll see you around, then.'"

"It's not that simple."

"Yeah, it is. Because you're just like Dad. You talk a big game. You act like you're tough and fearless, but when it comes down to it, you just roll over and give up. You don't fight for anything."

If James didn't fight for anything, then why were they in Vermont right now? James had spent the better part of a year rewriting Travis's book and another six months querying agents. He'd called in every favor he could to get the movie rights optioned. And this whole summer, everything he'd done, whether he should've or not, was all for Travis's movie. If that wasn't fighting for something, then James didn't know what was.

His phone rang. It was Esther. "I have to take this. We can discuss the plan for tomorrow when I'm done."

Theo stood and grabbed his hoodie off the bed. "I'm going for a walk."

"Did Will ever date Tony when he was younger?" Eo asked.

James opened the mini-fridge and pulled out his half-drunk soda from the drive up. "Of course not. Will hates Tony. And the feeling is mutual."

"Yeah, but maybe it's mutual for a reason. I was doing some more digging on Tony's phone and—"

"What do you mean? You don't—"

"Don't get your panties in a bunch. Did you honestly think I wasn't gonna put my own spyware on Tony's phone before I handed it over to you?"

"Fuck, Es. I knew I never should've trusted—"

"I found pictures—a lot of pictures. Most are of Derek, but there's a whole folder of Derek and Will together, and a few of just Will."

"What?"

"Check your email and call me back. I'll be home for another hour."

And then she hung up.

CHAPTER 53
WILL

Will sat on his balcony that evening with his guitar and a Manhattan. His fingers were bruised and sore from mindlessly strumming the same chord progression over and over again.

"What song is that?" Theo came and sat down in the other chair.

"What are you doing here?" James and Theo were supposed to be staying at a hotel.

"Your mom said I could crash here tonight. Uncle James and I sorta got in a fight."

Will leaned his guitar against the balcony railing. James must've told him what he'd said to Travis.

Theo picked up the guitar and perfectly mimicked the chord progression Will had been stuck on like a groove in a broken record. His fingers danced over the strings as he added flourishes and embellishments. When he stopped, he said, "I'm glad you're gonna put the old ending back, and I wanna be there tomorrow when you film it."

"I don't think that's a—"

"The plan was always for him to go into a nursing home when

things got bad. I was gonna visit him on his good days, because they said there would be good days. There were gonna be so many good days, especially at first. And then, when there weren't any more good days, when he no longer remembered me, only Uncle James was gonna visit him. And then he'd die there, behind closed doors. That was the plan. That was what the song was supposed to be about. *I'll take my life behind closed doors and give you an end that's only yours."* Theo plucked the low E-string, and it droned into the late summer evening. "But it was a lie. There were no doors."

Will's stomach felt like an elevator in free fall. James was right. Will didn't know shit about Travis.

"I wasn't supposed to know about the gene, but I overheard them talking about it one night when we were camping, and . . . It doesn't matter. The point is, even though there's a fifty percent chance I don't have it, in my dad's eyes, there was never any doubt. That's what pisses me off the most, that he blamed himself for something that might not even be a big deal. I could be fine. I could live to be a hundred. In fact, I went to this fortune-teller once, and she straight-out told me I was gonna be fine. I told Dad that, but he didn't believe me."

Will could tell Theo had more to say, so he sat there quietly and waited.

"Uncle James brought me with him to the hospital when Grandpa died. I was three at the time. I remember seeing Dad crying and thinking how weird it was because I didn't know grownups could cry, especially not my dad."

Jesus, Will's dad cried all the time.

"Then he saw me, and he stopped crying. Just like that. He even smiled. Sometimes, I wish they would've let me find out if I have the gene or not, just so Dad wouldn't have had to feel so guilty. Don't tell Uncle James, but I almost got the test on my birthday. I had the appointment and everything."

Will set his drink down, afraid he might spill it.

"Brice talked me out of it, though. And he didn't even bring up all that bullshit about insurance. He just said it was probably better to live with uncertainty and hope than the truth. But what if he's wrong?"

"He might be," Will admitted. "But it's a nearly impossible decision to make, which is why you shouldn't rush into it."

"Yeah, but if I do have the gene, at least I'll know my father didn't kill himself for no reason."

Will took a deep breath, trying to organize his thoughts. He didn't want to overstep, but he hated seeing Theo in so much pain.

"I can't speak for your father because I'm not him. I'm just the actor playing him in the movie. But if I were in his shoes, I wouldn't want my kid watching me suffer. I wouldn't want him to remember me like that. I know you think he did it for you, and maybe that was part of it. But is it possible that he did it for himself, too?"

Theo's glasses magnified the tears in his blue eyes. "I guess, maybe."

"Can I ask you something?" Will picked up his drink, but then set it right back down again.

"Sure."

"Would it be alright if I sang your song in the movie, the one you wrote with your dad?"

"You wanna sing my song?"

"If you don't mind."

Theo smiled, and it broke Will's heart in two. "I don't mind. I can teach you the guitar part right now if you want."

Will's fingers ached from playing all evening, but he said, "Really? That would be awesome."

WILL COULDN'T SLEEP that night, and he wasn't the only one. The TV in his father's room, James's old room, was on. Will couldn't make out what he was watching, but an ambiguous loudness pulsed through the wall. It was probably that *Desperate Housewives* episode again. Will thought about finding a white noise app on his phone. But instead, he got out of bed and knocked on his father's door.

"Come in."

It wasn't *Desperate Housewives*. It was *The Beautiful*. Will's father was watching Will's movie. And he was crying.

"Jesus, Dad, knock it off." Will couldn't find the remote fast enough, so he walked over and shut the TV off manually.

"I'm so sorry I never told you how good you are in this. Your work here is nothing short of astounding."

Will sighed and sat on the edge of his father's bed. "Dad, please."

"No, it's the truth. You're just so natural. I don't know how you do it. Maybe I'm biased because I'm your father, but you're the most heartbreakingly beautiful thing I've ever seen on screen. And I mean that. It's clear the title is supposed to refer to Derek's character. But it's you. You're the beautiful one, and I don't know how I never realized that before. Everyone else did."

Will grabbed his father's bottle of pills off the nightstand and read the label. "What's in these, ecstasy?"

"I wish I'd been more like you as an actor. You're so free. You never overthink anything. You make it look so easy."

Will set his hand on his father's leg. "Are you kidding, Dad? I overthink everything."

"Not when you're acting. When you're acting, it's effortless. I've been studying you. And it's like . . ." His father stared off into space for a long time, and Will thought maybe he was having another stroke, but then he said, "It's like all the puppet strings just vanish, and I can't figure out how. How do you do it?"

"Jesus, Dad, maybe you should space your painkillers out more. Don't take them all at once."

His father turned and adjusted the pillow behind his back. "There is a manilla envelope on the desk. I want you to have it."

Why was his father doing this to him?

"It's all of my old acceptance speeches, the ones I never got a chance to give. I want you to read them."

"Right now?"

The envelope sat on the desk like a bomb about to go off.

"If you don't mind."

Jesus Christ, could this day get any more depressing? Will walked over to the desk to retrieve the speeches. That was when he saw a second manilla envelope, one with Theo's name on it. "What's this?" he asked.

"That's between me and Theo. The other one's for you."

Will sat at the desk and opened the envelope meant for him, the brass tabs digging into his tender fingertips. He pulled out a stack of yellowing papers and started to read.

There was one speech from before Will was born, but the rest were after. In every single one, his father found some way or other to gush about Will and, to a lesser extent, Andy, too. He said being a dad was the best role of his life and that his son, William, was the best scene partner he'd ever worked with. *Sorry, Meryl*, he joked in one speech. *You'll have to settle for second best this one time.*

On the seventh speech, the one he'd written right after he was diagnosed with cancer the first time, he said, *I want to thank my family, my ex-wife, Donna, who is and always will be the love of my life; my youngest, Andy, who embodies everything that is pure and good in this world; and my oldest, William, who is the kind of actor I want to be when I grow up, natural, honest, and unyielding.* And the next two were just as bad, maybe worse.

Will slid the last one back into the envelope and wished he could trade places with his father, wished he could be the one dying.

"I always planned on being magnanimous," his father said. "I just never got around to it."

"We could always write one more"—Will set the envelope back on the desk—"just in case."

His father shook his head and laughed through bitter tears. "Nah, I'm done with all that. It's not important. And it shouldn't be to you either."

Will glanced over at the clock. "Well, we go again in five hours, so maybe don't be done just yet. Theo is counting on us. We have to get his song in the movie."

His father smiled. "Okay, well, in that case. But let's have fun with it, yes? Let's forget there are cameras and people counting on us. Let's just pretend we're running lines in the library, like old times. Fuck the Academy."

"Yeah, okay." Will tried to return his father's smile. "Fuck the Academy."

"Oh, and while we're on the topic of fun, I pulled some strings and got some top-notch talent to play the medical team."

Will rolled his eyes. "Oh, Jesus. Do I even want to know?"

His father gave him a wry smile. "Probably not."

Ten minutes before Will's alarm was set to go off, all the covers were yanked from his bed.

"Damn, papi. You never said you were packing." Enrique flopped down onto the mattress next to him.

"What the fuck, Enrique?" Will crossed his arms over his crotch and tried to cover up his morning wood. "What are you doing here?"

"It's Dr. Drake Ramoray to you." Enrique laughed and turned over on his side so his face was only inches from Will's. "Your dad said I could name my own character."

Will sat up in bed and pulled a pillow around to cover himself. "You're playing one of the doctors?"

"Yeah. I've always wanted to play a doctor. I only have three lines, but your dad said it's still important to create a fully realized character. So, get this, while Andy was driving, I came up with a killer backstory."

"Andy's here, too?"

"I'm talking, Will. Get this, in college, I was a major stoner and thought I was applying to nursing school, but I accidentally applied to medical school instead. And I got in, too, because I'm secretly very smart. I would've dropped out, but there was this girl I really liked, so I got my medical degree just to impress her. Of course, she wouldn't give me the time of day because of my stutter, you know, like Colin Firth in *The King's Speech*, but—"

"You're going to say your three lines with a stutter?" This had to be a dream.

"Seriously, papi, it's not polite to interrupt. Anyway, as I was saying, she wouldn't give me the time of day, but then I saved her cat's life with an emergency tracheotomy, and she fell madly in love with me, stutter and all. But, get this, the confidence I gained from having such a gorgeous doctor wife, and being a doctor myself, cured my stutter."

"That sounds awesome, Enrique. I can't believe you and Andy drove all the way up here for this."

"Well, technically, Nandi did most of the driving. Andy did the first leg, but then I found this bottle of Macallan's in my bag and—"

"Are you drunk right now?" Will hopped out of bed and started walking towards the bathroom.

"Fuck, papi, you're like super fit now. In *The Beautiful*, you're all skinny and boyish. But now you're a man. You're a real man, Will. Did you know that?"

Will stepped into the bathroom, but he couldn't close the door because his pull-up bar was in the way. "I should probably go shower."

Enrique turned his head and smelled his pits. "Yeah, me too." He took off his shirt and let down his man bun.

"Alone."

Enrique lay back on the bed with his hands behind his head. "Oh, I get it. You're still hung up on James. That's cool. My offer still stands if you want me to rough him up a bit."

Michelle and Annabeth loved the idea of using Theo's song in the movie. They wanted Travis to sing it in the hospital room as Bruce passes away, and they wanted baby Theo to be there, too, to show the multi-generational tragedy of it all, like a life cycle tableau. But that meant finding a child actor at the last minute. Theo suggested using his little brother, who was not only the perfect age, but lived close by. So that was what they did, even though Will's mom wasn't keen on involving Emily.

Enrique, Nandi, and Will's mother agreed to play the medical team, and Andy was set to play the hospice nurse who suggests they sing to Bruce as he dies. But first, they had to shoot the revised death scene, which was now the pre-death scene.

After the first couple of takes, Will went over to check on Theo. It felt needlessly cruel having him there, but Theo wouldn't take no for an answer.

"I'm fine." Theo was lying. He wasn't fine. He was crying. "And I know what you're thinking, but I'm not sad about the scene. I'm not all stressed out about dying. I'm really not. You're just so much like my dad. It's just, like, really weird."

They kept at it for the next three hours, take after take, and though Michelle gave them very little direction, Will could tell by the set of her jaw that she was far from satisfied.

"What are we missing?" he eventually asked. He peered over her shoulder as she watched the latest take on the monitor. "It's my 'I'm not putting Owen through this shit,' line, isn't it? Do you want me to try it smaller, more restrained, maybe like a silent thought accidentally voiced aloud?"

"No"—Michelle shook her head—"it's not that. We got that on the third take. And it's not Robert either. He's doing great, some of his best work, honestly. It's just these new pages. They're too perfect. It's too clean. It feels like a script."

Will nodded. He knew what Michelle meant, though he could hardly blame Annabeth. She'd had one night to revise the most crucial scene in the movie, and she'd had to write simultaneous dialogue that included the ramblings of a demented redneck.

"Maybe we should try having your father improvise." Michelle sat back in her chair and glanced over at Will's father in the hospital bed. The makeup team had outdone themselves: he looked terrible.

Will bit his lip. Robert Chapman thrived on preparation and control. He didn't improvise. "Really? I don't know if—"

"I know." Michelle took her hair down. "But let's try anyway."

She broke the news to his father, and Will had never seen him so scared in his life. It was like he was living out one of those nightmares where you're the lead in a play you've never heard of.

"Come on, Dad," Will said. "It might be fun, and we said we were going to have fun, right?"

"Right."

An hour later, his father was covered in sweat and his voice was hoarse from yelling. But he was doing it, even in a thick Vermont accent.

"Remember," Michelle told Will and Ryan before they went again, "you've been listening to your father rant like this for years. You don't hear him anymore. He's just the wet dog smell in your car. You're totally nose-blind to him at this point. I don't care if you talk over his funniest lines. Just keep the intensity."

Michelle wasn't sure what she was after, but claimed she'd know it when she saw it. So they went again and again. Enrique and Nandi rushed in time after time. Take after take, Will's Travis silently wrote his own ending, long shower and all, while Ryan's Jimmy tried in vain to be the supportive brother until it was too much, until he gave up and let Travis win. That was how they decided to play it. They wanted it to read both ways: as a quip said in anger and as a gift, as a promise to support his brother no matter what he decided.

Andy came up to Will shortly before they were set to break for lunch. "I don't think Dad can keep doing this. He's in a lot of pain, and he's refusing to take anything for it."

Andy had taken the news of their father's illness better than Will had expected. Instead of yelling at Will for keeping it a secret, he'd apologized. *I'm so sorry you've had to deal with this all on your own.* Now, to make up for lost time, Andy was acting like one of their father's nurses, constantly checking in on him.

"I know." Will glanced over at their father's pallid face. "I'll talk to him."

While they set up for the next take, Will walked over to his father. "Dad"—he sat down in the chair by the bed—"I know the painkillers put you to sleep and make it hard for you to concentrate. But you're not having fun if you're in pain, and we said this would be fun, right?"

"I can't." His father's face was pale, and it wasn't because of the makeup. "It'll ruin me for the rest of the day."

"So what? Your character is dead in the next scene. Besides, you said you wanted to be more free, right? What better way than this? And if it makes you forget your lines, who cares? Besides, you know this part. You could do it in your sleep. You could do it drunk and high. You just have to trust us. Trust yourself. We already have plenty of footage of you doing it through the pain. Now, let's try something new. Who cares if it works? It's going to be fun. And, if nothing else, it will make a hilarious addition to the blooper reel."

His father sucked in a breath, and it was like he was breathing in fire embers. "I don't know."

"I do. Think of it like jazz."

"I hate jazz."

Will chuckled and smiled down at his father. "Yeah, jazz is the worst. But the metaphor still holds. You're a professional. You know the theory. You know all of your blues scales in every key, major and minor. Now, it's time to let the music out."

His father closed his eyes, and before he could object, Will waved the nurse over.

"Action," Michelle said.

"Jimmy will be here in a minute," Will's Travis said. "Owen's sitter was late again."

His father smiled in a blissed-out, drug-induced euphoria. "Get me my gun. I'll shoot that fuckin' plane down myself, shoot it right out of the fuckin' sky."

Will turned his phone towards his father. "Look at him. No training wheels, and he's only three."

His father squinted at the phone. "Jimmy?"

"No, Dad, that's Owen, your grandson."

"They're coming for you, Jimmy, but I'm gonna shoot 'em out of the fuckin' sky."

The door swung open and Ryan came in. He pulled off his orange beanie and ran his hands across his stubbled scalp. "Not dead yet, I see."

"He's the one who took my fuckin' sock." His father hurled the cup of Jell-O at Ryan and hit him square in the face. It hadn't been planned, but Ryan didn't break character.

"Son of a bitch." Ryan clutched his eye.

"Dad, knock it off." Will tried to hold his father down, but he was stronger than he looked, and he reared up and head butted Will. Pain shot through Will's skull. Real pain. Jesus fucking Christ.

"Give me back my sock!"

Will didn't know what happened next, in part because he'd suffered a concussion, but also because it was fucking bonkers. Even later, when he watched it back on the monitor, he couldn't believe it. It was wild. It was unhinged. Half of Ryan's and his lines were swallowed as his father lost his shit. And yet, his father never broke character, not once. It was fucked-up and brilliant. And when he took his drink and began to silently aspirate, it came at the perfect moment, right as Will was saying, "Fuck this shit. I'm not doin' it. I'm not puttin' Owen through this. I'm not. There's no fuckin' way. I'll shoot myself in the head first."

"Awesome. That's just awesome." Ryan screamed so loudly it

obscured the fact that their father had stopped screaming and was choking to death. "You do that. Go be a martyr. Just be sure to make it look like an accident, okay? That way we can still collect the insurance money."

Will's Travis wanted to say something back, wanted to apologize, wanted to double down, wanted to hug his brother, wanted to punch him, wanted to tell him to go fuck himself, wanted to scream until his voice was hoarse. But instead, he unclenched his fists and let a single tear slide down his cheek.

"Shit." Ryan turned to look at their father. "He's not breathing. He's not breathing!" He ran over and tried to prop him up.

Will was supposed to run for help, but his feet wouldn't move. He stood there and stared as tear after tear fell from his eyes. Ryan turned to look at him, and even though Will knew what was supposed to happen next, knew they were waiting for his cue to come in, he didn't move.

He was frozen where he stood because it was going to happen. It was really going to happen. His dad was going to die, and it didn't matter if he called for help. It didn't matter if he forgave him, or if he made his father proud, or if they made a piece of art that moved the masses and won the hearts of the Academy. None of it mattered, not really. All that mattered were the moments, and there weren't many of those left.

Maybe if Will was still enough, inert enough, this moment wouldn't be able to escape his gravity. Maybe it would be trapped, like light in a black hole.

"Get help," Ryan screamed. His face was white, and his eyes were childlike and thunder-scared.

But Will didn't hear him. Travis didn't hear him. And he didn't move. He didn't call for help. He didn't want a doctor there, not for this. It was too personal. Because that wasn't just his dad. That was him. That was Theo. And it was too horrible, and too beautiful, and too special to share with a stranger.

"What the fuck?" Ryan dropped his father's head onto the pillow and ran to the door himself. He screamed into the recesses of the empty barn. "We need a doctor! He's not breathing! He's not breathing!"

Will was shoved out of the way as the doctors rushed in. Ryan's arms circled his chest and yanked him back. They'd betrayed him. They were taking his father's death for their own. He needed to stop them, to tear them off like the vultures they were. But Ryan wouldn't let him go.

"Let me go," Will screamed. "Let me go."

"Cut," Michelle said, barely more than a whisper, and the room went so silent all you could hear was the buzz of the lights.

Will wasn't sure how much time passed, seconds, maybe minutes. Later, they'd tell him he was suffering from a concussion. Ryan's arms fell away and someone else's took their place. He was crying again, and someone was patting his back.

It was his mother. His mother was hugging him and shushing him like a baby.

CHAPTER 54
JAMES

James was on his fifth episode of *The Golden Girls* when a key slid into the lock. Theo came into the motel room and set his bag on the floor.

"You're not staying at the house tonight?" James turned the volume down and flicked on the bedside light.

Theo shrugged. "Nah, I didn't wanna leave you alone."

Muted sunlight shone through the thin white curtains. "There's pizza over there if you're hungry." James nodded towards a box of Domino's.

Theo made no mention of their fight the night before, and neither did James. That was the Young family way—just act like it never happened.

"Any beer?" Theo headed for the mini fridge.

"Of course." James lifted a can from between his legs. "How did it go today?"

Theo grabbed a beer from the fridge and took the whole pizza box over to his bed. "Will sang my song." Theo's voice broke on the word song, and he started to cry.

James felt sick with anger. What was the point of Travis killing himself if Theo was just going to immerse himself in those final moments anyway? Why hadn't he listened to James and stayed home?

"It was so good," Theo said, his blue eyes liquid. "Can you do that for me? Can you sing to me? You know, if . . . ?"

The tears were in James's eyes before he could stop them. He wanted to yell at Theo, wanted to tell him that he shouldn't be thinking about shit like that, that he should be focusing on the positive, that he might not have the gene, but he knew it wasn't what Theo needed. So he wiped the tears from his eyes and said, "Okay."

CHAPTER 55
WILL

"Another?" Nandi held the pitcher of margaritas over Will's empty glass.

Will shook his head. He hated waiting, especially for bad news. And it didn't help that Enrique, Andy, and Ryan were splashing around the pool like they were on spring break.

"They're going to love it. How could they not? Even the rough cut Michelle put together is amazing. And the final scene is just . . ." Nandi trailed off and dabbed at her eyes. "See, I'm crying just thinking about it."

They'd shot the musical number a few times, and it had gone well. Then Michelle had had the idea to include Ryan, even though James hadn't been there when his father died. Ryan had entered on the second chorus, and though the harmonies had been far from perfect, the imperfection had made it even better. They'd all agreed the first take was the best because it was raw and messy and unrehearsed.

Will smiled and nodded, wishing he believed Nandi. He picked up his phone and was surprised to find only a minute had passed since he'd last checked.

The ball shot from the pool and narrowly missed his father, who was asleep on a lounge chair. "Sorry, Robert," Enrique said.

His father opened his eyes and smiled. Then he drifted back to sleep.

His mother came out half an hour later while Andy was in the bathroom with their father and the nurse. She'd been on the phone with the studio executives for the past two hours, and now she made a beeline for the pitcher of margaritas, which wasn't a good sign.

Will sat forward in his chair. "That bad, eh?"

"I'm just going to be blunt." As if his mother could be anything else. "They were very impressed with the footage, but they don't think they can turn a profit with you starring, not with your reputation the way it is. They're not even convinced the Academy will go for it as an awards contender, even with the narrative that it's Robert's last chance to win an Oscar. Plus, Derek is still under contract, and replacing him won't be cheap."

So that was it then. It was over. Will looked up and smiled at Enrique who, for once in his life, didn't crack a joke. But at least his father was still in the bathroom. They could still lie to him, tell him the studio went for it.

"They want you to do an interview," his mother said.

"Like late night?" Ryan asked.

His mother shook her head, and her hair was uncharacteristically messy, like a wasp's nest on fire. "No, not like late night. Probably *Dateline*, or maybe *20/20*. We'll have to see who bites."

They'd all bite. Of course they would. And they'd eat Will alive. He'd be like a puppy trying to swim across the crocodile-infested Nile.

"Fuck," Enrique said, which pretty much summed it up.

CHAPTER 56

JAMES

"Just fucking ask him." Es fell back on James's bed in frustration. She'd come over to James's apartment to sort through everything they'd found on Tony so far.

"You know I can't do that."

Will was filming his *60 Minutes* interview today and didn't need James being like, *Hey, I found a picture of you asleep in Tony's hotel room. Wanna tell me what that's all about?* James would come across like a jealous ex, which, to be fair, he kind of was.

The pictures of Will and Derek together made James's skin crawl. There had to be close to a hundred of them, laughing and flirting and looking totally in love. But the picture that hit the hardest was the one of Will asleep in Tony's bed. It was clearly a hotel room because the key sleeve was visible on the nightstand. Had Will grown frustrated with Derek's lack of action and taken comfort in Tony? Tony was a handsome man, after all, a total silver fox. And ten years ago, he'd been certifiably hot.

Or, maybe Tony had been jealous of Derek's attraction to Will and had decided to seduce Will to derail his and Derek's budding romance. On the other hand, maybe James was reading too much into it. Maybe Tony had only taken the picture to make it look like they'd been together, but they really hadn't been. Maybe he'd planned to show it to Derek to make Will look like the fuckboy Derek had accused him of being. After all, Tony was obsessed with Derek. He had so many pictures of the brawny movie star you could wallpaper a mansion with them without repeating a single one.

"Ask his mother, then."

James ignored Esther and the overwhelming desire to smoke a bowl. Theo was right. Apologies and explanations weren't enough. James needed to do more to fight for Will. He needed to take Tony down. But that was proving easier said than done.

Es sat back up and grabbed the laptop. "I told you, I think we're wasting our time. Tony must've figured it out and gotten himself a new phone. There is no way he hasn't made a single call in days."

"Then why didn't he delete the spyware?"

"Because he doesn't want us to know he knows."

"Isn't there facial recognition software that can identify these last two guys?"

They'd been able to put names to faces for all but two of the young men in Tony's photos. Unfortunately—or fortunately, depending on how you looked at it—all of them were of age.

"Maybe, if you wanna bring the cops in on this. But they're gonna wanna know how you got these photos. And they're probably at least eighteen anyway."

Es was right. *Goddamnit.*

Now, it was James's turn to flop onto the mattress in frustration. He stared up at the watermarked ceiling above his bed. He should just paint it himself. The landlord certainly wasn't going to do it.

"Wait a second. Holy fuck! Holy fuck!"

James sat up to see what Esther was looking at. She'd clicked out of the photos and had pulled up the video of Will and Derek leaving the elevator.

"What did you find?"

"Shh, hold on." She hit play, and once again James watched them step off the elevator and lock eyes. But then Es stopped the video. "There, look, on William's cheek."

Esther zoomed in, and though the security footage was grainy, especially at this resolution, there was the unmistakable smear of red lipstick on Will's cheek.

"And now look here." Esther pulled up the photo of Will asleep in Tony's bed, and there it was, though fainter, the same smear of lipstick. "It's the same. Tony must've taken this the night of the Golden Globes."

"What?"

Esther opened YouTube, and in a matter of seconds, she had Will's acceptance speech queued up on the screen. Julianne Moore was presenting, and as Will came up to accept the award, she planted a kiss on his cheek and left a smear of red lipstick.

"I don't think Chapman did it," Esther said.

What? How did Esther's brain work so fast? "What do you mean?"

"Listen." Esther queued up the second video, the one of Will and Derek arguing, and the moment James heard Will say, "I feel dizzy. I need to lie down," he understood, and rage coursed through his veins.

"That son of a bitch drugged him, didn't he?"

"I think so, which is why William doesn't remember anything. I don't think he did it. I think Tony did."

That didn't make any sense. Why would Tony try to kill Derek? He was in love with him.

"This is Derek's bed in the picture, not Tony's. Derek must've been in on it. Or maybe he left the room or something. Fuck, I bet that's it. I bet Tony thought Derek was gone, but he wasn't. Derek must've been about to catch Tony with Will, and Tony panicked and bashed him over the head."

Part of James was hearing Esther's words, but another part of him was so consumed with fury he couldn't form a single rational thought.

"That's why he stole the security footage," Esther said. "It wasn't to blackmail Robert and Donna, at least not initially. It was to save his own ass."

"I'm gonna fucking kill that son of a bitch. I'm not even joking."

"I'll help. But first, you gotta call Derek and get him to tell you where the fuck he was when this was all going down."

CHAPTER 57
WILL

Maybe Will needed an adult diaper. All this ass sweat was getting ridiculous. At least the stylist had the good sense to pick out a pair of thick black pants for Will to wear to the interview.

"Don't forget to smile," his mother said over the rim of her magazine. "You look less tired when you smile."

Will frowned. He'd spent most of the past week with his mother's PR team, and he didn't need any more advice clogging up his brain. Besides, maybe it wouldn't be that bad.

They'd gotten Stewart Webber to come out of retirement to do the interview. Not only was he good friends with Will's dad, but he was also a staunch opponent of cancel culture, probably because he'd lost a lot of good friends and colleagues in the #MeToo movement. There were even whispers that his early retirement had been an attempt to avoid the same fate.

His mother hated him, but even she thought he was a good choice to do the interview. She figured being interviewed by an old white man, the poster grandpa for misogynistic toxic-masculinity, might make Will appear more sympathetic by comparison.

"I need to use the bathroom." Will dropped his controller and ran from the room. Even *Mario Kart* couldn't take his mind off his impending public humiliation.

He pushed his pants to the floor, wadded up some toilet paper, and shoved it between his ass cheeks. He could do this. He could do this for his father, for Theo, for himself.

Tiffany knocked on the bathroom door a few minutes later. "You alright in there?"

"Yeah, I'm fine." Tiffany had come over for moral support, and she was driving them to the interview later. His mother was there, too, but only to protect her investment. It was costing her a fortune to make Will appear presentable.

Will's phone buzzed against his ankle, and he reached down and fished it out of his pants.

Will had a vague memory of calling Derek drunk the night before and leaving a three-minute voicemail. He felt guilty going after Derek's part, even though he wasn't doing it out of spite. He was doing it because his father didn't have time to wait for Derek to recover. He was doing it because Derek couldn't sing for shit and this was the only way to get Theo's song in the movie. He was doing it because, if he got to portray Travis, every time James watched the movie, he'd see Will.

"Hi." It probably wasn't a good idea to take this conversation on right now, but after the interview, it might be too late.

"Hi." Derek's deep bass voice rattled the wax in Will's ears. "I got your message."

"Yeah, sorry about that. I think I might have had a little too much to drink."

"I'm not surprised. You must be pretty nervous. I bet you've got real swamp ass right now." After all their love scenes, Derek was well-versed in Will's stress response.

"You have no idea. But listen, Derek, I want to explain because—"

"No"—Derek cut him off—"let's not do this now. That's not why I'm calling."

"It's not?" Will caught his startled reflection in the mirror. He looked like shit. He had dark circles under his eyes, and his face was puffy.

"No, I'm calling to tell you I did it. I fired Tony."

Will almost dropped his phone into his soggy underwear. "What? Really?" This was huge. Tony wasn't just Derek's manager. He was like a father to him. "What happened?"

"I'm sorry, Will. Tony was the one who leaked those stories about you." Derek paused, as if Will needed time to be surprised. He didn't. "He said he was doing it for me, that my career would be as good as over if people started sympathizing with you."

It made sense, in a twisted sort of way. A hero was only as good as his villain, after all. "I don't know what to say."

"You don't need to say anything. I never should've taken him back the first time." Derek's breath crackled through the phone. "I didn't know, Will, I swear."

"What do you mean, the first time? Have you fired Tony before?" The thought was preposterous. Derek didn't shit without seeking Tony's approval first.

"I did, the day before the Golden Globes. He said if I tried to pursue a relationship with you, it would destroy my career. He said I had to choose, and I chose you."

Will couldn't believe what he was hearing. This couldn't be real. Derek hadn't wanted a relationship with him.

"And then I lost, and I got scared, and I said a lot of things I shouldn't have. But I'm not scared anymore, and I want to take you out on a date. Can I do that? Can I take you out on a date?"

"Will," Miles called through the door, "the hair and makeup people are here. You almost ready?"

"I have to go. They're waiting for me." Will's voice came out weak and breathless. This couldn't be happening.

"Okay, well, I should be landing soon. Why don't I make dinner reservations for tonight? We can celebrate your interview. And we don't have to call it a date. We can just be two old friends grabbing a bite."

There were a thousand questions Will wanted to ask. But instead of asking one that might actually shed some light on Derek's revelation, Will asked, "Why are you back in New York already?"

Derek let out a chuckle. "I wanted to see you. That, and Tony has been crashing at my apartment in the city. I figured I should probably make sure he hasn't trashed the place or made off with my Oscar. As you can imagine, he wasn't too thrilled. I should've just taken it back to L.A. with me when I had the chance."

Will pulled the wad of toilet paper from his ass and threw it in the toilet. His damp underwear had grown cold, and a shiver rolled up his spine as he pulled them on.

"Anyway, break a leg. I mean that. I would never root for you to fail. I hope you know that."

Will threaded his belt through the buckle, still feeling like he was in a dream. Or was this a nightmare? "I do. Thanks, Derek."

CHAPTER 58

JAMES

James's phone buzzed in his pocket. Finally, the asshole was calling him back. James had left Derek over a dozen voicemails and just as many text messages. James wanted to go right to the police, but Esther thought they should wait until they talked to Derek first. They couldn't make their case to the authorities without sharing the videos, and if they were wrong, Will could go to prison.

But James was sure they were right. Maybe he could even surprise Will at his *60 Minutes* interview. It didn't get more romantic than that. Theo would be so proud.

"What do you want?" Derek asked, his voice a bad James Earl Jones impression.

"The night of the Golden Globes, did you leave Will alone at any point?"

"What?"

James tried again, this time slower. "In your room, did you leave him alone at any point?"

"Who are you talking to?" someone asked Derek on the other end of the line. Was that Tony's voice?

"Is Tony with you right now?"

"Yeah, why?"

"Okay, whatever you do, don't tell him you're talking to me."

Derek didn't say anything for a while and James heard footsteps and what sounded like a door opening and closing.

"If this is about Tony leaking the stories, I already know. He told me, and I fired him."

"You fired him?"

"Yeah, and he's not very happy about it. So, this isn't the best time—"

"Where are you?"

"In my penthouse. Why?"

"In New York or L.A.?"

"New York. What do you care? Will's not taking you back, you know."

This was bad. If Derek fired Tony, then there was nothing stopping Tony from leaking those videos and fleeing the country. Was that why Tony was back in New York?

"If you fired Tony, then why's he in your penthouse?"

"His flight doesn't leave for another couple hours. What's it to you?"

His flight? Shit. "Is he going to Morocco by any chance?"

"How the fuck should I know where he's going? What's this about? Why are you calling me?"

"Listen to me very carefully, Derek. I don't think Will is the one who attacked you. I think Tony is, and I think he's planning on fleeing the country."

"What the fuck is wrong with you? That's ridiculous."

"Did you or did you not leave Will alone in your room that night?"

"Yeah, but only for like twenty-minutes. I went down to the bar to get a drink and clear my head, and when I came back—"

"Someone attacked you, right?"

"Yeah, Will was waiting for me."

"No, he wasn't. Tony was. Will was unconscious. I think Tony drugged him. And I can prove it. Or I will be able to. But you can't let him leave."

"What?"

"I'll explain everything when I get there. Just don't let him leave. You got that? What's your address?"

As soon as they hung up, James threw open his closet door and started rummaging around for another pen recorder. But he couldn't find one.

Oh, well, his phone would have to do. And even if he couldn't get a confession, he could at least stop Tony from escaping.

"Where are you going?" Theo asked, pulling off his headphones as James raced past his bedroom. "Did Es leave?"

"Yeah, she had to go to work." James tossed Theo the keys to the 4Runner. "Why don't you drive? I have some calls I need to make."

CHAPTER 59
WILL

"So this is what New York City public schools look like inside." Will's mother stopped to admire the bulletin board at the top of the stairs of P.S. 65, where *Welcome Back* was written in bright yellow and blue die-cut letters.

It had been the publicist's idea to conduct the interview from Will's classroom. Will hated the idea of using his students as props to bolster his public image, but if he was going to get the shit kicked out of him, it might as well be in his classroom, where he was used to it.

Tiffany led the way down the hall towards Will's old room, Miles following closely behind her. As they passed the office, Mary appeared with a poster of Will's mother from an old *Sports Illustrated* centerfold. "Ms. Wells, it's an honor to meet you. Would you mind signing this for me?"

Will's mother smiled and took the pen. "I'd be happy to."

Mary set a hand on Will's shoulder. "Look at you all dressed up. How are you doing? They've been setting up in your room all morning."

Will swallowed the bile rising in his throat and smiled back. "I'm alright."

They made their way down the hall to Will's room, and he took a breath before looking inside. There was film and lighting equipment everywhere. Two chairs and a coffee table were set up in front of the library bookshelf. Behind one of the chairs, where Will kept his basket of markers, sat the puppet stand. Behind the other stood dinosaurs. They weren't Will's dinosaurs, though. They were Tiffany's.

Will turned to her. "Did you set my classroom up?" A few weeks ago, all the furniture had been piled in the center of the room. Now, it was exactly as he'd left it in May, aside from all the film equipment.

Tiffany shrugged. "Someone had to help the new girl out. You should've seen how she had it set up. It was like a racetrack."

It wasn't time to start, so after a brief meeting with the producer, they waited in Tiffany's room, where Miles busied himself building a block tower. King came in with tea and the basket of candy they passed around during staff meetings. Her hair was freshly colored, and she wore a light blue pantsuit Will didn't recognize. "William, aren't you going to introduce me to your mother?"

Here were two people Will had never thought would be in the same room together. He couldn't decide what was more likely, them bonding over their disappointment in Will or them fighting to the death like two beta fish placed in the same bowl.

"Mom, this is Principal King. Principal King, this is my mother, Donna."

"It's a pleasure to meet you," his mother said. "Your school is lovely."

King smiled, which, apparently, she was capable of. "Thank you. It's even more lovely when the students are here."

The producer stuck her head in the door. "We're ready for you."

LOVE ON THE D-LIST

STEWART WEBBER SAT in the chair with the puppets behind him and left the dinosaur backdrop for Will. He wore a pinstriped suit and a solid red tie. His white hair was parted on the side, and his thin spectacles rested on the tip of his nose. Two giant mugs of water sat on the table before him.

"William, it's good to see you." He stood to shake Will's hand as he came in. The cameras were rolling, so Will swallowed his nerves and smiled back. He was a performer, and this was a performance.

"Thanks for doing this." He took his seat and drank from his mug like the publicist had told him to do, like he was sitting down with a friend for coffee.

"Just so our audience is aware, we're conducting this interview from your former classroom in the Bronx, where you taught kindergarten for five years. Is that correct?"

Will set the mug back down. "Yeah, that's right."

Stewart sat up straighter in his chair. "But you recently resigned from your position. Why is that?"

Will hadn't been expecting this question to come so early in the interview. But he was prepared for it.

"I managed to keep a low profile for about a decade, but after I attended my brother's bachelor party last spring, I found myself back in the press again, and I didn't want to subject my students and colleagues to that sort of attention."

"So, you're saying it had nothing to do with the accusation that you're a bit of a loose cannon and use physical intimidation to make your students behave?"

Jesus, what was Stewart trying to do? They were supposed to be talking about why Will decided to take up teaching, not why he decided to quit.

Will's collar was tight around his neck, but he resisted the urge to undo a button. "Actually, that's exactly why I decided to leave. I didn't want lies like that to make my students and their families uncomfortable."

"So, you claim they are lies?" Stewart pulled his glasses from his face and leveled his gaze at Will. "Why should your students and their families believe that? After all, you have a bit of a reputation."

Will could hear the publicist's voice in the back of his head telling him not to get defensive, but that was easier said than done.

"I've always believed people should make informed decisions based on evidence, not reputation. And to my knowledge, no student, parent, or colleague has ever complained about my teaching style, which is not based on physical intimidation but relationship building. If you'd like, my principal is just down the hall. You can ask her yourself. I'm sure she'd tell you the truth, which is that I'm probably the least intimidating teacher at this school."

Stewart smiled. "That won't be necessary." He put his glasses back on and flipped back in his notepad. "Let's start from the beginning. You were born into acting royalty. Your father is one of the most celebrated actors alive today, with nine Academy Award nominations to his name. And before him, your grandfather, Richard Chapman, won an Oscar for his performance in *The Rabbit*. Your mother was an actress in her day and a Bond girl. And your brother is the star of the *Hollow Point* franchise. But you've only been in one movie." Stewart paused to look at Will expectantly.

"I'm sorry, are you asking me a question?" Will didn't mean to sound bitchy. But come on, what the hell?

"I guess what I'm getting at"—Stewart cocked his head to the side in mock sympathy—"is that you must feel tremendous pressure to live up to your family's legacy. But is that fair? Is it perhaps not time to let others shine?"

"Well, it's certainly true that there are fewer roles than actors." Will pulled gently at his pants and yanked them free from the cesspool of his ass crack. Jesus, he'd been in one movie. It wasn't like he was Meryl Streep, taking every good role for women over fifty. "And I'm not going to sit here and pretend connections don't matter, because they do, but—"

"It's fitting you should bring up connections," Stewart interrupted. "Ten years ago, you starred in an independent film called *The*

Beautiful, for which you won the Golden Globe for Best Actor. Back then, you claimed you auditioned for the role under a pseudonym because you didn't want an unfair advantage."

There was a hook in this breadcrumb, wasn't there? "Yes, that's right. I auditioned under the name William Reid."

"That's interesting,"—Stewart glanced down at his pad—"because I heard from a reliable source that *The Beautiful* was the first movie your mother produced. Anonymously, of course. Might that explain why you were cast over scores of struggling actors awaiting their big breaks?"

Will smiled to counter the smug look on Stewart's face. Their plan was backfiring spectacularly. What was going on? This wasn't an interview. It was an inquisition.

"That actually wouldn't surprise me at all. But it's news to me."

CHAPTER 60
JAMES

The moment James got off the phone with Robert, Theo turned to him with a gob-smacked smile on his face. "You're gonna win Will back by proving he's innocent, aren't you? This is so romantic."

"Don't leave the car. You hear me? Tony's already proven he's willing to kill to save his own ass, and I don't want you getting in the middle of this."

"Then shouldn't you have, like, a gun or something?"

"Derek's up there already. And Tony doesn't even know I'm coming. I'll be fine."

James crossed the street and entered the building. Derek had already told the concierge to expect him, and he checked James's ID, punched in the code for the penthouse elevator, and sent him on his way. As the elevator climbed, James made sure his phone was recording in his pocket.

The doors parted and the security gate was already open, so James stepped directly into the spacious loft-style penthouse.

The place resembled a basketball gymnasium. The floors were polished wood, and the exposed brick walls were at least twenty feet tall. Massive iron-clad windows let in giant beams of sunlight, as did the glass doors leading out to the rooftop garden.

It was clearly a bachelor pad. The furnishings were hyper masculine—a brown leather couch and an austere, wine-colored rug. The art was simple and modern, mostly non-descript geometric shapes and paint splatters.

"Why don't you come upstairs? Derek's waiting for you."

James froze at the sound of Tony's voice, and he turned to find the man sitting on a barstool at the kitchen island with a small silver handgun pointed at James's head.

Well, shit.

James considered diving back into the elevator, but the doors were already closed, so he did the only thing he could do—he put his hands up. His heart raced in his chest, and sweat coated his brow as Tony gestured toward the stairs.

"You go first," Tony said. "I'll be right behind you."

James walked, at gunpoint, up the stairs to the lofted bedroom. James half expected to find Derek's dead body. But instead, Derek lay handcuffed to the bed like some damsel tied to the railroad tracks, and he was very much alive.

When Derek saw James, he struggled against the handcuffs, which clanged against the metal bed frame. "Let me go, Tony. You don't want to do this."

"Sorry," Tony said, ignoring Derek. "Derek only had the one pair, so I'm afraid you're going to have to share."

James glared at Derek. "What is wrong with you? Why did you tell him I was coming? You're such a—"

"I didn't tell him. He must've been listening in on our call."

Tony smiled, and James knew Derek was right. Esther was probably right, too. Tony must've found the spyware on his phone and known they were closing in on him. No wonder he'd fast-tracked his getaway plan.

Tony had James uncuff one of Derek's hands and replace it with his own, so now they were both chained to the bed, the cuffs threaded through the bars of the metal bed frame. They lay side by side, James's right hand and Derek's left hand cuffed to the headboard above them. But at least they each had one free hand. Maybe Tony would come close enough for James to snag the gun.

"You do realize people know I'm here, right?" James said. "Do you really wanna add kidnapping to your list of crimes?"

Tony lifted the gun and pointed it at James's face. "What about homicide?"

Derek yanked on the cuffs and smashed James's hand into the bars of the metal bed frame. "Ow," James said. "Knock it off."

"Yes, Derek, relax. I'm not going to shoot you. Not if I don't have to. Now give me your phone."

Shit.

"You already have my phone," Derek said, like Tony was talking to him.

"Yeah, and I left mine in the car."

"I can see it in your pants. Now give it to me."

James used his free hand to reach around and fish his phone from his pocket.

"Unlock it and slide it toward me."

James did as he was told, and it took Tony less than two seconds to figure out James had been recording everything. "Well, let's just shut this off, shall we? And delete."

He proceeded to screw around on James's phone, and when he started typing something, James asked, "What are you doing?"

"Texting."

"Who are you texting?"

Tony smirked and set the phone down.

"Who did you text?" James asked again.

James had a feeling he already knew, and he cursed himself for being so careless. He'd told Robert and Esther where he was going. But what if Tony had texted them back and told them James had changed his mind, or that he'd gotten here and Tony was already gone?

Shit. That left Theo as their last hope, and James really didn't want him anywhere near Tony. *Please, Theo, just stay in the car.*

"You meant it for me, didn't you?" Derek said. "Did you slip something into my drink?"

Instead of answering, Tony grabbed the larger of his two suitcases and wheeled it into the hall and down the stairs, thudding on every single step.

Was Derek right? Was he the real target, not Will? James hadn't considered that.

"Why would Tony wanna drug you?"

"To kill me, obviously." Derek shifted on the bed, yanking James's hand into the frame again.

"Quit moving so much." James yanked back so Derek would know what it felt like. But that gave him an idea. If Derek could fit his arm through the bars, there might be enough slack for James to reach the bedside lamp. Maybe he could throw it at the window and get someone's attention. Though, they were practically in the friggin' stratosphere, so unless they wanted to alert the pigeons, they were probably shit out of luck.

"Ow, you fucking asshole. This is all your fault."

"No, this is all your fault. Did you know, while you were off getting drunk, your pervert manager down there was taking pictures of Will passed out in your bed?" Just saying the words made James's blood roil.

"What?"

"Yeah, now answer the fucking question. Why would Tony drug you?"

They were interrupted when Tony started climbing the stairs again.

"Aww, look, you're bonding. You'll probably be BFFs by the time someone finds you. Maybe you'll both realize you can do a hell of a lot better than William Chapman and decide to fuck each other instead." Tony yanked up the handle of his carry-on and wheeled it out of the room.

"I fired Tony the day before the Golden Globes because he said I had to choose, my career or Will," Derek said in a hushed whisper.

Jealousy bit at James like a swarm of fire ants. "And let me guess, you chose Will?"

But that was bullshit. If Derek had chosen Will, then why had Derek said all those nasty things to him? Why had he just left Will there, passed out and unprotected?

"I should've known Tony was lying. He said I needed to do it to protect Will. He said I had to tell everyone he'd already left my room. Fuck, I should've believed Will when he said he wasn't feeling well. But I just thought he was... Fuck, why didn't I believe him?"

James ignored Derek and tried to make sense of it all. If Tony was mad at Derek for firing him, he might have tried to drug him for any number of reasons. Perhaps he wanted to rape him or take incriminating photos to blackmail him with later. And then what, he found Will and switched targets? What if he took more than pictures? What if he—

"Guess what I found downstairs?" Tony entered with a roll of silver duct tape.

Shit. Tony was going to bind their other hands, too, wasn't he? So much for James's plan to smash the window with the bedside lamp.

CHAPTER 61
WILL

"Why wouldn't that surprise you?" Stewart asked. "Are you accustomed to your parents removing roadblocks for you? That must be nice. Not everyone has that luxury."

Will looked past the cameras to the line of cubbies beneath the word wall. Julian liked to hide in there when things got rough. Will would say, *Take some breaths and come out when you're ready*.

Will closed his eyes and breathed deep into his belly.

"It's okay, you can take your time answering," Stewart said.

Will kept his eyes closed and his breath steady. "Oh, I know. No one needs permission to breathe."

"I'm sorry, I beg your pardon."

Will ignored him and took his time. He did this during class, too. He liked to teach by example. Maybe his students would watch this later and say, *Look, Mr. Chapman is taking time to stop and breathe*.

"Okay." Will forced a smile onto his face. He was trained to deal with poorly behaved people, right? This was no different. "I'm going to answer your question. But first, let me ask you a question in return. Are you asking to be helpful or hurtful?"

"Excuse me?" Stewart leaned back in his chair like Will had bad breath.

"These questions you've been asking me, are you asking them to be helpful or hurtful?"

For a moment it looked like Stewart wasn't going to answer, but after a long silence he said, "Helpful."

"Okay, so how are they helpful?" It was like asking Julian why he thought dumping paint in the fish tank was helpful.

Stewart let a hint of exasperation seep into his voice. "This is an interview, Mr. Chapman. I'm doing my job, asking the questions our viewers want answers to."

Will smiled, and this time it was genuine. "Really? Because I imagine your viewers hardly think about me at all. I was in one movie, ten years ago, when I was eighteen. Now, I live in a small two-bedroom apartment with my best friend and spend my days helping kids learn how to read, write, and make friends. But to answer your question, I'm not surprised my mother would help me get a part in a movie because she's my mother and she loves me. And I'm not surprised she would keep it a secret from me because she knew how much it meant to me to do it on my own."

"And what about now?" Stewart kept his voice even and professional, but there was a hint of gloating in his tone. "I understand you're hoping to make a comeback by starring in your father's new movie. That's not exactly doing it on your own, is it?"

"No, it's not." Stewart wasn't wrong. But it also wasn't wrong to want these memories with his father, to want them preserved on film. "But the truth is, I'm less concerned about making a comeback than I am about working with my dad while I still have the chance. I've dreamed of being in a movie with him since I was a little boy. But I see your point about nepotism and privilege. It's one of the reasons I became a teacher. I wanted to leverage my privilege to help others."

"What about those who would say you only went into teaching to repair your tarnished reputation? That it was more about helping yourself than your students?"

Will's mother whispered something to Miles, and he took out his phone and started recording the interview. Tiffany was on her phone, too. This was going great, just great.

"You never really know someone's intentions, do you? You always have to guess. In my classroom, I use a social-emotional program called Conscious Discipline, and one of its central tenets is to assume positive intent. The idea is, since you have to guess anyway, why not guess something positive? Even if you're wrong, you'll still be in a better position to communicate your needs to someone than if you'd assumed the worst and put them on the defensive.

"Sure, you could assume I spent five years in college and five years in the classroom as some elaborate, decade-long plot to appear more sympathetic. And I'm sure there are some people who'll believe that. Or you could assume I like kids and want to help them learn. I can't control what others think and do. I can only control what I think and do."

"Like hitting your co-star over the head with a blunt object?"

Jesus, what the hell was Will supposed to say to that?

"Let's talk about that night. You told the police you went up to Derek Hall's room after the ceremony, had some drinks, and blacked out, that you don't remember a thing, even the argument you were heard having with Derek."

Will nodded.

"Was it ever more than friendship between you two?" Stewart removed his glasses, probably to symbolize the naked truth he was uncovering. "Or did you ever wish it was more than friendship?"

"I mean, duh." Will laughed freely. Fuck Stewart, and fuck public opinion. People were going to judge him no matter what he said, so he might as well tell the truth. "You've seen Derek, right? He's a total hunk. And he's a nice guy, too."

"Were you in love with him?"

You're just a pathetic fuckboy.

"I certainly thought I was at the time."

The truth was, Will had no frame of reference. Other than a few anonymous hookups, there'd only been Derek and James, and trying to sort out what was real and what was fake with those two was an absolute mindfuck.

Just a few hours ago, Derek had said the words Will had been dying to hear for over a decade. Will should've felt vindicated. It hadn't all been in his head. The connection he'd felt with Derek had been real and reciprocated. Yet, instead of vindication, Will only felt grief and loss. The boy who'd loved Derek, the boy who would've traded a year of his life for a single kiss, was gone, and he wasn't coming back. That boy was never going to get his happy ending because he no longer existed.

And the man Will had become didn't want to go on a date with Derek—not now, and not ever—because he didn't love Derek. He loved James.

Maybe it was Stockholm syndrome. Maybe it was staring into James's eyes for five minutes straight. Maybe it was nothing more than Will's mustache fetish. But whatever the reason, no one had ever made Will feel the way James had, like he was right where he belonged; like he was singing in the pocket, every note on pitch.

It had been surreal and absurd. Guys like James weren't interested in guys like Will. Yet, there had been moments, however fleeting, when James's affection and attention had elicited more than just disbelief and gratitude from Will. There had been glimmers of worthiness, too. James's constant assault of affirmation had actually started to work. Will had started to believe in himself again.

It was probably the reason James's betrayal had hit so hard. It had been devastating to learn that the one voice that had been singing Will's praises, the one voice that had managed to rise above the chorus of haters, had been lying the whole time.

Sure, if James was to be believed, he actually hadn't been lying. But it didn't matter. Either way, Will had experienced the high that comes from feeling wanted, needed, and cherished. Even if it had all been a deception. Even if he'd been bumped up to first class for nefarious purposes, there was no unseeing what he'd seen, no unfeeling what he'd felt. The damage had been done. He'd experienced how magical it could be, and he wasn't going back to his seat in steerage—not quietly, anyway.

Will deserved to be loved, and he was ready to fight for it.

"Do you ever wonder if jealousy played a factor that night? There are, of course, widespread rumors that you declared your love for Derek and he rejected you. But what if there was more to the story? What if you saw Derek with someone else that night, maybe even someone close to you?"

You mean like my mom?

"You know, I've wondered a lot of things over the years. But, if I'm being perfectly honest, I don't spend much time wondering anymore because it's not productive. It's not helpful. So, I've done the only thing I can do. I've forgiven myself for whatever may or may not have happened that night and moved on."

The second the words were out of Will's mouth, he realized they were true. They really were. The interview was a disaster, and the movie would likely fail as a result and take his father's last chance to win an Oscar with it. But Will would be okay. And if he could forgive himself, maybe he could forgive James, too. Maybe he was stronger than he thought, maybe even strong enough to risk another humiliating heartbreak.

"But is it your place to forgive yourself?" Stewart broke Will's reverie with an intense stare. "Isn't that up to those whom you've hurt with your intimidation tactics in the classroom and your violent actions outside of it?"

Jesus, what was wrong with this guy? Hadn't they already been over this? Will closed his eyes and breathed. When this was over, he was going to ask James out on a date. No, not James, Jimmy. Will was going to ask Jimmy out on a date.

Everyone expected James—cool, confident James—to take charge, to be their daddy, to be the hero of their romantic fantasies. Even Theo, who knew James better than anyone, gave him shit for just letting all his boyfriends walk away without a fight. But maybe Theo was wrong.

Maybe, when James had accused Will of being in a prison of his own making, waiting in vain for someone to come and break him out, he'd really been talking about himself. Maybe James was the one in a prison, a prison of duty, responsibility, and reparation.

Not only had James been kicked out of the house young, he'd also spent most of his adult life taking care of others: his father, his brother, and his nephew, not to mention all of his young boyfriends. He probably never stopped to wonder if maybe he needed to be taken care of, too.

That gave Will an idea, a cheesy, clichéd, totally embarrassing idea. He'd get Theo to trick James into coming to hear him play at some open mic night in Brooklyn. Only when James got there, he wouldn't find Theo up on the stage. He'd find Will. There had to be a country song for this situation. There was a country song for every situation. Will would find it and learn it and dress the part, too. Would assless chaps be pushing it too far?

"William." The intensity in Stewart's stare was now ninety percent confusion. "Let me rephrase that. Is it your place to forgive yourself, or shouldn't that be up to your victims?"

Okay, Will could think about James later. Now, he had to deal with this piece of shit douchebag. He was tempted to bring up the simmering allegations of sexual misconduct against Stewart, but that wouldn't be helpful, and in Will's classroom they strived to be helpful.

Will set his hands in his lap and rolled back his shoulders. "Okay, I think what we have here is a teachable moment. I am going to answer your question, but first I'm going to share what's going on in my head so you can better understand my earlier point about positive intent.

"You just doubled down on the accusation that I use physical intimidation tactics on my students, despite the fact that I invited you to ask my principal if there was any merit to those accusations.

And she's just down the hall, too. We could clear this up in two seconds. Now, I could assume a lot of things." Will could see Stewart wanted to interrupt him, so he talked fast. "I could assume you're not very smart and trust the word of a tabloid magazine over the only person with the authority to actually answer the question. Or, I could assume you're not interested in the truth, but in causing harm, that you think by repeating this lie over and over again people will eventually believe it, which, admittedly, is an effective strategy. One man used it to get elected president."

"I'm sorry, Mr. Chapman, but this interview is about you, not me or the former president."

"Or"—Will ignored him—"I could assume you're nervous and scared because you have your own public image problems to deal with and are hoping this interview will fix them. Now, do you see how I'm in a better position to help you grow and improve from this situation than if I'd said what initially popped into my head, which was some version of, 'Are you stupid or just a dick?'"

Tiffany stifled a gasp.

"Now, watch me communicate my displeasure in a helpful way." Will cleared his throat and locked eyes with Stewart. "You were hoping to fix your public image problems and get your career back on track, but you didn't know how to do it in a helpful way. You thought tearing someone else down would lift you up. But if you want people to like and respect you, you have to earn their trust over time by taking accountability for your actions, repairing the damage you've caused, and promising to do better in the future."

"Mr. Chapman, let me remind you again, I'm not the one being interviewed here, you are."

"Yes, I am." Will caught Miles's eye and returned his smile. "And to answer your earlier question, yes, it absolutely is my place to forgive myself. Even if my students and their families didn't love, respect, and trust me, which they do, and even if Derek, the man I'm accused of harming, hadn't forgiven me long ago, it would still be my place to forgive myself.

"Feelings of guilt and remorse are important, but their purpose isn't to comfort victims; it's to transform offenders. Once those feelings have served their purpose, once one has owned their actions, learned from their mistakes, and done their best to repair the damage, those feelings are counterproductive because they force one to wallow in the past, which can't be changed, instead of looking to the future, which can be changed."

Stewart leaned back in his chair. "Have you owned your actions? You spent one night in jail and three months in rehab. Assault with a deadly weapon usually carries a prison sentence of up to twenty years, at least it does for people without the wealth, fame, and powerful connections you have at your disposal."

Jesus Christ, this guy was relentless. And they'd probably edit out all of Will's best points, too. Oh, well, at least Miles was getting them on film. *Ah, so that's what his mother was up to.* She always was a step ahead. She was a bitch, but she was Will's bitch.

"I think you're conflating punishment with consequences. It's true our justice system didn't intervene, in large part because there was little to no evidence to suggest I'd attacked Derek. But setting that aside for now. I did suffer consequences for my alleged misconduct, namely the loss of my acting career. Punishment is remarkably ineffective at changing behavior because people have a tendency to shift the blame to the person or system punishing them instead of directing it inward. Consequences, on the other hand, especially natural consequences, keep the blame focused on the person responsible."

Stewart nodded and conceded the point, which could only mean one thing; he had something else up his sleeve.

"Okay, so here we are, ten years later, and you've forgiven yourself and moved on. You claim to have no recollection of what happened that night, so you've decided, why keep dropping a bucket in an empty well. Is that right?"

"Yeah, more or less." What if James said no? What if Will was too late? What if James was already seeing someone else? That would suck, but at least Will wouldn't have to wallow in what-ifs anymore.

"What if I told you new evidence has come to light about what really happened that night? What if I told you an anonymous source has come forward with portions of the missing security footage that not only places you at the scene of the crime, but shows you holding the weapon used in the attack, the very Golden Globe you'd won earlier that night?"

Will's mother was in the doorway, talking fervently to someone in the hall. She stopped at Stewart's question and looked into the room. Her face was as white as a sheet.

"What if I told you the video also provides a motive? You claim to have no memory of what happened that night. But tell me if this rings any bells. You found out Derek, the man you believed yourself to be in love with, was sleeping with your mother. You attacked him. You were so used to getting everything you wanted that the first time something didn't go your way, you decided someone needed to pay for your suffering with their life."

Before Will could answer, a chorus of shouts erupted outside in the street. Jesus, was he about to get hanged? Will pulled his eyes from the window and tried to focus on Stewart, but it felt like the walls were closing in on him.

Tony must've leaked the videos in retaliation for Derek firing him.

Stewart leaned forward. "Now might be a good time to take some of those deep breaths you're so fond of."

The shouting outside grew louder, and the producer, who was staring out the window, waved over one of the cameras to capture it on film. Will couldn't quite make out what they were saying, but it almost sounded like they were chanting his name.

Stewart glanced over his shoulder at the window, his eyes pinched in annoyance. He forced a smile and turned back around. "My apologies. There seems to be some sort of commotion going on outside."

Tiffany ran to the window and said, in her booming teacher voice, "Will, I think you're going to want to see this."

Well, there was no point sitting there any longer. It was over. Will's acting career was beyond dead. Hell, he might even go to prison. If nothing else, he'd at least spend the next several years in court.

Will rose from his seat. Stewart started to object, but Miles cut him off.

"Yeah, this is wild, Will. I recognize that one. It's the kid from our fridge."

Julian? Will ran to the window. And sure enough, there was Julian, dressed in his Catboy pajamas. He held his grandmother's hand and screamed Will's name repeatedly at the top of his lungs. And he wasn't alone.

There was Yareli, Jose, Awa, Brianna, and Denaisha. So many of Will's students and their families were gathered in the street below, and not just his most recent students either. There was Pedro, who was in the fourth grade now, and his dad, who always brought the most amazing fruit platters to events. Sierra's mom, who chaperoned every field trip, held a sign that read, *We love you, Mr. Chapman.*

There were other signs, too, and they really were chanting his name, though not the name that appeared on his SAG card, not William Chapman. They chanted, "Mr. Chapman! Mr. Chapman! Mr. Chapman!" And there, among the crowd, was Principal King, and Mary, and so many of Will's friends and colleagues.

Seeing them all there was like releasing a parachute. He was still falling, but the fall wasn't going to kill him. He was going to be okay. He was going to survive this because he wasn't alone. He had people who loved him, far more than he'd ever realized.

"Hey, Stewart, you're not going to believe what I just found out."

Will whipped around to find his father standing there in front of the cameras.

"Your anonymous source, who happens to be Derek's disgruntled manager, Tony Wallingford—whoops, guess he's not anonymous anymore—is actually the one who attacked Derek. And the reason my son, William, doesn't remember anything from that night is because he was drugged. William was unconscious at the time of the attack."

His father turned from his old friend and spoke directly to the camera. "All the proof you need will be provided in due time, and when that happens, both my son and I will happily sit down for another interview. But this one is over."

CHAPTER 62

JAMES

As James lay there—bound and gagged—he thought about his brother and their last weekend together.

The day before Travis had drowned, he and Theo had spent ten hours on the couch, finishing *Breath of the Wild*. It had taken them over a hundred hours in total, and when they'd defeated the final boss they'd jumped and cheered like they'd just won the Super Bowl. Afterward, the three of them had ordered pizza to celebrate.

Sometimes, James wondered if Travis had waited to finish the game first, if he had wanted to leave Theo with that memory in particular, the two of them playing video games and eating pizza. But other times, when James was feeling low, he would think about what had happened after Theo had gone to bed that night and blame himself for dragging Travis out to the bars.

It had started as a typical night out for them. They'd shot pool and played darts. But then, when it had been time to leave, Travis had gotten into a fight with the bartender, who'd insisted one of the bills Travis had given him was a ten, not a twenty.

James had been in the bathroom at the time. When he'd come

out, the police had already been called. James had tried to resolve the situation by slapping another ten onto the bar and dragging his brother outside. But before they'd made it five feet, Travis had broken free, shoved the money into some random guy's beer, and tossed it at the bartender's face.

"It's getting worse, isn't it?" Travis had said on the way home.

Tony came back into the bedroom and all thoughts of Travis vanished. Tony strode over to James, his face pinched in anger. He grabbed a corner of the duct tape covering James's mouth and yanked it off, which—with a thick mustache and two weeks' worth of beard stubble—hurt like a son of a bitch.

"It would seem your handsome nephew has decided to wait for you in the lobby, which is not going to work for me. My car is set to arrive in the next twenty minutes, so you can either make him go away or I can invite him up to join you and Derek on the bed. Your call."

Goddamnit, Theo. "I'll call him," James said.

"Okay, but if you try anything, I will shoot you."

"I said I'd call him."

Tony dialed and held the phone to James's ear. Theo picked up on the second ring.

"Good, you're not dead. What the fuck is taking so long?"

"Derek let Tony leave, so he and I have just been having a little chat." James looked over at Derek, gagged and bound on the bed beside him. "We've actually grown quite close in the last hour."

"What? Really? You and Derek?"

"Listen, I need you to do me a favor. Derek's called in an order for Thai food at a place called Thai Monsoon. It's not too far, just across the park, but they won't deliver. Do you think you can walk over and pick it up? It's already paid for. We'll eat here. You're gonna love Derek's penthouse. This place is sick."

"Why the fuck don't they deliver?"

"I don't know, bud. But according to Derek, it's the best Thai food in the city."

"Ugh, fine."

Theo hung up, and James let out a sigh of relief.

Before Tony could tape his mouth shut again, he asked, "Did you just take a picture of Will, or did you touch him, too?"

Derek squirmed at James's side and mumbled something unintelligible into his gag, which was more than Tony had to say for himself. All he did was reach for the roll of duct tape.

"I'm just gonna assume you did. I mean, why else would you clobber Derek, here, over the head? What, was he about to catch you with your pants down and your dick out? I used to think you were jealous of Will because Derek wanted him and not you. But maybe it was the other way around. Maybe you were jealous of Derek. Maybe—"

Tony placed a fresh piece of duct tape over James's mouth, shutting him up. "You honestly think I'd be interested in a scrawny little rat like William? You watch too many movies. I'm not some sexual predator. I was just doing my job, looking out for my client's best interests. I knew Derek's career would be over as soon as William found out about him and Donna. I tried to tell him you can't fuck a guy's mom and expect him to be okay with it. But he wouldn't listen. He thought William would understand and they'd live happily ever after. All I wanted to do was get Derek home before he ruined everything. But then William had to go and steal Derek's drink and pass out in his bed."

"Then why did you take his picture?" James tried to ask, but it came out as garbled nonsense, the duct tape pulling painfully with each word.

"I never wanted to hurt you, Derek. You know that, don't you? You're like a son to me. I was just trying to get William out of your room before you got back."

Derek mumbled something into his gag that James couldn't make out. But it sounded a lot like "Fuck you."

CHAPTER 63
WILL

"Let's take Tiffany's car," his father said, walking right past his limo. "We'll be less conspicuous that way."

"What's going on, Dad? Do you really have proof that it was Tony and not me?"

"I'll explain in the car."

His father shooed away his entourage, including his nurse, and they all piled into Tiffany's Ford Focus. Tiffany drove. Miles took the front seat. And Will and his father climbed in the back.

"Where to?" Tiffany asked.

"Derek's penthouse."

His father gave Tiffany the address, and she pulled out of her spot without even consulting Google Maps.

"Why are we going to Derek's? Seriously, Dad, what the fuck is going on? Did Tony leak those videos because Derek fired him?"

"Probably, but that's not important anymore. James has proof that you were unconscious when Derek was attacked."

"What do you mean, proof? Is there another video?"

His father pulled a bottle of pills from his pocket and swallowed three. "There is no easy way to say this, William. Tony has a picture of you on his phone from that night, and, according to James, you're obviously passed out in it. James thinks Tony must have drugged you."

Will didn't know what to say to that, but Miles did. "I'm going to fucking kill that asshole. I'm going to squeeze his neck until his eyes pop out."

Tiffany, meanwhile, caught Will's gaze in the rearview mirror and turned down the radio.

"He must've been upset that you won and thought he could derail the rest of your campaign by posting lewd pictures of you online," his father said.

"Or he's a fucking pervert," Miles offered.

"It was in Derek's drink." Will closed his eyes and pictured the glass in Derek's hand, the one Will had snatched and downed before Derek could even take a sip. "He was trying to drug Derek, not me."

"Why would he drug Derek?" his father asked. "No, my theory is, Derek was about to catch Tony in the act of taking your picture, and that's when he—"

"Derek fired Tony."

"I'm not talking about today. I'm talking about the night of the Golden Globes."

"So am I. Tony didn't want Derek to be with me, and Derek fired him because . . ." Will couldn't finish the sentence because it hurt too much. A whole alternate life, one where he and Derek had become the scandal of the century for a different reason, had died that night. And even though Will didn't want that dream anymore, didn't want that life, he still grieved its death.

"Maybe he planned to ruin you both, then. Maybe he thought he'd find you and Derek passed out, only Derek wasn't, and that's why he hit him."

Will was less concerned with why Tony did it than the fact that he did, because that meant Will wasn't an attempted murderer.

"Why are we going to Derek's?" he asked.

His father handed him his phone. "Look at the last message

LOVE ON THE D-LIST

James sent me and compare it to the others. Notice anything different?"

The last text read, *He's already gone. We're too late.*

Will looked up from the phone. What was so different about that? And who was gone, Tony?

"Look," his father said, taking the phone back and scrolling up to an earlier message. "James never uses punctuation. He'd rather send two separate messages than use a period, which is really annoying." His father pointed to a pair of gray text bubbles higher up the screen. "See?"

And if something happens to me who becomes the trustee then, read the first. And the second said, *Shouldn't there be a backup*

Sure enough, neither message had any punctuation, not even a question mark. What was his father suggesting, that someone was pretending to be James?

"I don't think James sent that message. I think Tony did."

"Why would Tony have James's phone?" Will's stomach tightened and his pulse quickened. Was James in trouble?

No, his father was just being dramatic. He didn't have a new film on the horizon to obsess over, so he was turning his real life into a movie instead. Tony wasn't violent.

Or was he? If Will's father was right, and Tony was the one who'd attacked Derek, maybe he was violent. Will had never liked Tony, but he'd never thought him capable of something like this.

"I don't know, but we're going to find out," his father said.

As Tiffany drove into Manhattan, his father explained that he'd already been on his way to the school when he'd gotten James's suspicious text.

"Don't you think maybe we should call the police?" Miles said.

"And tell them what, exactly, that we think our friend has been abducted because he started using punctuation? By all means, call them. But we don't have any time to waste. Esther, who is really quite resourceful—I mean, I'm glad she's on our side this time—

discovered that Tony not only owns property in Morocco, but that he recently applied for a Golden Visa there."

"So, what, he's planning to flee the country or something?" Miles asked.

"Exactly. Now, when we get there, I want you three to wait in the car. But keep your eyes on the door. Be ready to stop Tony if he tries to leave."

His father had this strange glint in his eye, the same one he got right before he was about to deliver an Oscar-caliber monologue. Was he enjoying this?

"And what are you going to do?" Will asked.

"I don't have much time left. And you know what that makes me? Dangerous."

Great, now his father was quoting lines from Andy's latest action flick. What the hell?

There wasn't any parking, so Tiffany pulled over in front of a fire hydrant and left the engine running.

"If I'm not back down in ten minutes, call the police. And if they won't do anything, call the paramedics. Tell them I've had another stroke."

"Dad, you're being ridiculous. If you're right—which I'm sure you're not—and Tony is holding James hostage, what do you expect him to do, buzz you up?"

"You forget that I'm not just your father. I'm also Robert Chapman. I'm pretty sure the doorman will be thrilled to help me surprise my dear friend and co-star, Derek Hall, with an unannounced visit."

Like Will could ever forget that his father was *the* Robert Chapman. "Fine, then I'm going with you."

"No, you're not. It's too dangerous. And besides, I need you down here to tackle Tony if he tries to leave."

"Let Miles and Tiffany tackle Tony. Actually, no one tackle Tony. You'll probably break his leg and get us all sued."

"I'm sorry, William, but this is something I have to do alone. I'm the one who got James mixed up in all this, and it's my responsibility to make sure he's okay. No matter what happens, just know that I love you, and I'm proud of you."

With that, his father, who was obviously fucking high, opened the door, climbed out of the car, and strutted across the street.

"Maybe we should get out, too. We can flank the doors," Miles said.

"Is that Theo?"

Will followed Tiffany's gaze to the tall, lanky boy with black-rimmed glasses walking right towards them. It was Theo.

Miles opened his door and narrowly missed slamming it into the fire hydrant. "Boy, where do you think you're going?"

Theo jumped about a foot in the air. "Fuck, you scared me. What are you doing here? Are you coming for Thai food, too? Is that Will?"

"Thai food?"

"Yeah, Uncle James just called and sent me to go get Thai food. Apparently, he and Derek are best buds now. Actually, can you guys drive me? The place is all the way on the other side of the park, and it's gonna take me forever to walk there and back."

Will had written his father's theory off as the delusions of a dying man. But why would James send Theo across town to get Thai food? There were plenty of Thai restaurants here on the east side, and places that delivered, too.

"Where are you going?" Miles called after Will, but Will didn't answer. He had to catch up to his father.

He ran into the lobby and jumped into the elevator just as the doors were closing.

"I told you to wait in the car," his father said, his body shaking from all the adrenaline.

"I know, but James did this for me, not you."

His father gave this some thought and then smiled. "Okay,

maybe you should come. I am on a lot of drugs right now. I'm starting to be able to see auras. Yours is red and gold, with a little purple on the top left. What do you think that means?"

THERE WAS no way to make a stealthy entrance, not with the pinging of the elevator announcing their arrival. But Will's father motioned for him to stay back while he stepped out into the apartment alone.

He looked around for a second, then beckoned Will to follow.

The place looked pretty much the same as it had ten years ago, although Will vaguely remembered the rug used to be white.

"You wait down here," his father said in a hushed voice. "I'll check upstairs."

"Why don't you both come upstairs?" Tony said over the railing of the loft. "It's a party."

At first, Will didn't see the gun, but then Tony lifted his arm and the silver glinted in the sunlight. *Fuck.*

Surely, his father noticed the gun, too, but he acted like he didn't. "We've got the building surrounded, Tony. You might as well give up now."

"Come on, Robert, we both know the building's not surrounded." Then, as if doubting himself, Tony walked over to the window and peered outside. "But it looks like my car is here early. That's convenient. Now, hurry up. I'm on a tight schedule."

Tony kept the gun aimed at them as they walked up the stairs to the loft. Will's chest seized when he saw not only James tied to the bed, but Derek, too. Their eyes went wide with shock at seeing Will and his father there. They both tried to speak, but it came out as garbled mumbles.

"There's some duct tape on the nightstand," Tony said, gesturing with the gun. "Robert, why don't you tie William to the chair? I'll deal with you after."

"You know what this reminds me of?" his father said, slurring his words. "The final scene in that god-awful movie I did, the one that shall remain nameless. You know the one I'm talking about, William." His father clutched his chest, like he was in pain. "My greatest shame."

"Are you drunk?" Tony asked. "I feel bad for you, William. I really do. Your father is about to duct tape you to a chair, and all he can think about is his legacy. Who knows, Robert, perhaps after you're gone, *Polly* will gain cult status. You know, one of those movies that's so bad it's good, like *The Room*. I wouldn't be surprised if that's the role you're most remembered for."

Polly was his father's lowest rated movie on Rotten Tomatoes, a silent, black and white murder mystery where only one character talks and appears in color: Polly, the parrot, who insists "the Devil did it." But that wasn't his father's greatest shame. That honor belonged to one of his more commercially successful movies, the thriller *The Day You Die*.

The lead actress, Olivia Osmond, had been injured during the shoot, and they'd suspended filming for six months. When they'd finally resumed, his father failed to replicate the Russian accent he'd been using. Only one critic had noticed, but to this day, his father wore the shame like a scarlet letter.

But this moment, right now, was in no way like either movie. Will was pretty sure the Devil hadn't done it, and seeing as they weren't on the rim of a volcano, and no one was about to go into labor, he failed to see the comparison. Unless...

No, he wouldn't. His father wasn't that reckless. Fuck, was that why he was acting drunk all of a sudden?

At the climax of *The Day You Die*, his father's character, a Russian mob boss named Nikolai, meets his end when a very pregnant Olivia pisses herself and pretends her water broke. Nikolai approaches to check on her, and she trips him and sends him plummeting into the magma chamber.

Will's father better not piss himself and get them all killed. *Just let Tony have his way.*

Will hated Tony with every fiber of his being, hated what he'd done to him and Derek. But as much as he hated Tony, he loved living more. Will was done looking backward, done letting that night define his life. All he wanted now was to start again, and to do it with James, if James would have him.

Will didn't think Tony would shoot anyone, not unless provoked. They just needed to cooperate and let Tony win, let him get away with it. Will didn't need revenge. He didn't need justice. He needed everyone to be okay.

The chair Tony wanted Will bound to was over by the bookcase, which displayed—along with a bunch of leather-bound books—Derek's Oscar.

Will sat in the simple leather armchair with the matching ottoman and placed his arms on the rests where it would be easy to bind them.

His father grabbed the duct tape off the nightstand and started walking towards Will, limping slightly. Will knew what his father was about to do, and a jolt of panic shot through his body. This couldn't be happening.

Will had only been ten at the time, but he remembered rehearsing the final scene from *The Day You Die* like it was yesterday, his father standing over him with a prop gun, Will waddling like a pregnant lady towards his would-be executioner.

Jesus, his father was going to get someone killed, most likely himself. Will had to do something. He had to stop this.

His father slowed and started to stumble. And then he collapsed.

Will's body flooded with adrenaline. There was nothing he could do now. Actually, that wasn't true. He could use the distraction and—

And what?

His eyes darted to the bookcase and Derek's Oscar, the golden man with the crusader's sword. No, he couldn't do that. That would be ridiculous. And he had another role to play now, that of the concerned son.

He jumped from the chair and tried to run to his father, but Tony turned the gun on him. "Don't move."

"Please, Tony."

"Nice try, Robert. But you're not going to win an Oscar for this performance either."

"Please, let me help him. I won't try to stop you from going, I promise."

"I said, don't move."

A wet spot bloomed on the front of his father's slacks. And a moment later, the smell of shit hit Will's nose. *What the fuck?*

Tony took a few steps closer, putting himself directly between Will and his father. "Come on, Robert, scene's over." Tony kicked his father in the leg.

When his father didn't react, Tony kicked him harder.

As he did, Will inched towards the bookcase. What was he doing? This was a terrible idea. The Oscar was still several feet away, and there was probably another ten feet between the bookcase and Tony. Will would never be able to close the distance in time.

But Will kept hearing James's words play out in his head, about how Will was in a prison of his own making. *No one's coming.* James was right. Will couldn't just wait around and hope for the best. He had to do something before his father's plan backfired and someone got killed.

Will stared down at his father, expecting him to scream from the bruising kicks, but instead, his eyes rolled back in his skull. *Damn, he really was good.* He almost had Will fooled.

Tony pulled his leg back to kick him again, and that was when his father struck.

It all happened so fast. His father swept his leg under Tony's and knocked him off balance, sending him reeling backward.

At the same instant, the gun went off and a cloud of white feathers billowed into the air, as if Tony had shot a swan or an angel.

To Will, the deafening bang was like a starting pistol, and he lunged for the Oscar.

But unlike in *The Day You Die*, Tony didn't trip and fall into a volcano. He also didn't drop the gun. He merely stumbled a couple of steps backward before regaining his footing.

Will's fingers closed around the golden statue just as Tony pointed the gun at his father's face. Tony's eyes were filled with rage, and there was no doubt in Will's mind he was going to pull the trigger.

"No," Will screamed. He hurled the statue at Tony with all his might.

Will wasn't an athlete. He'd never once played baseball. But Miles had made him throw enough fucking sandbags at the wall over the years that the motion was second nature, especially with all the adrenaline coursing through his body.

The statue careened through the air, flipped twice, and struck Tony just as his finger pulled the trigger. There was another deafening bang, and Tony's head snapped violently to the side in a spray of blood.

The gun fell from Tony's fingers as he collapsed to the floor. Will dove for it, certain Tony would shoot the rest of them, too, if he got to the gun first.

But then, to Will's complete and utter astonishment, his father picked up the gun and turned it on Tony. How was that even possible? Had Tony missed? Had Will managed to throw off Tony's aim in time? What about James?

Piss-soaked and shit-stained, his father rose to his feet. "It worked. Holy shit, it worked. That was amazing."

Will wasn't listening, though. He was already at James's side, checking him for bullet holes. "Did it hit you?" he asked, brushing away the mess of down that had settled over James and Derek like snow.

James tried to speak, but his mouth was still taped shut.

There were no obvious signs of blood, and both Derek and James were moving. Will reached up and pulled the tape from James's mouth. Perhaps ripping it off like a band-aid wasn't the best idea, but he needed James to tell him he was okay.

"Are you okay?" he asked. "Are you shot?"

"I'm fine." James gasped for air. "Holy fucking shit, you're ridiculous. I can't believe you just did that. You could've been killed."

Will's hands shook as he struggled to find the lip of the duct tape binding James's wrist. Meanwhile, his father shuffled over to the other side of the bed to help Derek.

"What are you doing?" Will shouted at his father. "Keep the gun on Tony. I'll untie them."

"It's okay, William. Tony's not a threat anymore."

Will glanced over his shoulder and saw Tony's body slumped on the floor, his face disfigured and bloody.

"What the hell, Will?" James said. "What was that? Did you guys plan that?"

Will turned away from Tony's motionless body and locked eyes with James. The bright green and gold of James's irises was like a tonic to Will's frenetic nervous system, and he took a deep, calming breath.

"What, have you never seen *The Day You Die?*" he asked, finally getting his quaking fingernail under the lip of the duct tape.

"I knew you'd get my reference," his father said, working to free Derek. "That right there was hands down my greatest performance ever. In fact, I'm seeing the movie in a whole new light now."

"You're friggin' ridiculous, Will, you know that? Both of you are."

"Well, nobody shoots my dad or messes with my man." Will unwound the final loop of duct tape and freed James's left hand.

It was only when he saw the wide grin spread across James's face that he realized what he'd just said.

James cocked an eyebrow. "Your man, eh?"

"No, I . . . I didn't mean . . ." *Fuck.* So much for surprising James with a romantic serenade.

James smiled. "Shut up and kiss me."

Using his newly freed hand, James fisted his fingers into Will's hair and pulled him down into what would've been the most epic kiss of all time had Will not just waxed James's lips with duct tape.

As it was, James winced and pulled away. "Ow, shit, that hurts."

"Sorry."

"Stop being sorry. We've been over this. Just come here." James pulled Will down again, but this time, instead of kissing him, he held Will tightly against his chest, squeezing him like a bear.

Will buried his face in James's neck and inhaled deeply, breathing in the familiar woodsy musk of James's scent, pine and smoke and apples. Yes, definitely apples. Will wished he could stay right there forever, his nose pressed against James's pulse, James's arm wrapped around him, but he pulled back and rattled the cuffs. "Now we just need to find the key to these."

"It's in Tony's pocket," Derek said.

Will had almost forgotten Derek was there. But he looked at him now, at the scar slicing Derek's eyebrow in two, a scar Tony had put there.

"I'm so sorry, Will. I should've believed you when you said you didn't feel well. I never should've left you there alone—"

"It's fine. You didn't know."

"I should've known. I just didn't—"

"What's important now," his father said, stepping away from the bed, "is that we did it. We stopped a monster."

"The part's yours, Will," Derek said, rubbing his raw and newly freed wrist. "I'm not going to fight you for it. In fact, I'm going to call the studio and demand they give it to you."

At that moment, Will didn't give a shit about the movie.

"I found it," his father said, pulling the key from Tony's pocket.

He handed it to Will, who reached over James and unlocked the cuffs.

The moment James's other hand was free, he reached up and cradled Will's face in his warm palms. "I'm gonna say something now, and I don't want you to freak out. I'm well aware this is one of those things you're not allowed to say this early in a relationship, or for the first time during sex, which means you're probably not allowed to say it right after someone rescues you, but I don't care. I friggin' love you, William Chapman. You don't even know."

Will's heart felt like it might literally burst in his chest. The love and reverence in James's piercing green eyes made Will's whole body buzz with gratitude and desire. "I love you, too." He pulled James against his chest. "I'm sorry I said all those—"

"Goddamnit, Will, if you say sorry one more fucking time, I'm gonna—" James paused to find the appropriate way to finish his threat.

Will pulled back and met James's gaze. "You're going to what?"

"Well, fine, empty threat. But just friggin' stop, okay?"

Will couldn't help but laugh. "Okay, sorry."

James glared at him.

"That was the last one, I promise."

Since Will couldn't kiss James's lips, he kissed his forehead and his closed eyelids. He kissed his cheeks and the tip of his nose. Still not certain this wasn't all a dream, he caressed the stubbled skin on James's neck and swooped his finger through the hollow between James's collarbones.

But it wasn't enough, not by a long shot. Will pulled James against him, wishing he could merge their bodies into one, like two lumps of playdough.

They stayed like that for a long time. James must've realized Will wasn't ready to deal with what came next because he made no moves to pull away. He just let Will hold him.

It wasn't until a cloud passed over the sun and the room grew momentarily dim that Will let go and followed James's gaze over to where Derek and his father were crouched over Tony.

Will's chest hitched, and a cold numbness crept into his bones. "Did I kill him?"

His father shook his head. "I'm sure he'll have one hell of a headache when he wakes up, and he's missing a few teeth. But I'm fairly certain he'll live to see the inside of a prison cell."

His father took a step back and wiped a bit of blood on his already soiled slacks. "James, why don't you call 9-1-1 while Derek finds me some new clothes to change into. Will, let Miles and Tiffany know we're okay. And then call your mother. She's never going to believe this."

"I should probably call Theo, too," James said, reaching up to turn Will's face away from Tony's body.

Will let his forehead fall against James's, and he closed his eyes and took a deep breath. They were okay. James was okay.

There would be more to come, a lot more. There would be interviews, both from the police and the press. There would be court appearances and a never-ending swarm of paparazzi. But that was okay because James loved him, and he loved James.

At that moment, nothing else mattered.

CHAPTER 64

JAMES

There was a knock at the door, and James glanced at the clock on his nightstand. It was a little before six. Will, Miles, and Tiffany were early. But that was okay. James was ready. He'd been prepping for the last half hour.

"It smells amazing in here," Tiffany was saying when James came out of his bedroom.

"Thanks." Theo stepped back to let them in, and James's heart leapt in his chest when he saw Will in a tight fitting long-sleeve T-shirt. Will's hair was nicely styled, and his jeans showed off the delicious curve of his perfect ass.

James came up behind him and kissed the nape of his neck. "You made it. Sorry the place is such a shit hole. I bet you're wishing we did this at your place right about now, aren't you?"

Will leaned back as James's arms encircled his waist. "No, not at all. And it didn't take us that long to get here."

"Yeah, and your place is huge," Tiffany said. "What is it, three bedrooms?"

"Yeah."

The place was not huge. The bedrooms were just slightly larger than the beds, and the living room barely fit a couch, a chair, and a coffee table. But the tiny kitchen, where Theo had been cooking all day, was functional, and there was a cute little dining area with a table that sat four.

"Make yourselves at home. There is something I need to show Will up on the roof. We won't be long."

"You're gonna love it, Will," Theo said. "He's been working on it all week. Actually, we should all go check it out. The meat's gotta rest anyway."

Miles must have caught the look in James's eye because he grabbed Theo by the shoulders and spun him around. "I don't think we're invited. Why don't you give us the tour and put some music on? Preferably something loud."

"What is it you wanted to show me?" Will asked as James shut the apartment door.

"You'll see."

James climbed up the ladder that led to the roof, unlatched the cover, and pushed it aside. He climbed through first before turning to offer his hand to Will.

"I still need to paint it, but it's pretty much done." He pulled Will through the rectangular opening and into the bright sunlight.

Will's eyes went wide. "What? You built this?" He walked over and ran a hand down the four-by-four post on the corner of the covered pavilion James had spent the past week building. "Did you build the swing too?"

"Nah, I bought the swing."

"Wait, don't you rent? Are you even allowed to build up here?"

"Probably not."

James's small three-story apartment building in Jackson Heights was right in the landing path of LaGuardia Airport. And at that very moment, a plane flew overhead, close enough to hit with a rock.

Using the distraction to his advantage, James pulled the bottle of lube from his pocket and tossed it to Will. "Think fast."

James stepped into the shade of his little rooftop pavilion and looked over his shoulder just in time to catch the wide grin that spread across Will's face.

"Are you serious?" Will took in their surroundings, all the windows that looked down on them, not to mention the planes flying overhead. The pavilion would provide some cover, but not complete, which made it semi-private and semi-public, just the way Will liked it.

"Dead serious. We gotta hurry, though. Do you want me like this?" James rested his elbows on the back of the swing and spread his legs.

"Wait, you want to try bottoming up here, right now?"

"All the way in, big boy."

"No. There's no way you're ready for a quickie. You have to build up to that. We'll get there, though. Tonight we can start with a bath and some candles and maybe go for just the tip."

James stood, unzipped his pants, and pushed them down to his ankles. "Hurry up and breed me, boy."

"What the fuck has gotten into you?"

"Well, I managed to get three fingers in a few minutes ago, if that's what you mean."

Earlier that week, they'd both gotten tested because nothing says boyfriend quite like barebacking.

James folded his arms across the back of the swing and rested his head on them. "Come on, fill me up, buttercup. I wanna feel your load inside me. That counts as sexy talk, right?"

"You're ridiculous."

James closed his eyes, and for a moment, he feared Will was going to chicken out and leave him bent over and bare-assed, but then Will's legs brushed up against his, light as feathers.

"You look so fucking sexy right now." Will pushed James's T-shirt up until it bunched around his armpits and proceeded to kiss his way down each vertebra.

James kept his eyes closed and focused on his other senses: the traffic in the street, the wind, the soft buzz of Will's zipper as he yanked it down, the snap of the lube cap opening. Something tapped against James's leg, and it wasn't until he felt the stick and release of pre-cum that he realized it was Will's erection.

The wood smelled fresh and green, and the obscene spurt of lube sent a shiver of anticipation up James's spine, which still tingled from Will's kisses.

"You better tell me if it hurts." Will's slick hand reached around and gripped James's cock, squeezing hard to show he was serious.

"I will, now just fuck me already. I'm already warmed up."

"It's a good thing you're cute because I'm not going to tolerate this whole warming yourself up nonsense. Eating ass is one of the best parts."

James held back a snicker. He loved when Will got into character.

But the smile fell from James's lips when he felt the round tip of Will's cock press against his opening. He took a deep breath and bore down slightly. He could do this.

Will's hand gripped James's shoulder, and instead of plunging into him, Will pulled James back onto his dick, inch by inch. There was pain, but there was also this glorious sense of fullness. A dick was so much better than bony fingers. Longer, too.

James's breath grew quick, but then he remembered to relax, to keep each exhalation long and languid. He wanted to ask how close they were. Were they halfway in? More than halfway? But he didn't want Will to stop.

Will leaned forward, and his breath was hot on James's neck when he said, "You're so fucking beautiful. And you're doing great. We're almost there."

Will stood up straight again, and the pressure built as he slid deeper inside.

But it wasn't enough. James wanted to feel Will's legs pressed flush against his own.

And then Will pulled out.

"Don't," James said.

"Relax, I'm just putting more lube on."

James opened his eyes and followed the spiral of a knot in the wood. He wasn't mad. He was just impatient. Why was Will being such a gentleman about this? Just fuck him already!

Will must have read James's mind, because this time he wasn't quite so timid. He pushed back inside James, and his fingers dug into James's skin, as if he hoped to distract James from the pain. But it wasn't pain, not really. It was something else. It was like a flash fire. It cooled as fast as it burned.

"There you go. Almost there." Will tightened his grip on James's shoulder and the fullness grew tenfold. James was dizzy from it. "Fuuuuck," Will moaned. "I love being inside you."

And there it was, complete and utter fullness, burning and cooling. Will's legs were flush against James's. His hip bones pressed into James's ass. Then Will leaned forward and his body lay heavy on the bare skin of James's back.

Will softly bit the skin at the nape of James's neck. "You did it. All the way in."

James was pretty sure it didn't get better than this, this sense of being so close to someone, to have them literally inside you. But it did. As euphoric as those first few minutes of slow closeness were, they paled in comparison to the frenzy with which Will fucked him.

There was no more pain, only fire and friction and this pulsing, throbbing numbness.

Will placed his hands on James's lower back and pressed down, changing the angle. And holy shit. What was that? And why did it feel so good? Was that his prostate? No wonder guys liked bottoming so much. Why had no one ever told James it could be like this?

It was sensory overload, the fullness, the smell of the untreated wood and the way it mixed with Will's scent, sweet and citrusy, the grunts of pleasure Will let out with each deep thrust, and the little moans that escaped James's own lips.

James wasn't touching himself, yet he was about to come anyway. "Oh, shit, I can't stop it. I'm gonna come." He reached between his legs and gripped his cock hard, trying to squeeze off the eruption building inside him.

"Do it," Will said, his voice music and gravel, and James obeyed.

Every muscle tensed, and it was like his whole body was coming. He emptied himself onto the bench of the swing in quiet, choking gasps. They mixed with Will's grunts, and he could feel it. He could feel Will coming inside him.

Will collapsed onto James's back, and his arms encircled him. They stayed like that for a while as their heavy breathing slowed. And as Will's softening cock slid out of him, James told himself it was okay because they could do this again as often as they wanted. The future was theirs.

"Are you okay? Did I hurt you?"

"Are you friggin' kidding me? That was the hottest thing ever. I'm so beyond okay. Holy shit."

Will's mouth found his, and between kisses he said, "Next time, I won't be so gentle. I'll roll you up like a cinnamon bun and drill you like a jackhammer."

James laughed at the absurd image. "Is that a promise?"

WHEN THEY GOT BACK DOWNSTAIRS, they discovered their viewing party had more than doubled in size. Robert, Donna, Andy, Nandi, and Enrique had joined Miles, Tiffany, and Theo, and they were all stuffed into the tiny living room like olives in a jar.

James glared at Theo.

"Don't blame the boy," Robert said. "You're family now, and that means unannounced visits. Get used to it."

"I'm glad you guys are back. This calls for a toast." Donna

uncorked a bottle of champagne, and white plumes spewed out, streaking across the narrow strip of carpet in front of the coffee table.

James gave Will's hand a squeeze. "Your family is ridiculous. I suck a dick and my dad disowns me. You top your boyfriend and get champagne."

"Wait, really?" Andy sprang from the couch and wrapped James and Will in a giant hug. "That's even better. Was it the Botox? It was, wasn't it?"

"No, you took my advice, didn't you?" Enrique said, joining the group hug.

Everyone was looking at them and smiling like they knew something James and Will didn't. James really had taken Enrique's advice, but he wasn't about to share that fact with this lot.

"I'm so happy for you both," Donna said. "My news isn't nearly as exciting as that. But it's still pretty fucking exciting. I was talking to the studio execs this morning, and they want you, William. They want you to finish the movie. And don't worry about Derek. He's going to play Emily's new boyfriend, Chris, the one she runs off with."

Donna didn't bother waiting for Theo to get glasses—which was probably for the best since they only had coffee mugs—and drank straight from the bottle before passing it to Nandi.

James had never doubted they'd give Will the part. The guy was a friggin' hero and, as far as James could tell, the greatest actor alive. How could they not give him the part? James was dating a friggin' movie star, an honest-to-god movie star. In fact, he'd just been fucked by a movie star.

The champagne made its way over, and James drank it like it was meant for him, like taking a dick called for champagne. Maybe it did.

There was a knock at the door, and Theo leapt up to answer it. "I'll get it."

Esther stepped into the crowded apartment with a bottle of bourbon. She took one look at the room full of celebrities and said, "I probably need to sign something to be here, don't I?"

"Not unless James wants you to," Robert said. "It's his home."

Esther handed the bottle of bourbon to Will. "Is this gonna be awkward because of the whole getting you fired thing?"

Will laughed, and James literally felt weak in the knees. God, he loved that man. How was this his life? What had he done to deserve this happiness?

"You also saved my ass. I say we crack this bottle open and call it even."

"Works for me. But no ice. Ice is for lightweights."

"Right? Now, tell that to James. He still insists on drinking that watered-down excuse for beer."

"Hey, leave my beer out of this."

Tiffany turned up the volume on the TV. "It's about to start."

There wasn't room on the couch, so James sat on the floor and pulled Will onto his lap. He still couldn't believe these assholes had traveled all the way out to Jackson Heights. If they wanted to make a party out of watching Will's *60 Minutes* interview, they could've done this at Enrique's penthouse or Robert's place in Chelsea. Even Donna's room at the Four Seasons was probably bigger than James's apartment.

But the gesture wasn't lost on James. For so many years, it had been just the three of them—Travis, Theo, and James. And then just the two of them. But now, he and Theo had been welcomed with open arms into this big, totally dysfunctional, fiercely loyal family.

What would Travis think if he could see them now? He'd probably laugh his ass off. He'd be proud of James, but not for landing a wealthy movie star. No, he'd be proud of him for getting his head out of his ass and letting his heart take the lead for a change. He'd see how happy Theo was and breathe a huge fucking sigh of relief. And then he'd be at peace.

James would've expressed his gratitude aloud, but he didn't want to risk making half the men in the room cry. Seriously, it was embarrassing as hell to witness.

Instead, he pulled Will closer, hooked his chin over Will's shoulder, and licked his ear.

"Jesus, stop doing that. It's gross."

Will tried to squirm away, but James tightened his grip, his chest rattling with laughter. "You can punish me later. I've always wondered what happens to a cinnamon roll when you take a jackhammer to it."

EPILOGUE
WILL

The telecast went to commercial break, and Will considered making a dash for the restroom. But he couldn't go now. His category was next, and if he wasn't there to smile for Bradley, he'd look like a sore loser.

James set his hand on Will's shaking leg. "I still think you're gonna pull off the upset. In fact, I'm willing to bet big on it."

This was one bet Will was sure to win. His category, Best Actor, was stacked that year. He was up against Daniel Day-Lewis, who'd come out of retirement to delight audiences with his portrayal of charismatic funnyman Dick Van Dyke in *The Centurion*; Denzel Washington, who starred opposite Cate Blanchett in a remake of *The Lion in Winter*; Jim Broadbent, who was *Peter Pan* in the least problematic version of that story ever told; and the frontrunner, Bradley Cooper, who'd lost sixty pounds to play a coked-up former ballet dancer in *Periwinkle*. So, Will was safe from giving anymore speeches.

He'd already had to give one on his father's behalf, and it had been torture. He'd had to just stand there awkwardly waiting for everyone in the Dolby Theater to stop applauding and sit their asses back down.

The academy liked to spread the wealth, and their movie, *Between the Boy and the Body*—the new title after *Sundowning* was deemed too obscure—had already won Best Supporting Actor, Best Adapted Screenplay, and Best Director. They weren't going to give it Best Actor, too.

Besides, Will had been perfecting his loser's smile all awards season. So far, Bradley Cooper had taken home the Golden Globe, the Critic's Choice, the SAG, and the BAFTA awards for Best Actor.

His mother had warned him this might happen, even after Will had swept most of the regional critics' awards, including New York and L.A.

"Sometimes, it's not about giving the best performance," she'd said, "but about whether or not it's your time. You're barely thirty. You'll have plenty of other chances to win an Oscar, and everyone knows it. Just be glad you got nominated."

The nomination was great, but it paled in comparison to the real prize—a fuck load of new movie offers. Still, while life was pretty damn awesome, there was room for improvement. And Will knew exactly what he wanted next, and it wasn't an Oscar.

"Okay, how about this? If I win, I'll agree to hike the PCT with you in the fall. But if I lose, you and Theo have to move to the Hamptons with me."

"Hey, don't drag me into this," Theo said. "I don't wanna live way the fuck out there."

"No, it's going to be awesome," Will said. Theo was starting to become famous in his own right, and Will wanted to save him from the many perils of being young, hot, and popular in New York City. "We can even put a recording studio in the house."

"Can we lose the desk and put a pool table in the library?" James asked.

James was missing the point of a library, which was a place of peace and learning, not sport. But relationships were about compromise. "Sure, but I get to pick the felt color."

"And can we get a dog, like a real one, at least sixty pounds?"

"Yeah, but it has to be a rescue."

James smiled and shook Will's hand. "Okay, it's a bet." He leaned in and whispered, "And whoever loses has to bottom in the limo after the ceremony."

"I can fucking hear you." Theo plugged his ears. "And if we're moving to the Hamptons, I'm getting goats, like those little baby ones in sweaters."

Theo was just bitter because he'd lost Best Original Song to Beyonce.

The commercial break ended, and Saoirse Ronan glided out onto the stage to present the award for Best Actor.

James took Will's sweaty hand in his. "For our anniversary, I'm gonna get you an ultralight trowel for digging shit holes in the woods. I already found one that's less than four ounces."

"Yeah, well, I'm going to get you a tortoise that's going to live a hundred years and shit all over your closet."

"You do realize you're ruining romance for me," Theo said. "Why can't you two just be normal and get each other bath bombs and drones and shit like that?"

Saoirse stepped up to the microphone, and even though Will knew there was no way in hell he was going to win, his heart fluttered in his chest.

"The best performances have the power to scare us, move us to tears, make us laugh, and make us hold on to the ones we love just a wee bit tighter. These five brilliant actors have shown us the staggering breadth of the human experience, from the bleak hollows of loss to the tears shed in moments of pure joy. Here are the nominees for best performance by an actor in a leading role."

The clips played, including Will singing Theo's song into the sterile hospital room, his son on his lap, his father's corpse beside him in the bed.

Will took comfort in the overwhelming amount of talent in his category. He was safe, and way too young to win anyway. Plus, Will was gay, and openly gay men never won Oscars, not for acting anyway.

"And the Oscar goes to"—Saoirse's finger slipped under the seal, and her eyes went wide—"William Chapman."

The whole crowd gasped, and somewhere overhead a voice said, "This is the first nomination and first win for William Chapman," but Will wasn't listening because all around him people were cheering and touching him and congratulating him. James leaned over and kissed him smack on the lips.

What the hell was going on? Did Will have another concussion?

"Get up there," James said, shoving Will out of his seat.

Somehow, Will made it up onto the stage without falling over or shitting his pants.

"Wow!" He accepted a hug from Saoirse. "Are you sure?"

She turned the envelope to face him.

"Okay, well, this is unexpected." Will smiled down at his fellow nominees and locked eyes with Bradley. "I'm so sorry."

Will took a breath to steady his nerves, and then started rattling off thank-yous as fast as he could. "I want to thank my director, Michelle Liu. You are such an amazing artist, and it was an honor to work with you. I want to thank and congratulate my fellow nominees. I respect all of you so much.

"Ryan, thank you for being like a brother to me both on screen and off. And Miles and Tiffany, your loyalty and support over the years have meant more to me than you'll ever know.

"James, I know you hate taking credit for anything, but this belongs to you more than me. None of this would've been possible without you, not the book, not the screenplay, and not the performances. And Theo, thank you for writing such a powerful song and for letting me sing it.

"But most importantly, I want to thank the real Travis Young. This is all because of you, all because you wanted something more for your son and wrote him a book.

"I want to thank my family, my brother, Andy, my adopted brother, Enrique, my sister-in-law, Nandi, and of course, my parents. I've been in two movies now, and my mom got me both parts. It's embarrassing, but true. Thanks, Mom, for being the first person to believe in me."

Will stopped to look down at his Oscar—his Oscar—and then up into the lights where he imagined his father standing and smiling. "And I want to thank my dad. When I was a little boy, I used to run scenes with him, and he'd say things like, 'Stop acting and just be,' and I'd be like, 'But, Dad, I'm not actually a dog,' and he'd say, 'Not with that attitude you're not.'"

Will promised himself he wasn't going to cry. But who was he kidding? He was a Chapman. Of course he was going to cry. So he gave in and let the tears flow.

"My dad was a masterful actor, and I know he didn't belong just to me, that I wasn't his only protégé. I know this because people keep coming up to me and telling me how much my father has taught them. And I'm like, 'Oh, no, please tell me he didn't make you piss on a fire hydrant, too?'"

Everyone laughed, and Will smiled, stemming the flow of tears. He was almost done.

"Lastly, to all my students, I miss you, and I love you."

Will was escorted backstage, but there was no time to process his win because, defying the odds yet again, *Between the Boy and the Body* took Best Picture.

Will was hauled right back up on stage and pushed towards the front, where his mother and Michelle stood. Ryan, Derek, Andy, Nandi, and Theo crowded in around him.

There wasn't time for long speeches because the ceremony had run over, but Will's mom and Michelle each said something brief that no one heard over all the whooping and carrying on.

People stood and screamed. There were hands on Will's back and hands in his hair, and someone picked him up. *Fucking Enrique.* And then Will spotted James in the front row with tears in his eyes. Why wasn't he up on the stage, too? He fucking co-wrote the book.

"I love you," James mouthed.

And Will mouthed back, "I love you, too."

The End

Acknowledgments

This book wouldn't have been possible without the support of my platonic life-mate and co-parent, Gillian Boudreau. Thank you for letting me monopolize your ten-minute breaks with random questions like, "What do you think is the most erotic yoga pose?" and "How would you describe the intersection between the physical and metaphysical responses of staring into someone's eyes for five minutes?"

I can't thank the writing duo C.N. Crawford enough for their encouragement, support, and inspiration throughout this process. This journey began for me when Nick told me to stop revising my first book already—I'd been tinkering with that one for about a decade—and just write something new. That something new is Love on the D-List. Thank you, Christine and Nick. A guy couldn't ask for better mentors. It just goes to show, you never know who you'll meet at a Mother's Day brunch. They might change your life.

I want to thank my editor, Jena O'Connor, whose developmental edits were spot on. You made my book stronger, and you made me a better writer in the process.

Of course, I have to thank my two proofreaders, Kylie Hammell and Ebonee Bell, who did so much more than just fix my typos. Kylie, your validation came right when I needed it the most. And Ebonee, your simple suggestion forever changed one of my favorite characters for the better. You may have even saved his life.

Genevra Black, thanks for helping my Gen X self be less offensive and for putting on your editor hat while you gave my manuscript a sensitivity read. I'm so grateful we met, and I hope we can work together again.

Lastly, I need to give a big shout-out to my first readers, Elizabeth Gillman, Steven Carter, James Holstad, Cara Griffin, Mary Lovejoy, and, especially, Tristan Moriarty, who, in addition to reading his first gay romance ever, also took my author photo at a moment's notice. It takes more than just true friendship to read someone's debut novel and give them honest feedback. It takes guts and faith. What if it'd sucked and you had to make up nice things to say like, "I like the font you chose," and "Wow, your book about gay men actually sort of passes the Bechdel test?" Thank God it didn't come to that, right? Right?

About the Author

J.R. Barker writes quirky m/m romances with humor, heart, and heat. He graduated from Cornell University with a degree in Earth and Atmospheric Sciences and a concentration in creative writing. And before you ask, no, every spicy scene is not about thick columns of basalt and volcanos erupting.

J.R. spent twenty years as a classroom teacher, and now he writes full-time from his home in Portland, Oregon. When J.R. is not writing romantic dramedies and dramatic comedies, he hikes with his handsome dog, Orlando, who is a stereotypical chapter one romantic hero—cocky, willful, misunderstood, and, secretly, very sweet.

J.R. spends most of his free time parenting his young son—doing his best to voice every superhero and villain ever invented—but he will, on occasion, put himself out there on the dating scene for "research." To learn more about J.R. and join his mailing list, head to jrbarkerbooks.com. And if you message him on any dating apps, you best have a face picture.

Printed in Great Britain
by Amazon